ACHERON SALVATION

KEN LOZITO

ACOUSTICAL BOOKS LLC

Published by Acoustical Books, LLC

KenLozito.com

Cover design by Jeff Brown

IF YOU WOULD LIKE TO BE NOTIFIED WHEN MY NEXT BOOK IS RELEASED VISIT

WWW.KENLOZITO.COM

ISBN: 978-1-945223-46-4

CHAPTER ONE

QUINTON and his crew rushed their sleek shuttle past a field of decrepit, broken-down spacecraft, searching for anything remotely intact enough to be worth investigating.

"I still say we could make do finding what we want out here," Guttman said in a voice that was always a tad too loud for normal people.

"That's why you're not a scout," Becker replied, keeping his gaze on the main holoscreen.

Oscar snorted a little.

"You think that's funny?" Guttman asked.

"As a matter of fact, I do," Oscar replied.

Quinton heard the sounds of a quick scuffle from the two men who sat at the rear of the shuttle.

Oscar laughed while Guttman growled.

"Okay, seriously. Stop," Guttman groused. "You always gang up on me. I've had it!"

The two salvagers wrestled for control, with Guttman using his short, stocky frame to its fullest advantage. Oscar managed to slip away with a grin, but Guttman spun around and his gaze zeroed in on Oscar.

Becker looked behind them and shook his head, pressing his lips into a thin line as though he were considering whether he was going to have to get out of the copilot's chair. Too much time in the shuttle meant tempers were at an all-time high.

"Okay, Guttman," Quinton said, "we'll do it your way."

Guttman stopped advancing on Oscar.

"There, you see," Oscar said, gesturing toward the front of the shuttle.

Guttman frowned and scratched the patchwork of a beard that grew over his flabby jawline. His belly stuck out beyond his chest, and he narrowed his protruding eyes suspiciously.

"But do me a favor first," Quinton said. "If you can detect whether or not any of these ships have a working power core *and* their main engines are operational, I'll take us there immediately."

Guttman bit his lower lip, shook his head, and glanced at the holoscreen next to his seat.

"Go on, take a look," Quinton said.

Guttman slid forcefully down into the chair and reached toward the holo-interface. Then, he banged his fist on the side panel. "I can't."

"Why not?"

"You know damn well why not."

If any of the ships had active power cores, they would already have detected them. The ships had been out there for a long time, waiting for the people of Three Moons Shipyards to either bring them in for refitting or scrap them altogether. Bringing depleted power cores back online took time they didn't have and required equipment they hadn't brought.

"What about the engines?" Quinton asked. He twisted around and looked at Guttman.

Guttman sneered and glared at his holoscreen. "You're not as smart as you think you are. There are some good prospects out there, like that HK light freighter over there. That one could work for what we need."

What we *need*, Quinton thought derisively. His three passengers had, over the past few months, helped him get the *Wayfarer* space worthy. This whole operation was his way of paying them back.

"You won't do it. You won't take a look."

Quinton glanced at Becker.

"We don't have time for this," Becker said.

"I knew it," Guttman groused.

"Why don't you do us all a favor and just shut up."

"Come back here and make me!"

Becker shot to his feet. "My pleasure," he growled.

Quinton grabbed Becker's thick, muscular arm, stopping him from going anywhere. Becker was tall and liked to fight, but he was no match for the cybernetic avatar that Quinton was housed in. No amount of implants or strength enhancements could compete with the enormously powerful, advanced composites of his avatar. Despite superior strength, speed, and intellect—something the others might question, but Quinton did not—frustration could get the better of them. They'd been cooped up together for a long time without shore leave, and they all needed a break but had decided they'd much rather steal a ship. Becker, Guttman and Oscar wanted to get whatever ship they could find to get away from him, and Quinton tried not to take it personally.

"Let me go," Becker said, his deep bass voice deadly quiet.

"Calm down, this will only take a second. What if Guttman's right?" Quinton asked.

Becker glared at Quinton's hand and then his gaze slid back to Quinton. When Quinton let go, Becker sat back down in the copilot's seat.

"You shouldn't encourage him," Becker said.

"What the hell is that supposed to mean? I'll tell you what,

Becker, I'm finished. I'm finished with all this. We're done," Guttman said.

"Hey, come on," Oscar said quietly. "Calm down."

"No, I'm serious. All of you walk all over me, and I've had it. I went along with it because in the Union we had each other's backs, but not anymore. There isn't any Union for us, and I don't have to take this crap from anyone."

"We just have to get through this one last thing and then we can take a break," Oscar said.

Guttman shook his head. "It's always one more thing. Then it's, 'Shut up, Guttman. You're an idiot, Guttman.' Well, I've had it. I'm not doing it anymore."

Quinton used the maneuvering thrusters to change course, bringing the shuttle toward the HK. Tempers had been flaring for weeks, and this was just the latest in a long line of escalating blowups.

"Will you be satisfied if I take us to the HK?" Quinton asked.

Guttman crossed his arms. "I don't care what you do."

"Well, I'm going to take us to the HK—the ship *you* picked. If you think it's good enough to salvage, I'll leave you on it. Deal?"

Guttman raised his eyebrows.

"I'm serious. I owe all of you. If you want out that badly, then here's your chance," Quinton said.

Guttman licked his lips and his eyes gleamed. He nodded. "All right," he said and looked at Oscar and Becker. "You guys are going to miss me when I'm gone."

Quinton altered course to give them a better view of the HK. Guttman's grin died, and a bout of laughter bubbled from Becker's mouth.

"Oh, she's a good ship right there. What do you say, Oscar? Think you can fly her?" Becker asked.

Entire sections were missing from the light freighter. It appeared that salvagers from Three Moons Shipyards had decided to scrap the ship for parts, but it had looked nearly intact from their initial approach vector.

Becker stopped laughing. "Okay, are we done? Now can we stick with the plan?"

Quinton changed course. "Sticking with the plan."

Guttman slammed his fist onto the holoscreen controls and they went off.

"Hey, don't worry about it," Oscar said. "You've still got us, and we love you."

Guttman jerked his head toward Oscar, who was holding out a bottle of Sangorian Bourbon.

"Peace offering," Oscar said, raising the bottle as the liquid sloshed around lazily.

Guttman smiled and grabbed the bottle, popping it open to take a long pull. Then he offered it to Oscar. They passed the bottle around and even Becker took a drink. He glanced at Quinton.

"Keep it. It would just be wasted on me," Quinton said. He could taste the bourbon. In fact, he could smell it and knew it was worth all the sighs of pleasure from the others. He could take a drink and his sensors would report on the chemical components of the bronze liquid, but he couldn't enjoy it. It wouldn't take the edge off. That was just the way things were.

Becker handed the bottle back to Guttman and gave him a nod.

Then just like that, there was peace once again on the shuttle.

Quinton could have flown the shuttle by integrating with its computer instead of the physical flight-control systems. Personality Matrix Constructs—PMCs—were capable of direct machine interfaces, among other useful skills, and his prototype avatar was designed for the PMC interface. It was radically more advanced than the Consciousness Driven Android—CDA—he'd trained for in the Acheron Confederacy Navy. Quinton had been a commander in the ACN, which caused no shortage of friction with Becker and the others. They hated and mistrusted anything that had to do with the Acheron Confederacy, and it didn't matter to them that the confederacy had been gone for almost a century.

The outdated star charts on Quinton's ship had designated this sector along the Castellus Federal Alliance expansion route. For a century, Quinton's PMC had been in storage on a third-tier colony world. He didn't know how he'd come to be on that world, and he had no idea who had activated his PMC. His knowledge of the interworkings of the galactic region was woefully out of date. It would take time to put the pieces together, and his arrangement with Becker and the others had helped, but that deal was coming to an end.

"I never know what to think when you're quiet like this," Becker said.

"I was just checking the status of the *Wayfarer*."

They couldn't risk flying the *Wayfarer* into the shipyard's region where they might be detected by automated defenses. Although Quinton had his doubts about this, Becker was sure this was the case, and it wasn't Quinton's mission. Becker was calling the shots. Instead, they'd opted for a fifteen-hour journey on a shuttle—fifteen hours to breach the protected interior of the Three Moons Shipyards and fifteen hours of the bickering that came with being confined to small places. This didn't bother Quinton so much. Then again, he didn't have to put up with the smell. Three men in a small space... There was going to be a smell eventually, and there was plenty of ripeness in the shuttle. Quinton could just ignore his highly sensitive smell receptors. The others had no such luxury.

They flew toward a large installation that was built into the side of an oddly shaped asteroid. Thousands of docking ports covered the outside of the asteroid, and automated tugger drones guided various ships in for inspection and evaluation. The larger ships were docked along the perimeter and other designated docking ports. Small to mid-size freighters were escorted to open hangar bays. Quinton saw that the hangars were designed for certain ship types but not others. Some hangars held ships that were in various states of either repair or breakdown—he couldn't decide which.

"The shipyard's name doesn't resonate with this place," Quinton said.

Long-range sensors had detected six asteroids nearly the size of small moons.

Becker looked at him and shrugged one shoulder. "Are you surprised? Three Moons Shipyards is just a cover name."

"It looks more like a junkyard."

"It probably was at one point."

Quinton nodded. "Are you sure about this?"

"About what?"

"This," Quinton said, gesturing toward the video feed on the main holoscreen. "There have to be better ships out there than this."

"Oh, there are, but they'll also have more security measures in place to protect them, as well as trackers."

"I can deal with trackers."

"We'll find something. By the looks of things, we'll have our pick and can probably get more than one ship from here."

"If you say so," Quinton said, not convinced.

"You haven't been salvaging as long as we have. Ships like the *Wayfarer* are few and far between. More often than not, it takes the parts of multiple ships to get one in good working order. By that time, it'll have a new identification and won't show up on any rogue registry of stolen property."

Salvaging, or something directly tied to it, was the way of life in the post Federation War galaxy. Quinton didn't point out that they used to build things—ships, stations, colonies. Exploration and expansion were what galactic residents had striven for. Now, it was just this—salvaging for scraps.

"Does it bother you?" Becker asked.

Quinton shook his head. "It depends on who we're stealing from. The original owners of these ships are long gone, so is it really stealing?"

"So pragmatic."

"It's the least I can do," Quinton said.

He flew away from the larger docking ports. They couldn't fly the bigger ships with such a small crew. But that wasn't exactly right. Quinton could fly those ships with the help of his VI, Radek, but the point of getting a ship for Becker and the others was so they could part ways with him. PMCs were dangerous and sometimes unstable, and they experienced Quinton differently now. Despite months aboard the *Wayfarer*, their fear had dulled only a little. He'd even updated his appearance to look human down to the finest detail, but that had created more problems than it solved. Now they believed he was just pretending to be something he wasn't.

"Take us down near the maintenance access area," Becker said and then craned his neck toward the others. "All right, pay attention. From here, we'll explore the nearby hangars. We're looking for ships that've had some work done to them. The priority is the most intact ship we can find. With any luck, we'll find a few of them."

Quinton glanced at the layout of the central complex. "How do you know the ships in these hangar bays are any better than somewhere else?"

Becker smirked. "Trade secret."

Quinton made an *uh-huh* sound and plunged the shuttle toward an older Kappa freight ship, which still sported large bronze cargo containers that looked more like canisters. He increased their velocity, and the cargo carriers blurred past the video feed.

Becker went quiet, his mouth forming a grim line.

Proximity alarms sounded inside the shuttle and a warning flashed on the main HUD.

"You're going to kill us all!" Guttman said.

"Come on, Quinton, pull up," Oscar said.

Large shipping containers were mostly smooth walled except for the junction points where both interior and exterior sensor towers were located. These were essential for protecting the cargo and the shipping container.

The shuttle sped toward an island of towers.

"I don't know, I'm feeling a little unhinged," Quinton replied. "You know, there are several open comms channels." He updated the HUD to show the Three Moons Shipyards secure transmissions, as well as the command-and-control comlinks used for their drone workforce. "I'm sure I can tweak the control signal and find out why this area is so important."

Becker shook his head and Guttman shouted for him to stop.

"Do you think their comms systems can detect a rogue PMC interference if I attempt system access?"

"For the love of—Just answer him," Guttman pleaded.

Seconds went by while the shuttle sped toward the towers.

Becker looked at Quinton. "Go ahead. See what happens."

Damn it, Quinton thought. Becker was calling his bluff.

Quinton's tactical VI presented a course for him to fly through the towers. Becker watched, his face deadpanned. Guttman and Oscar's groans became louder but then were cut off as Quinton cranked up his frame rate. His perception of time accelerated so quickly that it slowed down for everyone else. Seconds in normal time dragged out while Quinton executed evasive maneuvers that narrowly avoided the towers. The inertia dampeners squealed, throwing up alarms as the shuttle jerked through the plot Quinton had programed. Maneuvering thrusters fired in concert with the mains that were beyond anything a mere pilot could execute, making use of systems— including artificial gravity—to assist with obstacle avoidance.

Quinton's frame rate returned to normal and Guttman's scream was cut short. They'd made it through, but the maneuver had pinned everyone to their seats. His passengers were jostled but would otherwise be okay.

Becker shook his head to clear it. "And you wonder why we can't wait to get our own ship."

"That hurts. You could have just answered the question."

"You're right. I could have."

"You still can."

"Maybe."

"I'm still waiting."

Becker's lips lifted. "You can't stand not knowing."

Quinton sighed inwardly. Becker was right. He didn't want to give the former salvager the satisfaction of knowing that, but Becker's smirk meant he already knew.

He was being foolish. He thought he'd gotten his impulse response under control, which had been a real issue when he'd been trapped in an old garden bot. The limited systems access had so severely reduced his capacity that it had been a miracle he'd survived. But his current avatar was designed for a PMC. He had full access to his memories, but there were still questions he couldn't answer, although this was no time to charge down that particular wormhole.

Quinton flew them to the maintenance hatch and deployed the docking clamps. The others activated their EVA suits and secured their helmets. Quinton didn't have a need for protective outerwear since the avatar could function quite well in temperature extremes that included a vacuum. And he didn't need to breathe, so oxygen wasn't an issue for him. However, in order to conceal his identity, he updated the avatar's configuration to make it look like he was wearing an EVA suit as well.

Becker led them to the hatch and gestured for Quinton to join him. Guttman and Oscar waited behind them.

Quinton accessed the door-control systems. Bypassing the

pitiful security of the access control system was beyond easy; however, in order to cover their tracks, he brought up an access list of the previous systems that had used the door to gain entry to the hangars. A quick analysis filtered the entries by time stamp, and he picked the user or system that would most likely be used to access the door.

Quinton yanked the hatch open and they all went inside the complex.

"No alarms," Oscar said.

Becker looked at Quinton and nodded. "Good job." He then looked at the others. "The layout should be familiar."

Guttman nodded. "It looks like a Union layout."

"Where do you think Lennix Crowe got it from?"

The others shared a knowing look, and Quinton finally understood why Becker seemed to know where he was going.

Becker accessed his wrist computer, and both Guttman's and Oscar's highlighted with the data he'd sent them.

"You know, I could just access the system and probably find suitable ships quicker," Quinton offered.

"You know we can't risk that," Becker said.

Guttman and Oscar headed down the corridor away from them.

Becker went in the opposite direction and Quinton followed him.

"The security here's pitiful. They'd never know I was in the system."

"You're right because I don't want you in the system. Quinton, you told me you'd cooperate. We do this my way. If I don't need you to access the system, then I don't want you to do it. If we come up short, we'll try it your way. All right?"

They weren't concerned about whether Quinton could access the system. They were more concerned about whether his access would trigger alarms. Quinton wasn't sure he wouldn't trigger any of the PMC fail-safes that seemed to be in just about every computer system they'd come across. It was easier to hide his presence on the larger and more complex systems, but that wasn't the case here.

They spent the next few hours exploring the hangar bays that contained ships in various states of disrepair. Some of the ships had massive hull breaches while others were missing critical systems from main engine pods, life support, or the power core, and sometimes all three.

"Doesn't this bother you?" Quinton asked.

"Actually, it's kind of encouraging."

"How?"

"Because those components were removed to rebuild something else. We're looking for the ship they were rebuilding," Becker replied.

The salvager had removed his helmet because an atmosphere was being maintained. Quinton found this interesting since there was very little life on this part of the station. The air was cold, which was evident whenever Becker breathed.

A comlink registered to both of them.

"I think I found a good one," Guttman said.

A few moments later, Oscar joined them on the comms channel. "I'm not having any luck at all. I keep finding breakdown projects. No intact ships at all."

"It's all right, Oscar, I found one. You should head to my coordinates," Guttman said.

"On my way," Oscar said and left the comms channel.

"What did you find?" Becker asked.

"A Stellar Gypsy that has all the critical systems intact. Looks like it was going to be cleared for auction in another month or two. The modular layout is for carrying cargo," Guttman said, his voice high with excitement.

"That's a good find. Keep checking the systems and see if you can bring it online. Have Oscar do a double-check with you."

"Roger that," Guttman said and disconnected.

They headed to another hangar bay, and Quinton was starting to feel that his time with these people was just about up. He would help them get away from here if the ships they found were in working order. Then that would be it. That was the end of their arrangement.

"It looks like you've got what you wanted," Quinton said.

"Not yet. I know there's another ship over here."

"You know what they say about wanting more."

Becker frowned and shook his head. "No, what do they say?"

"Sometimes it's better just to accept what you have."

"One ship does not a fleet make."

"Is that what you want—a fleet of ships?"

Becker tilted his head to the side and peered into the hangar. He mumbled a response, and a subspace comlink opened from the *Wayfarer*.

"Go ahead, Radek," Quinton said.

Radek was his virtual intelligence assistant that actually resided within his Energy Storage System—ESS—but Quinton had left the sub-VI on the *Wayfarer* to monitor the ship systems.

"A massive broadcast signal has just reached this star system," Radek said.

"From where?"

"From the communications buoy in the system. The origin of the broadcast is unknown."

Becker looked at Quinton. "What's going on?"

"The *Wayfarer* detected a broadcast that came from outside the star system."

"I have analyzed the signal and confirmed that it's a PMC activation signal similar to the signal that activated you on Zeta-Six."

Quinton's thoughts scattered for what felt like long moments as seconds dragged by. Radek sent him a data dump of the signal detection and the VI's analysis. This contained standard comms initiation protocols, but it was looking for a particular acknowledgment before the rest of the data inside the signal could be reviewed. Quinton was a PMC and could provide the special acknowledgment but wouldn't risk it. There was no way for him to determine what else was inside the signal. There could be block protocols that could initiate changes in him and in Radek. It was too risky to do further analysis here, even if he increased his frame rate to maximum. He needed the computing resources aboard the *Wayfarer*.

The signal was almost here, and that meant there must be a PMC somewhere nearby.

Quinton looked at Becker. "We've got a big problem."

CHAPTER TWO

BECKER WAS STANDING inside a hangar bay and had just turned on the overhead lights when he suddenly went still and a wide smile lit up his face.

A golden hull nearly gleamed in the light. Heavy robotic arms were frozen over the rear of the ship, and it looked as if several large sections of the hull plating had been completely replaced. The ship almost completely filled the entire hangar bay.

Becker raised his wrist, reading his amber-colored holoscreen, and grinned. Quinton cleared his throat and Becker tore his gaze away from the ship. "What did you say?" he asked, his eyes sliding back to the holoscreen.

"I said, we've got a big problem—"

"Yeah, baby!" Becker pumped his fist and looked at Quinton. "Critical systems are all intact. Someone even restocked atmospheric filters for the life-support systems. There's enough fuel in the power core to take us away from here. Jump drive," Becker paused and whistled. "It's got a Paxton Series 15 drive—"

"Becker! You're not listening to me. We've got a big problem," Quinton said. Becker raised his eyebrows and looked at him questioningly. "Radek detected a PMC activation signal heading this way."

Becker blinked several times and leaned forward. "What? Heading this way, or…"

Quinton brought up his own holoscreen and showed Becker the trajectory of the signal. It would reach them in less than ten minutes.

Becker's gaze darted to the ceiling, his lips pressing into a white slash. Then he looked over at the ship with longing eyes. "Yeah, but that doesn't mean there's a PMC here. Right? The signal that activated you went through thousands of star systems before you were reactivated."

"That's true, but activation signals aren't sent out randomly. At some point, there was an ESS in this star system," Quinton replied.

Becker swore and took a few steps toward the ship, then turned back toward Quinton.

"Think about it. This system was used for scrap. It's a good place to hide something, especially during the Federation Wars."

Becker bit his lower lip a little and then sighed explosively. "Can you help me with the ship?"

"I don't think you understand."

"I do. Can you help or not?"

"That signal is going to trip the security protocols for the entire area. Then, Three Moons security teams are going to swoop in after they initiate a lockdown. No one can afford to have a PMC roaming around their operations, especially if the Sentinels are tracking the activation signal."

"Have any Sentinels been detected?"

Quinton couldn't believe Becker was being like this. Normally, the spacer was much more cautious. "Not yet," he said finally.

"So we have time. Have they initiated a lockdown?"

Quinton rolled his eyes, then licked his index finger and held it in the air as if trying to gauge the way the wind would blow. "How should I know? I told you I wasn't in their systems. What the hell, man? We've gotta get out of here."

"No!" Becker said and stomped toward the ship. "It's a damn Diamondback Trailblazer. There's no way I'm going to…" He raised his hand to his ear and opened a comlink to the others. "What's your status?"

"I've just begun the startup sequence for the Red Sun freighter. Oscar found a Mercury class star jumper a few hangars away from me," Guttman replied.

"Things are heating up. Can you switch to emergency startup sequence and use maneuvering thrusters to get to the waypoint?" Becker asked.

Quinton heard the atmospheric scrubbers running through a cycle overhead. Radek was still feeding him updates via the subspace comlink. By all outward appearances, no alarms had been raised.

"Guttman," Oscar said, "you don't need to wait for the power core to come online if you've got emergency backup power. You can bring up minimal systems while the power core comes online."

Becker ran toward the Diamondback and initiated the maintenance override to gain access to the ship systems. Quinton walked away from the gleaming hull and headed back to the corridor. Not directly interfacing with the station's computer systems was keeping him in the dark, and he walked over to the access terminal near the hangar bay entry. The interface came right up and there were no alarms. What was taking them so long? The activation signal must have been detected by now, but he couldn't confirm it because he wasn't patched into the station.

Overhead, the atmosphere scrubbers cycled again, sending a gust of air into the hangar.

Quinton squatted and placed the palm of his hand on the floor, increasing the sensitivity of both his auditory system and his sense of touch. He began cataloging the sounds and subtle vibrations through the floor, increasing his frame rate slightly to give himself an edge in analysis and reaction time. He couldn't increase it too much, or detecting anything out of the ordinary would be all but impossible. He just needed a slight edge.

Becker shouted an impressive stream of curses and hastened away from the ship. From Quinton's perspective, Becker wasn't moving very fast. He partitioned his efforts so he could interact with Becker while still doing his analysis. Multitasking like this made him more reliant on his VI assistants, which could sometimes be a challenge.

"Who the hell rips out the entire backup system?" Becker said and frowned. "What are you doing?"

"I'm listening."

"For what?"

"To see if anyone's coming."

Becker shrugged. "Oh that. Don't worry about it," he said and walked past Quinton.

Quinton stood up.

"I'm patched into the system," Becker said, waving his arm up and down, and the amber holoscreen flashed. "No alarms." He grinned.

This was too much. Quinton was often accused of being reckless, but seeing Becker's flippant reference to station security was downright alarming. "Wait a second."

"Can't wait, Quinton. There's another hangar this way. Thanks for the ride. We'll take it from here. You can head back to the shuttle."

Guttman and Oscar paused their own conversation.

"Goodbye, Quinton. It's been great," Guttman said, and then a bout of laughter bubbled out over the comlink.

Oscar grinned. "Woohoo! Thanks for the memories."

Quinton shook his head and hastened to follow Becker.

"I thought we'd never be rid of him. We're almost free, boys,"

Becker said and started jogging down the corridor. Without warning, he lost his balance, as if the floor had dipped heavily to one side.

"What the…" Quinton muttered and blocked out the jeering from the others.

He heard a faint humming sound far down the corridor that sounded more like an echo. A soft breeze blew overhead again, and Quinton glanced at the vent. Becker stumbled ahead.

The others were laughing uproariously and spouting random words.

"I could never leave my body. Women would miss me too much," Oscar said.

"They'd have to get past your bad breath," Becker quipped.

This led to them all speaking at once.

"Hey, morons!" Quinton shouted. "Put your helmets back on. You're being gassed."

He had to repeat himself two more times before his inebriated companions acknowledged that he'd spoken.

"I got your helmet right here," Guttman said mockingly.

"Wait a minute. Is that why I'm feeling so good?" Oscar asked with a long sigh. "God, I really needed this. Just needed to cut loose and be still. I couldn't handle being on that smelly shuttle anymore."

Quinton bet they were just sitting on the floor, taking it easy.

The hell with this, Quinton thought. Becker stumbled and fell, and Quinton quickly caught up with him. He pulled him forward and palmed the helmet controls on Becker's spacesuit. The helmet protracted, and clean air began pumping into the spacer.

Becker groaned for a few seconds, and Quinton spared a moment's satisfaction, knowing the headache that awaited him. There were still no alarms, which Quinton no longer believed was possible. Time to break his promise. He cranked up his frame rate to the max and infiltrated the Three Moons' computer systems. One of the advantages of being a PMC was the ability of directly accessing any computer system. Energy-state data storage meant that he could access the data at the speed of light. Quinton's PMC actually resided inside an ESS. Essentially, he was a being of light with the strong perception of being human. The leuridium core could power his ESS for a thousand years. Quinton's VIs helped manage the brain-to-machine interface, which also included accessing external computing systems. The risk of accessing the current systems was the enhanced detection capabilities for PMC infiltration. Those capabilities hadn't been well developed when Quinton was uploaded into an ESS. A century and several brutal wars later, he'd awakened to a galaxy vastly different from the one he remembered. Memories of his old life stirred, as if sensing his attention, but he ignored them. No use dwelling on the past. Whatever the past was, it was gone. At least that was what a friend had told him once.

Quinton blew past the pitiful security protocols. Civilian-grade security was no match for his capabilities, nor were they designed to be, and he obliterated the PMC detection protocols for anomalous activity before the system had a chance to detect him. Computing limitations could always be tied to the system they resided on. Quinton's platform had been created through the Acheron Confederacy Navy's advanced research projects initiative. The Acheron Confederacy hadn't been the most powerful federation in the galaxy, but its technical base was ahead of the curve with research and development it had carried out in secret. Quinton's cybernetic avatar outclassed most computing systems he'd encountered. His VI henchmen infiltrated and confirmed that the station's automated defenses *had* been engaged.

The lockdown protocols were designed to function even in the event of successful infiltration. This made things more complicated. Initiated security measures, which included atmospheric contamination, functioned on isolated systems that were now offline, and he couldn't simply kill the lockdown protocols.

They'd have to be physically reset. They functioned as such for the purpose of remaining undetected and thus able to operate in isolation. Those systems had their marching orders and there was no central command authority to stop them.

Clever.

Quinton brought his frame rate back to normal. Becker was breathing deeply.

"I said to put your helmets on," Becker snapped.

"I'm already on the bridge," Guttman said. "You should see this thing. This is it. This is my ship. I think it was going to be someone's luxury ship. Not anymore. The carpets feel amazing. I just need to take off my other boot."

Becker pushed his brows forward in frustration.

"I bet it's good," Quinton said.

Becker glared at him.

"Quinton, you have no idea. My bed on the *Wayfarer* was nice enough, but this is amazing," Guttman said while letting out a moan of pleasure. "Heh, there's wetness on my cheek."

Quinton tried not to imagine Guttman stripping off his spacesuit.

"Hey, have you closed off the ship? Are you ready to take your new ship out for a ride?"

Becker glared at him. "Are you trying to get him killed?"

Guttman groaned with effort. "Yeah... No. I'm not sure."

"You'd better get to it if you want to keep that ship."

"You're right. Is someone coming?" Guttman asked. He sounded like he was climbing into a seat.

"Yup. They're on their way. I'm sending you a set of coordinates. Enter those into the navigation system and switch to the ship's life-support systems," Quinton said and muted the comlink to Guttman. "He probably doesn't have his helmet or his spacesuit on, for that matter. The only way he's gonna make it is to escape on that ship. His head will start to clear once he's off the station's umbilical."

"Hey, there's lights outside," Oscar said.

Quinton accessed the video feed. Oscar was sprawled on the floor, looking as if he'd just rolled on the ground. Quinton traced the source of the flashing and saw three oval-shaped security drones flying through the corridors. He accessed the door-control systems and closed off the corridor.

He looked at Becker. "Security drones."

Becker unholstered his blaster and Quinton did the same.

A comlink broadcast came through the station's communication systems.

"What the hell was that?" Becker asked.

Quinton recognized it immediately, even though he didn't want to believe it. It was the acknowledgment of a PMC activation signal. Somewhere in this facility, a PMC was coming online.

CHAPTER THREE

"What's happening?" Becker asked. He kept his gaze down the corridor with his weapon ready. Ribbons of flaxen light radiated from both sides of the corridor, separated by adjoining sections that were locked together.

"There's a PMC coming online," Quinton said and tacked on, "I think."

"What do you mean 'you think'? Don't you know how it works?"

Quinton brought up the standard operating procedures for PMC reactivation on his HUD.

"We're slightly more complicated than the standard computing core."

There was a loud clang against the bulkhead door farthest from them. Several more clangs reverberated through the corridor, followed by a bright flash as the security drone began cutting through the door. The video feed showed that an armored unit with eight legs, like a spider, had seized the door while it used a plasma cutter to slice through it. As if sensing it was being watched, one of the drone's crimson optics spun toward the camera. Then the video feed went dark.

Quinton and Becker hastened away from the door.

"That's right, you're a sophisticated piece of—"

"Be careful how you finish that statement," Quinton warned. "Right now, I'm trying to keep all of us safe. Oscar is staring at the back of his hand like he's never seen it before, and Guttman has stripped off his spacesuit down to his underwear. Geez, there's a stain on his belly. Does he ever not get food everywhere? Not to mention the security drones that are converging on our location. If you want to take your chances without me, I can live with it."

Becker glanced behind them.

"Eyes front. We're turning here," Quinton warned.

They increased their pace and ran past another set of bulkhead doors. Quinton tried to close them, but they wouldn't respond to his commands.

"They won't shut."

Becker slowed down. "We'll have to close them manually."

A metallic slam echoed down the corridor. The drones were through, and Quinton saw them race through the opening at breakneck speeds.

"Come on, it's too late for that," he said.

They ran along the corridor, Quinton matching Becker's pace.

Guttman's cough sounded through the comlink. "We're green across the board."

Becker cursed. "Guttman, hang on a second."

"It's all right. I locked out the console he's sitting at," Quinton said.

"How?"

"Comlink. I've uploaded the waypoint coordinates to the nav computer."

"What's with these straps? I can't move!" Guttman shouted.

"Sit still," Becker ordered.

"Guttman, guess what?" Quinton said as they ran. "There are

a group of female Servitors on that ship, and they're heading to the bridge right now to help you out."

"Really?" Guttman asked with awe in his voice. He sounded like he was twisting in his seat to look for them.

"Yup, there are six or seven of them on their way right now."

"But no one is supposed to be on the ship."

Becker shook his head. "They come with the ship. It's part of the luxury package. Enjoy it. They can't wait to meet you."

"I will," Guttman said, sounding like he was drifting off to sleep.

Quinton muted the comlink so Guttman couldn't hear them.

"Good thinking. That ought to keep him occupied for a while," Becker said.

Servitors were genetically enhanced humans that exemplified physical beauty, and their services extended beyond primal pleasures to nurturing psychological and emotional wellbeing. Quinton had yet to actually meet one. They'd encountered an agent who had disguised herself as a Servitor and had had no shortage of admirers, with Guttman first and foremost among them.

Quinton pulled Becker to the side just as a red particle beam singed the wall where his head had been and returned fire with stunning accuracy. Two of the flying security drones tumbled out of the air and crashed. The third dropped toward the ground and flew near the wall. Quinton couldn't get a clear shot at it.

"Where's the other one?" Becker asked.

That was a good question. The big spider-drone should have been with the others. More and more of the video feeds were cutting out and going offline, blinding him. How could a glorified scrapyard have such a comprehensive response for intruders?

"I don't know."

They kept running.

"Are we close to Oscar's location?" Becker asked. He was starting to breathe heavier.

"Hey, you don't have to worry about me. I found a ship," Oscar said.

The pilot had been quiet this whole time. The video feed of the hangar bay showed Oscar sitting in a small, two-person aircar that rested on a raised maintenance platform. The entire engine was in pieces on the floor, and it looked as if it had been in the process of being gutted for parts. Quinton saved a quick recording of Oscar sitting in the aircar, attempting to engage the flight controls. He was acting as if the vehicle was actually moving.

"He's not going anywhere," Quinton said, bemused, and sent the video feed to Becker.

Becker grinned for a few moments and then frowned. "The bulkhead doors are closed— the video feeds just dropped for the surrounding corridors."

Charging into the area where several spider-drones were attempting to reach Oscar wasn't a great idea. They were armed, and Quinton wasn't sure their blasters could penetrate the drones' armor.

"We have to get to him," Becker said. "We can't leave him like that. All they have to do is vent the hangar bay and he's dead."

Quinton used the comlink channel to Oscar's wrist computer to access the aircar's computer systems. It still had emergency power, which was fortunate for Oscar. He engaged the canopy and a protective shield protracted over Oscar's head, sealing the inside. The aircar's life-support systems came online, and Oscar stared at the roof of the vehicle with a mixture of awe and bewilderment.

"Now sit tight," Quinton said. His voice boomed over the aircar's sound system. "Don't touch anything."

"I wasn't... I wasn't going to," Oscar replied.

"Can you lock him out like you did Guttman?" Becker asked.

"I can't, but I did enable the first-time-user preference interface." If Oscar accessed the aircar's controls, he'd spend twenty minutes answering new-user prompts.

They raced to the end of the corridor, where it split into two different directions. A spider-drone sped toward them and Quinton cranked the bulkhead door shut. The drone slammed into the door with enough force to put a sizable dent in it. They moved fast, but Becker continued to breathe heavily, and Quinton wasn't sure how long the spacer could keep up the pace. He was certain Becker wouldn't appreciate an offer to carry him.

There was another broadcast from the PMC being activated. It was broadcast on all comlink channels, and Quinton was able to pinpoint its source.

"Why is it doing that?" Becker asked.

"It's not the PMC. It's the VI that's sending out a general broadcast. It's probably because the ESS is unable to be installed into a host, so the VI is requesting information on how it should proceed," Quinton said.

"Well, can't you tell it to shut up? Tell it this was an accident and it should shut down."

Quinton felt a flash of irritation ignite amid his thoughts. The utter disdain that Becker and the others had for PMCs sometimes rubbed Quinton the wrong way. PMCs were alive. They were actual people. They weren't machines that should be shut down until it was convenient. The fact that they were being used as pawns was the source of growing irritation for Quinton. He'd been in the same situation when he was brought online. He'd been hunted as a result, and he was very lucky Radek had taken matters into his own virtual hands or he wouldn't be alive.

"I'm not doing that."

"What? Why not?"

"Because it's not a machine. How would you like it if I knocked you out every time you wanted to wake up? Dose you up with drugs to make you unconscious just because you had the audacity to wake at an inconvenient time." The words came out harsher than he intended them, and Becker was taken aback.

"All right, I get it," he said evenly, "but we've got to save Oscar."

Quinton opened the control interface for the maintenance platform where the aircar was located. He ordered it to lower one side so the top of the aircar faced toward the hangar doors. The hangar bay door-control systems were still online, so he ordered them to open. The hangar bay quickly depleted its atmosphere and Quinton initiated the aircar's emergency egress system. The passenger compartment of the aircar was also an escape pod. Its thrusters exerted enough force to carry it beyond the hangar bay doors and out into space.

Becker watched the video feed, his eyes wide. "What have you done?"

"Oscar is safe. He's got thirty-six hours of O2, which is more than enough time for us to pick him up. I'm not leaving without that PMC."

Becker knew better than to argue with him.

Quinton scanned the walls and found a maintenance access tunnel. He bypassed the security mechanism for the door, and they entered, having to bend over a little to fit inside the small space. Quinton closed the door and waited for a few moments, hearing the security drones race by, none the wiser.

"We're clear," Quinton said quietly.

Becker led the way since they didn't have room for Quinton to squeeze ahead.

"Straight on for a hundred meters. Then left," Quinton said.

Becker quickened his pace. Quinton noticed that he kept glancing toward the ceiling.

"Minimal monitoring in here. They're probably reliant on drone check-ins rather than monitoring these tunnels," Quinton said.

Becker nodded. "How'd you know these tunnels were here? Did you see it on their system?"

"This isn't the first time I've done something like this."

"Now there's a story I'd like to hear."

"Later," Quinton said. Despite Becker's disdain for the pre-Federation War galaxy, he was keenly interested in what Quinton had done for the Acheron Confederacy Navy.

"How are we getting this PMC out of here?" Becker asked.

They reached an intersecting tunnel and Becker gestured for Quinton to lead.

"You don't want to take the long way back to the shuttle?"

"Not really."

Quinton heard the clatter of the security drones as they went by in the corridor, detecting four of them. He tried to detect a comlink session being used by the drones, but there wasn't any. They must be coordinating using a line-of-sight comms, but without any video feeds in the area, he had no way of confirming his hunch. Whoever designed the security response for Three Moons had taken their job quite seriously.

"How far do we have to go?" Becker whispered.

"Just a little farther," Quinton replied and then added, "The fun part will be going back into the corridor."

"Why do we have to go back?"

"Because it's the only way to get outside."

"You didn't say anything about going outside."

"You didn't think the PMC was in here?"

"Yeah, I kinda did. I figured it was on a ship that had been brought in or in some kind of cargo stored here. Nothing goes to waste in places like these," Becker said.

"Not a bad guess, but still not right."

"You told us the activation signal propagates through a star system's communication infrastructure, so it didn't need to know precisely where a PMC was stored."

"That's right, but this one came directly here. To this asteroid, in fact," Quinton said.

Becker didn't reply because they were nearing the maintenance hatch that would let them back into the corridor. Quinton leaned toward the hatch and listened for a few moments. He looked at Becker. "Okay, it sounds clear. There's an exterior hatch and airlock a short distance from here. We'll take that to the asteroid's surface. Then it's just a few hundred meters away."

Becker nodded.

Quinton opened the door and they stepped into the dark corridor. The security protocols must have switched off the lighting, but Quinton could see in the dark and Becker's HUD could compensate for low-light conditions. They quickly ran toward the exterior hatch.

Quinton opened the hatch and saw an airlock a short distance from them. He stepped through the hatch, but something slammed into him from above and knocked him back into the corridor. As he was crashing into the wall, he cranked his frame rate up to maximum in order to quicken his perception of time and slow everything else down. Becker was just starting to flinch away from the doorway, and the spider-drone that had been hidden on the ceiling of the airlock was coming through the door. Quinton lowered his frame rate and aimed his blaster. At this point, his perception of time was still way above normal, but it wasn't at a standstill for everyone else. Plasma bolts shot from his blaster. His back hit the wall as the bolts hit the spider-drone's armored chassis. Quinton fired his weapon again as the spider-drone closed the distance. Becker was turning toward him. The jagged ends of the spider-drone's legs also had grabbers, which meant they probably performed maintenance, as well as security. The plasma bolts scorched the armored chassis but didn't penetrate it. He angled his fire toward one of the oncoming legs and blew the end off the body. Then the spider-drone was on top of him.

Quinton grabbed the nearest leg and twisted to the side. He jumped toward the ceiling, yanking the spider-drone's leg hard. Becker fired his blaster at it but missed. The spider-drone's leg bent at an awkward angle and Quinton let go, but it still had six legs. It stabbed him, and the hardened alloy penetrated his own armored torso. Quinton didn't feel pain, but he did register that the spider-drone could do some serious damage to him. The drone slammed him to the ground, and he rolled to the side, breaking the jagged foot off the drone's leg as he did.

The spider-drone tried to stab him again, but Quinton was too fast. He scrambled out of the way and stood up. More spider-drones were heading toward them from farther away.

"Go out the airlock!" Quinton shouted, making sure his speech came out in normal time so Becker would understand him.

Becker spun toward the hatch. He was sure Becker was moving as fast as he could, but he still appeared to be moving in slow motion. The spider-drones were able to move quicker than an unenhanced human, but Quinton's avatar had the advantage now that the trap had been sprung. He increased the power output of his blaster and took out three of the spider-drone's legs. With only one left, it couldn't do more than flail about. Quinton ran past it and into the airlock. He slammed the hatch shut and was through the airlock before the other spider-drones reached it.

The asteroid's terrain wasn't as uneven as he expected. Becker waited for him outside, and Quinton looked at him incredulously. Why wasn't he moving?

"I don't know which way to go."

Quinton shook his head. "Sorry about that," he said and closed the distance. He grabbed Becker by the back of his suit. "We've got to move."

They were at the edge of the artificial gravity field, but it was still half the standard one g. He took several steps to gain momentum and leaped. Becker used his suit thrusters to level them off and extend the jump.

The brownish, roughened terrain sped by as Quinton jumped into the air again. The PMCs location was on his HUD, and they were closing the distance.

"We've got company heading our way. Where's the shuttle?"

Quinton had had their shuttle on standby since they first arrived. He hadn't been convinced they wouldn't need to find another way off the asteroid.

"It's coming," Quinton replied. He'd tasked a VI to manage the autopilot so the shuttle would head to their location.

Quinton peered into the distance and saw what looked like an escape pod that had crash-landed onto the surface of the asteroid. It looked to have been there a long time.

"We're going to have to hold them off. Aim for the legs. They're vulnerable there," Quinton said.

As they closed the distance, they noted patches of bronze amid the blackened walls of the pod, which easily blended with the asteroid's surface. If there hadn't been an active comms signal coming from it, Quinton was sure he'd have missed it.

Quinton opened the escape pod's hatch while Becker fired his weapon at the spider-drones, but they dodged out of the way. Inside the pod was an ESS core suspended in a counter-grav cradle that had been designed for it. The decagonal shape of the leuridium core glowed with a bluish light that pulsed lazily.

"Why don't they send out a body with it? Seems short-sighted to me," Becker complained.

"I'll bring it up at the next PMC governance review meeting about improving their services," Quinton said.

He couldn't reach inside and just snatch it out of the cradle. There were defenses in place. He initiated a comlink using his own PMC protocols.

PMC offline.

VI designate Greta.

Quinton observed the spark of communication from Radek to Greta. Radek had to conduct the initial greeting, or Greta might not communicate with him.

PMC Quinton Aldren – G-Class.

Greta, we're here to retrieve you.

Understood. Clearance given to transport PMC Nash Harper into an acceptable host.

No host available. Hostile forces in the area. Need to transport.

Must confirm with COMCENT.

PMC Nash Harper will not be moved without a host.

"Damn it," Quinton said.

"What is it?" Becker asked.

"It won't allow me to retrieve it without a host."

Becker's mouth opened a little and he frowned. "We tried. Let's just leave it."

Quinton wasn't going to leave it. Greta was just following safety protocols, but he didn't have time for this.

"I see the shuttle," Becker said and then fired his weapon at a spider-drone. He hit one of the legs, but it hardly slowed down.

Guttman's comlink became active. "Someone's firing weapons at my ship," he said. His voice was clear. The euphoric effects must have worn off. "Quinton, what did you do? I can't control the ship."

Quinton sent a command to end the lockdown via comlink on Guttman's ship.

"Head to the waypoint," Becker said.

"I'm trying."

"Do the best you can. We're a little busy down here," Becker said.

"Fine," Guttman grumbled.

Becker kept firing his weapon at the two spider-drones as they continued to push closer to their position. They darted out of the way of incoming fire, staggering their approach.

Quinton glanced at them. "Hold your fire."

"Why?"

"I have an idea. I need one of them intact."

Becker glanced at the escape pod and his eyebrows raised. "You can't be serious. You're going to stick that thing into one of those drones?"

"Do you have a better idea?"

"How the hell are you going to do it?"

Quinton watched the spider-drones racing toward them, their legs propelling them across the uneven terrain with ease.

"I have no idea."

CHAPTER FOUR

"YOU ONLY NEED ONE OF THEM," Becker said and fired his weapon.

Quinton did the same, focusing his fire on the drone that had taken the most damage. The spider-drone's legs were built in sections, so unless they shot them out near the body, the thing could still move.

The other drone stopped and shot its particle beam toward them. Quinton took out its leg, cutting off the deadly beam, but Becker cried out in pain. The spacer went down and dropped his weapon. Quinton ran over to him. He had seconds before the spider-drone reached them. He'd taken out the drone's weapon so it would have to come in close. The fact that it wasn't retreating meant that it expected reinforcements soon.

Becker clutched his shoulder. His suit was venting atmosphere. The suit's self-repair functions began working, closing the hole, but it would do nothing for the pain.

Becker would live.

Quinton turned toward the drone. "Now it's your turn."

He scanned for any comlink signals and didn't detect

anything. The drone was cut off from whoever had activated it. It still had six of its legs, and he needed to disable it without destroying it. Quinton increased his frame rate and searched for an access panel. The elliptical armored body had ridge lines, so it was difficult to see every surface. He ran a quick tactical analysis, which gave him two possible locations for the access panel, neither of which were easy to get to.

Quinton reduced his frame rate but kept it high enough that his own reaction times were faster than the drone's and then rushed toward the creepy critter. Its crimson optics blazed as it darted toward him. Had he surprised it? He darted to the side and fired his weapon, obliterating one of its legs. The spider-drone dropped off-balance, and Quinton took out another of its legs. Then he slid underneath its body, grabbing its underbelly. The drone spun around, trying to find him, and then slammed its body onto the ground in an attempt to knock Quinton lose. When that didn't succeed, the drone dragged its underbelly along the rough terrain. Quinton glanced up and saw that the drone was heading toward a deep crater.

Quinton saw the access panel, which required special tools to open. How thoughtful of them. The nanorobotic alloy that comprised his "skin" hardened, and Quinton pierced the armor. He tore off the panel and shoved his hands inside. The spider-drone might not have had an active comlink, but it couldn't protect against the physical access that Quinton now had. He quickly found the command-and-control subsystem and overrode it. The spider-drone stopped struggling, but that was the easy part. The hard part was that they were both sliding toward the edge of the crater. Quinton pushed his feet toward the ground, trying to slow them down, which didn't help in the slightest. The low gravity hampered his movement. Rather than slowing down, he was flying over the surface.

Quinton muttered a curse. More Three Moons security forces

were on their way, and Guttman was getting attacked on a ship with only emergency power. Oscar was in an escape pod waiting to be rescued. Becker was hurt, there was a PMC coming online, and he was soaring toward a deep crater. Maybe he needed to rethink his life.

The spider-drone's body jerked to a halt and Quinton's legs flung out from underneath it, but he held on.

"I've got you," Becker said.

His voice came over the comlink. He'd shot a grappling tether, which attached to the armored body of the spider-drone, and Becker quickly reeled him in. Quinton felt a slight increase in gravity as he was brought back into the field.

"Thanks. I owe you one," Quinton said and dragged the spider-drone back to the escape pod. The shuttle had landed nearby.

Becker's suit was blackened at the shoulder and the spacer grimaced in pain. "I can't stop you, but this isn't a good idea," he said, jutting his chin toward the escape pod where the PMC waited.

Quinton didn't reply. He walked back to the pod and peered inside. "Greta, I have a temporary body available for the ESS."

Unacceptable.

"We don't have a lot of options. It's got a sensor interface that should help. I've got extensive materials back on my ship, but you've got to trust me."

The VI seemed to consider this for a few moments and then the shield protecting the ESS core powered off. Quinton used the cradle to transfer the core to the open panel of the spider-drone. The core burrowed deeper into the chassis and began the PMC startup sequence.

"Come on," Quinton said.

They went to the shuttle and Quinton secured the spider-drone in the rear cargo hold.

"Radek," Quinton said sub-vocally so no one else could hear, "restrict access from that PMC until we know more about what we're dealing with."

"Understood, sir."

Quinton engaged the shuttle's flight controls and they rose upward. He swung the shuttle around so its cannons were locked onto the escape pod and fired. It blew apart. If anyone came to investigate, they wouldn't find much evidence of what had happened here. Swinging the shuttle back around, he spotted the last spider-drone limping back toward the station. He fired the mag cannons again and destroyed it.

Quinton updated the main holoscreen with both Guttman's and Oscar's comlink locations.

"How you holding up?" Quinton asked.

"I'll live," Becker said while studying the holoscreen. "Oscar is closer."

Quinton nodded.

Becker activated Oscar's comlink. "Hey, Oscar, are you awake?"

Becker had to repeat himself.

"Yeah," Oscar answered. "Ouch. Yeah, I'm here. I guess they gassed us," he said in a quieter tone.

Quinton flew toward the escape pod. It didn't take long to catch up with its slow speed.

"We're almost to you. Is your suit intact? Do you have your helmet?" Becker asked.

"No," Oscar answered irritably. "Damn it! No helmet."

"We don't have enough room for that escape pod in here," Quinton said.

"We'll need to tether it to the cargo holder."

Oscar groaned and there was a sound of him checking the compartments. "I've got something—Yes! They've got an emergency head covering in here. I can open the hatch and make it to the shuttle. Just let me know when."

"Stand by," Becker said and looked at Quinton. "I'll go back to the rear airlock."

"Like hell you will," Quinton said and stood up. "With that shoulder of yours, I'll end up losing both of you. Sit tight."

Becker clamped his mouth shut and didn't protest any further. "Release the controls. I can still fly the damn shuttle."

Quinton waved without turning around as he headed to the rear airlock. "All yours."

About a minute later, Quinton was in the airlock, facing the deep dark. An automatic tether was attached to the back of an EVA utility belt that had suit thrusters. The aircar escape pod was a short distance away.

"All right, Oscar. Time to open up," Quinton said.

Oscar chuckled. "I didn't know you cared, but this isn't the time or the place for us to confess our truest feelings for each other."

Quinton smiled. "You know what I like."

Oscar laughed, and the hatch to the escape pod popped off with a puff of atmosphere. Quinton deployed a tether toward the open hatch and Oscar attached it to his suit. He pulled himself out of the pod and Quinton retracted the tether.

"Gotta move it," Becker said.

Quinton increased the speed of the retractor, then caught Oscar and pulled him into the airlock.

"We're secure. Go," Quinton said.

They went inside the shuttle and Oscar sat in one of the rear seats. "Thanks, Quinton," Oscar said with a heavy sigh.

Quinton gave him a nod and returned to the pilot's seat.

A message from Radek appeared on Quinton's internal HUD.

"The PMC would like to speak with you," Radek said.

"Tell him we're in the middle of a situation and I'll talk to him after it's resolved," Quinton replied. It was disorienting enough for a PMC to be brought online, and the experience was going to be compounded by the fact that whoever was stored in that PMC was stuck inside a spider-drone.

"I'm afraid he's insisting— He's overriding my control."

"What is the meaning of this! You can't keep me in the dark. Who is this?" the slightly modulated voice asked.

Quinton should have anticipated that Radek might not be able to keep their new guest in the dark.

"Ready to take over?" Becker asked.

"Not yet," Quinton replied.

Becker glanced at him.

"Hey, I asked you a question," the PMC said.

Quinton muttered a curse. "Calm down. My name is Quinton Aldren. I'm the one who saved you."

"Saved me? Did something happen to the transport ship? What happened to the *Kendrick?*"

"What's your name?"

There was a pause for a few seconds. The PMC was still coming online.

"Nash Harper."

"Okay, Harper, call me Quinton. What's the last thing you remember?"

Becker flew them toward Guttman's comlink signal.

"Deployment orders… I can't remember. I should be able to. The *Kendrick* was taking us to a major offensive with… Wait. I don't know who you are. I shouldn't be talking to you," Harper said.

Harper had limited access to his memories. Ordinarily, Quinton could sympathize with that, but right now he just didn't have the time.

"Harper, I don't have time to go into this with you. I need you to be patient."

"I don't have to listen to you!" Harper exclaimed.

The PMC tried to seize control of the shuttle's computer systems, but Quinton had anticipated that and locked him out.

"I can't let you do that."

"How did you do that?"

"I promise I'll answer all your questions," Quinton said. He wasn't going to share his complete identity because he wasn't sure which federation Harper was from. Even though he hated to keep Harper ignorant of that information, it was for his own good.

Quinton initiated a comlink with Harper's VI. Then he initiated a PMC integrity check via the stored procedures that were part of the VI suite.

"Hey, I don't consent to this. I'm going to stop—" Harper went quiet as he was brought offline. The integrity check would take a few hours to run. It was unlikely that it would improve Harper's mood, nor would it make him less suspicious of Quinton, but he had no choice.

"Okay, I've got it," Quinton said, and Becker returned control of the shuttle's flight systems to him.

"What happened?"

"Nothing. He's just a little confused," Quinton replied.

Becker's gaze darted toward the interior cargo hold, and his hand went to his blaster. "Are we in danger?"

"What? No, put that thing away before you hurt someone," Quinton said.

Becker looked unconvinced.

"I told you I took care of it," Quinton said.

The *Wayfarer's* shuttle was a fast ship, capable of greater speed than the luxury ship Guttman was so keen on keeping.

Guttman was flying through a scrap region, attempting to lose the Three Moons security force that was chasing him. He wasn't doing a bad job of keeping them at bay. Becker activated Guttman's comlink and they heard him spouting a steady stream of curses. He was talking to himself, questions and all.

Quinton heard Oscar chuckle from behind him and he snorted. Even Becker cracked a smile.

"Hey, Baby New Year," Quinton said, "we can hear you."

Guttman stopped speaking. "Oh good, now you've got something else to make fun of me about."

"Well, you're the one who stripped off your suit so you could be…" Quinton paused a moment. "I think you said you just wanted to be free."

Oscar laughed and Quinton joined him as Guttman growled.

"All right, that's enough. Guttman, were you able to charge the jump drive?" Becker asked.

"Charge the jump drive! Why didn't I think of that? Of course, I did. And it was the first thing those damn security forces shot."

"Are they the ones…" Quinton began to say and then stopped.

"What! Go ahead and say it. Have a nice laugh. You idiots are going to miss me when I'm gone. Do any of you know how to cook? Enjoy plain old nothing from now on."

Quinton glanced at the others. "He does have a point. I think we should save his ass. Let's put it to a vote."

"A vote! I swear, Quinton, I'm going to find a way to get you back. So help me, I'm going to find a way."

"Right, then," Quinton said. "A vote. Oscar?"

"Yeah, let's save the little guy."

"That's one for yes. But he just threatened me, so I've got to give it a hard no. What about you, Becker?"

Becker shook his head. "Stop messing around."

Quinton mimed disappointment. "Looks like it's your lucky day. I guess I'm in the saving mood today. Guttman, we're coming up on your six. When I tell you…" He paused.

"Say again, Quinton, you cut out," Guttman said.

"Oh, sorry about that. When I tell you…" Quinton said and paused again.

"What? What did you say? What do you need me to do?" Guttman asked. After just a few moments, he said. "You're messing with me? Damn it! I'm going to kick—"

Quinton flew a trajectory that kept Guttman's ship in his line of sight most of the time. Guttman was weaving his way through space junk, as were the two ships pursuing him. Radek put up a flight path that Guttman and his pursuers would most likely take.

Becker tried to answer Guttman, but Quinton muted his comlink and fired the shuttle's mag cannons in controlled bursts, hitting the partial hulls of ships that were in the area and altering their trajectory, which put them in the paths of the security ships. They had elongated snouts like a dart and only had single occupants. One of them managed to avoid the space debris, but the other crashed into it and tumbled off course. The damage to the ship must have been severe because the pilot used his escape pod.

The remaining security ship executed a tight maneuver that swung the front of the ship, pointing it in the shuttle's direction. Quinton fired the mag cannons again and altered course, removing them from the path of the security ship's return fire.

They both missed.

"Guttman, you're in the clear. We've given them something else to chase," Quinton said.

"Nice of you to finally show up," Guttman replied.

Becker looked at Quinton. "You know he's not going to let this go."

"I know."

"Don't you think you pushed things just a little too far?"

"We all have a flaw. Several, in fact."

The security ship was on an intercept course, and Quinton initiated a comlink to it.

"Something isn't right," Guttman said.

"What's wrong?" Becker asked.

"I'm not... I can't. Nothing is responding. Did you lock me out?"

Quinton shook his head. "That's not me."

"Shit," Becker said. "Listen to me. Head for the nearest escape pod."

"What! No! This is my ship!"

"Listen to me, or you're going to die. They triggered a dead-stick remote override, but it won't affect the escape pods because they're on a closed system," Becker said.

Guttman cursed. "Core containment is failing," he said. He sounded like he was running.

The security ship was trying to angle its approach to the shuttle to get a clear shot, but Quinton wouldn't let it. When the ship's comms system acknowledged his broadcast, Quinton got into the security dart's systems. He quickly shut everything down and then jettisoned the escape pod.

The luxury light transport ship flashed as the core containment went critical and the ship exploded.

"Guttman, are you there?" Becker asked.

Silence.

Quinton executed an active scan sweep, but there were too many objects for the shuttle's scanners to identify an escape pod.

Becker called out to Guttman two more times, but there was no response. He leaned forward, peering at the video feed on the HUD.

"Guttman, please respond."

"Ha ha! How do you like it? Now come and get me," Guttman said.

They were able to track the escape pod using Guttman's comlink; however, there were no emergency supplies aboard, and Guttman had to ride the entire trip back to the *Wayfarer* in the pod. No one was too disappointed, though. Undergarments notwithstanding, there were just some lines that shouldn't be crossed unless absolutely necessary.

Oscar brought Becker the first aid kit and applied a healing pack to his shoulder.

"No signs of pursuit," Quinton said.

Becker frowned. "That doesn't seem right."

Quinton had the shuttle going max speed, so the trip out would be much faster than the way in had been.

"I thought so too. I have Radek monitoring their communications from the *Wayfarer*. He'll let us know if he learns something we need to know."

As they traveled back to the *Wayfarer*, a brooding silence descended on the others. They were leaving empty-handed despite all their preparations, including picking the target that was both the most likely place to find a ship worth stealing and with a small enough operation that it wouldn't bring the ire of any major players in the galaxy.

Quinton was just as perplexed about how the events had unfolded as the rest of them.

"You didn't know anything about this activation signal?" Becker asked.

Oscar looked at him. Both he and Becker were thinking the same thing—that he had somehow known about it.

"No, I didn't know."

Becker pursed his lips while he considered Quinton's response.

"I'm serious. I had no idea that an activation signal was coming. You can review the communication logs on the *Wayfarer* if you want, but I'm telling you the truth. This wasn't me."

Becker nodded and Oscar relaxed. "The timing is suspicious."

Quinton exhaled. "I don't know. I guess you're right."

Oscar cleared his throat. "I just want to put this out there. Whatever you might have seen me doing in that aircar, it wasn't me. I mean, I'm not responsible for that, so let's just keep it between us."

Quinton put up the video recording of Oscar pretending to fly the aircar. "I don't know. This is pretty compelling stuff."

A grin bubbled up from Becker's mouth. He leaned toward

the holoscreen as if taking a closer look. "Certainly looks like Oscar to me."

Oscar's cheeks reddened. "So, any chance I can persuade you to delete that recording?"

Quinton paused in thought. "There's one thing I've learned from all of you—that everything has a price. Make me an offer."

Oscar bit his lower lip and looked away.

"It had better be good," Quinton said.

CHAPTER FIVE

THE SHUTTLE'S maximum speed would have cut their travel time to the *Wayfarer* in half, but they hadn't accounted for Guttman's incessant humming. Guttman was alone in an escape pod and had hours to entertain himself. When he worked, he hummed a lot, along with muttering snippets of conversations or anything he was thinking about at the time. This was occasionally broken up by singing, which would crescendo where he inserted the names of random objects into whatever song he was singing. Becker had muted Guttman's comlink a few times, but then the trapped spacer would get lonely and reinitiate a new comlink session to bypass the muted one. Quinton didn't have the heart to remove that capability. Too much isolation wasn't good for anyone, and they were in this together, even if it meant enduring the colorful nuances of Guttman's personality. They all had them, but that didn't mean he couldn't lessen the duration of their travel time. Quinton uploaded an intercept course to the *Wayfarer's* nav computer, and the star jumper was on its way to them.

"Not that much longer," Quinton said.

Guttman stopped humming. "Thank God," he said and looked at the holoscreen.

"Can I ask you a question?"

Guttman leaned away from the comlink video feed with suspicion. He had the look of someone who'd been a frequent victim of playful baiting and wasn't eager to be the target again. But he also had an insatiable need to take the spotlight. He enjoyed the attention.

Guttman looked away from the camera and sighed. "I'm really not in the mood."

"Headache still bad?" Quinton asked.

Guttman nodded and massaged his temples.

The escape pod hadn't been stocked with supplies, and Guttman made sure everyone knew about it. There was also no food in the pod. Guttman had been lucky that its life-support systems were operational, but the pod was far from being suitable for anything like sustained occupancy for more than a few hours. Waste disposal was a real concern because the pod had been stripped of its management system. Whoever had been refitting the ship must have been working on the life-support system and had been in the process of replacing key components.

"All right, what is it?" Guttman said. "Go on, ask me what you were going to ask me."

"Oh, that. Don't worry about it. It's not important."

"Quinton, don't you do that. I hate it when you start to ask a question and then don't. It's annoying."

Quinton experienced an immediate urge to remark about Guttman's singing, but both colossal restraint and sympathy for someone who was cut off from everyone else made him decide not to.

"Okay," Quinton said.

Becker and Oscar didn't look over at him, but they were definitely listening. There wasn't enough room in the shuttle to avoid it.

"Why strip off your space suit? Why did you do it? I mean,

what was going through your mind when you decided that enough was enough—get this thing off me?"

Guttman snorted a little and then shrugged. "It was the inhibitor. Trace amounts of—"

"I know all that, but what I'm trying to understand is why after achieving the point of 'I feels so good' you'd take off your clothes?"

Oscar swung around in his chair to face the video feed. "That's a good question."

"I don't know."

"Come on, think about it. I genuinely want to know," Quinton said.

Guttman didn't reply right away, and the seconds ticked by for two full minutes. "Freedom," he said quietly.

Quinton's eyebrows knitted together in a thoughtful frown. "Freedom? I'm not following."

Guttman looked at the camera. "You wouldn't, but *they* know what I mean."

Quinton glanced at the others. Becker didn't look at him, but Oscar looked away and nodded a little.

"We're always stuck in a ship or space station," Guttman said. "We've got to wear our safety gear because everything is old. You never know when something is going to break. We've only got entertainment modules to remind us of the open sky."

"Why don't you just go planetside somewhere?" Quinton asked.

"Where?"

Quinton looked at Becker. "You told me there were habitable worlds out there."

Guttman forcefully exhaled through his nose, and it sounded like the pressure release of an environmental system purge. "Yeah, right. They're tightly controlled with more restrictions than you'd have off-world if you wanted to change your mind. I told you I want freedom—swim in a lake without seeking a permit and swim naked if I wanted to," he said and pointed a finger at the holoscreen. "Just don't. You asked and I'm answering."

Quinton raised his hands in a placating gesture. "I'm pretty sure we can find something like that. Maybe not a planet, but surely one of these space stations has a module that offers the same thing."

Guttman banged his fist down beside him and leaned toward the camera. "No, you don't get it. I don't want to pay an hourly credit wage to buy an illusion for a few hours. I want the real thing, whenever I want it. I don't want to swim in water that's been recycled. I want hot springs. I want a lake with a mountain range nearby. On a planet without anyone breathing down my neck about it."

A somber silence settled on the others that Quinton couldn't help but notice, and he wouldn't attempt to cheapen it with a snarky comment. Guttman had given him a real answer, and the sentiment was clearly shared by the others. They probably didn't want the same things, but they shared the spirit of the desire for what they wanted. It reminded him of Maelyn. She'd been after information about colony worlds that the Acheron Confederacy might have kept hidden from the rest of the galaxy.

Becker turned toward him. "We need to talk."

"I'm not going anywhere. Talk," Quinton replied.

"That—PMC," Becker began. Quinton was sure he'd been about to say 'thing,' but instead he said, "Harper. Is he stable?"

"I don't know. The integrity check is still running, and it'll help repair him if there's degradation," Quinton said.

"If those measures really worked, the Federation Wars wouldn't have happened."

"I'm not going to disable him because you're afraid."

"Damn it, Quinton, this is serious. These are real concerns. You might have beaten the odds, but that doesn't mean he will," Becker said and tilted his head toward the rear of the shuttle.

"I told you I'd keep an eye on him."

Becker tapped his fingertips on the console in front of him. "I know you're trying to do the right thing, but you need to trust what I'm saying—what we're all saying. There are reasons PMCs are shunned."

Quinton eyed him. "That hurt my feelings."

"I'm serious."

"So am I. You think I like that you guys have this deep-seated fear that I'm about to go insane?" The others went still. "Sure, I joke about it. Sometimes it's even funny, but I haven't done anything to deserve it. And PMCs were more than stable…" He'd been about to say, "where I came from," but that wasn't as accurate as "*when* I came from."

Becker pursed his lips and nodded. "Like I said. You beat the odds, but that doesn't mean everyone else can. And," he said, holding up his hand when Quinton tried to speak. "And, even with your experience, it wasn't a sure thing. The *Wayfarer* doesn't have another one of those bodies in it."

A proximity notification appeared on the HUD. The *Wayfarer* had finally reached them.

"It doesn't, but that doesn't mean I'm not going to try to help Harper."

"You stuck him in a security bot," Becker said.

"It's more of a combination maintenance and security bot. Three Moons Shipyards were quite practical about the whole thing," Quinton said. Becker glared at him. "Look, you can check out the bot when we get back aboard the *Wayfarer*. It'll take Harper time to acclimate to a new body. I removed the more dangerous limbs from it. Also, we'll need to explain to Harper what he's woken up to."

Becker leaned back in his seat and scratched his chin. "The fact remains that you don't know who we're dealing with."

Quinton didn't reply.

Oscar leaned forward. His short, dark hair had blond tips.

"Quinton," he said, calmly, "we just need to be careful. What if Harper tries to take control of the ship?"

Quinton thought about how Harper had circumvented Radek's control to speak with him. "I understand."

"We need more than that. We need a plan," Oscar said.

"What do you mean?"

"He means," Guttman said, "we need a way to stop Harper from killing the rest of us if he decides we're a threat."

"He's right," Becker said. "The fact of the matter is that we're vulnerable. We can't access the ship's systems the way you can."

"But I wouldn't let him do anything like that. And besides, what do you propose? One of you guard Harper at all times with a weapon?"

"I thought about it, but it's not practical. We need a fail-safe. Something that can disable him if we need it," Becker said.

"I don't believe this. Harper isn't even awake yet and you want me to strap a bomb to the spider-drone to address the possibility that he might do something to you? Does that sum it up?" Quinton asked and looked at all of them. "By that logic, we should all be sitting here with our weapons pointed at each other. How does that behavior build any trust or even cooperation?"

"Do you think it was any different on the *Nebulon*?" Becker said and gave him a long look. "Maelyn had a security system on her ship that would have disabled the agricultural bot you were in if you'd proven to be unstable."

"She did, but she also gave me some time to process the situation, which is what I intend to do for Harper. The *Wayfarer* doesn't have a suppression system like what was on the *Nebulon*, so we'll just have to do the best we can with what we've got."

Becker looked as if he wanted to press the issue, but Oscar spoke first. "All right, let's just table this discussion for now. Okay. Let's get back on the ship, get cleaned up, and have a bite to eat. Then we can come at this again after we've had some rest."

"I, for one, could go for some food," Guttman said. "But I could probably hold off on a shower."

"No!" Quinton, Becker, and Oscar shouted at once.

Guttman looked at the video feed innocently. "If you guys are sure."

"Yes!" They said in unison.

Guttman chuckled. With the exception of Quinton, they had all achieved a certain level of ripeness that could only be cured by some vigorous scrubbing.

"I'll make sure Harper is under security lockdown with restricted access to the ship," Quinton said.

He was the *Wayfarer's* captain, so the decision was up to him. Everyone else was a passenger, but Quinton knew the value of crew cohesion.

Becker brought up the scan feeds from the *Wayfarer* and put them on the shuttle's HUD.

"They let us go," Quinton said.

"I know. What I can't figure out is why," Becker replied.

Shipyard security had chosen not to send more ships after them beyond the initial pursuit.

"Were there other pirates in the star system?" Oscar asked.

"That's what I was looking for," Becker replied. "Nothing has been detected, and we're too far out to see what they're doing now."

Oscar shook his head. "It doesn't make sense."

"No, it doesn't," Quinton agreed. "I had Radek record their comms chatter. There might be something in there. Can you guys take a look? You might see something I'd miss."

Quinton could access data faster than anyone else on the shuttle, but what good was that if he didn't know what to look for. He needed their expertise. "The only thing I keep wondering about is why their security measures were so good. I mean, it was well thought out—almost military in their response."

Becker nodded. "It was better than I thought it was going to be for an independent shipyard."

"Maybe it's not independent anymore," Oscar said.

Quinton considered that for a few moments. "There was nothing to indicate it's a Union shipyard."

Becker shook his head. "It's not Crowe's Union."

"The Collective, maybe," Oscar suggested.

"I'll have Radek compile a list of names based on the comms data. Maybe something will jump out at you," Quinton said.

The others agreed. The lack of response from shipyard security bothered Quinton. It meant that they were more worried about something else than they were about being robbed. It could be that the PMC activation signal had thrown their response teams into disarray. It was definitely worth considering.

Later, Quinton stood before the main holoscreen on the bridge of the *Wayfarer*. Shortly after they'd returned to the ship, he executed an emergency jump that had taken them out of the star system. He'd also moved the spider-drone into the maintenance workshop where Greta continued running the integrity check of Harper's PMC. Since coming aboard the ship, she had partnered with Radek and leveraged the *Wayfarer's* computing core to quicken the check.

The door to the bridge opened and Becker entered. He'd expected Becker would be joining him. The man was a workhorse and would make a good ship captain.

Quinton gave him a once over. "I thought you wanted to get cleaned up?"

Becker looked at the information on the holoscreen. "I'm more interested in figuring out why they let us go."

Quinton nodded.

"The only reason I can come up with is that they were worried about something else. I'm not sure what, though. Is this all Radek has been able to find out?"

"Yes. It looks like they were expecting—at the very least—a Sentinel scout ship to survey the area," Quinton said.

Becker peered at one of the data windows and expanded it. "They recalled all their ships and shut down operations."

"Is that how Crowe's Union would've handled it if the activation signal had gone to one of their operations?"

"I'm not sure. There was no standing protocol on what we should do in that eventuality. Contrary to what just happened, PMC activation signals aren't that common."

Quinton considered it for a few moments. "Maybe the activation signals are more common than we thought."

"Or maybe this is a recent development. We've been out of contact for a while."

"True. I'd like to know if a Sentinel scout ship *did* show up in that star system. It wasn't worth the risk of sticking around, but I am curious. Based on this information, I have to think that whoever was running Three Moons Shipyards had expected the Sentinels to show up. Maybe they were prepped by somebody."

"Like who?" Becker asked.

"The Collective."

"Three Moons was an independent operation. The Collective doesn't prioritize the successful operations of independent companies."

"Unless they were recently acquired by them," Quinton said and shook his head. "It's just a thought. You know more than I do about how the salvager operations mesh together."

"Well, for one, they don't all wear a badge that makes it abundantly clear they're with the Collective. So, if there *is* a partnership, it might be kept secret."

"Why?"

"There's competition between different salvager operations. It's not uncommon for someone to create opportunities from the misfortune of others."

Quinton nodded. "All right, no giant sign that says who their affiliation is. We might not be able to figure this out from this data. I thought you might have had an insight into it since you picked this target."

"I thought so, too, but I'm coming up short."

"Well, there's nothing that matches Crowe's Union, so we know Lennix had nothing do with this," Quinton said.

He noticed that bringing up Becker's former employer didn't make him as anxious as it used to.

"I'd recognize Union data transmission, so we're covered on that."

"So where do we go from here?" Quinton asked.

"I was thinking that we need to go to... Find some place to get some current news, but I'm not so sure that's a good idea right now."

"Harper?"

"Harper," Becker agreed. "I don't think it's a good idea to bring him anywhere he could be detected."

"We can't stumble around in the dark forever. Remember, I'm trying to fulfill my end of our agreement. You, Oscar, and Guttman all helped me put the ship back together."

"It looks like we won't be rid of each other as fast as we thought."

"You say that like it's a bad thing."

Becker shrugged a meaty shoulder. "We have different goals, Quinton. It's not personal."

"I know it's not," Quinton said but suspected otherwise. "We agreed to keep helping each other out to get you a ship. As for Harper, you don't have to be involved in that."

"As long as we're all on this ship, we're all involved in it. When is the integrity check going to finish?"

"In another hour."

"Is that normal?"

"That's what the analysis should tell us." Becker considered this for a few moments and Quinton continued. "You've got time. Go get cleaned up and I'll meet you in the workshop. We can question Harper together."

"Won't that take longer?"

"That depends on Harper, doesn't it?"

Becker nodded and left the bridge.

Quinton studied the data on the screen. Sentinels were the product of the Federation War. They were the answer to the PMC menace that was infecting the galaxy. Something had made PMCs unstable, and Quinton had no idea what that was. When he was uploaded before the Federation Wars began, becoming a PMC had been highly revered. They'd been necessary to the survival of the Acheron Confederacy Navy.

Sentinels roamed the galaxy in groups, hunting for PMCs and any type of technology that was remotely related to them. If the Sentinels determined that there was a PMC presence on a ship or space station, it was destroyed. There were no communications, and any inquiries were ignored. But Quinton had communicated with a Sentinel once, and it wasn't an experience he was eager to repeat. The best thing for him to do was to find another DNA vault and regrow his body. The only problem with that plan was that he had no record of his DNA. But one problem at a time. He'd given Becker the impression that Radek was overseeing Harper's integrity check of his PMC, but that wasn't entirely true. Quinton was also monitoring the results as they came in. There'd been a degradation of the PMC that he was in the process of trying to repair, and that was why the integrity check was taking a bit longer than normal.

Quinton left the bridge and headed toward the workshop.

CHAPTER SIX

THE ESS that stored Nash Harper's PMC must have been damaged, but Quinton couldn't figure out how. He stood in the workshop where the spider-drone sat in a maintenance cradle.

"The ESS is intact and operational, so how come PMC stability scores are so low?" Quinton asked.

Radek was the lead interface of Quinton's own virtual intelligence and had taken the form of a holographic sphere hovering in the air. "In the absence of detectable damage to the ESS, the stability scores are only indicative of the PMCs current state but don't demonstrate what those scores would have been when it was first created."

Quinton bowed his head. No one else was in the workshop. "Is that just a fancy way of saying that Harper could have been unstable when he was uploaded?"

"That is one possibility. According to Greta, there was an update to Harper's ESS that was only processed once he was activated."

"Do the logs indicate when they received the update?"

"Negative. It could have been queued for the entire time the escape pod resided on the asteroid."

"What did the update do?"

"Specifics are unknown, but it did use the mergence protocol," Radek replied.

Quinton wanted a triple shot of that Sangorian Bourbon Oscar had on the shuttle. Maybe the ship's VR could reproduce the whole bourbon experience for him.

Mergence protocol was used to provide PMCs with updated mission data and skillset augmentation. "Does Greta know if that's causing the instability?"

He preferred to speak with Greta directly, but the VI was focusing all her resources on mapping Harper's PMC so she could keep him functioning. Mergence protocol, once initiated, couldn't be undone. Quinton knew the theory of how it was supposed to work. It was meant to build upon the experiences of other PMCs to increase their functionality. It required thorough personality mappings, and only PMCs that had similar mappings could be integrated without affecting the original host's identity.

Harper's stability scores were borderline concerning. The only way to make a better assessment would be to bring Harper out of the maintenance routine, which Quinton intended to do once the others arrived. Harper might just need some time to adapt to his situation.

Quinton was integrated into the ship's systems, which included knowing the locations of the crew for emergency purposes. This data was available to anyone, and Becker and the others insisted on having an area of the ship where they could have privacy. This included their quarters, as well as one of the common areas, and allowed them to meet without worrying about whether Quinton would be monitoring them. He understood the need for privacy, but sometimes he did wonder what they talked about. He respected their wishes, even though it was his ship—unit cohesion and all that. They didn't exclude him from those areas of the ship, but they had certainly relaxed more now that barriers had been established.

Quinton glanced at the spider-drone. Harper was going to have to learn how to use it until they could find a better host for him. No doubt the others were discussing this among themselves.

The biometric readings on the ship indicated that Becker, Oscar, and Guttman were on their way to the workshop. A short time later, the door opened and the three men walked in. Guttman and Oscar carried assault rifles while Becker had decided to keep his heavy blaster holstered on his side.

"Armed and dangerous, I see," Quinton said.

"Just in case," Oscar said and took up a position that gave him tactical coverage of the maintenance cradle.

Guttman—fully clothed, thankfully—rested his stocky russet frame against a countertop on the other side of the workshop.

Becker walked over to Quinton's side. "Ready when you are."

Quinton looked at the others. "How about we don't have itchy trigger fingers."

Oscar adjusted the strap of his rifle so it swung behind him. Quinton knew that Oscar could have that rifle ready in seconds, but the show of faith wasn't lost on him.

Guttman shook his head. "I'll hold onto it," he said. He wasn't pointing his weapon at the spider-drone, which was Guttman's idea of "good enough" cooperation.

Quinton thought about his own reactivation. Harper was lucky they'd found him. At least there weren't any hunter mechs trying to kill him. He'd just have to deal with a little mistrust.

"All right, the maintenance cycle is going to expire," Quinton said.

The spider-drone's legs spasmed a few times, and Quinton stepped toward it. "Harper, can you hear me?"

There was no response.

"Harper, you're coming out of an extensive maintenance cycle. Give yourself a few minutes to get acclimated."

The spider-drone's ocular units on the armored torso moved.

The others went still. Guttman lifted his rifle a little, but Becker gestured for him to lower it.

"It's just a mobility startup check. The same thing happens on any bot or mechanized suit," Quinton advised, and the others relaxed.

"Where am I?" Harper asked. His voice was tight, as if he was straining.

"You're aboard my ship, the *Wayfarer*."

The ocular unit was able to spin, so Harper could see the room while his body was still locked in the maintenance cradle.

"Your movements are restricted. This is as much for your own protection as it is ours."

"This isn't a humanoid avatar. Why have I been installed here?"

Quinton frowned. They'd gone over this before Harper had agreed to go through the integrity check. "Your ESS was stored on an escape pod we found on an asteroid. There wasn't anything else for us to use."

"This doesn't make any sense. This bot feels strange. Why was I activated then?" Harper asked, sounding slightly less strained.

"Let's take this one step at a time. What do you remember?"

The spider-drone's body jerked as Harper tried to move. "Get me out of this thing. I need to move."

"Not yet."

"Why not?"

Quinton stepped closer. "You already know this. You're in the wrong kind of body and it's going to take some practice to get used to it. I promise I'm going to let you out of the cradle, but I need you to cooperate. One step at a time."

A sound that seemed to be a mixture of a sigh and a growl came from Harper.

"I know it's frustrating. Remember your training."

"I do," he replied. "I do remember."

"Okay, let's start with your name and rank."

"Nash Harper, Lieutenant, Acheron Confederacy Navy. Tactical engagement specialist."

"Thanks for that. I'm Quinton Aldren, Commander in the Acheron Confederacy Navy. I'm a G-class PMC."

"Commander," Harper said. "G-class. Have I been assigned to your command? What fleet?"

"What do you mean?"

"Commander, you should already know. Galactic class PMCs were designed to utilize other PMCs as part of their command structure. Which battleship cruiser are we on? Is it the flagship ACS *Javelin*?"

Quinton considered Harper's response for a few moments and could guess what Becker and the others were thinking.

"Another one," Guttman said softly, but not quietly enough.

The spider-drone swung its gaze toward him. "Who are you. Are you a civilian?" Harper asked and looked at Quinton. "Why are civilians aboard an ACN warship? They don't have clearance."

"Clearance? You don't even know what kind of ship you're on," Guttman said.

"That accent," Harper said, and the spider-drone jerked toward Guttman. "Jordani!" he snarled. "Why isn't he shackled. Is he an intelligence asset? He doesn't look like it, but it could be a disguise."

Quinton was starting to think that he should have met with Harper alone.

Guttman chuckled, and Quinton glared at him. "Not helping."

"Commander, I need the mission briefings for our fleet deployment," Harper said.

Becker exhaled and looked at Quinton. "This is going to take a while. Maybe we should give you guys a few hours."

"Appreciate the backup," Quinton replied.

"I think you've got this, *Commander*."

The spider-drone's head turned toward Becker. "Insolence is not to be tolerated in the ACN."

Becker inclined his head. "Oh, I apologize."

Guttman laughed and walked toward them.

Harper shifted his focus to Quinton. "You're out of uniform."

"A lot has changed," Quinton replied.

The others started heading for the door.

"Must have. Admiral Browning wouldn't tolerate such lapses," Harper said.

The others froze mid-stride and turned around.

"Did he say Browning?" Oscar asked.

Guttman grumbled a reply.

Grand Admiral Elias Browning had been a war hero with accumulated victories over the Jordani Federation. Then he, along with several fleets, had broken away from the Acheron Confederacy to start a deadly campaign that spread across multiple federations. Browning went from the most renowned war hero to the vilest war criminal and was directly responsible for the Federation Wars. Quinton had tried to locate historical records to find out what had happened, but there wasn't much left. The Federation Wars had spread so rapidly that much of the old federations were gone, leaving mere shadows of what they'd once been. The galactic consensus was that Admiral Browning had unleashed his armada of PMC-enhanced ships on an unsuspecting galaxy. The lines of enemy and ally had been dissolved. Quinton had been uploaded into a PMC before all this, predating the Federation Wars, so he'd been prepared to fight the Jordani. Now the question was: when had Harper been uploaded?

"Have you served Admiral Browning?" Quinton asked.

The ocular units tilted to the side in what was reminiscent of an incredulous stare. "Of course. The battle of the Darcaya Star System brought the Jordani to their knees, breaking their hold on the galaxy."

Guttman spoke quietly to Becker, but Quinton ignored him.

Harper turned toward them.

"Never mind them for a second," Quinton said. "What do you remember?"

"Commander, this is highly irregular. All the ACN had been committed," Harper said and paused. "You're not an officer in the ACN."

"Yes I am. You've seen my credentials."

"That doesn't explain how you don't know about the single most important fleet engagement in the history of the confederacy."

"That's because I was uploaded before the campaign."

Harper considered this for a few moments. "You're one of the early ones. Why haven't you received a mission update?"

"I don't know. What I need to know is the last thing you remember. What were your orders?" Quinton asked.

"My orders?" Harper said. "I haven't received them."

"But did you have an—"

"Wait! There was a recruitment recall notice. Those were my last updates."

"What was the recruitment for?" Becker asked.

Harper regarded the spacer for a moment.

"It's fine. I want to know, too," Quinton said.

"It was for a major offensive, something more dangerous than the Jordani. Admiral Browning was assembling a new task force."

"Do you know what the objective was?"

"No, those details would be given after."

Quinton glanced at the others. Becker opened his mouth as if he were about to speak, but he didn't say anything. Then he looked at Quinton, his mouth forming a grim line.

"Do you know what this means?" Becker asked.

Quinton nodded once. "I do."

"I'm glad you guys do, but I don't," Guttman said.

"I agree with my friend here. I'm not following," Oscar said.

"Harper was uploaded just before the Federation Wars. He served that bastard Browning," Becker said.

The spider-drone's legs jerked as it struggled against the maintenance cradle's restraints.

"I don't know who you are," Harper snarled, "but I'll strip the flesh from your bones if you say another word against Admiral Browning." The last of that utterance came out in a deadly whisper—the kind of tone that men killed over. Harper wasn't making an idle threat. He meant what he said.

Guttman and Oscar raised their weapons.

"Don't," Quinton said. "He doesn't know. Lower your weapons. Now!"

Guttman and Oscar still held their weapons but weren't pointing them at Harper.

"I'm going to bring Harper up to speed. It's best if you guys weren't here," Quinton said.

"Sounds good to me," Guttman said and headed for the door.

Oscar and Becker stayed where they were. Then Becker looked at Oscar. "Come on, we need to find another place to get a ship of our own," he said and looked at Quinton. "We'll be on the bridge."

Becker headed for the door, but Oscar gave Quinton a sympathetic look. "Good luck," he said and followed Becker out of the workshop.

Quinton turned toward Harper.

"Commander, permission to speak freely."

Quinton was really going to have to do something about the military protocol Harper was clinging to—though not *exactly* clinging to. It was representative of the world he'd known, and now Quinton got to take it from him. Lucky him. He thought about Simon, the young technical specialist who had helped him understand that the galaxy he remembered was no longer around. Then there was Maelyn, captain of the *Nebulon*. He'd been impatient to find out the state of the galaxy, but she'd been quite deliberate in how that information had been revealed to him. It wasn't the first time Quinton had been managed. His career in the military had made him familiar with operating on a need-to-know basis, but when he'd been reactivated, the situation had been different. His access to his own ESS—his memories—had been restricted. There had to be something similar going on with Harper, but Quinton wasn't sure to what extent. There was only one way to find out.

"Go ahead, say what you will," Quinton said.

"You can't trust those men. They should be off your ship immediately."

Quinton leaned back against the workbench across from the cradle. He regarded Harper, and his hands came to rest on the cool metallic countertop. "They're not so bad. You'll understand more when you hear what I've got to tell you."

"Understood, Commander."

Quinton sighed. Time to pull the healing pack off the wound before it was ready. This was going to hurt.

"That's the first thing. There isn't an ACN anymore…"

CHAPTER SEVEN

MORE THAN TWELVE hours had elapsed while Quinton gave Harper a crash course on the galaxy he'd awakened to. He tried to be as patient with Harper as possible, but the news that the world Harper thought he knew was gone couldn't be processed over the span of mere hours. They hadn't spent the entire time talking. Quinton had unlocked the maintenance cradle from the spider-drone, giving Harper some time to get acclimated to it.

There were obvious shortcomings to using the spider-drone, but Harper was adapting well to the new body. He was aware of the danger that prolonged use of the spider-drone meant but seemed to bounce from subject to subject. He'd focus on what had happened to the ACN for a while and then shift his attention to how to make the best use of the spider-drone.

Harper regarded him. "How long do you think I'll have to stay in this?" he asked and raised one of the legs. The spider-drone's legs had multiple joints, and Harper was able to not only wave the leg as a gesture for attention but also pivot the joints. On the ends of the legs were grabbers that Harper made mimic a human hand. The fingers seemed to meld into one another to form three elongated appendages that were capable of latching onto things. Quinton ought to know because several spider-drones had tried their best to dismember him.

"We'll try to find you a replacement as soon as we can."

"Good, because it doesn't feel right. I can use it, but Greta says there's some diminished capacity from the ESS interface into the drone's onboard central processor."

"What does it feel like?"

Harper took a few steps around the workshop. The spider-drone had four legs, which were enough for it to move around with. Quinton wondered if mobility would have been more of a challenge for Harper if the drone had retained all its appendages. The agricultural bot Quinton used had been humanoid and had a few useful capabilities. Its main problem had been that it was ancient and not designed to have a PMC installed into it.

"Like I'm wearing someone else's shoes that don't fit right," Harper said. "It's not all bad. The mobility interface is actually pretty good. I don't need to focus on moving each individual leg. I can focus on where I want to go, and it does the rest. There are interface errors, though. I'm working my way through them. I guess it's going to take some time and practice."

"Let me guess—you get an error whenever you try to make a micro expression."

"Micro expression?"

"Facial expressions—some quirk or habit that is unique to you—but the bot is unable to fulfill the request. That really used to annoy me," Quinton replied.

Harper paused for a moment. "I just added those errors to the ignore list."

Quinton had done the same, but he recalled that they still had a way of sneaking to the forefront.

Harper walked toward Quinton and seemed to regard him. "They didn't have anything like what you're using when I was uploaded."

Quinton's cybernetic avatar was made from advanced

composites that were incredibly powerful but duplicated natural human musculature. The skeletal structure was a duplicate of a human skeleton, but again, was many times stronger. The bones were hollow to allow for molecular circuitry and power transmission. Nerve impulses moved literally at light speed, which was around a hundred times as fast as the chemically transmitted impulses of the human body. But despite all the advances, no computer could fully match the brain's interconnections. The ESS was the means by which much of the "thinking" ability of a PMC worked. Quinton's and Harper's personalities and experiences were stored in an energy-state, the limitations of which were expressed in how the ESS was able to integrate into a host machine.

"I wasn't expecting this. The ship was on the Starbase Endurance and had been designed for PMC use," Quinton said.

"Lucky for you."

Quinton remembered his battle with the Sentinel fleets. He'd thought he was about to die. At the time, he'd felt as far from lucky as one could possibly get, but he didn't correct Harper.

"You're the lucky one," Quinton said.

"How?"

"Virtual environment for one. The *Wayfarer's* computing core has plenty of capacity for you to function within a virtual world. There are some configurations already set up. I haven't..." Quinton paused. He didn't want to tell Harper that he hadn't tried them because he didn't need them. "There hasn't been time for me to try them out."

"Why would you?" Harper said and was quiet for a few seconds. "I'm sorry, sir. I know you're trying to help. I just... They really blame Admiral Browning? Everyone hates him?"

"There isn't a lot of love for him out there."

"Still, how can one person be responsible for the Federation Wars? Do you know how crazy that sounds? We were fighting the Jordani and winning. Victory was all but assured. There were going to be Federation Accords for peace. That was what was going to happen."

"It doesn't make sense to me either, and the records are lacking. The facts are that, for whatever reason, Browning began raiding strategic targets across the galaxy. That much is clear."

"I don't believe it."

"Did you know him personally?"

"No, but... He took care of the people who served under him. He was ACN to his core."

Quinton had never served under Browning, but he'd known him by reputation. He thought he would have been transferred under Browning's command, but this was unclear. He remembered the selection process for PMC candidates. They wanted experienced naval officers. He hadn't been the highest-ranking officer to go through the selection process, but he had made it through all the qualifiers to be in the final pool of candidates. He didn't remember anything after that. Presumably, this was when he'd been uploaded into an ESS. How he ended up on a fringe system hidden away on a third-tier colony world was anyone's guess.

"I keep calling you 'sir,'" Harper said.

"It's all right."

"I don't know if I can stop, Commander."

"Harper, it's going to take time. You've been awake for less than a day. Give yourself time to get acclimated."

The spider-drone didn't move, and this bothered Quinton. There were very few people who could remain completely still for any length of time. Movement was part of being human, and he was tempted to query Greta for a diagnostic review of Harper.

The drone's ocular units looked away from Quinton. "I know, sir."

Quinton moved so he was standing in front of Harper. "The war we were meant to fight is over. We missed it."

"What's left for us then? What are we supposed to do?

Everyone we knew. Our families. All those people are just… gone," Harper said. His voice sounded thick. "How did you deal with that?"

"I had restricted access to my memories. It wasn't until I'd integrated with the starbase that those memories were even available."

"I… I can't ignore it like you can."

"I didn't ignore it. It wasn't until I ended up here that I accessed those memories. Greta can help regulate them to help you cope with it. Radek did the same for me. I gave myself time."

"You increased your frame rate."

"Yes, but after a while, I decided that longing for a world that was gone wasn't going to help me. I haven't forgotten them. If you remember fighting the Jordani, it's not the first time you've lost people."

"I'll have to try that," Harper said. "Commander… Quinton. Thank you for helping me. I'd like to be alone now, if you don't mind."

"You're welcome. It's fine. I'll be on the bridge. Come join us when you're ready."

"About the others—they don't trust me. They think I'm like those other PMCs they've been taught about."

"You're right; they don't trust you," Quinton confirmed. "Your access to the ship's systems will be restricted for the time being."

"You don't trust me either?"

Quinton regarded him for a few moments. "I want to trust you, Harper. This is my ship, and the lives aboard it are mine to protect. We'll take it one step at a time and go from there. Try not to take how the others react to you personally. They have real reasons for their prejudices. I don't agree with them, but they've spent a lifetime learning to survive in this galaxy, and we're the newcomers."

"When you put it like that, it makes much more sense. I'll remember what you said, sir."

Quinton left the workshop and headed for the bridge. He walked past the galley where Oscar and Guttman were eating. Guttman's voice echoed through the corridor. The man had one volume to his booming voice.

Quinton glanced inside the galley as he walked by.

"How many times do I have to tell you? Say it, don't spray it," Oscar said.

Guttman leaned back. "Sorry, but you should have seen it."

Quinton walked onto the bridge and found Becker standing in front of the main holoscreen.

Becker looked at him and then glanced at the clock. "How'd he take it?"

He'd put on a fresh set of clothing—all black, as if the spacer had some sort of aversion to anything that had color to it. He looked as if he'd gotten a few hours of sleep; however, his deep-set eyes were still tight with stress, same as Oscar and Guttman. They were wound up too tight. Something was going to break.

"He wanted to be alone for a while."

Becker titled his head to the side once. "I guess he has full access to his memories."

"Most of them."

Becker nodded and crossed his muscular arms over his chest. "That's...something else. You were out of it in the beginning, but Harper was ready for action. Is that normal?"

Quinton snorted and shook his head. "Normal," he said and sighed. "Yeah, you could say that. We were fighting a war. We needed to be ready to get up to speed quickly, sometimes in the middle of a fleet engagement that was already in progress."

"Sometimes I forget that you were an officer."

"It's all part of my disguise."

"You don't fit the profile."

Quinton looked at him, slightly amused. "What profile is

that? Ramrod straight with a giant pole shoved up my ass? Come on, we're not all the same, you know."

Becker arched an eyebrow. "Did I hit close to the mark or something?"

Quinton was irritated and it surprised him. "Something like it."

"Get over it. I've met former military before—the old-timers who managed to survive and the ones who'd been trained by people who'd actually been in the military when there were real federations and star empires around. They all had a certain command authority."

"Oh, you want me to be more decisive. My way or the airlock," Quinton replied.

"Something like that."

"You know how you told me that agents of the Collective don't roam around advertising who they work for? Well, it's something like that."

"You were a commander in the ACN. You commanded a ship and perhaps a battle group—maybe even something approaching an actual fleet. You know how to fight."

"What's your point?"

"Just that you don't act like an officer."

Quinton simply stared at him for a few moments. "Noted. Thanks for that. Would you like me to tell you what you act like?"

"Harper really has you twisted up inside. Maybe you need some downtime."

"Maybe."

"Before you go, what's Harper's status?"

"His access to the ship's systems is restricted."

Becker nodded. "Good," he said and glanced at the holo-screen. "We've been trying to find a secondary target."

"Any luck?" Quinton asked, thankful for a change in subject.

"No."

"There are star systems in the nav computer that might have ships. We could try one of those."

"That's the problem. The nav computer's astrogation charts are decades out of date. They need to be updated. We'll need to find a data beacon and then choose a target from there," Becker said and looked at the main holoscreen again. He shook his head, annoyed.

Quinton moved to stand in front of him. "You know, speaking of command experience, you—everyone—needs to calm down. A data beacon isn't a bad idea, but what about heading someplace where we can get off the ship for a while?"

Becker's gaze slipped into some sort of calculation while he considered it.

"I know you want to get your own ship and get off of this one, but think about what just happened. You're all so desperate to move on that it almost cost you everything. What good is finding a ship if you're not alive to enjoy it?"

Becker unfolded his arms. "I'll talk about it with the others."

Quinton grinned. "You think Guttman and Oscar are going to pass up shore leave?"

Becker rolled his eyes. He knew Quinton was right. "What about you? What are you going to do?"

The door to the bridge opened and Harper walked in. The spider-drone's armored chassis was the same height as Becker's chest. The spacer looked at him, and Quinton noted that he'd positioned his hand near his blaster.

"What about the activation signal?" Harper asked.

"What about it?" Quinton replied.

"We should trace it. Figure out who sent it."

Quinton shook his head. "No one sent it."

"How do you know?"

"It's just some latent protocol from a remnant facility that the Sentinels are likely destroying right now to make sure it doesn't happen again."

Becker looked at him but didn't say anything.

"We need to be sure," Harper said.

Becker walked toward the door. "I'll leave you two to work this out."

Quinton resigned himself to a long conversation that would ultimately end up increasing Harper's frustration, and Quinton couldn't blame him. At one time, he'd also wanted to track the activation signal.

CHAPTER EIGHT

COLO JAKIN STEPPED onto the elevator and the doors shut, blocking out the crowded common area of the residence deck that served as the premiere living space on Chiba Station.

A bubble of space surrounded Colo, which he hardly noticed. A woman on the elevator regarded him curiously. She wore a spacer's pale gray flight suit, and her dark hair was cut short. She whispered something to her companion, another spacer, and Colo ignored them. They must be among the latest tours from the temporary habitation deck for frequent visitors of the station. Colo glanced at the woman. She had either been owed a favor by some higher-up in Chiba Station Affairs, or she'd found a valuable claim that warranted a tour of what the good life meant on Chiba.

The elevator chimed as it reached the central terminal, which was the heart of the station. Colo stepped out of the elevator and set a brisk pace.

"Excuse me," someone called out from behind him.

Colo ignored them. He didn't have time for this.

Hastening footsteps followed him, and then there was a tap on his shoulder. Colo glanced behind him.

The woman from the elevator looked at him evenly. "Are you the dockmaster?"

Here it comes, Colo thought. "In about fifteen minutes."

The woman frowned as she kept pace with him.

"I was told that you're the dockmaster."

"I'm off duty."

The woman nodded. "I'm Captain Waymire—"

"Let me just stop you right there, Captain," Colo said. Why did these ship captains always start with their rank, as if that carried any weight on the station. "Official inquiries into salvage licenses have to come through the Chiba Ministry of Affairs."

Captain Waymire's thin lips lifted in amusement. "I already have my salvager rights for Kizu Star System and the cluster, for that matter. I'd like to talk to you about expanding those to include more of my employer's ships."

Colo's eyebrow arched with curiosity. "Who do you represent?"

"Okan Consolidated."

"I've never heard of them."

"We seek to expand our operations here."

There was always someone looking to jump to the front of the line. "Talk is cheap. Who's your backer?"

"My backer?" she asked, feigning confusion.

Colo rolled his eyes and quickened his pace. "That's all the time I have," he said, heading toward the security checkpoint for Chiba personnel.

"We're funded by Esperon."

Colo stopped and gestured for her to come closer. "Anyone can throw out a name. Give me the ID of the signatory."

Waymire inclined her head and made a passing motion from her wrist computer toward him. The signatory's ID appeared on Colo's wrist computer and he was able to determine the authenticity with the data he had on file.

He looked at her and shook his head. "Next time, lead with this."

"I didn't want to appear pretentious."

"But ambushing me at central was fine," Colo said and sighed. "Okay, you'll still need to take this through central processing. I'm sending you a guest pass to get you through security."

"I appreciate your help, but that process will still take many weeks or more."

Colo pursed his lips. Waymire knew her stuff. Going through official Chiba channels *would* take months. Meanwhile, she'd be limited to the common claim regions for salvage runs.

Waymire stepped closer to him. "Perhaps a few sessions at the pleasure dome."

Colo laughed. "Planetside? Are you kidding me? No."

"What is it you want?"

"Ten percent of your claims for the next year."

"Three percent for six months."

Colo shrugged and began to walk away.

"Five percent for ten months."

Colo turned toward her. "Make it seven and you've got a deal. Otherwise, enjoy the next few months of minimal profits."

"Six percent," she said, and Colo started to walk away, "with a signing bonus of twenty-five thousand."

Colo regarded her for a few seconds. She was serious. She likely had several leads to a salvager's treasure trove. "All right, you've got a deal," he said. Then he transferred a different contact from Chiba's regulator office to her. "Welcome to the Collective, Captain Waymire."

Waymire inclined her head and transferred the credits into his account.

Colo headed to the Chiba's Docking Authority control center. He stifled a yawn as he walked through dingy corridors that no amount of maintenance cleanup crews or atmospheric scrubbers could fix. He thought about his encounter with Captain Waymire, wondering who else she'd sought out as she started up her operations. Colo had walked away, suitably compensated for fast-tracking a new request through bureaucratic channels. He made a mental note to add Waymire to the list of contacts he needed to keep an eye on.

The doors opened to the wide expanse of Chiba's Docking Authority, which was the gateway for any ships that wished to conduct shipping and salvaging operations in the sector.

He glanced toward the massive viewport that showed Boros's grimy, fungus-laden atmosphere. The colony world was fifty years into a substantial terraforming effort that still required more than twenty-five years before the atmosphere was even breathable. The planet looked like an old stain. Colonists crammed together to scrape out a living in dome-covered cities. Spacers came to Boros when they had nowhere else to go. Colo hadn't been anywhere near the immigration offices in years. Once had been enough. He had no need to look at the putrid desperation of people clamoring for a living wage that only guaranteed they wouldn't starve. Of course, they hadn't realized that when they committed to helping build a better tomorrow.

Colo glanced at an image of Boros before the terraforming initiative had begun. Instead of a sickly yellow, the atmosphere had been a reddish brown from an overabundance of carbon dioxide. The image was meant to show how the colonial populace was helping the terraforming effort. This also included a data overlay, with real-time feeds from atmospheric sensors deployed across the planet.

Other than the influx of desperate spacers on Chiba Station, eager to trade in an existence aboard a ship for a cramped HAB unit, there were colonists who had managed to scrape up enough credits to return in hopes of finding work that would get them a ticket to another star system. The risk was that if they couldn't find any work or couldn't afford to wait on the station for a ship captain in need of additional crew, they were taken back planet-side to start the process over again—a process that could take years. Outgoing communications from the standard colonist was monitored and altered before it was routed into the star systems communications network. There was a price to pay for their ignorance.

A tall, narrow-shouldered man hastened over to him.

"Welcome back, Dockmaster Jakin."

Colo frowned and gave the man a once-over. He noted the stim-induced intensity to the man's gaze. "Malachi, have you been at it again?"

Malachi pressed his virtually nonexistent lips together, and his pale cheeks colored. "I was ahead. There were ups and downs, but I was so far ahead."

Malachi was a Chiba Station coordinator who had become somewhat obsessed with wagering on various sporting activities sponsored by station authorities. "Sounds like you should have quit while you were ahead."

Malachi sighed. "I was so close. It just kept getting better and better."

"How much were you up before you lost it all?"

"How do you know I'm not still up?"

"Because you showed up to work today, and you're wearing the same uniform as yesterday," Colo said and gestured to a stain near the Chiba Station patch.

Malachi glanced down and began scrubbing the stain with his fingers. "I thought… Never mind."

They walked to the control center. "How much?" Colo asked again.

"Five thousand."

"You lost five thousand credits?"

Malachi shook his head. "No, I was up by five thousand. I lost closer to eight."

"Taking a hyperlane to Boros, I see."

Malachi blanched. "I might have a problem."

"Might?"

Malachi shook his head. "I'll stay away. I'll even take a different way home."

Colo didn't think Malachi was going to be successful. The adverts had a way of finding almost anyone. Just a little nudge during a journey and sure enough, Malachi would be back gambling away wages he hadn't even earned yet. A week or two at most, and his assistant would come to him, desperate for help. Colo wasn't sure if he'd help him or not. His last assistant had been much more pleasing until... Well, he let go that line of thinking. Assistants were easy enough to replace, and the good ones never stayed long. Malachi had potential, but he also had a lot of flaws.

"I have a couple of updates for you. One, there's a station-wide alert limiting broadcast communications."

"Another lockdown?"

Malachi nodded and sent the briefing to Colo. "Yes, but they've given this a top-tiered severity."

Colo opened the briefing on his wrist computer and quickly scanned it. "All right, all ship comms will be monitored for outbound broadcasts and routed to station security. What's next?"

"Inspector Ko Ji is looking for you," Malachi said.

Colo walked inside the command center. Thirty-six members of his staff waited at their workstations for him to officially take the handoff from the current command center staff located several decks below them. He headed for the raised platform where he oversaw operations.

"Did he say what he wanted?" Colo asked.

"He's upset about the cargo inspections schedule. He says he needs more staff for the increased workload."

Colo snorted. "Negative, the staff he has is capable of fulfilling the workload. And tell him there's no approval for overtime. If he doesn't like it, he can take it up the chain."

Malachi nodded. "Got it. Tell him to stop complaining and get to work."

Colo chuckled and regarded his assistant for a moment. Then he gestured for Malachi to come closer. "I'm sending an application to your wrist computer. It's an inhibitor for your finances. It'll force you not to exceed your budget allocation in the entertainment ward."

Malachi raised his eyebrows and his wrist computer beeped when it received the special program. "Thank you! Thank you so much. I don't know how I can repay you."

"Oh, you *will* repay me. We'll come up with something," Colo said.

Malachi swallowed and nodded.

Colo forwarded his credentials to Chiba Station's central computer. All Dockmaster duties now cut over to him and his staff. An instant later, there was a flurry of activity as docking requests filled up the queue, as well as flight plans for ships heading out. They needed to be reviewed and approved before the ships could leave.

Colo leaned forward in anticipation. One of the things he loved about his job was that sometimes a salvager managed to find something truly remarkable and valuable. For the next standard cycle, no ships could leave or dock without his permission. He loved his job.

The hours flew by, and Colo was busier than normal. The workload efficiency meter was high enough that he had to take part in more of the day-to-day part of operations, which meant fielding special requests that came in to his staff.

An unknown ship request entered his queue and a message appeared on his personal holoscreen from Malachi.

I think you need to take this one ;)

Colo's lips curved at the winky smiley face that also included the galactic credit symbol. Maybe keeping Malachi around was going to be a good idea.

Colo selected the comlink session for the unknown ship. "Welcome to Kizu Star System. This is Dockmaster Actual for Chiba Station. Transfer your ship registration and credentials now."

"Greetings, Dockmaster Actual," a woman replied, and a video session was added. "I'm Captain Mercy Gentry of the *Gypsy Clipper.*"

Captain Gentry looked barely old enough to process an astrogation update to a ship's navigation computer. She had long, dark hair, and her pale skin was nearly covered with body artwork that Colo couldn't make sense of, but it was her eyes that drew him in. They were alluring and dangerous, all wrapped up into one naughty-looking package.

Colo received the data he'd asked for and informed the "captain" of his name. "What is the purpose for your visit to Chiba Station?"

"Why does anyone come here? I'd like to file a salvage claim."

Colo nodded. "I see," he said. The ship was on an intercept course with the station. "There's a problem."

"What kind of problem. You do accept freelance claims?"

"We do for registered ships, which yours is not. You lack the proper permits to salvage anything in this sector."

"You're right; I don't have the proper permits. I'm transferring the data on our salvage claim to you now. We happened upon a derelict ship on our way to you. It didn't make sense for us to leave the cargo for someone else to find just so we can file paperwork that can clearly be done now."

Colo winced. "About that, Captain Gentry."

She narrowed her gaze and her mouth formed a grim line. "Is this where you give me some kind of bureaucratic red tape that robs me of fifty percent of the value of my cargo?"

"There is a hefty penalty for salvaging without a permit."

"This is ridiculous. I'm going to turn my ship around and

head to the nearest jump point. I'll find somewhere else that's willing to deal with me."

"No, you won't."

"Excuse me?"

"You heard me, Captain. You're not leaving."

"How do you intend to stop me?"

"Oh, I don't need to stop you. You're running low on fuel and supplies."

Her eyes widened. Colo didn't believe she was the real captain of that ship. More likely, she'd killed the original captain.

"Here's a tip for you, *Captain*. You contacted us using an unsecured comlink, which basically gave us access to your ship's systems. Now, we can't actually affect any of the systems, but we can query them for status, which I've done. So, forgive me if I find your bluff—excuse me—*assertion* in regard to leaving this star system bordering on the fringe of hilarity."

Gentry snarled a curse.

"Now, Captain, I can clear your ship to dock, and after an inspection of the cargo, we can calculate your penalty responsibility for salvaging without the proper permits."

"You're going to take half the value of our find."

"Look at it this way: at least you'll get to keep half."

She looked angry enough to spit plasma. "Fine."

"Excellent. Sending clearance for a secure docking bay. The inspectors will meet you at the airlock," Colo said and looked at her for a moment. "I wouldn't keep them waiting."

"Understood. *Gypsy Clipper* out," Gentry said and closed the comlink.

Colo laughed. Welcome to the Collective. Looks like his own bank account was about to get another credit bonus. As an incentive for enforcing the regulations, Chiba Station staff received a percentage of the value of the cargo, which could add up over the course of a pay cycle.

Colo's workload lightened as the hours went by, and he

checked the video feed of the docking bay where the *Gypsy Clipper* was undergoing a lengthy interior inspection by Ko Ji. The inspector liked to complain, but he was quite thorough at his job. Colo wouldn't put it past Gentry to try to hide the most valuable items they'd "found," but Ko Ji would find those too.

Malachi caught his eye and smiled, and Colo gave him a nod. He looked back at his holoscreen at an alert that appeared moments before a klaxon alarm screeched throughout the command center.

A comlink from Chiba Station's defense minister, Jocasta Sable, appeared. "Jakin! What have you allowed on the station?"

"I don't know what you mean. All docking requests have been filed to the central office, and broadcast comms are being monitored as you requested."

"I don't care about—Look at the damn system plot and tell me what you see!"

Colo brought up the system plot, which showed six additional ships. They must have just entered the system, but they were so close to the planet! No ship could have done that. He felt the blood drain from his face, and he looked at Jocasta in alarm.

"You brought a damn Sentinel strike force down on us!"

"That's not possible," Colo said and brought up the docking security dashboard on his personal holoscreen. It was filled with broadcasts. "This can't be right—"

Jocasta snarled. "There are broadcasts coming for practically every ship that has docked during your shift."

Colo accessed the space dock monitoring system and initiated regression analysis to figure out which ship had started broadcasting first. How the hell had he missed this? "I, I, don't know how this happened," he said and stood up. His mouth went dry.

The analysis finished running and a single ship name appeared.

Gypsy Clipper.

"I found where it started but—"

"But it's already spread, compromising other ship communication systems." Jocasta looked away and began barking orders to bring up the station's defenses.

People began fleeing the command center. They'd seen the ships that were heading for the station, and there was only one thing they could do. Malachi ran over to him. "The Sentinels are here!"

"I know," Colo said and gritted his teeth. What had Gentry found that started all this? He should have paid more attention to it. He'd known there was something wrong, and he should have trusted his instincts. "The ship you gave me began broadcasting a signal."

"A signal? Can't we shut it down?"

"Station security has been trying, but it keeps popping back up. It's spread to the other ships. It brought the Sentinels here."

"Can we send our own broadcast to the Sentinels? Tell them it's a mistake?"

"You're welcome to try," Colo said.

Malachi's gaze darted to a workstation and then he shook his head. "I'll stick with you."

They ran out of the command center. All Colo could hear was Jocasta's bitter assertion that there would be no escape for any of them. He glanced at the wallscreen that showed a live video feed from Boros. Already, there were thousands of escape pods en route to the planet's surface.

"We need to get to an escape pod," Malachi said.

"You think those people are gonna live, think again. There isn't enough room down there. All of them are choosing a slow death."

Colo ran down a corridor and stopped at a bot maintenance hatch. Malachi was right behind him.

Colo entered a special access code and waited a few seconds for acknowledgment. The hatch opened to a darkened interior.

He looked at Malachi. "I have a shuttle. This shaft is the quickest way to get there. Keep your arms close."

Colo didn't wait for Malachi to reply. He stepped into the maintenance shaft with one foot on each side of its darkening walls. Inhaling deeply, he leaped down, and air began to rush past his face. Indicator lights for each deck flashed by him in an orange blur. He plummeted downward at startling speeds. His heart started to race, he felt an ache in his gut, and his body became rigid. Then, the artificial gravity slowed his descent and his feet lightly touched the ground.

Colo heard Malachi screaming above him, and he hastened out of the way. He quickened his pace and glanced behind him. Malachi was crouched on the ground, panting.

"No time to waste," Colo said.

He ran to the end of the corridor and stopped at a hatch, quickly entering his access code. Malachi caught up with him and waited. Colo watched the status window shift to green once the atmosphere was cycled into the small docking bay beyond.

"I had no idea this was even here."

The door opened, revealing a small platform where a shuttle waited. Colo raced to the other side and entered through the access hatch. The shuttle was small. It only had two seats and a small storage compartment. Colo sat in the pilot seat and began the preflight checks. Malachi sat next to him and closed the rear hatch.

As the engines powered up, Colo sent the command to open the docking bay doors.

"How do we get out of here?" Malachi asked.

Colo jutted his chin toward the ceiling and grabbed the flight controls. "We go up."

The shuttle rose upward, and after a few seconds, they were outside Chiba Station where Boros's poisoned atmosphere came into view. Thousands of escape pods were streaking through it. Colo swung the shuttle around and increased the mains to the maximum, pressing them back into their seats until the inertia dampeners were able to compensate.

They flew along Chiba Station's massive structure. The shuttle's onboard flight computers helped him navigate through the station's outer structure. Colo set a course, and the flight plan appeared on the main holoscreen.

"You have a star jumper on standby?" Malachi asked.

"Always have a way out."

The star jumper was essentially an interstellar support module used for small shuttles to escape star systems. He updated their course, and they flew away from the station.

"My God!" Malachi said.

Colo saw two huge ships flying toward the station and noted massive weapons mounted center mass on each of those ships—spinal mounts, which were powerful weapons that needed to be part of a warship's superstructure or the ship would be torn apart when it was used.

Chiba Station had point defenses that were reliant upon smaller, rapid-fire mag cannons. He wasn't a weapons expert, but he was certain that Chiba Station was minutes from being obliterated.

Several bright, bluish flashes came from the Sentinel ships, as if a lightning storm had erupted from their powerful weapons. The bolts blew through the station and seemed to spread along the outer hull. There were several more flashes, building up in intensity, and then large sections of Chiba Station began to break apart and collapse in on itself.

Colo watched in horror as the bolts spread to the nearest escape pods, destroying them almost as soon as it reached them. The last thing he heard was Malachi whimpering, and then there was nothing. No last word. No last breath or even a thought. He felt nothing. Colo Jakin was nothing.

A GUNNISON FREIGHTER lingered at the edge of Kiva Star System. The captain and crew watched the Sentinels annihilate Chiba Station with grim satisfaction. Chiba Station had no strategic importance, but it sent a powerful message to its powerful backers—a message that was being sent throughout the sector. They watched as the wreckage of Chiba Station spread amid the destructive forces of Sentinel weaponry, forming a vast debris field that would orbit the planet. The Sentinels patrolled the area, systematically destroyed anything that crossed their paths, even after the broadcast signals that had drawn them into the star system went silent.

"That's enough," the captain said. "Execute jump coordinates delta. We've got more messages to send to Trenton Draven and the Collective."

CHAPTER NINE

Quinton stared at the spider-drone. He wanted to act like he'd misunderstood, but there was absolutely no chance of that, and Harper knew it.

"There has to be something," Harper said. One of the drone's legs tapped the ground, seemingly an outlet for a mental tick.

Guttman and Oscar pointedly looked away, as if suddenly finding the last swallow of Angorian ale worth further scrutiny.

"No, there is," Quinton said, trying to think up a response that would smooth things over.

"I've gone over the ship's diagnostic reports for most of the systems. The weapons systems and point defenses are all fully functional. All of you have done a thorough job with it," Harper said and looked at Guttman and Oscar, the latter of whom threw a nod his way.

Quinton thought a bit of deflection was in order. "Guttman, do you need any help with—"

"Nope, I've got it covered."

Quinton quirked an eyebrow. "Really, because I seem to recall several complaints on your part about the physical checks of systems as part of routine maintenance."

Guttman stood up and made a show of stretching his arms. "I did, but then—Oscar, yeah, Oscar brought up that it's good exercise. Movement is essential for optimal health," he said as he tried to suck in his gut.

"I'd be happy to help out," Harper said. "I've been checking those systems anyway."

Guttman's eyes went wide, and Quinton couldn't tell if the spacer was more shocked or afraid that he'd missed it.

Harper looked at Quinton. "You said I should make an effort. I'm making an effort, but this is ridiculous. Look at him." The spider-drone surged toward Guttman, who nearly jumped out of his skin. "Seriously, what are you afraid of?"

"I know," Quinton said. "If you wanted to murder poor Guttman, all you'd have to do is wait for him to go for his middle-of-the-night galley raid."

Oscar grinned a little and shrugged when Guttman threw him a scathing look. "You do have a pattern. We all do." He stood up. "Let's make it a group effort."

Guttman blinked several times. "Cross training, yes! That will work."

The two spacers headed out of the galley.

Harper looked at Quinton, who nodded his head toward the door. Without another word, the spider-drone followed them into the corridor.

Becker walked in and glanced at Quinton. "Where are the others?"

"Communal maintenance check. Strength in numbers."

Becker nodded and went to the meal console. He scrolled through what the fabricator could make with the supplies aboard and shook his head. "We need supplies."

Quinton didn't need to eat—or sleep, for that matter—but he still enjoyed the smell of food. He could consume food and even taste it, but it was wasted on him.

Becker made a selection and a few seconds later, some kind of brownish gruel squirted into a bowl. Quinton was able to smell a faint odor of cinnamon.

"It's not that bad. You could have chosen something else," Quinton said.

Becker sat down and began eating the protein-paste meal. "I'll live."

"We need a supply run," Quinton said. They'd let the supplies run low because Becker thought they'd be on their own ship by now. "You know, we could send a message to the DUC."

Becker finished eating and chased the paste down with some water. He then rubbed the top of his lip and stood up. "Too many strings."

"They owe you."

Becker shook his head. "No, they owe *you*. Anyway, how would it look if after all these months I sent a message to the Dholeren United Coalition requesting payment?"

"That doesn't change the fact that we were part of the mission."

"Oh, so it's okay if I tell Maelyn you're alive?"

That hit home. Quinton hadn't wanted to contact Maelyn for the same reasons Becker didn't want to get involved with the DUC. The DUC was always recruiting. Keeping Maelyn in the dark about their survival of the starbase's destruction had been Quinton's decision. Becker was right. They couldn't contact the DUC because by all accounts, Becker had gotten a ship—the *Wayfarer*. But Quinton had taken it with the promise of helping the spacer find a ship of his own.

"It's complicated."

"It's a big galaxy."

"The DUC probably doesn't have what you're looking for anyway."

Ships were among the most valuable commodity in the galaxy for anyone who wanted to be independent.

"Don't bite my head off," Quinton began, and Becker's eyes

narrowed. "I know you want off this ship. Why not take an interim job in someone else's operation?"

"Listening to our conversation last night?"

"Give me a break. I don't have to spy on you guys to figure out what you were talking about," Quinton said.

Harper had done it for him and reported it, but Becker didn't need to know that.

"I've already done that. I put in ten years in Crowe's Union. Worked my way up. I had multiple crews under me," Becker said.

Quinton nodded. "And then I showed up."

Becker looked as if he'd swallowed something sour. "You don't get it."

"What don't I get?"

"I had things in the works."

"Really," Quinton said dryly. "I wasn't there for long, but it looked to me as if Dante was going places and you were waiting for Crowe to let a few scraps fall your way."

Becker glared at him. They'd been through this before.

"You took a chance."

Becker grabbed his plate and threw it in the washer. Then he stalked out of the galley.

Quinton followed him. "You took a chance. You saw an opportunity to get what you've always wanted, and you took it. But it's proven to be much harder to reap the rewards, and you're going to stand there and tell me you'd rather go back to where you were."

Becker quickened his pace, heading to the bridge. He slammed his palm against the door controls.

"Plus," Quinton said, following him inside. "You fell for it, too."

Becker spun around. "For what?"

"We're men. She had a pretty face. You do the math."

Becker stepped toward Quinton. "I didn't do it because of Maelyn."

"Maybe not, but that's part of it—the promise of a big payout and, come on, she was... *something*."

"When we're done, you can go find her."

He'd considered it, more than once, but he always wound his way back to it being a bad idea. The more time that passed, the more that idea was reinforced. That, and now he had his memories—Nope, he wasn't going to do it. Mental trap avoided.

"Look, we can't keep going at this in the dark."

Becker spun around and brought up the main holoscreen.

"It's not going to work," Quinton said.

Becker ignored him and brought up a star chart.

"You're smarter than this. We need information. There has to be someone we can go to that has a lead for what you need," Quinton said.

Becker flipped through a few more star systems and then swiped them off to the side. He rolled his shoulders, stretched his neck, and let out a long sigh. "You're right, Quinton. This isn't working."

Quinton felt his lips lift in a tentative smile.

"I was hoping we could hit a few of the places I knew about, but we need better odds."

"Now you're talking! I had Radek query for sector comms buoys to give us a starting point."

Becker grinned. "Yeah, those are unreliable. News travels by ship. The buoys get the fluff."

"I know, but it'll give us the highlights. At the very least, we'll know if there are other reported instances of the activation signal."

They needed to avoid those systems so as not to cross paths with the Sentinels. They'd nearly killed him, and Quinton wasn't in any rush to repeat the experience. In fact, he preferred to avoid it altogether, and he'd get no arguments from Becker or the others on that front.

An audible chime overhead signaled a ship-wide broadcast. "Quinton, we need your help down in engineering," Oscar said.

They heard Guttman shouting in the background, which was answered by Harper.

"Now would be great."

"We're on our way," Quinton replied.

Both he and Becker ran out of the bridge, quickly making their way through to the belly of the ship.

"He's coming," Oscar said. "Hold on, he's right here."

Quinton rounded the corner. Harper had Guttman pressed against the sidewall of the reactor core. If the spider-drone pierced the sidewall, they'd have some serious problems.

"Guys! Is five minutes of peace too much to ask?" Quinton said.

"Tell him to put me down!"

The spider-drone's head spun toward Quinton. "He tried to deactivate me," he said and turned back toward Guttman.

Becker stood behind him. "Quinton," he said in a tone that said he'd better deal with this.

"Harper, what exactly happened?"

Guttman growled. "All I did was try to help."

Harper had one of the spider-drone's legs raised as if he were getting ready to skewer Guttman.

"Hey, look at me," Quinton said.

Harper didn't turn around, and Guttman continued to try to get free. His sidearm was on the floor nearby.

"Harper," Quinton said. Getting no response, he then spoke more forcefully. "Lieutenant Harper, you are a guest on my ship! If you'd like to remain aboard, you'll put Guttman down now!"

His combat HUD overlay measured the distance to Harper and gave Quinton several options with which to disable the spider-drone, but none of them guaranteed that Guttman wouldn't get hurt.

Harper cleared his throat and then stepped back from Guttman. The spacer sagged to the floor.

Quinton relaxed a little. "What happened?"

Harper backed away from the others. "He tried to access my control panel."

"Wait," Guttman said, rubbing the area where Harper had held him. "Hold on a second. An alert flashed on the panel and I was just trying to get a better look."

"After you said we'd all be safer if I went into standby."

"Until we found you a better body, is all. That's it. I was just making a suggestion."

"What's the matter? Don't you like spiders?" Harper said and tapped each of his legs in rapid succession on the floor.

Guttman's eyes became wide. "That's beside the point." He shook his head and glared at Quinton. "I want off this ship. As long as this—Harper is here, I'm not going to be."

"I can take you to the nearest airlock if you want," Harper said.

"That's enough," Quinton said. "What am I supposed to do here?" Guttman opened his mouth to reply. "It's a rhetorical question. We're stuck here. We *are*, and I expect a little more cooperation from all of you," he said and looked at the others. "You think getting off the ship at the next resupply depot is going to get you where you want to be?"

"I won't be *here*."

"Yeah, you'd be burning credits, hoping for another ship to arrive that'll take you with them. And that's only if they overlook the fact that all of you are on the run from Crowe's Union," Quinton said. He glared at Guttman and the spacer looked away.

"All right, you made your point," Becker said.

"I don't think I have," Quinton said and walked toward Guttman. "He's not going anywhere," Quinton said, gesturing toward Harper. "He didn't ask for this. He didn't choose to be here. Something turned him back on. It's like being born again, except you know a lot more."

Guttman backed up against the wall.

"Look at him!"

Guttman's eyes darted to Harper. The spider-drone remained perfectly still, and Quinton had no idea what he was thinking.

"You go on and on about how we should treat you with more respect. Isn't that right? How about treating Harper like he's a guy who's stuck in a bad situation? Maybe instead of treating him like he's about to go insane, you can find a way to help him out, or God forbid, make him feel a little bit welcome," Quinton said and looked at the others. "We weren't part of the history you know. I don't know what happened that caused the PMC degradation that gave rise to the Sentinels. I don't doubt that it happened, but this," he said, gesturing to all of them, "this constant mistrust and animosity stops now. You want off this ship so bad, fine. I don't care anymore." Quinton looked at Becker. "Go have your little meeting that's sure to follow and then get the hell off my ship. Good luck. See you later. I'm through with this bullshit," he said and exhaled. "Harper, come with me to the bridge. Now."

Quinton turned and left the others behind, Harper following without saying a word. They made it back to the bridge and Quinton glanced at the main holoscreen, which still had Becker's star system search on it. He inhaled deeply and rested his hands on his hips.

"Thank you, Commander."

Quinton winced and shook his head.

"I'm sorry. I keep doing that."

"It needed to be said," Quinton replied.

"I might have overreacted. I don't like how they look at me."

Quinton turned around. "Guttman can be a little overdramatic, but it takes two. You can't lose control like that. The only reason things didn't get worse was because of Oscar. He could have shot you. He chose not to. They're not a bad group if you get to know them."

"Why do you defend them? They just want to leave."

"I owe them."

"But it's still not right."

Quinton regarded Harper for a few seconds. "It's complicated," he said. He didn't want to discuss how PMCs were almost universally mistrusted and outright scorned.

"I'll do better, sir—uh, damn it."

Quinton ignored the lapse. "There *is* something I need from you."

"What do you need?"

"You need to be honest with me."

"I haven't lied about anything," Harper said, the tone of his voice rising a little.

"I mean by omission. That drone isn't meant to hold you. You know the rules. Greta is going to help you as much as she can, just like Radek does for me, but you can't lose control. Neither of us can."

"That's easy for you to say."

Quinton leveled his gaze at him. "You've been reactivated less than two days. Are you saying you can't handle the current situation?"

One of the spider-drone's legs tapped the ground in rapid succession. Did Harper even notice it?

"There could be others like me."

"And."

"We should be looking for them."

"No, we shouldn't."

"The Sentinels can't be that much of a threat."

"Harper, do me a favor. Never say that again. You don't know what you're talking about, and this is exactly what worries the others. There's a price to pay for ignorance. I know. I paid, and now you don't have to. Just trust me. If you can't do that, then at least be cautious."

"What happened?"

"Not right now. I'll tell you if you stick around long enough. I need a promise from you that you'll stay in control, and if you think you can't, then you'll back off."

The spider-drone's armored torso was tilted downward as if Harper was looking away. "I don't think I can make that promise."

"Why not?"

"I need to be able to trust myself."

"Yeah, and I need to be able to trust *you*."

"But you're worried that I'm not stable."

"All our lives are on the line if you're not."

"I don't understand."

"We're going to have to resupply. There are built-in security protocols that can detect PMC access. If you trip those alarms doing something you think isn't going to be noticed, it will invite unwanted attention and could give away our location to the Sentinels. Trust me when I say that you don't want that to happen."

Harper was quiet for a minute. "I promise I won't lose control with the others, but like you said, it goes both ways."

Quinton wanted to believe him, but he couldn't. This might have been because of the PMC integrity check he'd run on Harper, or the fact that he'd seem completely in control one moment and then would ask an obscure question in the next. He just needed Harper to stay in control long enough for them to find another body, or better yet, a DNA vault.

"Thank you, Harper."

CHAPTER TEN

Sometimes Quinton really missed sleeping—laying down on a comfortable bed and slipping off into oblivion only to wake up hours later refreshed and ready to take on the day. He didn't need to sleep in the traditional sense, but there was a rest cycle built into the upkeep schedule that Radek tried to make him adhere to. A quick frame rate increase when less than a second had passed in real time meant that he'd gone through his own rest cycle. Apparently, the human mind needed downtime to process information and to just wander on its own. Quinton knew the science behind it. The knowledge and importance of it had been drilled into him as part of his training, but the rest cycle was tied to having a normal human body. Most creatures had evolved to go through a rest cycle for the recuperation of the body and also for the brain.

Harper required at least ninety minutes for his rest cycle because of the limitations of the spider-drone. The drone's computer systems and hardware only allowed for increases in frame rate in a limited capacity. Even though Quinton could go through days without a rest cycle that took only seconds to achieve, Harper required it every eighteen hours.

A sound of exaggerated static came from shipboard comms. "Now hear this," Oscar said. "Captain, your presence is requested on the bridge immediately. All nonessential personnel should stay away. Guttman, the galley is off-limits—" Oscar's voice cut off. "Captain, hurry! Angry spacer is closing in."

Quinton chuckled. The star class jumper should have had a larger crew if he was concerned with routine maintenance and anything like maintaining a standing watch. They traded off duties and Quinton carried most of the slack. Over the last thirty-nine hours, Harper had helped them maintain the ship, and there hadn't been any more incidents.

Quinton walked past the galley on his way to the bridge, and Guttman nearly collided with him.

"We're not going to leave without you," Quinton said.

"Oh, I know it. Club Ranstead, here I come," Guttman replied.

The clipped cadence of the spider-drone came from farther down the corridor. Guttman glanced behind them for a moment.

"Good morning," Quinton said.

"Good morning, Captain," Harper replied. "It went better this time. I think the VR needed a little bit of tweaking. Greta has got it much better tuned."

The ship had a VR interface that had a pretty extensive library available. Quinton had never even tried it. Becker and the others hadn't been too keen to use it either.

Guttman looked at him for a second.

"The VR is available to anyone, Guttman. You can use it," Quinton said.

He shook his head, which surprised Quinton. Of anyone on the ship, he'd thought that Guttman would have embraced VR, but he'd always refused.

"There's a training VR that shows you how to use it," Harper said.

"I know how to use it," Guttman said and then added, "Thanks anyway."

Quinton felt one of his eyebrows twitch. Guttman had been almost civil in his tone toward Harper.

They went on the bridge and joined Becker and Oscar.

"Nice 'all hands,'" Guttman criticized.

"All we need is the captain," Oscar replied.

Quinton looked at the main holoscreen, which showed a rather small resupply depot. "It's a little underwhelming. Are you sure you'll be able to find an information broker here?"

Becker nodded. "These are the best places."

There was a small interface window waiting for Quinton's input. He had to transfer his captain's credentials, which would authorize payment to put in at Club Ranstead.

"It looks a bit run-down. Are you sure someone isn't going to try to steal this ship?"

"They might try," Becker replied.

"They won't succeed," Harper said.

"Pay the fee and no one asks questions. That's exactly what we need," Becker said and raised his hand, gesturing for Guttman to wait.

"I'm going to pay the fee. I can't wait to see what this place looks like on the inside," Quinton said.

"Are you sure that's a good idea?" Oscar said. "You coming with us, that is."

"Are you afraid I'll embarrass you or something? You're making me feel like your goofy cousin."

Oscar considered for a few moments, looking uncomfortable, and then looked at Becker.

"Let's get one thing straight—I'm coming," Quinton said.

"*We're* coming," Harper said.

That brought a few raised eyebrows.

"Harper, you need to stay aboard the ship. I'm pretty sure a spider-drone would garner attention we don't need," Quinton said.

Harper was silent for a few moments, and then he started laughing. "If you could see the looks on all your faces! Woo!" He shifted on his feet and a couple of his legs tapped the ground. "I know. I get it. I'll stay here and monitor communications. Maybe I'll find something interesting."

Quinton knew that the best way to get someone to cooperate, especially on a ship, was to give them something to do, and not something meaningless. That wouldn't work for anyone beyond basic intelligence. He glanced at Guttman for a moment. Harper had been a tactical officer trained in the Acheron Confederacy Navy, which had had one of the best trained navies in the galaxy. He might be a little biased when it came to that, but nothing he'd seen so far had changed his mind. Monitoring comms chatter among the locals was well beneath Harper's skills, but it could prove valuable if the effort paid off.

Quinton's outward appearance was human—dark hair, two meters tall, athletic, with a handsome smile. He had Radek engage the life-sign protocols that allowed the cybernetic avatar to simulate a live human. His body mimicked breathing that would increase if he exerted himself. His eyes blinked. He could even produce sweat if required, and he gave off body heat.

Quinton opened a sub window on the main holoscreen, which showed the ship's life-support system. On the bridge were the biological markers of four humans and one spider-drone.

"Good enough for you guys?" Quinton asked.

The others peered at the main holoscreen.

"That ought to work," Becker said.

Guttman walked over to him, peering at him as if he were trying to see through a facade. "That's creepy. Look at him. I would never have guessed."

Quinton held out his arm and Guttman touched it. "It's

warm. That's impressive. It's actually warm to the touch," he said, looking at Becker and Oscar.

Oscar walked over and gave him a nod, then raised an eyebrow. "We need a few more of these."

Quinton glanced at Harper. "I wish."

"Impressive," Becker said. "How long can you maintain it?"

"I'm actually not maintaining it. It's part of the onboard programming. I've just activated it."

"Nothing can interfere with it?"

"Like what?"

"I don't know. That's why I'm asking you."

Quinton snorted and gestured toward the image of Club Ranstead. "Yeah, like anything in there is going to have the ability to detect something wrong with me."

Becker shrugged. "Don't underestimate them."

"It looks like they cobbled together a few old mining platforms and installed several industrial HAB units."

"It's nicer on the inside," Guttman said.

Quinton authorized the credit transfer and received docking clearance. Oscar returned to the pilot's workstation and set a course.

"Have you been there before?" Quinton asked.

Becker shook his head. "Not Ranstead, but there are plenty of mobile resupply depots that travel throughout the sector. The reason this one is so far out in this star system is because of the Ashanti mines here."

"Never heard of them."

"They don't like visitors. Club Ranstead must have gotten clearance to be here; otherwise, a squadron of gunships would've convinced them of the error of their ways."

"I didn't realize these were Ashanti mines," Guttman said and looked at Quinton. "No visitors to their mines ever. They only use their own freighters to transport the exotic gases that they mine out of the star system—even if it's to transport to a larger freighter that has been contracted to bring it somewhere else."

Becker nodded. "They're one of few mining operations that know how to extract the gases. They operate throughout the sector. How they extract and refine the material is a closely guarded secret. Others have tried to figure it out, but it's a pretty lethal process."

"Okay, so no courses through the internal star systems unless we want to start trouble. Got it," Quinton replied and frowned. "How do the Ashanti bring people into their operation if everything is so secretive?"

"Carefully," Becker replied.

Quinton gave him a look.

"I don't know. They probably have multiple layers of operation, and only so many people are privileged to know the inner workings of their method of operation."

"What if someone wants to leave?"

"They're not allowed."

Becker's face was deadpanned, but Quinton didn't believe him. "Right, then. Time to go find an information broker. I, for one, can't wait to question them. Do we pay them for a session, or do they charge by the question? We don't have endless credits." Technically, they didn't have credits at all. Quinton had secured their funding from a Union creditor who had unknowingly transferred several transactions to them. It was nice of the Union to bankroll them like that.

Becker sighed. "I'm not sure of the inner workings of the Ashanti mining corporation. It depends on their role in the company and the level of knowledge of their operations. Now stop messing around. I don't need you to scare off any broker contacts."

Quinton had gotten what he'd wanted, which was an answer to his question, and nodded.

"Why would a broker be based here?" Harper asked.

"They're not here," Becker replied. "Contacting info brokers isn't the same everywhere. We're here to get a way to contact them."

"I didn't know that. I thought we'd be meeting them here," Quinton said.

"You thought wrong. They're secretive, and why take the risk if you don't need to with an in-person meeting?"

Quinton couldn't fault the logic, but he still didn't like it.

"I won't know the contact methods available until we go inside."

Oscar flew the ship to the docking platform. Once the docking clamps were attached to the hull, refueling hoses extended to the receivers.

Quinton authorized payment of the refueling operations and then looked at Oscar. "You didn't even scratch the paint on the hull."

Oscar pursed his lips and nodded once. "Would you expect any less? We're all professionals here."

A memory of Oscar pretending to fly an aircar that was secured to a maintenance platform came to his mind and he smiled. "I'll buy you a drink."

Oscar grinned and shook his head. "I think I owe you several."

Guttman was peering at his personal holoscreen with a look of intense concentration. He grunted a few times as he navigated the interface, then tapped the confirmation button. "Resupply order has been put in. Standard resupply for this class of ship."

"When are they going to deliver it?"

"It won't take them long. Probably within the hour."

Quinton looked at Harper. "You'll need to open the secure hatch and allow them to unload the order there." That way, they wouldn't have access to the interior of the ship.

"I can do that. Do you want me to store the supplies after they deliver them?"

"I'd appreciate it, but if something comes up, we'll get to it when we get back," Quinton said.

"Understood, sir," Harper said.

Quinton and the others went to the forward airlock. His biometric sensors showed the slightly elevated heart rates that signaled their anticipation and excitement at finally getting off the ship. Oscar and Guttman were chatting about where they would go first. Even Becker wasn't immune, and neither was Quinton, for that matter. He felt a slight pang of regret that Harper had to stay behind, but given his current form, there wasn't even the option of a disguise.

They all wore enviro-jackets that had hoods, which could serve as an emergency helmet should the need arise. One thing Quinton had learned since being reactivated was that most people in the galaxy had a general mistrust of their surroundings. There were redundancies built into any space structure, but this preparedness had spread to the individual level. This wasn't exactly new to Quinton. His experiences in the ACN had been full of preparedness plans, but warships were designed for going into dangerous places, and a state of readiness was expected. Civilians had never needed to bring that kind of preparedness into their daily lives. Merchant fleets experienced this to a lesser extent than federation militaries, but as they entered Club Ranstead, it was just another stark reminder of how the galaxy had changed.

The resupply depot's rounded design brought visitors into a central promenade. Ranstead's interior looked old. Small maintenance bots scurried around, performing maintenance tasks throughout the multileveled area. The interior wasn't overly large, less than a kilometer. Becker led them past various shops and eateries. The smells of cooked food sent out an enticing aroma.

Becker led them to a dimly lit place called Nunu's. There were plenty of spacers inside, and much of the foot traffic outside brought them to the restaurant and bar. They walked inside where multiple bars were located throughout the different zones, which seemed to follow a certain theme. Neon holographic themes lit up the walls and ceilings with such vividness that it was almost easy to forget where you were. Quinton thought this was the purpose.

Guttman inhaled deeply and sighed. "I need a drink."

Oscar agreed.

"You guys go on ahead. I've gotten a few nibbles on my initial inquires," Becker said.

"Do you want backup?" Quinton asked.

Becker shook his head. "Nah, it'll be fine. I'll call you if I need you."

Quinton nodded once and followed Guttman and Oscar. They headed for a warmly lit bar and sat on the stools. The patrons in the area glanced at them and then went back to their meals. Cheers erupted from a crowd of people that surrounded an area Quinton couldn't see.

A good-looking bartender, nearly covered with intricate body art, came over and took their meal orders. Guttman opted for an extensive sampler, while Oscar chose some kind of delicacy Quinton had never heard of. The bartender looked at Quinton expectantly.

"Got any local brews?" Quinton asked.

The bartender arched an eyebrow. "Really? I had you pegged for an import," she said with a wink and nodded. "I have just the thing for you, hon."

For the better part of the next hour, they watched Guttman devour plate after plate of "succulent delights," as he liked to call them. As if their jovial mood drew like-minded company, the spacers were soon swapping stories shared by people who lived and worked in the deep dark. There were cautionary tales or insights into sectors where there was salvage potential, which Oscar and Guttman seemed to lap up eagerly. More than a few times they looked in Quinton's direction. He'd give an acknowledging nod and raise his glass in a toast, but he didn't participate much, preferring to observe. There were others who also quietly observed. He kept an eye out for Becker, but he was nowhere to be seen. He considered contacting him through comlink but didn't. If Becker needed help, he'd contact them.

Quinton stood and gave up his stool to someone else, walking over to the outskirts. There was a cheer as Oscar and Guttman bought another round of drinks for their new friends. Quinton kept having the urge to move, as if he needed to expend some nervous energy. Being here triggered memories of shore leave when he'd been part of the ACN. The accommodations had been nicer, but the ambiance was the same. Spaceports had a commonality, as well as the people who frequented them.

Oscar and Guttman eventually yielded their places at the bar and moved toward the gaming section. The small crowd joined them. Quinton took another pull from his drink, which was more of a habit—something to do that came from a life-time of practice. He found that he kept looking for the familiar faces of friends who were long gone, casualties in a war he'd never gotten to fight. The artificial biological imperatives he'd activated as part of his human appearance were also reactive to his inner yearnings, and he inhaled deeply. He looked around at the spacers who came and left. Some navigated the sections, unable to find a place to temporarily occupy. Standing there alone holding a nearly empty drink made him feel borderline pathetic. With a shrug, he put a stop to the slight pang he felt for a life he hadn't gotten to live and focused on where he was. He took one last pull from his drink and set the empty glass down on the bar.

Quinton turned and decided to make his own circuit through Nunu's. Maybe he'd even find a place to occupy for a little while. He passed various iterations of the name Nunu's where the typography was altered to fit the theme of the area. There must be a history to the name of the place, but he doubted it was all that complex—probably someone who'd once owned the place, or maybe it was just easy for people to remember.

He smelled a familiar and complex floral scent that reminded him of summer nights and outdoor gardens. Glancing toward his right, he saw someone looking at him from beneath the cowl of a hood. Music saturated the area with a rhythmical beat. There was something familiar about her, even though he couldn't see her face clearly. He glanced down and saw lavender skin extending from her neck to the soft edge of her white blouse.

Quinton strode toward her. It was too much of a coincidence if it was who he thought it was, but he was going to find out, regardless. She considered him from beneath the hood for a few moments and then pushed it back.

Quinton was pretty sure the temperature of the room hadn't gone up, but he couldn't have sworn to it. Violet eyes, deep and mysterious, regarded him. Some women have a quality about them, something completely intangible and indefinable, which gets called a lot of different things. Quinton thought of it as heat, fire. It wasn't always about sex, but it often was, and it definitely was with the Servitor.

Quinton was extremely aware of her body and eyes. Her soft lips lifted only slightly, and then she removed her coat. Long, silky black hair seemed to shimmer in the warm light from above. She sat in a tall chair, and her long legs crossed beneath a dress that seemed to part, showing swaths of smooth skin. Her expression told him that she knew exactly what effect she was having on him.

"I was wondering how long it was going to take you to find me," she said.

"You look like someone I met before. I'll leave you to it."

"You don't have to leave," she said. Dark eyebrows raised and she tilted her head slightly. "Yes, you've been among my kind before."

"I wouldn't go that far," Quinton replied. He'd intended to

walk away. Becker should be done with what he was doing by now.

She smiled a little and extended her hand. "I'm Kandria Pavond."

Quinton felt his lips lift along the edges. He wasn't going anywhere, and they both knew it. He took the proffered hand and introduced himself, but then didn't want to let her hand go because of how her skin felt. For lack of a better description, she was perfectly proportioned. His avatar was fully equipped, and Quinton felt a rush of purely physical hunger that hit him suddenly. It was unexpected and perfectly natural.

"Would you sit with me?" Kandria asked, gesturing toward the seat next to her.

"Does anyone ever say no to that?" Quinton sat down.

"You looked disappointed when you first noticed me."

"Occupational hazard?"

Kandria simply stared at him, unperturbed by his quip.

"Like I said, I thought you were someone else. They pretended to be one of you."

Kandria lifted a dark eyebrow, and her face took on a thoughtful frown while she considered what he'd said. "Not something the average person could get away with. What name did she give you?"

"How do you know it was a she?"

Kandria smiled, and Quinton grinned. She had him there.

"Vonya Irani."

"I don't know her. You said she fooled you?"

"Not just me but a lot of people. A whole space station, in fact."

Kandria looked troubled. Several spacers walked by, watching them for a few moments, but she kept her attention on him. He was the lucky one.

She pursed her lips in thought.

"I guess it doesn't happen often?"

Kandria shook her head. Even that was done with an allure that made him forget where he was. "We go through a lot of training, which isn't easily replicated by the uninitiated," she said and then smiled at him. "Thank you for telling me about her."

"You're welcome," he replied. "I'm surprised you don't want to know more."

She shook her head. "No need, unless there's more you think I should know."

With that, Quinton wanted to tell her everything he did know, but he remained quiet for a few moments. "What kind of training do you go through?"

"Years of education that covers a wide range of subjects, in addition to our physical conditioning."

"When does the genetic modification happen?"

Kandria seemed amused. "When we've been initiated. About halfway through our training."

Quinton pursed his lips. "Are the changes permanent?"

"Some."

"I see."

"She betrayed you, this woman who pretended to be a Servitor?"

"How do you know it wasn't a Servitor?"

"It wasn't."

Quinton knew he was being manipulated. He was easy to read. Kandria knew her craft well and had the instincts to go with them. Betrayal wasn't a strong enough word for it. Vonya had tried to kill them. All of them.

"I didn't mean to upset you," Kandria said.

"It happens when people try to kill me."

Kandria looked away. "I see. Violence is too easy an option."

Quinton chose not to respond.

"I watched you over there," she said and gestured toward where Quinton had been with the others. "Your companions seemed to be enjoying themselves, but you, not so much. Why is that?"

"Does everyone just spill out their feelings to you?"

"Only if they want to."

"Yeah, I don't need to."

"That's fine as well. What else would you like to talk about?"

Warm violet eyes regarded him.

"Why are you here? Is Club Ranstead a preferred scouting grounds for Servitors?"

"I'm likely here for much the same reason you are. This was a convenient place to resupply, but I doubt that's the only reason you're here."

"I was told that Servitors seek to bring harmony to the galaxy."

"That's one thing we do."

"Right. Then why does it feel like you're trying to squeeze me for information?"

"I thought we were having a conversation," she said, and as if on cue, a ringlet of hair detached itself, coming to rest on her firm breast.

"Does it bother you that someone is out there doing a pretty good job of pretending to be one of you?"

Kandria considered it for a moment. "It's something that will need to be addressed, but this is hardly the first time it's happened."

"I'd like to find her."

"Then what?"

"That depends. Many people lost their lives because of what she did."

"You intend to murder her?"

"She deserves it. It's not something that's going to change."

"I understand the desire for justice."

"But you don't approve."

"There is always accountability. I regret that this person

utilized a Servitor's likeness in order to achieve her deception. It undermines what we're trying to do."

"Great, so would you be willing to help spread the word about her and then inform the DUC?"

Kandria shook her head and sighed with a saddened expression. "The Dholeren United Coalition welcomes all the wayward spacers. I will do what I can."

Quinton hadn't been expecting that response. Servitors were sometimes hard to figure out. He made Vonya's data profile available and sent it to Kandria.

"There, you have it."

Kandria opened her personal holoscreen and peered at the image of Vonya. She frowned. "The resemblance is remarkable."

"Could Vonya have been a Servitor and…" Quinton pressed his lips together for a moment. "Quit or something."

"No one ever leaves."

Quinton frowned. "I don't believe that."

"I understand why you'd think that. It takes years of training and dedication, especially if you're not born into it. Anyone who lacks dedication will leave long before they become a Servitor."

Quinton still wasn't convinced. "What if you wanted to?"

"I don't want to."

"But what if you did? What if you decided that you'd rather be in the company of one person and then elected to settle down, as it were."

"Are you inviting me to travel with you?"

Quinton chuckled. It was tempting, especially now that the question had been raised. "I don't think so. I've been down this road before, and it's not one I'm eager to repeat."

Kandria leaned toward him, and a slight blush appeared on her delicate cheekbones. "You stand apart. Men like you are rare."

Quinton felt the heat gather under his shirt. "You don't get rejected often, do you?"

Kandria giggled, sending wiggles everywhere. "Don't be silly. You didn't reject me."

She wasn't entirely wrong about that. She might not have really offered to travel with them.

"You're not like the other spacers. I don't know what it is exactly, but I get the feeling that you don't know what you want."

"I know what I want," Quinton assured her.

"You misunderstand. Most people think they know what they want, but they're often wrong."

"So, what's next for you?"

"Deflection is a normal tactic," she said and placed her hand on his forearm. "I hope you find what you need. Very often, it's not what you think."

"I guess I can say the same about you."

Kandria tittered a small laugh. "What do you think I want?"

"Honestly, I wish I could say it was me, but…"

"I have no doubt it would be a pleasant way to spend a few hours," she said, watching him.

He felt like an idiot. What would it hurt if he spent some time alone with Kandria? She was willing and there was a mutual attraction between them, so what was the problem? It wasn't as if he hadn't had the casual encounter before, and this avatar seemed more than willing and capable of rising to the occasion.

"I can't," Quinton said, imagining Guttman screaming at him for what he'd just done.

"Our time comes to an end, then?"

A comlink from Harper registered on Quinton's HUD.

"Are you trying to broadcast something?" Harper asked.

"No, why?"

"It's strange. I'm monitoring communications and there isn't a broadcast, but Club Ranstead has intrusion signatures that are actively scanning for your identity. They've enabled a communication-dampening field around the station. Pretty interesting method actually. It looks like something based off an old Til signature," Harper said.

"Wait a minute. You said my ID? Do you mean my description?"

"Nope. How would they know what you looked like anyway? No, they've got ID signatures."

"Wait, are you in Ranstead's systems now?"

There was a long pause. "Yes."

"Harper," Quinton began.

"Not from our ship. I'm using a neighboring ship's access."

Quinton closed his eyes.

"Is something wrong?" Kandria asked.

His entire conversation with Harper had occurred sub-vocally.

"You know that moment when a friend does the exact opposite of what you needed him to do? That's what I'm dealing with now."

Kandria smiled, her eyes glistening. "It can't be that bad. Maybe they had good reason."

"She's right," Harper said.

Quinton stood up. "Whatever reason he had isn't good enough," he said, and then added sub-vocally to Harper, "Get out of Ranstead's computer system right now, and erase any footprint you left behind."

"But Quinton, they have your identification."

"I know. I'll look into it. Do as I say," he said and cut off the comlink.

Kandria stood up. She leaned toward him and kissed the side of his face. "I've enjoyed speaking with you."

Quinton smiled. "I wish it could have been longer."

"Maybe some other time. What is your ship called? In case I learn anything about Vonya," Kandria replied.

He couldn't tell her, especially now considering what Harper had just discovered. "The DUC will be much easier for you to contact."

"You are correct," she said. "Perhaps our paths will cross again someday."

They parted ways. Quinton was heading back toward the others, and the Servitor was walking in the opposite direction. She had pulled her hood up, and in the dim lighting, she blended in with other people walking in the same direction. He saw Oscar watching him, his eyebrows raised in an unspoken question.

Quinton shook his head and held up his hand, making a circular motion with his fingers. Oscar nodded and spun around to get Guttman.

Quinton opened a comlink to Becker. "Are you close to being done?"

"Yeah, I was just about to come back to Nunu's."

"Don't. Just head back to the ship."

"What happened?"

"Harper detected a comms-dampening field around the depot, and they're looking for my identification."

"How the hell would they have that?"

"I have no idea. We've got to go."

"I'll meet you back at the ship," Becker said and closed the comlink.

CHAPTER ELEVEN

QUINTON WAITED for Oscar and Guttman outside of Nunu's. He looked around, watching the spacers walking by. None of them gave him a second glance.

Oscar walked toward him. "Guttman won't leave."

Quinton blinked several times. "What?"

Oscar sighed. "He's not coming back to the ship now."

Quinton stepped toward Nunu's, and Oscar grabbed his arm. "Don't do that," he said.

"We've gotta go," Quinton insisted.

"What's happening?"

Quinton told him about what Harper had discovered. "I don't want to leave without him, but I might have to."

"Listen, why don't you go back to the ship, and I'll get Guttman."

"You'll get Guttman?" Quinton repeated, sounding unconvinced.

Oscar nodded. "Yes, you don't get him. He likes to sound off and stand his ground, and I get it. We were hoping for a whole day here. He needs to blow off some steam."

"You think Becker will go along with that?"

"Yes, he gets it. If you go in there and drag him out, you'll cause a scene. You'll do the exact opposite of what you want and draw attention to yourself. I'll go in there and reason with him, but it might take a few more drinks."

Quinton glanced through the entry of Nunu's. The darkened interior had warm, ambient lighting, and the sounds of the patrons' lively conversations spilled out into the corridor.

"I'll get him to come. It's just going to take a little while. I'll let Becker know," Oscar said.

"Do you want me to stay?"

Oscar shook his head. "Not necessary. I've got this," he said and went back inside.

Quinton stood there for a few minutes, not knowing what else to do. Then he started walking back to the ship.

"Radek," Quinton said sub vocally, "what do you make of this? Are the ship's systems compromised? Is that how they got my ID?"

A small holographic sphere appeared on the upper right side of his internal HUD.

"Negative, the *Wayfarer's* systems have not been compromised, and the captain's identification you provided to Club Ranstead's systems is completely different. There are no associations with it."

"Then why do they have an intrusion signature based on my PMC identification?"

"Unknown. Perhaps if you accessed the signature, it would reveal more information," Radek replied.

Quinton had been thinking along those lines. He'd been trying to avoid accessing the depot's computer systems, but he didn't have much of a choice. Either they knew who he was and had reason to believe he'd come to the depot, or someone was casting a very wide net in hopes of finding him. Neither explanation sat well with him. How would whoever was doing this know he'd survived the Sentinel attack on the starbase? There might be another reason, something he couldn't think of yet. Radek was right. He needed to access Club Ranstead's computer systems.

Quinton considered his options for infiltrating their computers. He needed to access the security monitoring systems that were analyzing all communications on the depot. He could use a subspace comlink and insert a session, but they might detect it and he'd give himself away. He needed to be smarter than that. The best way to hide what he was doing on anyone's computer system was to utilize a system that was already connected. There were plenty of existing communication sessions that were near constant. He'd take control of one of those and use that, but he didn't want to be physically anywhere near his point of entry. He wanted nothing that could be traced back to him or his ship.

Quinton opened a comlink to the *Wayfarer* and accessed the communication systems. He found that Harper was still using a neighboring ship's access and killed the session. He sent Harper a message telling him that he was looking into it.

Since Club Ranstead's security had enabled a communication-dampening field, they were more than concerned that someone with Quinton's identification would begin broadcasting. This meant that they would be monitoring for it on any comms systems and not just outbound ship broadcasts. This might be easier for him to track than he'd thought.

Quinton looked around as he walked through the depot. Club Ranstead was just a resupply depot, and not a very large one at that. There were limited shops, but mostly it was designed for a temporary break from shipboard life. He spotted a general info terminal that anybody could use. The info terminal would certainly be monitored, but that was exactly what he was looking for. He created a specially crafted message that was an invitation for free drinks at Nunu's and then uploaded it to the info terminal. As people walked by, they were sent the fake invitation, which created a comlink session to the personal wrist computers that everyone wore. How best to hide than simply becoming the most average asteroid among a field of them? When people responded to the invitation, the comlink was confirmed, which gave him a valid communication session that could not in any way be traced back to him. He had a limited amount of time before the fake invitation would be purged from the info terminal, so he had to work fast.

"Okay Radek, let's see what we can find out."

Quinton unpacked an infiltration program that he uploaded into Club Ranstead's internal communication systems. He didn't need to take control of the security systems to determine what they were scanning for. In order for any intrusion signature to work, it had to analyze all communications that passed through it. All Quinton had to do was run his queries to the normal comlink sessions and allow himself to be scanned. This also allowed him to collect a snapshot of the intrusion signatures Club Ranstead security was using. He took a data dump of the entire signature set.

Quinton was still within view of the info terminal he had commandeered, and groups of people were checking their wrist computers as they came into range, many of whom headed in Nunu's direction. He grinned sub-vocally, thinking about all the people who were going there expecting a free drink.

Quinton did a quick analysis of the intrusion signatures, and it was just as Harper had said it was. Based on a Til signature, it was more a wildcard that could pretty much look for whatever anyone wanted to input. The intrusion signature wasn't anything particularly special, other than the fact that it had Quinton's PMC identification. He still had no idea how they had gotten it.

Becker opened a comlink to him. "Where is everyone?"

"I'm heading to the ship now. I had to take a slight detour. But Oscar and Guttman—" Quinton began.

"Oscar contacted me. I'm not seeing any alarms that indicate they're looking for us—you, that is—so I told them it was fine to stay where they were for a few more hours," Becker said.

Quinton made his way through the throng of people and then said. "Are you going to join them?"

"No," Becker said.

"I'll meet you back at the ship then," Quinton said and closed the comlink.

Quinton returned to the ship, and Becker was already on the bridge, sitting at a workstation that had multiple holoscreens up.

He glanced at Quinton. "What did you find out?"

"Somehow, they have my ID, and they're looking for any broadcast with it."

"What do you mean your ID?"

"Do you remember when the DUC had me do that automated challenge protocol?"

Becker nodded.

"They have that ID, the one that's associated with my PMC."

Becker frowned in thought and then rubbed his chin. "I don't know. It doesn't make any sense. The only people who would have a copy of that are the DUC and Maelyn. Can you check if the *Nebulon* has been to Club Ranstead?"

Quinton shook his head. "Don't you remember? Club Ranstead doesn't keep those kinds of records. No questions asked, and your visit will be purged. And even if Maelyn had a copy of my ID, there's no way she'd make it available."

"What if she was looking for you?"

"Even if she was, she's way more subtle than this. This is like using a quad-barrel mag cannon to take out a hatch. Sure, you'll open the door, but you'll destroy whatever's on the other side."

Becker considered it for a few seconds and then nodded. "You're probably right."

Quinton smiled. "And that admission didn't even hurt this time."

Becker rolled his eyes.

"This is reactionary. I don't think we're going to figure it out here."

The door to the bridge opened and Harper joined them. "What's reactionary?"

Quinton raised an eyebrow.

"The auditory systems of the spider-drone are pretty sensitive," Harper said by way of explanation.

"I was just telling Becker that the intrusion signature seems like a reactionary response to something."

"Tactically, that makes sense. But we don't know why it's appeared here," Harper said, then added, "Who uses an old Tilion security system anyway?"

At that, Becker sat up straight and spun his chair around. "What did you say?"

"I said the intrusion signature was Tilion, based on the Tilion Federation," Harper replied.

Becker looked away, glancing at the main holoscreen for a moment. The screen was displaying a live video feed of the docking platform and an exterior view of Club Ranstead. He shook his head and looked at Quinton. "It's not the Tilion Federation."

"Yes, it is. I've seen this type of security before," Harper said.

"I'm sure you have, but that was either before or shortly after the Federation Wars began. The Tilion Federation, or what was left of them, was absorbed into the Castellus Federal Alliance," Becker said.

"But you told me that both of those star nations are no longer around," Quinton said.

"They're around, but they're known as the Collective."

"The Collective?" Quinton repeated. "*The* Collective? The group Lennix Crowe was so worried about?"

Becker nodded once. "The Collective—Trenton Draven—wasn't happy with Crowe's Union."

"The Collective? Crowe's Union? Who are these people?" Harper asked.

Becker sighed and turned away from them. He opened a comlink and began speaking to Oscar.

"They're powerful organizations that were built upon the remnants of the old federations," Quinton said.

"How powerful are we talking about here?"

"They have fleets from whatever ships were still around after the Federation Wars," Quinton said, remembering that Lennix Crowe had attacked him on the starbase with several Jordani cruisers.

Becker closed the comlink and turned toward them. "Oscar and Guttman are almost back to the ship."

"Really?" Quinton said. "I thought they'd be a lot longer."

"I didn't ask, and they didn't say," Becker said.

Quinton started the preflight checks for the *Wayfarer*. If the others were on their way back, there was no reason for them to stay after they were aboard. The preflight check process wasn't entirely automated, but he could get it to a point where Oscar could take over once he was back. Quinton thought about Nunu's. There had been quite a few drinks consumed. If Oscar wasn't able to finish preflight checks, he'd have to do it himself.

"So, Club Ranstead is somehow tied to the Collective," Quinton said.

"At least in part, or they based their security protocols off a service that's a subsidiary of them. There isn't one big charter that joined them all," Becker replied.

"Have you been to any of the Acheron Confederacy core worlds?" Harper asked.

The question caught Quinton off guard. He hadn't been expecting anything like it. He shook his head.

"Maybe we should go back there. Maybe there's something we can use," Harper said.

"There isn't anything there," Becker said.

"How do you know? You just said you haven't been there," Harper said, his voice sounding a little defensive.

"No one goes there because there isn't anything left. Those worlds, like much of the old federation core worlds, were destroyed in the wars," Becker replied.

"I want to go there. I think we should go there next."

Becker glanced at Quinton and then looked back at Harper. "You think we should go there?" he said, unable to keep the incredulity out of his voice.

"Harper, I'd like to see it for myself, too, but now isn't the right time," Quinton said.

The spider-drone turned toward him. "It's never the right time. When will the right time be? I'm serious. When will the right time be?"

"Not today," Quinton replied. He wasn't going to be lured into Harper's longing to return home. It was contagious, and Quinton knew it was one of the things they couldn't do now. "We need to focus on finding you a new host or a DNA vault."

"This spider-drone isn't so bad. I'm repairing it," Harper said and gestured toward several of the damaged armored panels that had been patched up. "Why is it so hard to find a suitable host?"

"Harper, we've been over this. Many of the technologies that were developed for PMC use were destroyed by the Sentinels. We might be able to find something that's better suited for you than the spider-drone, but a DNA vault would be better. Then we can regrow your body and offload you into it. I want the same thing," Quinton said. He'd almost had a new body, but it was gone, as well as any record of his DNA.

"Do you think there are any more ACN starbases out there?"

It wasn't the first time Harper had loosely indicated that he was envious of the cybernetic avatar Quinton resided in. He wished there were a second one aboard that Harper could use, but he wasn't about to give his up. "I wish I knew."

"I still say the core worlds are our best chance—" Harper began and stopped. The door to the bridge opened, and Oscar and Guttman walked in.

"You won't believe what just happened," Guttman bellowed and then continued without waiting for a response. "Nunu's was overrun by a bunch of people seeking free drinks. There were hundreds of people in there. I don't know what's gonna happen. When we left, there were security forces en route."

"It was getting pretty rowdy," Oscar agreed.

"You're lucky you escaped," Quinton replied.

Guttman agreed, but Oscar gave him a sidelong glance.

"Oscar, I started preflight checks for you. Can you take over for me, please?"

Oscar stifled a yawn and walked to the pilot's workstation.

"I don't know about you guys, but I'm going to take a nap," Guttman said.

"That's going to be a hard negative on that nap," Quinton said.

Guttman turned around. "Why? What now?"

"We had a resupply delivery. All that stuff needs to be stowed or we'll lose it all. Unless you don't want any of that food and the other things you ordered," Quinton said.

"He's right," Becker said. "The rest of us will give you a hand."

Quinton feigned surprise, and Becker shook his head. "It'll go much faster if we all help," he said and then added, "Harper, come with us. You can help too."

As they headed off the bridge, Quinton stuck his head back. "Oscar, as soon as the preflight checks are done, we're out of here."

"I'm on it," Oscar said.

Over the next hour or so, they brought in the standard resupply cache from Club Ranstead. If Quinton hadn't been so concerned that the depot's delivery personnel would react poorly to seeing Harper, he would've had him bring it in. Once they were done, they headed to the galley, and Quinton and Harper watched Becker and the others drink some coffee.

"I miss coffee," Harper said.

"Me too," Quinton agreed.

"At least you can taste it."

"It's not the same," Quinton said and looked at Becker. "So, what did you find out about an information broker? Do you have any contacts?"

Becker sipped his coffee and sighed contentedly. "Yeah, I've gotten the contact protocols for five brokers. I need to review them to see which one would best fit the bill."

"Contact protocols? Why do you need to use that?" Quinton asked.

"Direct contact with an information broker never happens. We use these contact protocols as a way to establish temporary communications with someone else who has direct contact with the information broker. Actually, there're probably several levels more than that, but you get the gist," Becker replied.

Quinton considered this for a few moments. "All this to find a ship for you."

Becker glanced at the others. "Not just a ship for me. I want to go independent. I want to start my own salvage operation. Oscar and Guttman are going to join me. We'll be partners."

"It's not like we have much of a choice," Guttman said.

"I don't understand," Harper said. "Why wouldn't you have a choice?"

"They burned quite a few bridges helping me," Quinton replied.

"I was getting tired of it anyway," Oscar replied. Then he raised his mug to the others. "Partners."

"Everyone wins," Quinton said, and the others looked at him. "There's something I'd like to ask the information broker."

Becker set his mug down and crossed his muscled arms in front of his chest. "The session is limited. This is for everyone's protection."

"Please," Quinton said in an exaggerated tone. "How long will it take to get a few targets for ships?"

"I intend to get targets for ships, but I'm also looking for potential sellers."

"Either way, it shouldn't take too long. Would the broker have information about Sentinel activity?"

The others became still.

"Why do you want to know about that?" Becker asked.

"We should also ask about the activation signals. Maybe they can help us find where they're coming from," Harper said.

Becker shook his head. "It's too dangerous."

"Maybe for you, it is," Harper said.

"Hold on a second," Quinton said. "It can't be that dangerous. We're just asking if there've been reports of more signals being detected and if there's been an increase in Sentinel activity. If there has been, we need to know where so we can avoid those places. Those seem like reasonable questions to ask an information broker, especially if we're in the market for a new fleet of ships to start our new salvage operations," he said and paused for a moment. "I'm speaking figuratively here. I don't want to join your salvage organization."

Becker considered it for a few seconds. "You've got a point. I think that'll be fine."

"That's twice in one day. A few more, it might become a habit." Quinton smirked.

"You wish," Becker said.

CHAPTER TWELVE

"Oscar, execute emergency jump coordinates," Quinton said.

"Executing emergency jump coordinates," Oscar replied.

The *Wayfarer* slipped out of the compromised location in their third attempt to contact an information broker.

Quinton looked at Becker. "You still think I'm being too cautious?"

Becker peered at the main holoscreen. On it were the final moments of the communications drone they'd used to wait for the Angry Pilot to contact them.

"That's two no-shows and one attempted capture," Quinton said.

Guttman cleared his throat, hands clasped behind his neck. "What did you expect? This is the risk we take for using a broker. High risk. High reward."

Becker had gotten five contact protocols for different information brokers. Dagan and the Phantom Node hadn't even shown up. The Angry Pilot tried to capture them. That left two more.

"I expected them to take their fee and give us what we paid

for. Now, I just want to hunt down the Angry Pilot," Quinton replied.

Becker's glare had more frustration than malice to it, but he had this way of making Quinton think it was his fault, that the things that had gone wrong for Becker were somehow Quinton's doing.

"Guttman's right," Becker said.

Quinton gave him an exaggerated head nod. "That's right, I forgot everyone's an opportunist here. If you knew this going in, then why was the original plan just for us to put the ship right on the coordinates where anybody could ambush us? And you say *I* play fast and loose. This is downright reckless."

They'd decided to use communication drones to give them a layer of protection, which had paid off just now. Becker argued that those drones were the reason they'd had two no-shows.

Becker glared at Quinton. "Are you done?"

Quinton regarded Becker for a few seconds. The spacer was normally more cautious than this. He must really want off the ship. Quinton glanced at the others. Guttman gave him a can-we-get-on-with-it look.

"Right, good talk. Where to next?"

Becker looked at Oscar. "Set a course for Mortis."

Oscar looked at Quinton.

"Do it."

They would travel to the rendezvous coordinates and deploy another sacrificial comms drone. Hopefully, Mortis would be different from the other brokers they'd tried to contact.

"Fifteen hours' travel time," Oscar said.

Becker left the bridge and was soon joined by Guttman and Oscar.

"You shouldn't let them treat you like that, sir," Harper said.

Quinton looked at the spider-drone. "We're not in the ACN anymore."

"I still don't like it. They should be restricted to their quarters," Harper said. "Would you like me to initiate a lockdown?"

"No, Harper, that will not be necessary."

"Are you sure?"

"Yes, I'm quite sure," Quinton replied.

"Fine," Harper said, cramming a good bit of disapproval into one word.

Fourteen hours and forty-five minutes later, Quinton was still on the bridge. Harper had gone to the workshop to continue repairing the spider-drone. For the moment, he had accepted that there was a severe shortage of consciousness-driven androids out there that were capable of holding his ESS.

Becker walked onto the bridge and came toward Quinton. "It'll be better today."

Quinton snorted softly. "Only if our luck changes."

Becker chuckled.

Before the fifteen-hour mark, the others had joined them on the bridge. A secure comlink registered with the ship's communication systems.

"All right, here we go," Becker said.

They'd agreed earlier that Becker would take the lead communicating with the information broker.

A voice-only secure comlink channel opened, and a countdown timer appeared next to the comlink session. They had ten minutes.

"You're go for Mortis."

"We're in the market for a new ship," Becker said.

"You and everyone else. What kind of ships are you looking for?" Mortis asked.

"A freighter class, either light- or medium-bulk transport will suit our needs."

"What's your first choice?"

"A former auxiliary ship would be perfect. Something along the lines of a Proteus or Endeavor class," Becker said.

"Querying," Mortis said. After a full minute had run on the clock, he continued. "Compiling list and coordinates. Do you care if they have ship-launch fighters?"

"They're nice to have but not essential. We can acquire those elsewhere."

"Adding that to the query. What else do you need?"

"Can you also include a list of transport ships in this sector? I don't want to be traveling all over the galaxy for these things."

"Understood. I have the list available. Once credits are transferred, I will send it to you," Mortis said.

A data window appeared from within the comlink session. Quinton thought the price was rather high for just a list of information, but Becker quickly acknowledged it.

"Payment has been sent," Becker said.

A few moments later, Mortis replied. "Confirmed. What else?"

"Wait a second," Quinton said. "How do we know this list is any good?"

"The data provided is current as of right now. What happens after this is not my concern. It's yours," Mortis replied impatiently.

Harper put a text message up on the main holoscreen. *Comlink trace running.*

"Is there anything else?" Mortis asked, sounding as if he'd like to end the transaction.

"Yes, there is," Becker said. "We've been hearing rumors about rogue PMC activation signals. Do you have any confirmation about that? Is there a particular sector we should avoid?"

"I'm surprised you're not asking about the increased Sentinel attacks."

Becker glanced at Quinton for a moment. "We've been out of touch."

"You must have been. Have you been living on an asteroid somewhere? Never mind. Ships are in short supply, so I'd move quickly on the highlighted ships on the list I gave you. There isn't a lot of time."

"Thanks, Mortis. What about those attacks?" Becker asked.

"There's been increased hostility between the Collective and Crowe's Union. There's a lot of credits to be made if you've got any information the Collective is looking for," Mortis said.

"What kind of information?"

Mortis grinned. "That kind of data comes at a cost."

As if on cue, another charge appeared on the comlink. Becker acknowledged it.

"Confirmed payment," Mortis said. "The data we're seeing is that there have been increased Sentinel attacks, but they seem to be targeted at organizations associated with the Collective. Locations are coming to you."

"How are the Sentinels being used?" Quinton asked.

"The Sentinels respond to a broadcast with a PMC identification protocol."

Quinton's eyebrows shot up, and he looked at Becker, who had a similar expression. Lennix Crowe had figured out how to lure Sentinels by using Quinton's identification.

"So, if you have any information, I can broker the deal with Trenton Draven personally. It's a lot of credits. Enough to buy that whole list of ships if they were all available. What do you say?" Mortis asked.

Everyone on the bridge of the *Wayfarer* became extremely still. Harper turned to look at them. The broker had essentially promised Becker and the others enough credits to set them up for the remainder of their lives if they were to take him up on his offer. Quinton knew they wouldn't do it. If the offer sounded too good to be true, then it probably was. That, and he was right here. A betrayal would end their association with a deadly finality.

"I don't have any current information," Becker said.

"Understood," Mortis said. "One last bit of parting advice

before our time runs out. Make sure that whatever ship you get, you have adequate amounts of ammunition. Federation War tech is coming back online. There have been a lot of reports on it. There are also rumors that another incursion is going to start soon."

Quinton didn't know what that meant, but Becker seemed to.

Becker looked at Harper and gave them a nod.

The comlink session was severed, and Oscar executed a micro-jump. The trace hadn't reached the ship, but Quinton didn't want to take any chances. He'd given Oscar orders to leave the area as soon as they were done.

"Oh man," Guttman said, breaking the silence.

Quinton looked at them. "You know that feeling when there's an asteroid on the landing pad? That's all I'm getting right now."

Becker shook his head.

Quinton continued, "I would've been tempted by all those credits. I mean, you could get your own salvage operation."

Becker looked at Quinton. "We had a deal."

"We did."

"I don't understand," Guttman said. "How did Crowe get your ID?"

"Yeah, I don't understand that either," Oscar said.

Becker looked at Quinton and waited for him to reply.

"It must be from the starbase. Crowe used Sentinel tech to infiltrate the system through Vonya." Quinton stopped. "Vonya," he said and shook his head. "It's just the gift that keeps on giving," he said through gritted teeth.

"Who's Vonya?" Harper asked.

"She's a spy for Crowe's Union," Quinton replied. He was silent for a few moments. "I need to be alone. Go on. You've got a list of ships to look through and systems to review. You don't need to do that here."

Becker gestured for the others to go. Then he looked at Harper. "Hey, would you give us a minute alone?"

The spider-drone followed the others off the bridge.

Quinton cranked up his frame rate. He needed to think about this now and wanted to do it before he spoke with Becker.

"Radek, is what Mortis said possible? Can Lennix Crowe be using my PMC ID to lure the Sentinels into an attack?"

"In order for this tactic to work, Crowe's Union must know the location of a Sentinel Scout ship unless they have monitoring posts deployed. An alternative to this is that he has some kind of agreement with the Sentinels," Radek replied.

"I don't know about that. Interactions with Sentinels are usually one-sided."

"Agreed, if the Sentinels show up to a star system based on a broadcast with your PMC identification, they're already traveling with hostile intent."

Quinton knew what that meant. Sentinels would destroy anything to prevent an outbreak of what they called PMC spread. If they detected a trace of PMC activity on ship computer systems or even space stations, they would destroy them to prevent the spread.

"Do we have any data from the attack on the starbase that can confirm whether…" Quinton began and stopped. That wouldn't help. The intrusion signature had his PMC ID, so he didn't need to confirm that Crowe was actually using it. He was. Now, all he needed to decide was what the hell he was going to do. "Stand by, Radek."

Quinton slowed his frame rate down so he could speak with Becker. "What's an incursion?"

Becker frowned for a moment. "You just did that thing with the frame rate, didn't you?" Quinton nodded. "An incursion is when the Sentinels send out all their fleets to check inhabited star systems, looking for… anyone like you."

Quinton gritted his teeth. "Damn it!"

"That's not all, Quinton. If another incursion happens, a lot of people are going to die. There's no safe place. The Sentinels can misinterpret any advance in computing as being manipulated by a PMC."

Quinton turned away and paced across the bridge.

"What are you going to do?" Becker asked.

"Lennix needs to stop this. Does he know what he's doing?"

"He might not care. If Draven was hunting for him, he'd look for a way to take the pressure off."

"And having Sentinels attack Collective installations would take the pressure off?"

Becker nodded. "Yes. To anyone on the outside—meaning whoever didn't know what we know—the Sentinels are targeting the Collective. That can bring pressure from all kinds of former federations, as well as anyone who has a grievance with them."

Quinton considered this. He couldn't fault Lennix Crowe's logic. His back was against the wall, and he'd lost the one thing that would've given him an advantage, so he'd chosen the next best thing. Until a few moments ago, the galaxy had been completely open to him, and now it was being cut off.

"You can't run from this," Becker said.

"I know," Quinton replied.

"What are you going to do?"

"I don't know. What if the Sentinels thought they had me? What if they thought they'd gotten me? Would they stop attacking?"

"You want to give yourself up?"

Quinton shook his head. "No, but if I could find a DNA vault, I could put myself in a body and send my ESS to the Sentinels. Wouldn't they back off?"

Becker shook his head and raised his gaze to the ceiling. "That's the stupidest thing I've ever heard. What are you thinking? That's not going to get them to stop."

Quinton swore. "Because the Sentinels are also looking for copies of PMCs. Damn it. Who the hell came up with such an all-or-nothing solution? Who thought this was a good idea?"

"They were desperate."

Quinton laughed bitterly. "I know the feeling. What the hell am I going to do? We have to get Lennix to stop this."

Becker shook his head. "I don't know if he will. I don't think he will."

"He'd risk an incursion?" Quinton said and shook his head. "That's obvious. Wouldn't someone like the DUC and the other federation remnants try to get the Collective and the Union to stop their little shadow war they've got going on?"

Becker thought about it for a moment. "Maybe."

"Maybe! Are you serious? Aren't any of these governments proactive?"

"It's not that simple. I mean, they wouldn't even know where Crowe's Union is. Hell, I don't even know where their operations are anymore. Lennix might've taken everything away and hidden it."

"I need to find Lennix Crowe and get him to stop. Wouldn't the Sentinels realize they're being used? I wonder if this is related to more PMC signals being detected. That's like releasing anti-matter on a ship. We've got to do something. Maybe we need to do all of those things," Quinton said.

"Quinton," Becker said mildly.

"Maybe we can reach out to the other... DUC, or Trenton Draven, and tell him what's going on. Then we can—"

"Quinton."

He looked at him. "What?"

"We had an agreement."

"You help me repair the ship and I help you get your own."

Becker nodded. "That's right. We have leads to a ship now. That's enough for us. We can't help you take on Lennix Crowe, the Collective, and the Sentinels."

Quinton stared at him for a few moments. "That's it? You're just going to leave? You got what you wanted, so it's good luck, Quinton. Wish you the best. Is that what you're telling me?"

The door to the bridge opened and Harper ran inside. "Cowards!" he bellowed. "You should toss them out the airlock."

The spider-drone hastened toward them and Becker pulled out his heavy blaster, pointing it at Harper. The tip glowed orange. "You come any closer and I'll melt that thing you call a body. Do you understand me?"

Harper came to a stop. A panel opened from the armored torso and a micro-blaster used for demolition extended, primed and ready. "It doesn't change what you are. You're a coward, just like the others. You cut and run when things get tough. You're weak and pathetic. I bet you've never stood for anything in your entire life."

Becker snarled and shoved his blaster toward Harper. Quinton darted over and grabbed his wrist. A plasma bolt melted through several layers of the floor.

"Enough of this," Quinton said. Becker's blaster dropped to the floor. "Back off, Harper."

The spider-drone took several steps back, and his micro-blaster retracted back inside the armored body.

"Let go of me," Becker said.

Quinton let him go.

Becker held his wrist to his chest. He flexed his hand a few times and then retrieved his weapon.

"I'm going to take us to the nearest star system. You can make your own way from there," Quinton said.

Becker's lips compressed to form a grim line. "Fine," he said and walked off the bridge.

"Go on," Harper said as he left. "Scurry on back to the others." Then he walked back to Quinton. "I'm with you, sir."

Quinton threw a nod to Harper. He meant well. Harper was a soldier, and Becker and the others were survivors. Harper was willing to stand and fight, while the others seemed to know the price to be paid for making a stand. This might not be a fight

Quinton could win. He hated it. All of it. And he had no idea what he was going to do next.

He'd expected more from Becker. They'd been through a lot. And Oscar and Guttman would more than likely follow Becker's lead. So much for loyalty. When loyalty and survival collided, survival won. It was time for him to part ways with Becker, Oscar, and Guttman.

Quinton accessed the navigation interface and looked for the nearest star system that had a space station. They'd head there straight away, and then he'd have to come up with a plan.

CHAPTER THIRTEEN

"I say we take out Harper before Quinton can do anything about it," Guttman said.

"Guttman, come on," Oscar replied.

"What? He attacked Becker! He's got a weapon!" Guttman kept looking toward the door, his eyes wide as if he expected an attack to come at any moment. "I knew this was gonna happen. I just knew it."

"Yeah, right. You did not."

"Oscar, I'm telling you. I've had my doubts about Harper ever since Quinton brought him on board. He's not stable."

Oscar leaned forward, resting his elbows on the table. "Becker, what happened? Why did Harper attack you?"

Becker kept one of his hands by his blaster and sneered. "He called me a coward. He said we're all cowards."

Guttman stood up. "That's it. I say we go down to the bridge and teach that thing a lesson. I'm no damn coward. Who the hell —all of us are cowards?" he laughed bitterly and rolled his shoulder, stretching his neck from side to side.

"You need to calm down," Oscar said.

"You need to calm down," Guttman mimicked. He pressed

his fists onto the table and leaned toward him. "You can't smooth-talk your way out of this, hermano."

"Because your 'storm the bridge and teach them a lesson' plan is so much better. Get real."

"You know what you can do, Oscar," Guttman said with a snarl as he stepped around the table.

Oscar glared at Guttman and inhaled explosively as he stood up. "Is there something you wanna say to me? I'm right here. Go for it."

Becker stepped between them, planting a beefy hand on each of their chests. "Guys, enough. Knock it off. We can't do this."

Guttman glared at Oscar for a moment then backed away, jerking his head from side to side. Oscar held his hands up in a placating gesture and then rested them on his hips.

Guttman jabbed a finger in Becker's direction. "Why are you so calm about this?"

Becker gritted his teeth. "You think I'm calm?"

Guttman nodded. "I've seen you upset. Hell, I've seen you go after an entire crew, numbers and odds be damned."

"What do you want me to do? We can't stop Quinton."

"The hell we can't."

Becker leveled a gaze at him. "We can't, and he's not going to let us do anything to Harper."

"Guys," Oscar said, "Quinton doesn't deserve this. He's done everything he could to help us, and we made a deal with him. So, no, I'm not going along with anything that puts us against him. You can count me out of this."

Guttman scowled. "At least we know where you stand."

Silence settled between the three men for a few long moments.

"Oscar's right," Becker said, finally. "I've got nothing against Quinton. I just want off this ship. I want to move on. Don't you?" he asked, looking at each of them in turn. "I'm tired of all this. I'm just... sick of it."

Guttman seemed to gather himself up, getting ready for another outburst, but then he sighed, and his shoulders slumped a little. "I'd love to get off this ship and go somewhere quiet. Wait for this whole thing to blow over," Guttman said.

"Cowards," Becker said, acidly.

"What if he's right?" Oscar said, drawing their attention. "Harper. What if he's right? The whole 'cowards' thing. We're just going to run away. No, I mean it."

Guttman shook his head. "I'm not a coward."

"Not just you," Oscar replied. "All of us, and it doesn't stop there. What have we always done? We've seen it in the Union and even with others outside Crowe's Union. We wait for the upper hand. We strike when others are vulnerable, and we run when we know we can't win."

"I call that surviving," Guttman said.

Oscar nodded. "Yeah, but it doesn't make us brave. Maybe we are cowards. Not," he said, drawing out the word before Guttman could interrupt, "without good reason. We need to survive, but what if it's not enough?"

Guttman rolled his eyes toward the ceiling. "You're starting to sound like a DUC recruiter."

Oscar shrugged.

"What do you want us to do?" Becker asked.

"I don't know; but doesn't leaving Quinton on his own seem wrong?"

"Wrong," Guttman scoffed. "Not everything is about right or wrong. The longer we stay here, the more likely we're going to die on this ship. Did you forget what happened on that starbase?"

"You mean the one where Quinton defended all of us against a fleet of Sentinels? That one? The same where he got us to this ship so we could escape. Yeah, you're a real piece of work." Oscar shook his head.

"Oscar," Becker said, "I don't like it any more than you do. But we've got to be realistic here. There's nothing any of us can do about the Sentinels, Crowe, or the damn Collective. Nothing," he said and looked away. "Nothing we can do."

Oscar slipped his hands into his pockets and looked away.

"If I could think of something, I'd tell him. I'd even help him, but there isn't. Guttman's right. We're dead if we stay here."

Oscar took a few steps and then turned back to face the other two. "Harper might not be stable. We even thought Quinton wasn't for a while, but there's something in both of them, something we've lost. The way he looks at us… as if he's the only one to realize it. He's not."

Guttman glanced at Becker. "What's he talking about?"

Oscar walked toward the door. "I need to get some air."

"Watch out for Harper," Guttman said.

Oscar paused at the door for a few moments.

"He's right," Becker said. "We've got to watch our backs. Quinton stopped Harper this time, but we can't rely on him always being there."

Oscar exhaled explosively. He turned around, walked to his quarters, and closed the door.

"What the hell was that all about?" Guttman asked.

"Salvager's remorse."

Guttman glanced at the door to Oscar's room and sighed. "We need to keep an eye on him. That remorse can make you do stupid things," he said and looked at Becker. "So, what happens now?"

"He'll be fine. Quinton is going to drop us off at the nearest star system that has a station or resupply depot. From there, we'll have to make our own way," Becker said.

Guttman grumbled and sat down. He opened a holoscreen and began looking at star charts.

A few seconds later, Becker joined him.

QUINTON WATCHED the video feed of the passenger lounge on his internal HUD. Both he and Harper were still on the bridge. Harper had entered a rest cycle a short time earlier, and he'd be out for a few hours.

Quinton disconnected the video feed. Forget crew cohesion now. Maybe he'd be better off with the others off the ship. He still wasn't sure what to do. Should he try to stop Crowe? How was he supposed to do that? Did that mean hunting him down wherever he was? He'd have to find him first, but the *Wayfarer* wasn't that kind of warship. It had teeth, but there were limits to what he could do with one ship. Would somehow taking out Crowe stop the attacks, or would his second-in-command take up the same fight? A Sentinel incursion sounded bad for everyone, so why would Crowe risk it happening? There were risks, and then there were risks someone takes when they think they have nothing left to lose, but still, Quinton couldn't figure out what Crowe wanted to achieve. What was his endgame? If Crowe's back was against the wall, he had no choice but to fight. If Lennix Crowe was simply trying to get the Collective to back off, these attacks would be limited. Crowe would just be trying to prove a point and the attacks should stop.

Quinton glanced at the comlink control on his workstation. He needed Becker for this. Becker knew Lennix Crowe. He'd been part of Crowe's Union for years. But then he looked away and shook his head. Only a few hours ago, he'd told Becker he was going to drop them off at the nearest spaceport, and he doubted Becker or any of the others wanted to speak to him. He considered bouncing ideas off Radek but dismissed it.

The door to the bridge opened. Becker stepped inside and stopped. "We need to talk," he said and looked over at Harper for a moment. "Alone."

"He's in a rest cycle, so we can talk here."

Becker walked toward him, his blaster holstered on his hip. Quinton did a quick query for the others. Guttman was in the galley, preparing a meal, but he also had a weapon nearby. Oscar was in his quarters.

"All of you are armed now?" Quinton asked.

"I don't want any trouble."

"Right."

"None of us feel safe around Harper. That's just the way it is."

"Unacceptable," Quinton replied. "Argh—It's my turn. I'm not going to allow everyone to walk around my ship armed and moments away from a fight. That's no way to live."

"I'm not giving up my weapon."

Becker didn't change his posture at all. He was simply stating a fact.

"Put your weapons back in the armory. Argh—again, it's my turn. There are palm stunners available. Use those for self-defense while on the ship."

"Palm stunners."

Quinton nodded. "Yeah, palm stunners. I tweaked them so they'll have no problem with… They'll work. That's all you need to worry about. I'm not going to have people blowing holes in my ship."

Becker considered this a few moments. "Do they work on you?" he asked, his tone light.

Quinton lifted his lips.

Becker snorted. "All right, fine. I'll let the others know," he said and paused. "Quinton, things got out of control."

"You think?"

"I do."

"What did you want to talk about?" Quinton asked, preferring not to kick the old drive coil.

"Iskevian Spaceport," Becker said and gestured toward the main holoscreen. A star chart appeared, showing the *Wayfarer's* coordinates and a plot to the spaceport. "It's not associated with the Collective, so it should be relatively safe. From there, we can find our own way."

Quinton looked at the coordinates. He hadn't actually picked a spaceport to leave them at yet. "Sounds good," he said and sent an update to the nav computer.

The data on the main holoscreen refreshed, showing the updated destination. Twenty-nine standard hours and they'd be at the Sunta Nebula where Iskevian Spaceport was located.

Becker nodded a little and a thoughtful frown appeared.

"There's something I'd like to run by you," Quinton said.

"All right."

"It's about Crowe. Do you think he realizes what he's doing?"

Becker pursed his lips in thought. "Yes. Even if he didn't, Carradine would know."

"Who's that?"

"Nate Carradine is Crowe's advisor. They've been partners for a long time. He keeps his head and is strategic. Crowe wouldn't do something like this without Carradine's input," Becker said.

"Okay, I'm just trying to understand what Crowe's doing."

"There's been increasing tension with the Collective."

"I understand that. He could just be doing this to get them to back off."

"Maybe."

"You're not filling me with a whole lot of confidence. If Crowe's ambitions are to rival the Collective, then he could push his advantage. Meaning that he'll continue to lure Sentinels to Collective targets and eventually force Draven to surrender."

"He could just be doing enough damage to the Collective to get them to back off."

"True," Quinton said. "But Crowe is also ambitious. If he's got someone like Carradine advising him, then I think whatever he's trying to do is more elaborate."

"What do you mean?"

"You know more about sector politics than I do, but there are power players out there. These attacks are public. Crowe isn't making a secret of what he can do. He's only hitting Collective targets, but the risk is shared by everyone if the Sentinels begin another incursion. Draven must be getting pressure from everyone else to negotiate with Crowe."

Becker nodded slowly. "I see where you're going. Yeah, I think that's accurate." He pressed his lips together and nodded again. "Yeah, that makes a lot of sense."

Quinton arched an eyebrow. "You don't have to sound so surprised."

Becker grinned a little. "I'm not... not really. But then these attacks would stop. Crowe would account for this in his overall plan."

"Precisely," Quinton said. "At first, I thought I'd need to find a way to stop him, but now I'm just thinking that he'll stop on his own once he gets what he wants."

"You mean you hope he stops."

"Well, yeah. If a Sentinel incursion is as bad as you say it is, then Crowe can't want that. What good is a power grab when the end result is much worse than the current state of affairs? He's proving a point."

"And locking in a target on his back. This isn't going to sit well with anyone."

"They don't have a choice."

Becker sighed and shook his head. "What are you going to do?"

"About Crowe, I'm not sure. I need to find a CDA for Harper."

"A CDA?"

"Consciousness Driven Android. They were designed for PMC use. It's either that or another DNA vault."

"I've never come across a CDA. My guess is that the Sentinels destroyed them first, as well as anyone who made them."

"Maybe they missed a stockpile somewhere."

Becker looked away a few moments and then turned back toward Quinton.

"This isn't your problem, Becker. That much is clear."

Becker looked as if he were going to say something but decided against it and walked away. "We'll store our weapons in the armory," he called out over his shoulder as he left the bridge.

Quinton didn't reply. He looked at their destination on the main holoscreen, feeling a spike of irritation at the thought of Crowe using his identity. How could he stop him? Harper didn't have time for Quinton to hunt down Crowe and stop the use of his ID. Crowe would no doubt have redundancies in place. Sometimes the best course of action was simply to do nothing, but it went against his instincts. He wanted to do something about it. There had to be a way to take away Crowe's ability to use Quinton's PMC credentials to lure the Sentinels.

"Radek, there are some things we need to work on."

CHAPTER FOURTEEN

EVERYONE on the *Wayfarer's* bridge became quiet. They'd just made the final jump to Iskevian Spaceport located near the Sunta Nebula. The advantage of building a spaceport away from any star systems was that ships were able to jump in relatively close proximity to the spaceport. Even a jump drive with the tiniest of range could jump within a day's journey. The *Wayfarer's* jump drive could bring them nearly on top of it, which is exactly what Quinton intended to do. Becker advised against it. No need to irritate spaceport security. They wouldn't be there long. The others would fly the shuttle to the spaceport and Quinton would remote-pilot the shuttle back to the ship.

"You can't be serious, Oscar," Guttman scoffed.

Oscar ignored him and looked at Quinton, raising his chin. "I'm saying that I'd like to stay on and help you. It's the least I can do. You've saved my life more than a few times. I owe you."

"You don't owe me anything," Quinton replied.

Harper stood on the other side of the bridge near an auxiliary workstation. He'd connected to the ship's systems using the data port.

"Don't do this," Guttman said and gestured toward Becker.

"We're going to be partners. The three of us. We need you with us. Stick with the plan."

"He's right," Becker said.

"We can still be partners. I'll catch up with you guys later," Oscar replied.

Becker looked at Quinton.

"This is news to me."

Becker considered Quinton's response for a few moments and looked at Oscar. "Anytime, Oscar. You're always welcome to fly with us. I mean that."

"Thanks, Becker," Oscar said and looked at Guttman. "You two take care of each other."

"You're insane," Guttman said and gave Oscar a playful shove.

Becker walked over to Quinton and extended his hand. Quinton shook it. "Good luck, Quinton. Take care of yourself."

"You, too."

Becker and Guttman left the bridge, heading for the shuttle.

Quinton walked over to Oscar. "Are you sure about this?"

Oscar smiled. "Already trying to get rid of me?"

"No," Quinton chuckled. "It's not that," he said and glanced toward the doors to the bridge. "They're not wrong. It's going to be dangerous. You're probably better off with them, keeping down low until all this stuff blows over."

"Maybe, but then again, maybe not."

Quinton nodded once. "All right, Oscar. Thanks for sticking around."

Quinton returned to his workstation and sent a standard check-in to Iskevian Spaceport to inform them that they wouldn't require docking services. Then he sent a flight plan for the *Wayfarer's* shuttle where two passengers would disembark.

The docking clamps released the shuttle and Becker flew them to the spaceport.

He put a video feed of the traffic heading to the spaceport on the main holoscreen. They weren't far from the port, but The Eye of Sunta filled the view. It was a nebula that resembled an angry red eyeball amid a gas cloud that spread hundreds of lightyears across. The fringes were wreathed in pale gold that gradually became an expanse of blue until finally giving way to the crimson central region. Millions of years would need to pass before it might actually become a star, or possibly a brown dwarf. Either way, Quinton wouldn't be around to see it. Still, it made for a stunning backdrop for the spacers who lived on the spaceport.

"You know, I could have flown them there," Oscar said.

Quinton snorted. "Are you a glutton for punishment?" Oscar's eyebrows raised a little. "For the next half hour, you'd have had to endure Guttman's comments about how you just made the biggest mistake of your life."

"And that I should reconsider… yeah, I know."

"I can get the shuttle back to the ship."

"Where do we go from here?"

"I was thinking of Seginus Prime," Quinton replied.

"Seginus Prime?" Harper said, speaking up for the first time. "I thought we were looking for a DNA vault."

Quinton had a list of coordinates for possible DNA vault locations he'd gotten from the DUC. When he'd been aboard the *Nebulon*, they hadn't checked all the locations. Instead, they'd gone to a set of coordinates that had been locked away in his ESS.

"Not yet," Quinton replied. "Seginus is home to Golden Taos. They specialize in refurbished droids."

"Do you think they'll have CDAs there?" Harper asked.

"CDAs?" Oscar asked.

"CDAs are short for Consciousness Driven Androids. They were designed to host PMCs," Quinton said and then looked toward Harper. "Probably not, but you never know. What they will have is a service bot that will be a better fit to store your ESS. Then we can search for a DNA vault."

"How far away is Seginus Prime?" Oscar asked.

"Just a few jumps from here. It won't take long, which is a good thing."

"Why is it a good thing?" Harper asked.

Quinton wasn't going to mislead Harper. "Keeping you in that spider-drone isn't healthy."

"It's not so bad. I'm getting more used to it. Having access to my own VR helps. I've made it like I'm remotely operating this old drone," Harper said.

"Still, Greta's diagnostic reports are concerning. Operating a spider-drone for the short term is fine, but not for ongoing usage. Degradation is highly probable."

"I know. I've seen my VI's reports. She doesn't let me forget it. Degradation leads to instability and the eventual breakdown of the PMC."

"What about finding Crowe?" Oscar asked.

"I don't know, Oscar. I spoke to Becker about it. I think Crowe is playing a dangerous game, but I don't think he intends for it to get out of control," Quinton said and paused for a few moments. "I'm not sure how to find him. I thought about sending a crafted message through sector comlink channels, but who knows how long that could take."

"You couldn't use your credentials, so how would he hear about it?" Harper asked.

"I wouldn't use mine," Quinton said and glanced wryly at Oscar. "I could always use Guttman's." They shared a laugh. "To answer your question, Harper, by the time any data made its way back to me, Crowe would be long gone."

"There are higher priorities, such as tracing the activation signals," Harper said and stopped.

Quinton's gaze darted to the main holoscreen. The tracking signal for the shuttle disappeared, quickly followed by all inbound and outbound ship traffic from Iskevian Spaceport.

"The ship broadcasts are gone! Where the hell did they all go?" Oscar asked.

Quinton initiated a subspace scan pulse and found the shuttle, but there was a delay and a lot of interference. "It's still there," he said and activated the direct laser communicator since subspace was unavailable. "You have to abort. Turn the shuttle around. Come back to the ship. The spaceport is under attack."

"Can't get a signal lock. You're breaking up. Repeat. You're breaking up," Becker replied.

Quinton increased the laser comms output and repeated himself. Then he followed up with a data packet and received confirmation of receipt.

The plot on the main holoscreen changed.

"Disruptor field is active, sir," Harper said.

Several bright flashes came from the spaceport. Someone was attacking it.

"Oscar, get us on an intercept course with the shuttle. We need to close the distance before we jump out of here," Quinton said and began activating the *Wayfarer's* weapons systems.

"Course laid in, but the nav computer won't let me execute emergency jump coordinates after. It's like I'm locked out," Oscar said.

"It's the disrupter field. We'll need to breach it before we can jump," Quinton said and engaged active scans.

"Sir, let me run the scans. I can narrow the scanner range for the field disrupter generators," Harper said.

Quinton handed off control of the active scans to Harper. "Update the tactical plot as soon as the generators are detected."

"Radek, run analysis on scan data."

"What priority?"

Quinton looked at the tactical plot on the main holoscreen. Disruptor field generators had been deployed within the vicinity of the spaceport, and more appeared, which meant they'd been in hyperspace before the field had gone active.

"Sentinel ship signatures," Quinton answered finally.

When he'd last engaged the Sentinels on the Starbase

Endurance, the tactical data had become part of his ESS before being transferred to the *Wayfarer*. PMCs were designed with knowledge sharing in mind, which included the retention of tactical data from engagement with enemy forces.

Outbound ships weren't able to engage their jump drives because they were caught in the disrupter field. Instead, they flew as fast as they could, hoping to breach the field long enough to execute a jump. It's what Quinton intended to do but doubted the civilian ships had the capability of detecting the field generators. They'd be flying blind. Civilian ship captains might not even know to look for the field generators.

Quinton heard Oscar speaking with Becker over a direct communications link. The disrupter field affected subspace comms.

"Tell him to get a move on it or I'll leave him behind," Quinton said.

The tactical plot updated with enemy ships—two destroyer class ships and five scout class ships. Not the best odds, but it could be worse.

"Sir, the hostiles are focusing their bombardment on the spaceport. They're not targeting the fleeing ships at all," Harper said.

"That's good. It'll give them a chance to get away then," Oscar said.

"Wouldn't be so sure about that," Quinton replied.

Powerful particle beams punched into the spaceport, cutting through escape pods and small ships that couldn't get out of the way fast enough. Quinton clenched his teeth. They didn't have the firepower to take on the Sentinel scout force, and there was nothing he could do for the spaceport. In a short time, it would be completely destroyed.

"Radek, were there any broadcasts detected with my identification?"

"No broadcasts detected by our comms systems."

Something had brought the Sentinels to the spaceport.

"Harper, give me a firing solution for field generators. We'll need to take out enough of them to escape the field," Quinton said.

"It will be difficult, sir. New field generators keep appearing on the plot."

"Standard blanket ambush tactic. Pick a direction heading away from the fighting and then we'll use best speed."

"Understood, sir," Harper replied.

"Where are they coming from?" Oscar asked.

"They're deployed in hyperspace. Once they transition to normal space, they disrupt communications and prevent ships from using their jump drives."

"How long can they keep this up?"

Quinton frowned. "Long enough," he said.

"What about the other ships? The spacers are trying to run away. Isn't there something we can do to help them? Can't you disable the field generators somehow?" Oscar asked.

The only way to disable the field generators was to destroy them. Not even the Sentinels could disable them, at least they shouldn't be able to. The generators would complete their scheduled run before going dormant. He couldn't destroy all the field generators. There wasn't anything he could do. They were outclassed but not nearly as bad as the freighters that were trying to escape.

"The shuttle just docked. Becker and Guttman are back aboard," Oscar said.

Quinton looked at the main holoscreen, and at the same time, he'd integrated with the ship's systems. He became aware of the data even before his cybernetic avatar could register that he'd seen the information on the holoscreen.

The Sentinel destroyers had split up, each attacking the spaceport from different vectors. The scout ships were scattered between them, focusing on destroying the spaceport's point defense systems—a task they'd soon be finished with—and then they'd begin focusing on the fleeing ships.

Quinton altered course to give him a clear targeting vector of the destroyer.

"Commander," Harper said, "that's the opposite course I've already laid out."

"Targeting priorities have changed," Quinton said and activated the *Wayfarer's* main weapon. A new holoscreen appeared in front of him.

Becker and Guttman came onto the bridge.

"Let's get out of here…" Becker said, his voice trailing off. "Wait, why are you attacking?"

"You better strap yourself in," Quinton said.

"We were better off in the damn shuttle," Guttman growled and hastened toward the nearest seat.

Quinton kept their speed constant. No need to give away what he was doing.

"They're going to detect us," Guttman said.

"No, they won't," Quinton said. "That's the unfortunate effect of using disrupter fields. It blinds them as much as it does us."

"Unless they've figured out a way around that limitation," Becker replied.

"They'd have to have invented a whole new field of physics if they have."

Quinton flew the *Wayfarer* along a trajectory, using the spaceport to prevent the Sentinels from noticing them.

"Commander," Harper said, "the design of those destroyers is based on ACN Leviathan class."

As Harper shared the information he had on the destroyer, Quinton merged the data with his own knowledge base and updated his firing solution.

"So that's what's on the upper deck," Becker said.

"What's on the upper deck?" Guttman asked.

"It's a tachyon lance," Quinton said.

"Oh, that explains it," Guttman said.

A secondary reactor came online, and its status appeared on the main holoscreen.

"I was wondering where the power draw was going to come from," Becker said.

"You've seen this before?" Harper asked.

"Not on a ship this size. Crowe was trying to get a lance working on one of the Jordani cruisers they'd found."

"That's never going to work. Jordani Federation ships didn't have the capability of producing the power required," Quinton said.

"And this ship does?"

Quinton didn't reply. He authorized the power tap and tasked a VI to manage the power flow. It had to be carefully monitored or it would overload the ship's power systems.

"Field is stable," Harper said.

"Prepare to route the power to the lance," Quinton replied.

He aligned the ship to be within targeting range and then fired the lance. The focus emitter arrays locked into position and the lance became active. High energy-focused particle beams more powerful than what the Sentinel destroyers were using pierced the armored hull of the ship. Quinton kept the tachyon lance active while it burned through the interior of the destroyer, making its way to the computing core.

"Oh my God, you're using a power tap, but that's prone to —" Becker said and was cut off.

Klaxon alarms blared and red flashing lights came on. Power levels from the tap spiked to critical levels. A shudder could be felt throughout the ship.

"Closing the tap," Harper said.

The tachyon lance stopped. The system had overloaded and needed a cool-down cycle.

"You've disabled their ship," Oscar said. "Look, it's not firing anymore. It's on a collision course with the spaceport."

"Hot damn," Guttman said. "I didn't know this ship could do that."

"Not for long. We can only sustain the lance in short bursts," Quinton said.

The power tap was still drawing power.

"I can't get the tap to close. There are fluctuations on the other end keeping it open," Harper said.

Quinton altered course and engaged maximum thrust. The reactionless drive kicked in and they began flying away from the spaceport.

"Can't we finish them off?" Guttman asked.

"We can't," Quinton replied.

"Then why did you attack in the first place?"

"To cause confusion. They weren't expecting anything like what just happened."

"Yeah, but if you can do it once—"

"No, Guttman," Becker said. "He just gave the spacers a fighting chance to get away."

Quinton tried to disrupt the power tap, but it wouldn't disengage. Siphoning power from higher dimensions ran the risk of erratic power surges that could force the tap to remain active. There was only one way to dislodge it.

"Go to your own life support," Quinton said.

The others engaged the emergency life-support systems from their seats. Emergency helmets protracted over their heads.

The power tap wouldn't disengage because there wasn't enough negative energy to disrupt the field. Quinton sent a burst of negative energy into the tap, and the ship's main power reactor began to drain. He quickened his frame rate exponentially. Capacity alerts sprang into his consciousness, which he had to ignore or he'd lose the ship. His army of VI assistants each made their analysis of the power tap available to him. It was as if he'd become aware of hundreds of analyses at once, and within the multitude of data he found a pattern. There was always an order to the universe, even if he was incapable of understanding it without Radek's help. Quinton siphoned off more negative energy from the ship's main power core and then ordered his VIs to insert the negative energy in bursts into the power tap. The effect was instantaneous. The field to the higher dimensional energy began to lose its hold and then the channel closed.

Quinton's frame rate snapped back to normal. The main engines stopped and they went to emergency power throughout the ship. Becker shouted his name.

Quinton held up his finger. "Harper, get ready to execute firing solution alpha."

"Firing solution ready."

The entire system had to be reset, which was mostly automated on the *Wayfarer*. At least it was supposed to be.

Quinton cursed and stood up.

"What can we do to help?" Becker asked.

"Follow me," he said and ran off the bridge.

Becker and Guttman followed him. Harper and Oscar stayed on the bridge.

Quinton made it to the maintenance hatch and slid down two decks. He opened a comlink to Becker and Guttman. "We have to restore main power before we can do anything else. The whole system is overloaded. I had to use up most of the core to sever the power tap."

"Okay, manual reset," Becker replied.

Quinton assigned a set of power relays to each of them. The *Wayfarer* wasn't a huge ship, but there were six relays spaced throughout the ship. The purpose of the relays was to route power away from the core in the event of an overload. Quinton was pretty sure the reqs had meant something along the lines of catastrophic overload. Even as fast as he could move, he couldn't physically be in more than one place at a time.

He ran to the relay, which was in the overload position, looking like an exposed cylinder a meter across. He rotated the cylinder, shoved it back into place, and continued. By the time he got to the fourth relay, Becker and Guttman had gotten to theirs.

Quinton initiated the power core reset. A violent shudder vibrated the walls and floor around them.

"Sentinel scout ships are firing on us," Harper said.

Quinton brought up the tactical plot and saw that the scout ships had launched a kinetic bombardment. They were just out of point defense range and were maintaining the distance.

Clever.

Quinton routed emergency power to missile tubes and granted Harper access to the missiles so he could directly interface with them. Small swarmer missiles launched in large volleys. That ought to buy them some time and overwhelm the scout ships' point defense systems.

Systems began to come back online, and Quinton started to head back to the bridge.

"Quinton, the jump drive coils won't align," Oscar said over comms.

"On my way," Quinton said. "You should get main engines back soon... There they are."

"I'm on it," Oscar said and began initiating the main engine restart.

Quinton stopped in the middle of the corridor. "Radek, I need a jump coil diagnostic."

"Complete," Radek replied. "The ship has taken damage near the jump drive."

"Can we bypass the damaged coils?"

"Negative, there are too many coils out of alignment, and there are whole sections that would breach safety protocols."

Jump drives required a minimum number of coils in order to fold space. Since none of them wanted to be obliterated while they tried to make the jump, he'd have to come up with a solution.

"Show me the damaged sections," Quinton said.

Radek showed him a schematic of the jump drive and the sections of coils that surrounded it. One section had overloaded. He studied the schematic and an idea came to mind. There was a part of his brain that sought to solve problems regardless of survivability. It simply presented a solution, and some chance of survival was better than no chance.

"I'm sorry. It's impossible for the ship to jump until the coils are repaired. Time to replace the damaged sections will take repair drones a minimum of twenty-two hours. Shall I begin the repair cycle?" Radek asked.

"Negative," Quinton said and started running toward the drive core.

He passed Becker and Guttman.

"Where are you going?" Becker asked.

They weren't able to match his stride.

"I'm going to kick the jump drive. You should head back to the bridge," Quinton said.

As he ran down the corridor, he checked Harper's status. His utilization was near the limits of the spider-drone, even with the help of the ship's computer system.

He opened a comlink to Oscar.

"Main engines are online. We're moving. Harper won't respond to me," Oscar said.

"He's busy. Just make sure the ship stays on course."

"Oh good. Disrupter field generators are going offline. The scout ships are falling behind, or at least I think they are. Without scans, I'm not exactly sure of their location. They're not firing on us anymore. The jump drive is still offline."

"I'm going to take care of it. You'll need to act quickly."

"Me? Won't you be able to initiate the jump from where you are?"

"I might not be able to," Quinton said. "I don't have time to go into it. Just be ready as soon as the jump drive status changes."

Quinton closed the comlink. One thing that had been drilled into him since he'd first served aboard a warship was that shipboard diagnostics, while very informative, couldn't solve the mechanical problems on a ship. They were advisors and could only function amid a rigid set of controls. This limitation was one of the founding principles that PMCs had been designed to overcome.

Quinton hastened through the bulkhead doors and into the jump drive chamber. The coils' housing units were mounted to both the floor and the ceiling with enough space for Quinton to squeeze through, though the space was normally occupied by maintenance drones.

"One Sentinel scout ship disabled," Harper said, "but the other one is on its way. It disabled the remaining swarmer missiles. It must have analyzed my attack pattern. I can't spare any more missiles."

"It's fine. Focus on the disrupter field generators."

"Yes, sir," Harper said and paused for a moment. "Sir, what are you doing—"

"Focus, Harper."

"Right, sir."

The comlink severed.

Quinton quickly made his way to the interior of the jump drive coil system. The entire jump coil housing units were offline, but Quinton couldn't see any visible damage. He took control of several maintenance drones and sent them to do a physical inspection. They'd initiate repairs if they could. Quinton continued forward and stopped at the sections that couldn't be bypassed. The Sentinel mag cannons had penetrated the outer hull and into the chamber. They weren't venting atmosphere because emergency shields had been initiated to compensate until the hull was repaired.

Quinton severed the jump coils' housing units so they were no longer part of the jump drive system. Between doing that and overriding all the safety protocols, he forced the ship's computer system to report a green status for the jump drive. That was the good part. The bad part was that he had to stay here with the jump drive to physically bridge the connections between the damaged sections. The avatar was capable of withstanding a significant but brief power surge. He just needed to hold on long enough for the drive to work.

"I don't know how you did it, but jump drive is green."

"What are you waiting for?" Quinton asked, then checked the tactical plot on his internal HUD. They were seconds from breaching the weakening disruptor field. Active scans showed the Sentinel scout ship pursuing them.

"Initiating jump," Oscar said.

Quinton detected the power spike in the jump drive as it spooled up. The jump drive distorted space surrounding the ship and then folded it, allowing the ship to travel to the emergency coordinates. The initial folded space from the drive was so intense that the jump drive had to be shielded from the rest of the ship. As folded space expanded to fill the distorted space, it became less dangerous. Quinton felt as if his entire body was being disassembled on the molecular level, every atom stripped away. His last thought before being pulled into darkness was that maybe he should have sent Harper to fix the damn jump drive.

CHAPTER FIFTEEN

System diagnostic running.

The words appeared amid the darkness of his thoughts. Where was he?

Veris initiation complete.

Cybernetic repair cycle has completed successfully.

Leuridium power core stable. Irreparable damaged sections have been removed.

Energy Storage System functioning nominally.

Personality Matrix Construct has passed all integrity checks. Integration optimal.

System startup complete.

Autonomous mode has been activated.

"Hello, Quinton," Radek said.

Quinton opened his eyes. He saw the curve of an opaque ceraphome door less than a meter in front of him and heard Becker and the others speaking in the room beyond.

"What happened?" Quinton asked Radek sub-vocally.

"Over seventy percent of the cybernetic avatar had been damaged beyond the capacity of the onboard repair capabilities of the unit."

"Seventy percent!"

Quinton looked down to see that he was in the avatar's storage container aboard the *Wayfarer*. He raised his hands. They looked like his own hands but for the chrome-colored "skin" of the advanced composites that comprised his musculature. His full sensory interface was working, which meant he could see, smell, and feel. He rubbed his thumb and forefingers together, noticing the muscles in his arms moving in a perfect copy of true flesh and blood.

"Seventy point four eight zero one—"

"I get it," Quinton snapped. His leuridium power core had been damaged by the jump drive.

His avatar provided the most protection in the chest area where his ESS was stored. The cybernetic avatar's design was based on a human body and, much like evolution, had developed the skeletal framework of musculature to protect the most critical parts of a person—the brain, heart, and lungs. The avatar was similar.

He'd almost died. Really died, as in utter destruction to the point of never being able to come back. Death. Finality. Quinton felt a shiver sweep down his spine. He'd known it could happen, and he understood the risks when he'd gone into the jump drive chamber to fix the coils. He thought there was a good chance he would survive, but seventy percent damage to the avatar... It had been more than a mere close call. Death had torn open the door, and the only thing that prevented it from claiming him was the design of the avatar whose built-in safety protocols were part of the base system his PMC used.

Quinton blinked his eyes several times while he considered his mortality. If he'd died, would he have felt anything? He doubted his death would be like when a flesh-and-blood person died and a bunch of chemical reactions occurred in the brain as the body shut down. What would his last moments have been like? Would he experience all the thoughts and feelings as one's life flashed before their eyes at the moment of death? This was the second time he'd almost died, and neither time had he experienced any of the things he'd expected to feel. He hadn't thought about his life or anyone, remaining focused on what had to be done. It was a hollow and empty feeling, and it worried him. He didn't like it. Maybe the engineers who designed PMCs had overlooked something.

"I've detected a severe spike of emotions," Radek said.

Damn VI, monitoring everything about him. He cursed inwardly.

"You think! How the hell should I react?"

Radek didn't reply, and Quinton heard Guttman speaking.

"If we'd gotten to that spaceport an hour earlier, we'd be dead," Guttman said.

"Yeah," Becker said in agreement.

"Makes you think," Oscar said.

"What? That leaving might not be the best option right now?" Guttman asked.

"You tell me."

Guttman sighed.

Quinton heard someone walking toward the holding container where he'd been rebuilt.

The outline of Becker's large, dark shadow came closer, as if he was trying to peer inside. "Is this going to work?"

"How should we know?" Guttman said.

"I don't know," Oscar said. "I know it's not just a storage container, and the menu options indicated that it could repair the damage."

Becker stepped away. "I don't know what else to do."

"There's always Harper."

"No, thanks," Becker replied. "I wish we had someone like Tolman or Fisher with us."

"Geez, Tolman," Guttman said. "He thought he could crack any secure system."

"All tech experts are like that," Oscar said.

"I know. We could use their help."

"Tolman had the worst breath. He could smell up a room with stink, it was so bad," Guttman said and grinned a little.

"Fisher had that head tick where he almost constantly nodded when he was working. It was distracting to be on runs with him," Oscar said.

Becker chuckled. "Yeah," he said. "What about that kid… Simon?"

"Oh yeah," Oscar agreed. "Webb. Simon Webb. He was good. Really good. Figured out that Quinton was a PMC before anyone else did."

"Yeah, but he's loyal to the DUC," Guttman said.

"He was, but I think he was more loyal to Maelyn Wayborn," Becker said.

"The boy had a crush, you think?" Guttman asked.

"Probably," Oscar replied.

"She was… impressive," Becker said.

Quinton updated the avatar's configuration so he looked like his normal self. Skin tone, hair, and even his eyes were all back to normal. He commanded the door to open and the others looked at him.

Quinton stepped out of the container and regarded them. "I almost died, and you ladies are talking about who likes who. What are you, a knitting circle?" He grinned and the others joined in.

"Good to have you back," Becker said.

"I guess I have you guys to thank for that."

Becker glanced at the others. "Yeah, we carried all the… pieces and assembled them in the chamber."

Quinton winced. "I guess I owe you all around."

"Shit," Guttman said, exhaling forcefully. "You pulled all our asses out of the fire again."

The others nodded in agreement.

"Maybe leaving isn't the safest choice after all," Quinton said.

Becker's eyebrows raised, and then he shook his head. "You were listening to us."

Quinton snorted. "Well, yeah. Wouldn't you? I mean the conversation was just so fascinating." He smiled and then added, "It wasn't that long. I'd only just come out of it and Radek was bringing me up to speed. Where's Harper?"

"He's in the middle of a rest cycle," Becker replied.

Quinton made an uh-huh sound. "And is everyone getting along?"

Becker's expression went flat, as did Guttman's.

"We've been repairing the ship," Oscar said. "There was significant damage in certain areas. Harper and the repair drones were able to fix the coils' housing units. They've made a lot of progress on that front."

"How come you never told us that this ship had a power tap or a damn tachyon lance?" Becker asked.

"It didn't seem relevant," Quinton replied. Becker and the others frowned. "I'm serious. You remember the condition the ship was in after... you know. But it wasn't essential."

"I've never heard of a power tap on a ship this size," Becker said.

Quinton nodded. "Evidently, there's a reason for that."

"Yeah, but you were able to disable a Sentinel destroyer!" Guttman said.

"Only because we took them by surprise. Once they report in, they'll be ready for it," Quinton said.

"Still," Becker said, leaning back against a workbench and crossing his arms. "It would have been nice to know."

Quinton shrugged. "Now you do. Consider yourself on the inside track now," he said and regarded the others for a few seconds. "Iskevian Spaceport was supposed to be independent, as in not part of the Collective."

Becker nodded. "They're not." Guttman and Oscar agreed.

"They're run by the Omicron Coalition. No ties to the Collective at all."

Quinton's eyebrows pinched together. "Then why did the Sentinels attack? What were they doing there?"

"I have no idea," Becker replied. "I've checked the ship's communication logs and there weren't any broadcasts."

"We might not have been there long enough."

Becker nodded. "That's what I was thinking, too."

"Then why would Crowe target the spaceport? Is there any strategic advantage that I don't know about?"

"I can't think of anything," Guttman said.

"Same here," Oscar replied.

"Only if Crowe was trying to make the rest of the galaxy aware that he could hit them, as well as the Collective," Becker said.

Quinton considered it for a few moments. "In order to get others to pressure Draven and the Collective to give Crowe what he wants."

Becker pressed his lips together for a second and tilted his head to one side. "I don't know. I mean, that's pretty ruthless, even for Crowe. He still needs to continue his business after this shadow conflict with the Collective is resolved. What good does it do him if instead of creating pressure for Draven, people started going after Crowe?"

"Who do they hate more?"

"Good point. Crowe could be banking on the perception that the Collective left him with no choice but to do these things."

"That's still pretty damn ruthless. It's too much," Quinton said and looked at the others. "He's gone too far. How many people have to die before they stop?"

"I agree," Becker said. "The other groups aren't going to take this lying down. There's probably already some mobilization going on, but the problem is the Sentinels."

"What about them?" Quinton asked. "Besides the obvious, I mean."

"If groups of spacers start mobilizing for a fight—and there's already increased Sentinel activity—Crowe would be the least of our worries. Once an incursion starts, there's no stopping it," Becker said.

Quinton needed to know more about the previous incursion. He wanted to question it because he didn't want to believe it was as bad as the others feared, but he'd be wrong. The certainty of it was written on the faces of Becker and the others, and he had to trust that.

"Then we need to stop Crowe."

"How the hell are we gonna do that?" Guttman asked.

"We find him."

"Yeah, and then what?"

"That depends on where we find him. We take him out ourselves, or we get others to help us do it," Quinton said.

Crowe was using Quinton's PMC identification to lure the Sentinels into attacking unsuspecting targets. He still needed to help Harper, but he couldn't ignore this. If he could figure out how Crowe was doing it, he could come up with an effective countermeasure. But if he could find Crowe, he could stop what he was doing at the source.

"We can't do this alone," Becker said.

"I know, but we can't advertise what we're doing either."

"Agreed. We'll need to come up with a plan," Becker said.

"We?" Quinton regarded them all for a few moments.

Becker looked at Guttman, who gave him a nod. "Looks that way," Becker said.

Oscar cleared his throat. "For the record, I was already going to help Quinton with this."

Becker looked at Oscar with mock severity. "And your point is?"

Oscar smiled. "I'm better than both of you. You just wanted

to leave, but I stayed." He looked at them, nodding his head in a self-satisfied way. "I think you both should tidy up my quarters for the next month, for starters."

Becker rolled his eyes. "Yeah, you win, buddy. Oscar is the winner."

Hearty laughter bubbled out of all of them.

"It's about time someone acknowledged it. Don't you feel better now that you did?"

These were the moments Quinton liked the most—the cama- raderie and surety of purpose. It reminded him of his time in the Acheron Confederacy Navy, but at the same time, it was differ- ent. These were different men than the spacers he'd served with.

"You're right. I'm getting all weepy-eyed," Becker said.

"Now you've done it. The big guy does care," Quinton said.

Another round of chuckles. Then Becker gave him an appraising look. "Are you back to normal now?"

"As normal as can be expected."

"I'm serious. You were in bad shape."

"Well, I don't want to repeat the process. Spare materials were used to patch me up, but it was a close thing," Quinton said. "Were you worried you'd be stuck with Harper?"

Becker looked at him solemnly. "I'd be lying if I said I wasn't concerned. I think you need to keep a closer eye on him."

"Unbelievable," Quinton replied. "He helped defend the ship and you still don't trust him."

"I don't, and I'm sorry it bothers you," Becker said. Quinton looked away, but Becker stepped in front of him. "I'm not trying to cause trouble. All I'm saying is that you need to keep a closer eye on him."

"I do. He has restricted access to the ship's systems."

"So did you on the *Nebulon*, but you still found a way around that," Becker said and held up his hand in a placating gesture. "I know this is different. I've been checking some of the logs."

Quinton looked at him for a long moment. Becker knew

what he was doing when it came to ships. He'd figured out that Vonya had betrayed them to Crowe. "All right, you've got my attention. What did you find?"

"Nothing."

"Nothing," Quinton repeated.

"That's right. Nothing. He's covering up what he does in the ship's systems. Not completely. There are some log entries, but something isn't right."

Quinton thought about it. Oscar and Guttman were silent.

"I figured you'd know more about it or might be able to check into it. You know, watch out for it," Becker said.

"You mean spy on him."

Becker shrugged. "If he's got nothing to hide, you won't find anything, but if you do find something, wouldn't you rather know before it escalates into something dangerous?"

"We're just asking that you check into it," Oscar said.

"All right, I will," Quinton said.

CHAPTER SIXTEEN

LENNIX CROWE HAD SPENT MORE time on *Union Cruiser Savage* than he had any other ship in a long time. Pragmatism had become the need, which required his presence in leading offensive operations against the Collective. He glanced around the conference room. The faded glory of a blue and gold crescent star adorned the walls, and smooth, gleaming surfaces surrounded a holotank in the middle of the room. He shifted in his seat. These chairs weren't nearly as comfortable as the ones on his previous flagship. *Savage* was a warship through and through, which provided very little in the way of creature comforts.

Multiple holoscreens were sourced above the holotank, showing the people who were essential to the Union. Crowe's Union was more than just another assembly of extensive resources fueled by salvage, mercenary, and shipping operations. It was very much his Union, but it was also theirs. No amount of compensation could guarantee loyalty. Belief in the mission was what held the Union together, which was more crucial now than it had ever been.

There was a shift in movement along his peripheral vision

that tugged at his attention. Carradine leaned forward, peering intently at his personal holoscreen.

Lennix looked back at the speaker highlighted on the holoscreen. "Continue, Captain Nakada."

"Our scouts have confirmed that the Sentinels are no longer in the Kizu Star System, and Chiba Station has been destroyed. A few of the domed cities of Boros Colony were damaged from the battle, but the Sentinels ignored them for the most part."

"Have the salvage teams begin recovery operations immediately," Lennix said.

"Understood, sir. We've alerted newsnets about the attack and expect the Collective to send recovery teams," Nakada said.

"They'll be too late, I think," Lennix replied, the edges of his lips lifting a little. "Excellent work, Captain. Convey my congratulations to your crew."

"Thank you, sir," Nakada said.

Carradine cleared his throat and looked at Crowe. "I'm sorry to interrupt, but I've just received the latest intelligence briefings."

Lennix regarded him with eyes of burnt almond and nodded. Then, he turned toward the holoscreens. "Senior captains remain. Everyone else can go. Resume normal daily operations."

Many of the holoscreens disappeared, leaving a dozen senior Union captains.

Crowe looked at Carradine. "What have you got for us, Nate?"

"Operation Undermine continues to be highly successful. Draven has become preoccupied with protecting his assets, but he's still scouting for Union operations in multiple sectors. The losses we've sustained were expected, but the damage to the Collective has been much worse. For anyone else, it would have been catastrophic."

The Collective was the single largest independent salvage, mercenary, and trade conglomerate in the galaxy. They rivaled the remnant federations and star empires throughout the galactic sectors.

"No doubt Draven is feeling the pressure," Lennix said.

"But there have been some alarming developments," Carradine replied. "We'll need to confirm some of these, but there have been reports of Sentinel attacks on unauthorized targets that have nothing to do with the Collective."

"Could someone else have found a way to copy our attack?"

Carradine shook his head. "I've reviewed the mission reports. Our method is contained. In fact, the only thing Draven's intelligence agents have been able to figure out is the initial broadcast that's tied to the attacks. They've pushed out security updates in an effort to block it, but they're still blind to our tactics and methodologies. It'll be easy to circumvent their security measures, but we need to address the issue of these other places being attacked by the Sentinels."

"Where else has been hit?"

Carradine gestured toward the holoscreen where a new subwindow appeared.

Lennix's eyes widened. "This many? Are you sure about this?"

Carradine nodded. "We need to validate some of these accounts, but they're only the attacks we know about. There could be more."

"The primary risk always was that the Sentinels would increase their patrols in known population centers."

"That's true, but the attack patterns are almost exactly the same as our methodology. We'll be blamed for all of them."

Lennix cursed. He stood up, clenched his teeth, and interlaced his fingers atop his head. "We've been double-crossed."

"It would seem so," Carradine agreed.

Lennix released his hands and peered at the report again.

"They're going to blame us for these attacks," Captain Nakada said, and the other senior captains agreed.

Their goal had been simple. They had to get the Collective to back off and allow them to keep building up the Union. He hadn't meant for the Sentinels to begin widespread attacks. Their operations, while it had risks, were designed to be precise within a wide range of targets to convey a clear message to the Collective, as well as anyone who supported them. The Collective maintained their operations through populated galactic sectors right alongside everyone else. They'd been careful to avoid the most populated star systems.

"Should we continue with Operation Undermine?" Nakada asked.

Lennix inhaled deeply, holding his breath for a few long moments before he released it and looked at the others. "Continue with existing operations. Hold on any new targets until we get more information."

The senior captains acknowledged their orders and the various comlinks disconnected, leaving Lennix alone with Carradine.

"It doesn't make any sense," Lennix said, finally.

Carradine knew to wait him out while he gathered his thoughts. "Desher delivered exactly what he promised us, but we were nearly there on our own. We only needed him to get us across the finish line by using that PMCs identity we pulled from the starbase, but he never promised anything else."

Lennix shook his head. He'd never liked dealing with information brokers, and Admen Desher wasn't any different. "This is what happens when we go into business with someone we don't really know."

"Desher gave us what we needed to survive."

"It has to be him," Lennix said and paused for a few seconds, considering. "What I don't understand is why. Why would he do this? What does he gain by it?" Lennix asked and shook his head. "We need to find him. He needs to be neutralized."

"We could release his identity. Let Draven hunt him down for us," Carradine said.

Lennix thumped his knuckles on the edge of the holotank a few times. "No one will believe us, and too many questions would be asked. Our shadow war with Draven hasn't been as clandestine as we'd hoped. We need to circulate a profile of Desher's ship and then broadcast an anonymous bounty for any information about it."

Carradine frowned in thought. "He'll know it's us looking for him."

"That's fine."

Carradine nodded and looked away for a few seconds.

"That look," Lennix said. "I'm not going to like this, am I?"

"It's just a thought."

"I've learned long ago to trust those instincts of yours. Let's hear it."

"The same instincts that advised you to deal with Admen Desher?"

"Nate, just get to the damn point. The sooner you tell me about this idea of yours, the sooner we can do something about it."

Carradine sighed. "What if—and I stress *what if*—Desher himself is a PMC?"

Lennix's thoughts flatlined as he contemplated. "Can't be. There's no way."

Carradine raised his eyebrows. "Consider the possibility for a moment."

"Fine. Consider away for me then."

"All right. Desher understood exactly what we were trying to do."

"That makes him clever, not a PMC."

"He's familiar with Sentinels and their protocols."

Lennix shook his head a little. "Still not conclusive."

"I'm not going for irrefutable. However, if I'm right, there's more at work here than an information broker gone rogue."

Lennix frowned in concentration. "That still doesn't explain what he's trying to do."

"What if he just wants to agitate the Sentinels? Maybe even trigger an incursion," Carradine said.

Lennix's eyes went flat. "All the more reason for us to find him. Lay a trap of our own and get rid of him. But I still think we're only seeing a partial picture here. We need more information."

"Agreed on all counts."

Lennix placed his palms on the edge of the holotank and rocked back and forth a few moments. All communications with Desher had been secured to protect both their identities. He glanced at Carradine as his mind made mental leaps of logic. "Nate, I really hope you're wrong."

Carradine swallowed hard. "I do, too, for both our sakes."

If they weren't wrong, they might have encountered a PMC from the Federation Wars, but unlike Quinton Aldren, Admen Desher could be the kind that the Sentinels were meant to hunt down and destroy.

"We need to proceed carefully," Lennix said, "as much as we can."

CHAPTER SEVENTEEN

"A successful jump," Oscar said.

Quinton read the report on his personal holoscreen. Oscar was right. "Run a full diagnostic on the drive and coils. We need to make sure we've worked out all the issues."

"The preliminary reports look good. Coils are properly aligned and are operating within acceptable safety parameters," Harper said.

"And the bypass?" Quinton asked.

"No errors reported."

They'd had to reduce the number of jump coils, which affected how far they could travel. The *Wayfarer's* range was still vastly superior to most ships, according to Becker, but what did he know? He'd only spent the bulk of his life on ships.

"That's good. We're still operating without any spares, which isn't ideal. Our effective range is going to diminish if we don't get more. That is, unless any of you know how to make some and have been holding out on me," Quinton said and eyed them all for a moment. "Couldn't hurt to ask, I guess. Let me know if the diagnostic turns up anything else."

"Understood," Harper replied without including "sir" or "commander."

Quinton wasn't sure if this meant that Harper was beginning to accept the circumstances as they were, or he'd simply forgotten. Quinton had given him more to do on the ship, which he knew worried the others, but Harper needed to be invested in what they were doing. Relegating him to the background was only going to hasten the degradation of his PMC. Quinton understood the struggle, although Harper dealt with it in his own way. It was going to have to be enough.

Quinton looked at Becker. "Once we confirm that the drive is good to go, we can go after your old boss. How do we find him?"

"You're not going to like it."

"If you say we have to go to another information broker, I'm throwing myself out the airlock... and I'm taking you with me."

"It's the quickest way to get information. They compile it from multiple sources. You want to find Crowe fast, then this is the way," Becker replied.

"No, it's not. It's convenient at best. I'll grant you that."

Becker's mouth twitched in annoyance. "I hope you've got a better idea."

"I might. I was thinking we cut out the middleman and go for the source."

"How do you propose we do that?"

"How about I make him an offer he can't refuse?" Quinton said, and Becker simply stared at him. "Send him a message—a specially crafted message that can only be opened by him."

"How would that work?" Oscar asked.

"It's simple," Harper said without looking away from his workstation.

"Yes," Oscar prompted.

The silence stretched, and then Harper turned the drone's optics over toward them.

Quinton nodded encouragingly.

"Yeah, it's simple. Just have him authenticate the message in such a way that confirms his identity. I imagine with your intimate knowledge of the Union, this task shouldn't be that difficult," Harper said.

Quinton smiled and looked at Becker. "There you have it."

"Okay, that could work, but—"

"We'll send a bunch of messages to all the old Union contacts you guys can think of. I expect that at least some of them are still being monitored by Crowe," Quinton said.

Becker glanced at Oscar. "Maybe," he said, sounding unconvinced.

Quinton frowned. "What do you mean 'maybe'? Crowe is a businessman. He needs resources even as he strikes at Collective targets. There's no way he can do this without a supply line of some sort from multiple sources for redundancy. We'll give him a way to contact us."

"You can't be serious. We can't just wait for him to reply."

Quinton gave him an incredulous look. "Duh. No one said anything about sitting here doing nothing. We've got plenty of other things to do. But I want to know how you plan to get him to authenticate."

Becker leaned back and his seat reclined a little. He rubbed his chin while he thought about it. "Crowe has likely increased security, so trying to slip past those measures might be more trouble than it's worth."

"Okay," Quinton said slowly.

"If the message came from me, that might make it through the chain," Becker said.

"Becker, are you sure about this?" Oscar asked.

Becker shrugged and then nodded. "We left. Crowe knows it. We're not dead, and sure, maybe we can keep operating under the scanner and not get noticed by the Union, but I'm starting to not care. That doesn't mean I would put myself on Crowe's tactical plot, but I think he's got enough going on that wanting to get revenge on a couple of former employees is a little beyond him right now. Like Quinton said, Crowe is a businessman."

Quinton stood up and clapped his hands slowly. "Wow," he said. "You finally realized that Crowe doesn't own you."

"I never thought he owned us, but it was more profitable and safer if we stayed away. At least until your sorry ass came along," Becker said.

Quinton remembered how scared Becker and the others had been about leaving the Union on the promise that it would be worth their while. It had taken a lot longer to collect on it, but this was the first time any of them had mentioned that moving on from Crowe's Union might not have been as detrimental to their health as they'd previously thought.

Becker looked at Quinton and smiled—not just a companionable smile but one he recognized.

"You're going to make me pay for this, aren't you?"

Becker nodded. "Duh," he said, mimicking Quinton. "With interest… a whole lot of interest."

"And here I thought we were working for the good of the galaxy."

"That doesn't mean we have to go broke doing it. Plus, I'm providing you a valuable service. My connections are going to help you get past all the standard bureaucracy and go right to the source."

Quinton snorted. "You're laying it on kinda thick, aren't you? I mean… what if you can't deliver? That would really be… hmmm, what's the word I'm looking for? Ah, yes—unfortunate." He smiled. "I'd need to be reimbursed," he said, "with interest. A whole heck of a lot of it."

"You won't be sorry you made this deal."

Quinton grinned.

"Enough already," Oscar said. "Quinton, what are you going to include in the message?"

"A strongly worded letter advising him to stop or else," Quinton replied.

Oscar blinked several times, and Quinton continued. "A couple of things, actually. Definitely a message from yours truly, but also a few things to infiltrate his communication systems."

"Don't broadcast a signal to the Sentinels," Oscar said.

Quinton nodded. "Of course not. That goes without saying. No, I thought I'd utilize a tactic that Vonya released on the starbase. Something persistent. Something that will seek out exactly how they're signaling the Sentinels and either remove it altogether or change the targets. I haven't decided what I'm going to do. I might do both of them, maybe more... You know, use a randomizer, so the options are always different. Their security systems will have trouble tracking that."

"You can do that?" Becker asked.

"Yeah."

"I guess I'm a little surprised. Who'd have thought that a commander in the Acheron Confederacy Navy could do that," Becker replied.

"What do you think we do? Roam the decks barking orders when we're not on the bridge stating the obvious or being tyrants to our officers?"

Harper's chuckle blossomed into a hearty laugh, and after a few moments, Quinton joined him. Then he looked at Becker.

"All right, there was some of that. I know *I've* served under my fair share of those commanders. But there was more to the ACN than simply having the most capable weapons. We lacked ships, so we had to make the ones we did have more capable than other federations, empires, or star kingdoms. This included data warfare. Infiltration systems were something we were the best at."

Harper looked at Quinton. "I'm so glad to hear you say that, sir. I was beginning to think you'd forgotten."

Quinton *couldn't* forget, and sometimes it was a curse, but not always. "I didn't forget," he said and looked at Becker. "Anyway, yeah, we're multi-talented. I'll have it ready by the time we jump within range of a galactic comms net."

"I never really thought about it. That you also could do that stuff," Becker said.

"Me either," Oscar agreed.

"Yeah, we're all full of surprises," Quinton said.

The temperature in the room seemed to decrease a little, as if the mood had shifted as it sometimes did when they were all faced with the fact that they were from two very different worlds —one of which had existed before the Federation Wars that devastated the galaxy Quinton had woken up to where the survivors of the Federation Wars limped onward in a struggle to survive and rebuild what they could.

They went back to their workstations and Quinton sat in the commander's seat, beginning to craft the message he wanted Lennix Crowe to receive. He drew from his brief experience aboard one of Crowe's space stations when he'd been stuck in an old agricultural bot. He added a few extra options for the worm to be more reactive once it infiltrated Crowe's Union ships. He'd had to draw from his experience as a tactical officer where he'd specialized in cyber warfare. The standard communication and systems protocols hadn't changed that much since the Federation Wars. The Sentinels were part of the reason for the stagnation, but PMC detection systems had been more developed since he'd been uploaded. He could have crafted a message that embedded a specialized version of one of his VIs, but he didn't want to risk detection. He'd settled for a dumbed-down reactive version of the worm and hoped for the best. He had Radek check his work to make sure the outcomes he expected were the ones that would actually happen. Radek did this by creating virtual environments and testing thousands of outcomes in seconds.

"Quinton," Oscar said.

Quinton turned in his seat to look at him. "Yes?"

"I have a list of coordinates that will put us in range of a galactic comms net. Do you want to check them over?"

"Pick one," Quinton said.

"You got it."

The ship made another successful jump without any issues with the drive coils or the drive itself, and it was reasonable to believe that the jump drive would continue to work reliably moving forward. If only they could guarantee everything else would go as smoothly.

"Are you ready yet, Becker?" Quinton asked.

"Just finished. You can upload at any time."

Quinton authorized the upload to the comms net. He also allowed various updates, including navigational data and other data from the lone comms buoy.

"Radek, analyze the data we've just received and let me know if there's anything we need to take a look at," Quinton said.

Oscar laughed, reading something on the holoscreen in front of him. He looked at them and shrugged. "They're still broadcasting messages about ship warranties backed by—you're going to love this—Three Moons Shipyards!"

Quinton grinned, as did Becker.

"I don't understand," Harper said.

"Three Moons Shipyards was where we found you," Quinton replied.

"I know that, but why would ships need a warranty?"

"They don't," Oscar said. "It's just another way for someone to scam credits from spacers."

Harper went back to his work.

"When do you want to go to the next buoy?" Becker asked.

"I have Radek running a few queries," Quinton said and twitched his chin toward Harper.

"I can see that, you know," Harper said. "I thought you realized that the spider-drone has an option for omnidirectional viewing."

"So, we can't sneak up on you. Got it," Quinton replied.

"Don't you get disoriented if you enable that option all the time?" Becker asked.

"I do, but that's why I have Greta monitor it for me," Harper replied.

Quinton glanced at Harper thoughtfully, experiencing an urge to test that omnidirectional viewing option of his but filed that away to try later. He wondered how much of the spider-drone's onboard computer was being devoted to giving Harper the peace of mind that he wasn't going to be attacked.

"Yeah, we need to find Harper a better body," Quinton said.

"What about the DNA vaults?" Becker asked.

"Yeah, well, we'll look for both, but stopping Crowe from starting a Sentinel incursion is the top priority," Quinton said.

"Quinton," Radek said, "I've found something that I think you should see."

"Put it on the main holoscreen."

"It's a recent distress beacon," Radek said, and a data window appeared for them to review.

"Looks like an automated message," Quinton said and frowned. "That can't be right. Radek, are you sure about this?"

"The distress beacon is authentic. It's an Alari Star Council outpost."

Harper walked over to them. "An Alari message here?"

"Who are they?" Becker asked.

Quinton looked at Becker for a moment. "I guess they're not around anymore. They were a small star nation that the Acheron Confederacy had trade pacts with."

"More than that," Harper said. "They were our allies."

"That must have been after I was uploaded," Quinton said. He accessed the other communication logs from the comms buoy and nearly stood up.

Becker looked at him. "What? What is it?"

Quinton put the data on the main holoscreen. "There was

another PMC activation signal. Short burst. Source unknown. It was just recorded about forty hours ago," he said and frowned. "The distress beacon became active shortly after."

"It's not active anymore," Becker said.

Quinton checked the coordinates of the distress beacon. They were within jump range.

"Quinton, the beacon is no longer active," Becker said.

"The outpost could be old and it malfunctioned."

"Yeah, or the Sentinels have already taken it down."

"Who... not it," Quinton replied.

"I meant the signal."

"We're going to check it out," Quinton said. "Oscar."

"Right, plotting a course," the pilot said.

"Not right on top of it. Let's be a little cautious with our approach. Just in case," Quinton said.

"I'll let Guttman know," Becker said.

The jump drive status appeared on the upper right corner of the main holoscreen.

"Hey, Oscar, also—"

"Have an emergency set of coordinates ready to execute in case there are hostiles in the area."

"I knew there was a reason I kept you around."

"That's because I'm the best."

"I won't forget it."

Becker closed his comlink and looked at Quinton. "Guttman is heading to main engineering."

"Good idea," Quinton replied. They'd been reliant on maintenance drones that Quinton and the others could control, but considering their last encounter with the Sentinels, those measures weren't enough.

Becker rubbed his forehead and squeezed his eyes shut.

"What's wrong?"

Becker shook his head. "It's nothing. Just a headache."

Quinton looked at him for a moment. Becker had taken a

blow to the head during the Sentinel attack. He was lucky that a headache was all he'd walked away with.

"Ready to execute jump," Oscar said.

"Make it so," Quinton replied.

The ship emerged into the outer fringes of a star system with a blue giant main sequence star. Initial scans revealed a few rocky planets orbiting extremely close to the bright star. The planets' compositions must be highly dense with extensive deposits of metals, or the star's gravitational forces would have prevented those planets from forming in the first place. There were three gas giants in the system, each with an assortment of moons, but the star system was otherwise unremarkable. Quinton had expected to detect a few mining installations on the interior planets, but there weren't any. Not a bad place to station an outpost.

The plot refreshed on the main holoscreen as new scan data was brought in. Quinton traced the distress beacon to one of the gas giants.

"That can't be right," Becker said.

"That's the source of the beacon."

"The outpost could be on one of the moons," Oscar said.

"It's not," Quinton replied.

"Did the beacon use some kind of repeater like how we tracked the ACN starbase?" Becker asked.

"That's a good point," Oscar said. "They probably wouldn't want to give away their position."

"Are you guys finished guessing?" Quinton asked. "I can just tell you if you give me a chance." He looked at them, and Becker gave him a get-on-with-it look. "It's a distress beacon. Unless someone is trying to ambush us, the location of the outpost is fine. Yes, by the gas giant is probably right. They could move the outpost into the upper atmosphere if they needed to. It's not unheard of, depending on what the outpost is used for."

"Why don't we do an active scan of the system, just to be sure?" Oscar said.

Quinton refreshed the passive scan data on the main holo-screen. "Because we're not the only ones here." Someone had entered the system ahead of them.

"Sentinels?" Becker asked.

"I don't know," Quinton replied. "It's just one ship. We'll need to go in quietly."

Quinton accessed the communications system and there were no broadcasts coming from the outpost. The star system was already quiet.

"Then it's not an ambush," Becker said.

"Yup," Quinton replied.

If there had been other ships in the star system waiting to see who investigated the emergency distress beacon, they would have already closed the trap for the other ship. The beacon and the outpost were real, and there was at least one PMC who'd come online.

"Oscar, take us in," Quinton said.

"Aye, Commander. Taking us in," Oscar replied.

"Harper, monitor for other ship activity."

"Aye, Commander," Harper said.

Someone had reached this star system ahead of them and weren't giving away their position. They'd have to get closer to the outpost to see if they were there.

CHAPTER EIGHTEEN

THE *WAYFARER* FLEW on a direct intercept course to the Alari Star Council outpost. They needed to make up for lost time. Rather than spending the better part of twenty-seven hours to reach their target destination, Quinton executed a micro-jump that closed the distance. The gas giant's colorful belts of pale green to yellow with a few brownish reds filled the view on the main holoscreen. The planet was surrounded by a few large, distinct rings where several of its natural satellites carved a path through the dust, ice, and rocks.

Quinton deployed a reconnaissance drone that would maintain its position beyond the atmosphere and passed control of the subspace session over to Harper, who would continue monitoring it.

A HUD overlay appeared on the main holoscreen, which showed their best guess as to where the distress beacon had come from. Quinton activated a focused active scan pulse through subspace toward the targeted region. The scan widened until they received a positive scan result.

"The outpost is in the thermosphere in one of the darker belts," Quinton said.

"Won't it be crushed?" Oscar asked.

"No… well, it can if it goes deep enough, but the darker belts are older and less dense than the lighter regions."

Becker cleared his throat. "This ship wasn't designed to fly into the interior atmosphere of a gas giant."

"You're right, but we only need to reach the outpost and then we'll be protected by its artificial gravity field. It's gotta be massive if it's positioned here," Quinton replied.

"It had better be, to compete with a planet that size."

"They were designed for it."

"Assuming the outpost hasn't been damaged," Becker said and then held up his hands, palms up. "I know. I know. Let's just get on with it."

"Take us in, Oscar," Quinton said.

He continued to review the scan data of the Alari outpost as the ship flew toward it. They couldn't actually see it, but the sensors detected it several hundred kilometers inside the atmosphere.

Quinton opened a comlink to engineering and Guttman answered. "Expect a power spike to the inertia dampening system."

"Understood," Guttman replied.

Quinton closed the comlink, and Becker looked at him quizzically. "Nothing, I just haven't heard Guttman use so few words before."

"Yeah," Becker said and turned back toward the main holoscreen.

The live video feed was replaced by a three-dimensional schematic rendering of the outpost from the incoming sensor data. Quinton diverted power to the ship's artificial gravity field, creating a bubble of resistance to the gas giant's powerful gravitational pull.

He checked the ship's communication systems. They hadn't received anything from the outpost. He'd initiated several broadcast hails to the outpost, but they hadn't been answered yet.

The Alari outpost was built into the bottom of a metallic asteroid that had likely been mined out for that purpose. The bottom was essentially a large, cylinder-shaped habitation unit, two kilometers wide that narrowed toward the bottom.

"I'm not detecting any active weapons systems," Harper said.

"Understood," Quinton said. He had access to the same scan data, but Harper was speaking the updates aloud for the benefit of Becker and Oscar.

"I guess the fact that they're not shooting at us is as open an invitation as we're likely to get, but how are we going to get inside?" Becker asked.

Quinton looked at Radek's analysis of the sensor data. "A docking port isn't ideal. I'd rather find a hangar bay... There, I've found one," he said and updated the waypoint.

Oscar flew them toward it.

More scan data revealed that the outpost's lower decks were significantly damaged, but the upper decks still had power. They hadn't received any response to their hails, so Quinton scanned subspace frequencies for a data connection within the vicinity of the hangar bay doors. He found one almost immediately and accessed the door-control systems. A quick analysis of the doors showed that they weren't secure. He sent a docking request. The door-control systems would only engage the open-door protocols if they were authorized by the outpost's central command. Quinton inserted an override that put his data session between the door-control systems and central command, which allowed him to grant his own docking request. Their lack of security was his gain.

"Hangar bay doors are opening now," Quinton said.

Oscar flew the ship toward them, and in a few moments, they were safely within the outpost's artificial gravity field. The ship's power draw returned to normal.

Oscar deployed the ship's landing gear and set the ship down. The hangar bay doors remained open so he enabled the atmospheric shield, which worked, but the hangar bay didn't fill up with a breathable atmosphere.

"Looks like we'll need suits for this one," Quinton said.

"I won't," Harper said.

"Harper, I need you and Oscar to stay with the ship."

"I thought I was coming with you. There could be PMCs on this outpost. There might be a body for me to use."

"Yes, we'll look for that, but I need you to monitor the recon drone for Sentinel ships, and we also don't know where the people who arrived before us went. I need you to stay here," Quinton said.

Harper was quiet for a few moments and then said, "Yes, Commander."

Becker stood up. "Guttman is on his way to the airlock."

"Oscar, you're in charge while I'm gone," Quinton said.

"Harper and I have got this, but don't take too long," Oscar said.

Quinton and Becker left the bridge.

"I saw what you did there," Becker said.

"We need an established chain of command; otherwise, everything just falls apart," Quinton replied.

They met Guttman at the portside airlock, and Quinton waited for them to put on their EVA suits. They'd opted for plasma assault rifles instead of their hand blasters.

Harper contacted him through comlink. "I'd like to deploy a few more recon drones to see if there are any other ships docked with the station. I'll have them fly close enough to the outpost that they'll stay in its gravitation field."

"Good idea. Let me know if you find anything," Quinton said and closed the comlink.

They entered the airlock and waited for it to cycle. When the outer airlock doors opened, Quinton walked out first and glanced around. The hangar bay was empty except for their ship. He gestured for Becker and Guttman to follow.

"You know what I don't get," Guttman said.

"I don't even know where to begin with that one, but I guess I'll have to start somewhere," Quinton replied.

Guttman snorted. "I'm serious. Where'd everyone go? Why would they abandon this place?"

"They were probably recalled by Alari High Command," Becker said.

They walked across the hangar toward the deck officer's office a short distance down the corridor.

"That's what we always assume," Guttman said. He walked over to the nearest workstation and brought it online. "I want to know why. Were they attacked, or did they just …? I don't know, leave or something."

"I'm not able to access their computing core, so I don't know why they decommissioned the outpost," Quinton said.

"That's just it. If they decommissioned it but left it intact, they might have expected to come back," Guttman said. The workstation holoscreen powered on. "You're right about the computing core. The alerts say it went offline," he said and frowned. Both Quinton and Becker peered at the holoscreen. "It went offline when the beacon stopped. It looks like someone tried to bring this outpost back online."

"That's good enough for me. That means they're still here," Quinton said and headed for the door.

Becker followed him and then stopped in the doorway. "You coming?" he said to Guttman.

Quinton stopped and looked through the clear ceraphome window to the office. Guttman stood near the workstation. He started walking toward them and then went back to the work-station.

"I know the computing core is down," Guttman said, "but the workstation has local storage. I'm going to see if I can find some supply caches nearby. There might be a good find there, especially if they really planned on returning."

Becker nodded. "Let us know if you find anything."

The adjacent corridor was lit by emergency lighting.

"Think he'll find anything?" Quinton asked.

"If there is something to be found, he'll find it," Becker said. "He's got a good head for finding valuable cargo."

"I doubt there will be any ships here."

"Agreed, that would be too convenient. Even if there were any, I doubt they'd be in good working order. Certainly not space worthy," Becker replied.

They made their way through the outpost, and a short while later, they entered a central section where there were elevators that actually had power to them.

They entered the elevator.

"Destination?" a modulated voice asked.

"Central operations," Quinton replied.

The elevator doors shut.

"I guess these are on an isolated system," Becker asked.

"Evidently."

The elevator sped upward.

"You don't know?" Becker asked.

"Of course, I know. Do you really think the elevator needs to be in contact with the computing core to operate?"

"Yeah, I did."

Quinton considered it for a few moments.

"What?" Becker said, annoyed.

"I was just thinking that this is what it must be like for you to explain to me how things work," he said and nodded a little. "It's a great feeling. I could get used to it."

Becker rolled his eyes and shook his head. "Sometimes... sometimes you're a real ass, you know that? Just answer the damn question."

Quinton just looked at him.

"You don't have to be such a jerk about it." Becker gritted his teeth and stepped toward him.

Quinton grinned. "All right. All right. I'll stop. Geez, that's some kind of temper you've got there."

Becker backed up to the other side of the elevator and glared at the wall. "Never mind, I don't want to know. The sooner..." He mumbled the rest.

"Okay, Becker, come on. I'm just kidding around. It's what we do."

Becker swung his gaze toward Quinton, gritting his teeth.

"Some military bases are different. They have systems that can work autonomously if they need or as part of a complex system. The designers built in redundancy in the event of being cut off from critical infrastructure. It's how the ACN designed their star-bases. That's why the base we were on could still function, even though it had suffered from severe weapons damage."

Becker's gaze softened a little. "Thank you. That's all you had to do."

"What's the matter with you?"

"Did you ever check into Harper's use of the ship's computer system?"

Quinton hesitated and frowned.

"I don't believe this. You never checked."

"I meant to. I just haven't gotten around to it yet."

Becker leaned toward him. "You don't forget anything."

But Quinton had forgotten. "I'll do it as soon as we get back on the ship."

"Do you need me to remind you?"

"No. I said I'd do it and I meant it."

"I don't believe you. Radek, are you there?" Becker asked. Radek's holographic sphere appeared. "Great. Can you remind Quinton to check on Harper's use of the ship's computer system for me, please?"

"Reminder is set," Radek said.

"Excellent. Make it daily until the task is done," Becker said.

"Acknowledged. Reminder preferences updated."

Quinton's gaze darted between Becker and Radek. Then he chuckled. "Thanks, Radek," he said.

Becker smiled, white teeth gleaming amid the dark skin inside his helmet. "You brought this on yourself."

Quinton laughed. "I guess I did."

He received a comlink request from Harper. Quinton answered it.

"The drones were unable to locate any other ships docked with the station," Harper said.

"What about the other hangar bays? Does anything look like they've been recently used?"

"Negative, Commander. I've recalled the drones."

"Understood. Thanks for the update," Quinton said and told Becker.

"Maybe they already left or weren't able to get inside the outpost," Becker said.

"Come all this way and just give up?"

"If they're salvagers, they might. Whoever came here knew what they were getting themselves in for. I wouldn't risk my ship to come here, and with news of increased Sentinel activity, they might have decided it wasn't worth the risk either."

"Unless the ship didn't stick around."

Becker frowned. "Boarding party."

Quinton nodded.

"That's a hell of a risk to take. We should warn Oscar."

"They're already monitoring for any ships that enter the area," Quinton said.

The elevator chimed as it reached the central operations deck. He tried to access the outpost's security system to see what was beyond the elevator door, but the system was offline.

Quinton's reactions were startlingly fast, well beyond the capabilities of even the most enhanced human. As the doors opened, he had a little over a second before a barrage of plasma bolts rapid-fired at them. Quinton threw himself toward Becker, knocking him into the wall. Then he leaped off the wall, propelling himself to the other side of the elevator. He'd caught sight of two automated defense turrets that had risen from the floor in the middle of the corridor beyond.

Quinton increased the power output of his assault rifle and fired a quick three-bolt burst. One of the turrets exploded. The other turret pinned him into the corner.

Becker recovered from being shoved into the wall and looked at Quinton, nodding his head toward the remaining turret.

The turret stopped firing and Quinton burst from the elevator, firing his weapon in a suppressing spray. His shots were accurate, but they didn't need to be. He was the distraction. Becker destroyed the second turret.

Central operations was a few dozen meters away. No other defense turrets appeared, and Quinton couldn't detect any power cables that led to more turrets on standby—not under the floor or hidden inside the ceiling.

"Why don't you hang back while I scout ahead?" Quinton said.

Becker nodded and kept a pace several meters behind him. Quinton peered through the clear ceraphome doors and saw several rows of workstations beyond. He scanned for local computer systems and they were offline, but someone had enabled the defense turrets. He reached the door first and took up a position just outside the doorway.

"See anything?" Becker asked.

A few metallic storage containers sat beneath several large holoscreens.

"Yeah," Quinton said. "Cover me from here while I go take a look."

Becker hastened to the other side of the wide doorway and kept out of sight.

Quinton palmed the door controls and walked into the operations center. The interior was a large round room that was more akin to a command center. The black Alari Star Council emblem shone from the holoscreens.

Quinton scanned the layout and didn't detect anyone inside. He walked toward the storage containers. They looked familiar. He went to the onboard controls and brought up the status interface. They were CDA storage containers. Inside each of them was an android designed to house a Personality Matrix Construct. There were two of them here. If they had an ESS inside of them, then there were two PMCs here.

Quinton detected a PMC broadcast that seemed to be coming from the other storage container. He walked over to it but didn't acknowledge the broadcast. The contact protocol wasn't one he was familiar with. The storage container lurched forward hard, knocking Quinton several meters back.

"Stay away from it!" a deep voice boomed.

Quinton bounced off the workstation and stumbled to the floor. Before he could regain his feet, something heavy and mechanical bounded toward him, fast. Quinton lifted his rifle. He glimpsed a pair of CDA red robotic eyes in battle mode as it grabbed the end of the rifle and tried to yank it out of Quinton's grasp. He held on as the CDA pulled him off the ground and flung him toward the wall. He spun in the air and his shoulder bore the brunt of the impact.

Quinton regained his feet. "Wait!" he shouted.

The CDA charged. "You can't have them, Agent of Harding!"

Quinton had just enough time to see Becker coming through the doorway, weapon raised. Quinton threw his rifle at the CDA's face and slid forward, tripping the android and scrambling onto its back.

"I'm here to help you, dammit!"

The android spun and pushed himself up, trying to knock Quinton off.

A plasma bolt hit the wall behind them.

"Hey!" Becker shouted. "Either you stop moving, or I start shooting at those storage containers. Which is it gonna be?"

The CDA craned its neck toward Becker and stopped.

"Becker?" said a familiar feminine voice.

Quinton stood up. Two spacers came out from behind the storage container. Both held a hand blaster, but neither of them was aiming at anyone. The leader looked at Becker and then at Quinton. From inside a clear face shield, celestial blue eyes widened in recognition.

"Quinton?"

"Hello, Maelyn."

CHAPTER NINETEEN

THE NERVOUS SHIFTING of Quinton's feet revealed his discomfort as he looked at Maelyn. She lowered her hand blaster and stepped toward him, stabbing him with a poisonous glare full of fury and betrayal. It was the betrayal that Quinton felt in his gut. If he had to choose between a hand blaster and the look in her celestial blue eyes, he'd choose the blaster.

"You're alive," she said, sounding as if she couldn't believe it. Then she glanced at Becker. "You're both alive."

"Guttman and Oscar are fine, too," Quinton said, and her gaze swung back to him.

The second spacer approached and stood next to Maelyn. Quinton recognized Simon as the face shield became translucent.

Simon's eyebrows raced upward, and then he smiled. "Quinton, is that really you?"

Maelyn raised her hand blaster, pointing it directly at Quinton. "That's a good question."

"It *is* me. I realize this is probably a shock to you both," Quinton replied. Maelyn didn't lower the hand blaster, and Simon looked as if he couldn't believe what he was seeing. "I can prove it to you. Simon, you helped me when I was stuck in that agricultural bot from Zeta-Six," he said and looked at Maelyn. "Were you able to find those colony planets from the data repositories on the Endurance Starbase?"

Simon stepped forward and took a good look at Quinton. "I... How did you survive? Where did you...? You look so real, like flesh and blood, but that body must've been destroyed."

Quinton nodded. "It was. My PMC was transferred via subspace into an ESS in this cybernetic avatar."

"You can't trust him," said the CDA that attacked him.

Becker still had him covered with his plasma rifle.

Quinton looked at the CDA. "I think we've gotten off on the wrong foot. I'm Quinton Aldren."

The CDA regarded him. "You could tell me you were Admiral Elias Browning, and I still wouldn't believe you, Agent of Harding."

Quinton frowned and glanced at Maelyn and Simon for a moment. "I don't even know what that is. What's an Agent of Harding?"

The CDA looked at Maelyn. "You said you came here to help me. If you mean that, you'll shoot him. You can't trust anything he says. Agents of Harding are the enemy."

Quinton shook his head and grinned. "She's not going to shoot me," he said and looked at Maelyn. "Right?"

For a few moments, Maelyn appeared as if she was seriously considering it.

"Walsh," Simon said, "this is Quinton Aldren. He's not an agent of anything."

"Walsh," Quinton parroted, quickly exploiting the advantage of a name, "I came here because of the PMC activation signal. I'm actually here to help you. Simon is right; I'm not anyone's agent. How can I prove it to you?"

Walsh regarded him for a few seconds. "PMC authentication. You denied my initial request, but it's the only way. Then you'll know who I am, and I'll know exactly who you are," he said and looked at Maelyn. "Be ready to act."

Quinton was a little bit amused but also annoyed at the same time. Whoever Walsh was, he was deadly serious. Quinton looked at Maelyn. "It's me, Maelyn. Don't shoot me."

She smiled, but it didn't reach her eyes. "Go on, Quinton. Prove it."

Quinton inhaled deeply and sighed.

"Would you look at that!" Simon said excitedly. "You can mimic our behaviors. You didn't need to take that breath. It's a mental stimulus for releasing tension. That's amazing. I'd really like to know more about this avatar."

Quinton smiled a little and then looked at Walsh. "Here it comes." Opening a data comlink to the CDA, he transferred his PMC authentication. PMC authentication protocols drew upon unique identifiers that were encoded into his ESS. They went well beyond a simple data handshake that conveyed credentials. It was something that couldn't be forged. This was to prevent anyone from impersonating another PMC.

Walsh's credentials appeared in his HUD.

Walsh, Corvax, Alari Navy.

Specialization—defense tactical command.

Walsh frowned for a few moments and then stood up straight. "Commander, please accept my apologies. I had no idea that you were a Galactic class PMC of the Acheron Confederacy Navy. I have an update for you, sir, when you're ready to receive it."

Becker snorted and lowered his weapon a little. "Oh my God, not another one."

Maelyn lowered her blaster and returned it to the holster on her hip. "What do you mean 'not another one'?"

"We've encountered another PMC who believes Quinton is his commanding officer."

Maelyn regarded Quinton for a few moments. Her expression gave nothing away beyond the fact that she was furious with him.

Walsh cleared his throat. "Commander, I must insist."

"All right, what have you got to tell me?" Quinton asked.

Walsh gestured to one of the storage containers nearby. "The PMC in this container is of vital importance."

"Who is it?"

"This is Commander Isobe Misako. She's an ACN intelligence officer who has a mission briefing to give us when she's brought back online," Walsh said.

Quinton nodded and gestured toward the other storage container. "And who's in this one?"

"That's Lieutenant Chloe Bradshaw, also in the Alari Navy."

"Are there any more PMCs here?"

"I don't think so. I knew I was going to be stored with Lieutenant Bradshaw and that Commander Misako was going to join us. But that was before..." Walsh stopped and frowned for a moment. "The Federation Wars," he said. "Agents of Harding were everywhere. We are preparing to make a major offensive."

"Were," Quinton said. "The Federation Wars were a long time ago."

"But that's not possible. We were to be part of the vanguard."

"Who's we?" Becker asked.

Walsh looked at him for a moment and then turned back to Quinton.

"Go ahead. It's all right," Quinton said.

"You don't know..." Walsh said. "You don't know about the offensive? You've never heard about the Agents of Harding?"

"I was uploaded before the Federation Wars. I was supposed to serve in Grand Admiral Browning's Freedom Armada for the final assault in the Wildner Sector in the Jordani Federation."

Walsh looked away and considered this for a few moments. "You're one of the early ones. Before the Agents... Before Harding."

"Before Harding did what? And which Harding are we talking about here?" Quinton asked.

"Miles Harding, the original PMC. The one who paved the way for all of us," Walsh said.

"Miles Harding," Becker said. "*The* Miles Harding, the hero of the Federation Wars?"

Walsh turned toward Becker so fast it seemed like his body had simply jerked in one direction. "Harding was no hero," he snarled.

Becker glanced at the others. "Boy, have you got a lot to learn. And you think Browning—"

"Becker!" Maelyn said. "Not now. This isn't the time."

Becker's mouth hung open a little, as if he'd been about to form a word but didn't.

"No, don't stop," Walsh said. "What were you going to say about Admiral Browning?"

"Maelyn's right," Quinton said. "We can sort this out later. This isn't the safest place for us to be right now."

Walsh looked at Quinton and nodded. "Understood, Commander. There's a lot you must be brought up to speed about."

Becker shook his head. "He's not the only one. You really think whatever mission you had all that time ago still applies today? Don't you realize you've been on standby for five or six decades? Whatever your mission was, it's over."

"This is one of the contingency plans. The mission parameters might've changed, but the mission hasn't," Walsh insisted.

Quinton looked at Becker. "Come on. We don't need to do this right here. We can sort this out later." He looked at Maelyn. "We can sort everything out after we're off this outpost. Agreed?"

"Fine," Maelyn said. "We have a shuttle."

"We have a ship in the hangar bay. You sure your shuttle is going to survive the trip? The outpost is barely maintaining its altitude," Quinton said.

Maelyn rolled her eyes and shook her head but didn't respond. Instead, she walked over to Becker. "I need to talk to you," she said and headed for the door. Becker looked at Quinton, shrugged, and then followed her.

Walsh walked over to one of the storage containers and activated the counter grav option from the controls. The storage container began to hover above the ground, and he did the same thing for the other one.

"Are there any unoccupied CDAs here in the outpost?" Quinton asked.

"There should be some spare units, but the computing core is down," Walsh said.

"That was me," Simon said. "I had to take it down because there were hundreds of systems bleeding power. I had to reroute them into other systems or disable them to keep the outpost here. Actually, I was trying to get it to go back to its original orbit but couldn't. The outpost did have an orbit well above the atmosphere before Walsh tried to bring it back online."

Quinton nodded. "Did you also enable the defense turrets in the corridor outside the operations center?"

Simon flinched. "Whoops. I'm sorry about that. We thought the Sentinels might try to board this place."

"The Sentinels send in boarding parties?"

"Sometimes."

What would be the point of that? The Sentinels that Quinton had encountered had simply destroyed their targets. He hadn't thought they were capable of carrying out other kinds of missions.

"You almost got us," Quinton said.

"To be fair, we didn't know you were here, and we didn't know you were alive. Why didn't you contact us?" Simon asked. He'd been about to say "her," meaning Maelyn, but he'd switched it at the last second.

"It's a long story, Simon. It really is. Becker and the others helped me get the ship running, and then it's just been one thing after another," Quinton replied.

Simon regarded him for a few moments. The spacer's boyish looks had thinned out some, giving way to the more mature man he was becoming. Experience had aged him, and Quinton realized he wasn't going to accept such a shallow response.

"Can we talk about this later?"

Simon swallowed hard. "We thought you were dead. That you sacrificed yourself. It was hard on all of us, but it was especially hard on her. She deserved better."

Each of his words was like a concussive blast directed at his chest. He *had* sacrificed himself. At least he'd meant to. He'd thought it was better to just leave well enough alone and everyone could move on.

"Fine, I'm the bad guy," Quinton said. "But what I need now is a CDA unit because we rescued another PMC that's stuck in a spider-drone. Will you help me with that? His name is Nash Harper, and he's on my ship. Remember how it was with me? How hard was it to keep it together? He has access to his memories…most of them, but he's stuck in a damn spider-drone. I'll let you beat up on me for the length of one voyage, but first, we help him. Does that work for you?" Quinton asked bitterly.

Simon brought up his personal holoscreen, and Quinton watched as he accessed the outpost's local computer system. "There's another unit in storage. I can have it sent to the hangar bay where your ship is. You just need to tell me which one."

Quinton transferred the hangar bay's location.

Simon watched the screen for a few moments and then nodded. "It's on its way.

Quinton looked at Walsh. "All right, let's get these guys out of here. I'll help you with the storage containers."

As they guided the containers out of the operations center, Quinton glanced toward Maelyn and Becker speaking quietly by the elevator. Becker looked like he was doing most of the talking.

His avatar had a highly acute auditory system, and he could have listened in on their conversation, but he didn't bother. He could guess what was being said.

Quinton received a comlink request from Oscar.

"Harper asked me to contact you. A Sentinel scout force has entered the system. They're on their way here. I hope you found what you were looking for," Oscar said.

"We did," Quinton said and quickly filled him in. "Tell Harper that we have a CDA unit on its way to the ship. We can begin the transition once we get out of here. We're on our way back."

As they reached the elevator, Maelyn and Becker became quiet.

"Sentinels have entered the system. They're on their way here now," Quinton said and looked at Maelyn. "Where's your shuttle?"

Maelyn looked as if she were about to say something but the elevator doors opened. She walked inside and the rest of them followed.

Quinton positioned himself next to Maelyn. "Are you going to ignore me?"

"No, I'm trying not to shoot you," she replied. Then she moved to the other side of the elevator.

Quinton shook his head and glared at the status window in front of him.

CHAPTER TWENTY

QUINTON'S HEAD tilted to the side. He'd done nothing wrong. Nothing. He resisted the urge to look in Maelyn's direction. She could stare at the elevator doors for as long as she wanted.

Shoot him?

He didn't owe her anything, so why did it feel like he did? He'd delivered on his end of the bargain. The DUC had gotten what they wanted, and he'd been under no obligation to remain in contact.

Focus, dammit, he chided himself. The Sentinels were in the star system. It was only a matter of time before they figured out where the distress beacon had come from, and that would lead them here.

He hadn't been able to contact Maelyn after the battle on the ACN starbase. They'd needed to repair the ship, which had required more time than any of them thought it would. After that, he'd decided to put off contacting her and the DUC. She was jumping to all kinds of conclusions. He shook his head and ignored another spike of irritation.

"Simon," Quinton said.

"Yes?"

"Where is the *Nebulon*?"

Maelyn looked at him. "It's on the other side of the system with the star between the ship and us."

"The plan was for you to recall it when you'd left the outpost?"

"Seemed like a good idea at the time."

"The Sentinels will probably focus their efforts here," Quinton said. But it was understood that it wouldn't be safe for the *Nebulon* to jump anywhere near this area, and they couldn't escape the Sentinels on the shuttle. "You can dock the shuttle with the *Wayfarer*, and we can rendezvous with the *Nebulon* after."

Maelyn didn't have any other options, and they both knew it.

"Unless you've got a better plan," Quinton added.

Maelyn shook her head. "No, I don't," she said and looked at him. "Thank you."

Quinton thought he kept the surprise from his face but couldn't be sure.

"Awkward," Becker snorted. "Couldn't resist."

"Thanks, buddy. Glad to know you always have my back."

Becker tapped the side of his head, giving him a two-finger salute. He glanced at the elevator's destination. "I didn't see a hangar bay at that location."

"There isn't one," Simon said. "It's more of a maintenance bay. The shuttle is small enough to fit inside."

Quinton watched as Becker glanced at the storage containers and Corvax. "You'll be able to fit all this in the shuttle?"

Simon frowned.

"We'll be going with Commander Aldren," Corvax said.

Maelyn looked at him. "You have an open invitation to come with us if you want."

"Thank you for your assistance, but the situation has changed."

"Of course," Maelyn said.

Becker leaned toward Quinton and raised an eyebrow. He nodded a little by way of acknowledgment.

The elevator reached its destination and the doors opened. There was a long corridor beyond, with emergency lighting flickering in some places along the way.

Quinton looked at Corvax. "It might make more sense for us to split up. The key is to get everyone safely out of here, including them," he said, gesturing to the storage containers. "They'll fit on the shuttle, and you can come with Becker and me to the ship. This way, when the Sentinels attack, we'll know they're safe."

Corvax's artificial jade-colored eyes considered this from the metallic chrome-colored alloy of the CDAs head. "Yes, Commander."

Quinton hadn't meant for it to be an order but didn't argue the point. "Let's get them to the shuttle."

They exited the elevator and guided the storage containers down the corridor.

Oscar opened a comlink to Quinton. "The Sentinels took out the recon drone and have just micro-jumped. They're on their way here."

"Understood," Quinton replied and closed the link.

The Sentinels were definitely within weapons range. They quickened the pace. The door to the maintenance bay was still a long way. They should just turn back to the elevator and head to the *Wayfarer*. Maelyn wouldn't like sacrificing the shuttle, but he didn't think she'd be opposed to the idea.

"Hold on. Stop," Quinton said. "We should turn back—" He stopped speaking.

A broadcast appeared on almost all comlink channels seemingly at once. His frame rate increased to maximum, and a cyberattack alert appeared on his HUD. Radek had increased Quinton's frame rate.

"Remote hack attempt buried in the broadcast. The highest probability is that this is of Sentinel origin," Radek said.

To protect himself, Quinton had changed his avatar's communication protocols to route all message traffic through a virtual sandbox. The analysis occurred so fast that there was hardly any kind of discernible latency—certainly not for general commlink-type attempts.

Quinton reviewed the report. The Sentinels were trying to exploit a vulnerability that existed in the mere acknowledgment of an initial comlink request. They were also trying to broadcast on multiple subspace frequencies in order to overwhelm the receiving system in hopes of bypassing standard security protocols. He didn't know what the remote hack would do if it succeeded, and he didn't have time to fully investigate it now, even with his frame rate set to maximum. He initiated a data comlink to the others and uploaded a set of instructions to disallow all outside communications. This would effectively sever existing outside comlinks and prevent new connections from being made.

He received an almost instantaneous response from Corvax. The CDA's communication configuration was to deny all comlink attempts until they were deemed safe and the PMC accepted.

Quinton turned his attention to the storage containers that held the PMCs on standby. They both had active comlinks to the Sentinels. He cursed inwardly and raced to sever their connections. He was able to sever one of them quickly, hopefully before the Sentinels were able to execute whatever payload they'd included in the message.

He was too late for the second one. He knew it. Corvax knew it.

The Sentinels' malicious code was even now running its exploits on the vulnerable PMC in standby. Quinton tried launching a trace to protect the PMC inside, but the Sentinels had gotten their foothold and they wouldn't be dislodged. The PMC was being reactivated and there was nothing he could do to stop it. He tried to think of a solution but couldn't. Any attempt he made to stop the PMC from coming online was overridden. This entire confrontation had occurred at the speed of light, and less than a second had elapsed in normal time.

Quinton grabbed the container before anyone could react. He saw the occupant's name on the status window.

Commander Isobe Misako—Acheron Confederacy Navy Intelligence.

Quinton shoved the container toward the maintenance bay doors where the *Nebulon's* shuttle waited. As the container began its journey, he uploaded new security protocols to the *Wayfarer,* hoping he'd been in time. He couldn't wait for the acknowledgment. As soon as the updated protocols had been delivered, he forced a communication reset for the *Wayfarer's* systems. Oscar would probably freak out, but Harper would be able to explain it to him.

Quinton lowered his frame rate back to normal time. The others were about to look at their wrist computers.

"What have you done?" Corvax asked. He'd taken several steps down the corridor, chasing the container with Misako inside.

"There isn't anything I can do for her. The Sentinels have corrupted the PMC," Quinton said, and sent him Radek's detection report for the remote hack attempt.

Corvax received it and looked at the container. "The mission."

"I know," Quinton said. "We have to go back. We can't go that way."

Simon peered down the corridor. "Wait. What happened? That container is coming online. The PMC is being reactivated."

"I'll explain," Quinton said. "You need to trust me."

He urged them back toward the elevator.

Becker came to his side. "Guttman is back at the ship. The Sentinels are positioning themselves to begin their assault."

No sooner had the words come out of his mouth than the emergency lighting in the corridor dimmed.

"Run!" Quinton shouted.

Corvax pushed the storage container with Bradshaw inside toward the elevator. Simon jumped on top because the CDA could move much faster than they could run. Becker did the same. Quinton scooped Maelyn up and carried her to the elevator.

The floor shook beneath his feet as the Sentinels began their bombardment of the outpost.

CHAPTER TWENTY-ONE

CORVAX PUSHED the container through the elevator doors, and both Becker and Simon leaped off. Quinton and Maelyn were right behind them. He set her down, and the doors closed. Quinton accessed the elevator control system via the local data port and initiated an override of the safety protocols to accelerate the elevator.

The deck numbers flashed overhead while the elevator raced to the upper hangar bay. If he hadn't altered his own security protocols under advice from Radek, he might have been in some serious, irreversible trouble.

Maelyn looked at him with a curious expression. "What happened?"

Quinton had to sever all comlinks from the *Wayfarer* while the communication system reset.

He looked at Maelyn. "What is it about us and elevators?"

She regarded him for a few moments, and then he saw a flicker of recognition in her eyes. Her lips lifted a little, showing hints of a smile.

"The Sentinels attacked us," Quinton said, gesturing toward Corvax and the storage container. Becker held his plasma rifle raised slightly. "Radek detected it, and I was able to stop it before they could do anything."

Becker glanced at Corvax. "What about him?"

"Commander Aldren warned me before the attack came."

Becker frowned. "This is from the increased frame-rate thing."

"It allows him to process information much quicker than we can. His perception of time is orders of magnitude above ours, and probably theirs," Simon said, inclining his head toward Corvax.

Maelyn glanced at the storage container. "What about them?"

"I wasn't fast enough," Quinton replied. "The comlink for PMCs in storage is open to receiving information. I was able to disconnect the comlink sessions for Bradshaw, but by the time I got to Isobe Misako, it was too late."

"Couldn't you reverse whatever the Sentinels did to her?" Simon asked.

"Not without corrupting the PMC," Quinton said.

The elevator slowed down a few moments before it stopped at the deck with access to the upper hangar bay. He'd had to tweak the artificial gravity field so the rapid stop didn't slam them all through the metallic ceiling.

"Comms are still down on the ship," Becker said. He looked away for a moment. "I've got Guttman. I let him know we're on our way. He says there's a problem with the reset you did."

Several loud pops sounded progressively closer to their position, and Quinton accessed the recon drones Harper had deployed. He could see the Sentinel ships through the atmosphere of the gas giant. Particle beams penetrated through the atmosphere and sloughed through the outpost's armor. The pops came from rapid decompression as the particle beams penetrated the armor. The beams were heading toward them. Either the Sentinels had guessed where they were, or they were just luckier than everyone else.

The emergency lighting dimmed, and station-wide alerts boomed from overhead. *Unable to maintain orbital locations. Main engine failure for units twelve through eighteen. Outpost will reach crush depth in fifteen minutes. Abandon the outpost. Proceed to the nearest escape pod or egress point for transport. Abandon the outpost.*

The announcement ended as they ran out of the elevator and down the short corridor that led to the hangar bay.

"Simon," Quinton said and gestured inside the deck officer's office. He turned to the rest of them. "Go on. We'll be right there."

Simon joined him in the office. Corvax headed to the ship, guiding the storage container. Maelyn and Becker waited outside the office.

"Doesn't this outpost have any weapons?" Becker asked.

"No, decommissioned outposts don't have weapons on standby," Quinton said and gestured for Simon to go to the workstation. "Did the CDA unit make it to the hangar bay?"

Simon accessed the workstation. "Yes, it's waiting for pickup. It's on the far side of the bay," he said and stood up.

"Not so fast," Quinton said. He heard more pops coming from below the elevator. They were fainter, as if smaller. "You took the computing core offline. Did you leave yourself a way to bring it back?"

Simon frowned. "I can, but we need to get out of here."

"We can't leave yet. If we do, the ship won't last long," Quinton said.

Becker looked down the corridor and cocked his head to the side. "Do you hear something?"

Quinton walked toward the doorway and listened. Then he looked at Simon. "Can you set up remote access to that workstation?"

Simon nodded.

"Good, do it and head to the ship."

A sound of metal being torn apart came from the elevator. The lights flickered inside and the doors closed.

Quinton lifted his plasma rifle and stood next to Becker.

"What do you want me to do?" Simon asked.

"Divert power to the remaining engines. Overload them. We need to get all the thrust we can to break through the atmosphere," Quinton said.

Something slammed the elevator doors, causing them to bend outward, straining against the metallic frame.

"Holy shit," Becker said and backed up.

They backed down the corridor and into the hangar bay. The elevator doors burst open, bending outward as a CDA forced its way through. Crimson eyes gleamed through the flickering amber lighting. It was the CDA that housed Commander Isobe Misako of ACN Intelligence, except it wasn't her anymore. She meant to kill them. The Sentinels must have corrupted her PMC and were controlling her. It was either that or she was one of those Agents of Harding Corvax had accused Quinton of being.

Quinton fired his rifle and Becker did the same. Maelyn and Simon ran toward the ship.

The CDA leaped up, scrambling along the ceiling before dropping back to the ground. Then it bounced from one side of the corridor to the other while propelling itself forward. It moved so quickly that they couldn't get a clear shot.

"Go!" Quinton shouted and increased his frame rate. This wasn't a fight Becker could survive.

Quinton darted to the side and fired his weapon, anticipating where the CDA would go next. Radek enabled a multitude of combat VIs, all with sapient combat simulations active. Misako must have had hers engaged, which was why she'd been able to dodge the rapid fire of their weapons.

Misako tried to alter course as she received the glancing blow of a plasma bolt from Quinton's rifle. The damage only blackened the metallic alloy of the CDA's protective and apparently armored skin. The standard Consciousness Driven Android that Quinton had been trained to use wasn't a battle-bot. It had been designed to give the PMC a sensory experience akin to that of their original human body. At some point during the Federation Wars, this had changed.

A violent shudder went through the outpost's floors and the walls, as if the entire structure was experiencing extreme turbulence. Sudden rises and drops made fighting the CDA all but impossible. The others should have reached the ship by now. All Quinton had to do was make it there so they could leave.

Quinton turned and ran out of the corridor. Misako would be close behind him. The floor pushed upward at a nearly constant rate, causing him to lose his balance temporarily.

"Need more time before the ship can safely leave the outpost," Radek said.

Simon had been able to divert power to the engines, and they were pushing the outpost upward. If Quinton went inside the *Wayfarer* now, leaving Misako outside, she could cause more damage and possibly disable the ship altogether.

Quinton veered off course, running away from the ship. He either needed to keep the CDA busy while the outpost reached a safe altitude for the ship's escape, or he needed to stop it for good. What if he could disable it? Misako must still be inside the CDA. She must be fighting against what the Sentinels had done.

Quinton came to a stop and turned around, initiating a comlink broadcast to the CDA like he'd done with Corvax earlier. He included his PMC authentication and identity. Corvax had responded to the fact that Quinton was a Galactic-Class PMC with command authority.

Misako stopped coming toward him. The red gleam of the CDA's machine eyes seemed to take on more of a human-like cast to them. It was working. Misako must be fighting back.

"Commander Misako, what is your mission?" Quinton asked.

He stepped cautiously toward her.

Misako's gaze jerked toward him. "Stop the spread!"

The CDA lunged toward him, knocking the barrel of the plasma rifle to the side as Quinton fired. She shoved him backward and Quinton flew through the air. He landed near the atmosphere shield, coming dangerously close to the crushing depths of the gas giant's atmosphere beyond. The shield could only contain the atmosphere. Ships and any other objects, including him, could go through the weak shield with almost no resistance at all.

Quinton looked at his plasma rifle. The barrel was bent, and the status window showed a great big failure message. He hastened away from the shield.

Misako hadn't spoken to him; that was the Sentinels. He'd communicated with them before. The CDA slowly approached him, as if each step was a struggle.

"Commander," Misako said. "I can't stop them."

A data comlink to the CDA became available and Quinton uploaded his own VIs to help fight the Sentinel hack. He tried to think of something else he could do. He'd been able to counter the Sentinels that had infiltrated the starbase's computer systems, but he'd gradually lost control, and it appeared that Misako was losing the same battle.

The CDA lunged toward him, but the attack was slow and the movements were off, as if the inner battle with the Sentinel was spilling over into the physical struggle. Quinton easily blocked the movement but stepped back.

The data comlink disconnected and Misako grunted with effort, as if she were trying to lift something heavy. Quinton stood there, unsure how to help, but a dark knowledge was growing inside him that insisted he knew what he had to do. He couldn't bring Misako on the ship. She was lost to them. The Sentinels had taken her away, and yet he couldn't make himself leave. He didn't know Isobe Misako, but her authentication confirmed that she'd been in the Acheron Confederacy Navy.

Misako stepped toward the shield in short, jerky movements. She wasn't trying to survive anymore. She was trying to die. She knew she was lost and didn't want to be an instrument of the Sentinels.

A bright flash raced past the area outside the shield. The Sentinel scout ships had resumed their bombardment. Quinton gritted his teeth and glared upward where the Sentinel ships waited. He couldn't stop them. Not like this. Not here.

"Commander," Misako said. She was right at the shield. Her arms flailed as if she'd lost control of them. "Polaris Op," she muttered and then lunged through the shield.

Quinton saw the CDA fall away, and he screamed with the primal defiance that came when facing predators. He calculated the rate of her fall and tried to imagine the last moments she'd feel as the gas giant's crushing gravity squeezed the CDA with the PMC inside.

He flung his broken rifle through the shield, then turned around and ran toward the rear loading ramp of the ship. More bright flashes from the Sentinel's bombardment lit up the hangar bay. They were targeting the last location where their agent had been.

Quinton ran up the loading ramp, and it started closing as he reached the top. He headed for the bridge.

"Oscar," Quinton said, "take us out on my mark." He'd reconnected to the ship's computer system and used the ship's sensors to detect the Sentinel attack pattern. "Now!"

The ship's engines engaged, and Oscar flew them out of the hangar bay. He maintained altitude while the outpost continued to ascend and then flew away while the Sentinels continued to bombard the outpost. They hadn't detected them. Once the outpost breached the gas giant's atmosphere, the Sentinels would destroy it, if they hadn't managed to do it before, and that was the *Wayfarer's* narrow window of opportunity to escape.

There was no minimum safe distance because they couldn't

keep the ship inside the gas giant's atmosphere. The Sentinels might not detect when they left the atmosphere, but they would almost certainly detect the jump.

The others on the bridge were quiet, which was both sobering and appreciated.

"Breach the atmosphere and execute emergency micro-jump," Quinton said.

"Aye, aye," Oscar replied.

The *Wayfarer* increased its altitude amid the gas giant's atmosphere, and tumultuous storms were beginning to tax the inertia compensators. Their power core had to balance the need between the jump drive charging and the increased velocity.

The ship emerged from the gas giant's atmosphere, and Oscar increased their velocity, accelerating their distance from the planet. Then he executed the micro-jump that took them away from the planet, the Sentinels, and the ghosts of the past.

Quinton uploaded a second set of coordinates into the navigation computer. He looked at Maelyn. "Send these to Kieva. She'll be able to meet us there."

Quinton remembered the *Nebulon's* capabilities. It would take them a little bit of time to catch up with them, but at least the Sentinels wouldn't be anywhere near them when it did.

Once Maelyn had sent the message to the *Nebulon*, Oscar executed the first in a series of jumps.

Maelyn walked to Quinton. "I need to speak to you."

"And I need to check on my ship," he said and began to walk away from her.

"Captain's Privilege," Maelyn said.

Quinton came to a halt and glanced around the bridge. Becker, Oscar, Guttman, and Simon looked at him. They expected him to comply. Captain's Privilege was a practice of cooperation among ship captains in this post-Federation War galactic society. He was expected to have a private meeting with the visiting ship captain while they agreed on an acceptable outcome. It was meant to be a civilized negotiation, but he suspected Maelyn had something else in mind. She was still angry that he hadn't contacted her or the DUC after the destruction of the starbase, but he was thinking of Misako and how the Sentinels had infiltrated and corrupted the PMC. If he hadn't acted so quickly, they might have overwhelmed all of them. He'd been in a fight like that before, and it was like slowly suffocating while the world closed in around you.

Quinton looked at Maelyn. "Fine then. Follow me," he said and left the bridge.

CHAPTER TWENTY-TWO

QUINTON ENTERED the ready-room that was just off the bridge. He hardly ever came into this room. There was a clear ceraphome desk with a small half-dome holoscreen projector on the left side. He walked around the desk and glanced at the charcoal-colored couch on the far side of the room. Two lounge chairs with gray memory foam were positioned across from the couch. There was an empty coffee mug on the desk. Becker used the office occasionally and must have left it.

Maelyn followed him inside and closed the door.

He was inside the ship's systems and quickly read through the most critical of alerts. Repair bots were already at work patching the hull. The damage was from the previous encounter with the Sentinels while they destroyed another space station. The life-support systems were in need of attention, particularly the atmospheric scrubbers. The cartridges needed to be replaced. He thought he'd asked Harper to take care of that. Quinton couldn't misremember anything. Becker had been right about that. However, he could ignore certain things. He'd need to find out why Harper hadn't performed one of his assigned duties. The spider-drone was on its way to the rear cargo hold. No doubt that

Harper was excited to be transferred into the CDA from the outpost.

"Quinton," Maelyn said softly, and he looked at her.

He hadn't forgotten how beautiful she was. He couldn't forget the curve of her magnificent jawline as it met her neck and then down to a set of collar bones that he'd sometimes imagined kissing. He'd first seen her through the optics of an old agricultural robot and then from the video feeds of the *Nebulon* and on the ACN Starbase Endurance, which included the last comlink where he thought he was about to die. Quinton wasn't sure what it was about the shape of her eyes, her mouth, the soft skin of her cheekbones and the adorable dimple that presented itself when she laughed. He was well past the time in his life when the attention of a beautiful woman made him stammer incoherently, but he'd been powerfully attracted to her. Maelyn was athletic, with a woman's curves that his cybernetic optics drank in the sight of, whether he wanted them to or not. On the starbase, he'd tried to imagine what it would have been like to see her with his own eyes in a freshly regrown body based on his DNA. He'd memorized every curvature of her body and the natural curl to her long, thick, chestnut hair. His smell receptors reported the familiar chemical breakdown of the floral scent of her preferred soap. Quinton could ignore his memories but not forget them, and seeing Maelyn in her pale flight suit that hugged her curves reignited all that attraction.

The sophistication of the mapped consciousness into a PMC was such that it included things beyond behavioral patterns. Quinton wasn't a scientist, but he knew what he felt, even without the biological chemistry that would have been present if he'd been in his own body. He didn't know how it worked. Perhaps it was a function or interpretation of his VI assistants to help him retain his humanity. He wasn't sure, and it probably didn't matter.

Maelyn's eyes took in the sight of him, and her biometrics

showed a slightly elevated temperature from her lips and face, even her hands. This could be because she was angry with him or hurt by the fact that he hadn't contacted her. Quinton could access a plethora of biometric data, but none of it could tell him what she was thinking.

"Can we sit down?" she asked.

Quinton gestured toward the seat on the opposite side of the desk.

She glanced at the seat but then shook her head. "I was thinking over here," she said and walked over to the couch near the wall.

Quinton walked around the desk and sat in the plush chair near the couch. "How does…" he began. He'd been about to ask how this was supposed to work, but that wouldn't have gone over well. He shook his head a little. "I know you want to talk, but now might not be a great time."

One of Maelyn's eyebrows twitched up a little, but her expression was guarded. "The ship is safe. Oscar is piloting through the set of jump coordinates you gave him. Becker and Guttman are going to check on critical systems. Simon is probably helping them as much as he can. So, I ask you, why put this off?"

This was his ship, and he wanted to do it himself. He looked away from her. "I don't know. It could be that there are three PMCs aboard my ship, and I really need to talk to them. There would have been a fourth, but she got infiltrated by the Sentinels." Quinton sighed and swallowed hard, lifting his gaze toward her. "And there's you."

She leaned forward a little. "We'll get to that. What happened to Commander Misako?" she asked.

Quinton gritted his teeth. "I didn't get to her in time," he said and told her how the Sentinels had successfully initiated a remote hack that gave them access to Misako's ESS, which led to the corruption of the PMC residing there.

Maelyn pursed her lips for a few moments. "So, your security measures saved not only your own life, but the lives of three more people. Not to mention that you protected the rest of us when they attacked, but you're full of fury because there was one casualty instead of five, including a PMC you'd already rescued before," she said and waited for a few moments. "You need to cut yourself a little bit of slack, Quinton."

Quinton's eyes went skyward. "When you put it like that, it sounds… heroic. I was so close to stopping it. With this avatar and my frame rate so high, I should have been able to prevent it."

Maelyn shook her head. "God, you're so arrogant."

Quinton frowned. "What?"

"Arrogant! Your ego is as big as an entire star system. Would you listen to yourself? You didn't even know the Sentinels could do this. No one knew they had this ability, and yet here you are beating yourself up about it. I'm calling rubbish on the whole damn thing. Misako's death is tragic, and I'm not making light of that, but the fact remains, Quinton, you aren't perfect. You just don't like—"

"To lose," Quinton finished. His lips lifted a little. He wasn't sure which was more frustrating, the fact that she'd just thrown his own words at him or that she was right. Dammit, she was right. "I understand what you're saying. I do. But the Sentinels…"

"They're the real enemy."

"Misako was an intelligence officer, you know. She had a mission briefing she was going to deliver. She had answers."

"I know. I was there when Corvax told you."

He'd been close to getting some answers. Was there a mission or a purpose for PMCs being reactivated? He'd been prepared to just let go of those questions, but knowing he'd been about to get some answers gave rise to a molten frustration deep inside him— frustration that was tied to the reality that everything he'd known was gone. He wanted to make the Sentinels pay for that and much more. And now, Lennix Crowe using some form of Quinton's identity to lure them into becoming his own personal strike force meant that Quinton couldn't just walk away.

He stood up. "I need to speak with Corvax. He might know more about the Federation Wars and Admiral Browning. Maybe he can shed some light on this whole mess. I know I sure as hell can't."

He took a few steps toward the door.

"Why didn't you contact me?" Maelyn asked.

Quinton stopped with his hand stretched toward the door controls.

"After the battle. You survived. Why didn't you meet me at the waypoint coordinates? We waited for Becker and the others, too. We waited a long time," she said.

The way she said "we" was synonymous with the word "I." She'd waited there. She'd waited for him.

Quinton turned toward her. "The ship wasn't as space worthy as we thought. Becker, Guttman, and Oscar helped me repair it. In exchange, I was going to help them get a ship of their own."

Maelyn stood up. "Was the communication system malfunctioning?"

Quinton regarded her for a few moments. "Maelyn," he began.

"Don't," she snapped. "Answer the question."

"I intended to contact you, but I knew you thought I was dead, and so did the rest of the DUC. I started thinking that maybe contacting you wasn't the smartest thing to do."

Maelyn glared at him. "The smartest!" she snarled. "The smartest... Are you...What kind of idiotic, flawed logic led you to that? I really want to know."

"You got what you wanted—colony worlds for the DUC to start settling, rebuilding and all that, including whatever tech you managed to get off the starbase before the attack."

Maelyn closed the distance between them. "You're unbelievable. You think that the only reason I helped you was to get access to the Acheron Confederacy's secret colony worlds project? Did you forget the fact that I got as close as possible to disobeying orders from the DUC admiralty to help you? Did you forget that part? I convinced Admiral Brandt that it was worth helping you not only so I could help the DUC, but to help you, you idiot. I stayed at the waypoint for weeks, hoping that maybe you'd found a way off that damn starbase. Then I spent months trying to find other PMCs who might have been reactivated and lost in a galaxy they didn't understand. PMCs like you."

Quinton's thoughts flatlined. Her words seemed to strike him with tiny molten bolts of plasma. Individually, they didn't kill, but together they knocked him off his proverbial feet. He'd really stepped in it. She'd been something he'd really needed at the time, and he'd rewarded her friendship with nothing. It was worse than that. He'd abandoned her. "I didn't know you did that," he said. "You thought I was dead, right?"

"I did, but I also thought that maybe... maybe you'd found a way to escape."

Quinton opened himself up to a star system full of second-guessing the decisions he'd made since first waking up on the *Wayfarer*. Every path had led him to this moment—him feeling like an idiot for hurting someone who cared for him.

Great job, Quinton, he said sarcastically to himself.

He kept trying to think of a way to make it up to her. Simon was right. Maelyn deserved better, and he should have known that. As he looked at her, he realized there wasn't anything he could say that would undo any of it.

"I'm sorry," he said. "I'm really sorry."

The edges of Maelyn's lips tugged downward in a grim, hurtful line.

All the reasons he'd used to convince himself that not contacting Maelyn was the right decision were shallow and worthless. He could hear his father's words echoing from a life-time ago: *Quinton, when you're right, you're right, but when you're wrong, admit it. Be man enough to admit it, and you'll be a better man for it.*

Quinton exhaled deeply. "You're right, Maelyn. I should have contacted you and let you know I was alive. What I've done is inexcusable. I promise to return you to your ship, and after that, you can do whatever you want."

Maelyn's tongue quickly glided over her lips, and her head tilted to the side. Her celestial blue eyes stabbed him in the chest. "You avoided me because you thought that once I found out you were alive, I'd try to get you to do something else for the DUC."

Quinton frowned, feeling like he was about to be ambushed, but there was no avoiding it. Sometimes he had to just take his blows as they came, and this was no different. "Yeah, I did. Am I wrong?"

Maelyn looked away, disappointed. "No, I would have tried. And you could have said no if I had."

That stung him. She was right to be furious with him. Hell, he was furious with himself. He was better than this. Now he just felt like a coward, which he wasn't. He'd made a mistake, and he wouldn't repeat it.

"What else do you want me to say? I said I was sorry. I meant it. I'll take you to your ship and then you don't even have to see me again."

Maelyn shook her head. "It's not that simple."

Some foolish part of his brain came up with the idea that making a stupid little joke in an attempt to deflect from the situation would be good, but he banished that idea to a black hole in his mind that he set aside for his truly awful ideas, never to be heard from again.

"Okay," Quinton said. "Do you want to sit back down?"

"No!"

Quinton flinched a little. "Okay then."

Maelyn gritted her teeth and balled her hands into fists. "You're such a jerk." She used an angry tone, but there was also a hint of something close to amusement in spite of her fury. It was a long way from forgiveness, but it was something.

"I am," he agreed. "I'd let you use a palm stunner on me, but I don't think it'll have an effect—"

Everything else Quinton had been about to say he couldn't because he'd dropped to the ground. He couldn't move his arms or legs. Multiple alerts snapped to existence on his HUD, demanding his attention.

Maelyn smiled sweetly and squatted down next to him. Something silver flashed in her hands, and she regarded him for a few moments, appraisingly. "Did that hurt?"

He hadn't felt pain, but the cybernetic avatar did register the disruption of the molecular bonds that made his cybernetic musculature work. There wasn't any damage, other than to his pride because he was helpless. He felt like he was floating in a pool, but he couldn't move.

Maelyn waved the palm-sized disruptor in front of him. "I wasn't sure it was going to work on you."

She adjusted the disruptor field and he could move his head.

Quinton grinned bitterly. "All right, now that you've had your fun, turn it off."

Maelyn pursed her lips in thought, and her eyes flashed playfully. "Oh dear, I don't know if I can. This is so much fun. Maybe I'll just keep the field engaged while I go take a walk."

"You wouldn't—Maelyn!" Quinton shouted as she headed for the door.

He quickly disabled the door controls, locking her into the room with him.

Maelyn spun around and grinned, enjoying this a little too much. She glanced at the door, and he thought she was deciding whether to leave him or not. He'd disabled the door controls, but he was also sure she could figure out a way to override them.

"You deserve much more punishment than this," she said.

Quinton glared at her, but it had no venom in it. "Maybe a

little more, but let's not get away from ourselves here. You've had your fun. Now turn off the disruptor field."

Maelyn sashayed over to the couch, sat down, and crossed her legs, looking at him with indifference.

"What more do you want? I already said I was sorry," he said. "You know, being trapped on this ship with Becker, Guttman, and Oscar was no picnic. Most of the time, they're complaining. It never ends. They're worse than a bunch of first-year cadets on training rotation. If I could have exchanged them for you, I would have. I know it was wrong now."

Maelyn's lips twitched, this time in a good way. Maybe she'd even forgive him... eventually. As the minutes dragged by, he began to wonder how long she was going to keep him like this. He wasn't going to ask.

Maelyn nodded to herself. "Now we can negotiate."

"Negotiate?"

"You owe me," she replied.

Quinton chuckled. "And you say *I'm* unbelievable. I'm not negotiating anything until you turn off that disruptor."

Maelyn considered this for a few moments. "You should consider installing a ship-wide suppression system like I have on the *Nebulon*. It would have prevented something like this from happening."

"Maybe you can give me the name of a few reputable installers who can be trusted to upgrade my ship."

Maelyn nodded again and then turned off the disruptor field. The alerts on Quinton's HUD vanished as the avatar's cybernetic musculature returned to normal. He stood up and eyed her warily. Then he sat down.

"I didn't see that coming."

"I know," she replied and just looked at him for a moment. "Let's set the personal stuff aside for now."

"Okay." Quinton nodded.

"You're aware of the increased Sentinel activity throughout occupied sectors of the galaxy?"

"We knew they'd become more active, but it's because of Lennix Crowe and the Union's conflict with the Collective."

"That's part of it, but it's getting worse. Sentinels are targeting places that have nothing to do with the Collective."

"Why?"

"I haven't received an update about what DUC intelligence has uncovered in their investigation."

"Is this an incursion?" Quinton asked and then quickly added, "Becker told me about them."

Maelyn ran her fingers through her hair, brushing it away from her face. "It could be the beginning of one, yes."

"The only way I can think of how Crowe got my identification was from the Sentinel code he used to take over Endurance Starbase. It lured the Sentinels there. He must have figured out a way to make it work, then came up with a deployment protocol to use against the Collective."

"He must have had help."

Quinton frowned. "You mean from outside his organization?"

Maelyn nodded.

"So he hired someone or forced someone to figure it out. Does it really matter how?"

"Yes, it does. If we can figure out who helped Crowe, then we can also figure out a way to reverse what's been done."

"We've been working on stopping Crowe," Quinton said and told her about the specially crafted message he had spreading through galactic communications channels.

"Crowe wouldn't want an incursion to happen."

"I wouldn't be so sure about that. We hunted for a Jordani battle group that was wreaking havoc across inhabited star systems. They were commanded by a real brutal bastard. He'd conduct raids among civilian ship traffic using them as shields, knowing full well that our ROE prevented us from engaging them."

"How did you stop them?"

"The civilian ship captains used their ships as weapons. They flew them into the Jordani warships, freeing us to engage. The point I'm trying to make is that sometimes the person leading doesn't care about the damage they're doing. Crowe might have reached his limit."

"Or he might be in over his head. What was a tactical advantage is now out of his control."

"Maybe," Quinton said. "He still needs to be stopped."

"Take a look at these intelligence reports gathered over the past few months. There has been increased Sentinel activity and also PMC activation signals," Maelyn said. She activated her personal holoscreen and a galactic star map appeared. "These icons are where Crowe used the Sentinels to target Collective installations. Now I'm adding in the other star systems where the Sentinels also attacked." Quinton watched as more star systems were highlighted, and they were equal to the number of systems Crowe had attacked. That couldn't be a coincidence. "Now, here are the reported sightings of Sentinel scout ships throughout the region, and keep in mind that these are only the ones we know about."

The star map updated again, showing vastly more sightings of Sentinel ships.

"I take it that this is more than what's normally reported?"

Maelyn nodded. "They're hunting for PMCs."

"I don't suppose you've found a way to log activation signals."

Maelyn chuckled. "Funny you should ask." The star map updated again with dozens of signals. "There's a clear correlation between increased Sentinel presence and an increase in PMC activation signals."

Quinton peered at the data on the holoscreen. He had Radek

conduct his own analysis, which also concluded the high probability that these activities were interrelated.

"Do you see the correlation?"

Quinton nodded. "A correlation exists, but we still don't
know what it means."

"They're in response to one another."

"How?"

"The Sentinels have always searched for PMCs and the
remnant tech associated with them. Their activity increased after
Crowe started using them as a weapon."

"Right, so if we stop Crowe, then the Sentinels should stop."

"What about the activation signals? Something triggers them
in response to the increased Sentinel presence."

"What if it's just the Sentinels triggering the activation
signals?" Quinton said. "As a way of exposing people like me."

"If that were the case, the Sentinels would be present wherever the activation signals go, and that's not happening."

"Have you been able to trace the activation signals?" Quinton
asked.

"Some, but not to the source. We've been trying to beat the
Sentinels to the locations in hopes of rescuing the PMCs before
they're killed."

"And."

"It's complicated," she said.

"Complicated?"

"Yes, it wasn't just danger from the Sentinels that we had to
be concerned about. We didn't know if the PMCs being reactivated were stable. The Alari Outpost was the closest we'd gotten.
It was touch and go even before you showed up. Corvax was a bit
on edge when we arrived."

Quinton remembered how disorienting it was when he'd
been reactivated. "What is it you want from me?"

"Something is triggering the reactivation signals after decades
of silence. Don't you want to know who or what it is?"

"I'm more interested in stopping Crowe."

"That might be harder than you think."

"I'll find him, and I can guarantee you that he won't enjoy the experience."

"Quinton, spaceports, stations, refueling depots, colonies and the like are all closed off to you. You can't go to any of them."

He looked at her and frowned. She was serious. "I'm pretty sure I can provide the local authorities or governing bodies a set of credentials that they won't second-guess."

Maelyn shook her head. "I'm sure you can, but your ship is unlike anything that's registered. That's something you won't be able to fake. They're not allowing anything that doesn't match up in their data repositories to come anywhere near a docking port. Security forces and measures are in full operation. I've seen them fire on ships to prevent them from reaching them. No one wants to give the Sentinels a reason to destroy what's left."

"We'll have to agree to disagree on that."

"Come back to the DUC. You can help us track the PMC activation signals."

"No," he replied.

"That's it? No, 'I'll think about it?' Just, no?"

"Yes," he said and held up his hands in a placating gesture. "Hear me out and stop fingering the disruptor. You're making me uncomfortable."

Maelyn interlaced her fingers and rested them on her lap.

"I volunteered for the PMC program to protect the Acheron Confederacy, to help Admiral Browning defeat the Jordani Federation and its allies. Now you think that because I woke up years after those battles have been decided I should just take up another cause and fight for that? That's what you're asking me to do."

He regarded Maelyn for a few moments and she nodded.

"Yes," she said.

"I don't want to. In fact, I'm choosing not to. Wait a second," he said as she was about to interrupt. "I just want out of this. The galaxy wants people like me gone, and looking at the aftermath of the Federation Wars, I'm a little inclined to agree with them. If I could help the others get out of this and back into a human body, then that would be all right with me."

Maelyn inhaled and sighed. Then she stood up. "You've made your point."

Quinton stood up. He was a little surprised that she wasn't belaboring the point.

"You said you wanted to talk to Corvax. Let's go do that. Do you mind if I come along?" she asked.

Quinton eyed her suspiciously, and she looked innocently back at him. Why did it feel like she'd given in too easily?

"Fine with me," he said, and they left the room.

THE *WAYFARER'S* entry to both the armory and the workshop was located in the cargo area, where the weapons were stowed and locked in their cabinets. The workshop walls were lined with storage cabinets and two metallic tables for equipment maintenance and repair. The workshop, like most of the ship, sported pale, sleek lines with burnished copper accents.

Quinton slid down the ladder between decks and saw Walsh Corvax standing near the CDA storage container, which hovered several feet off the floor. The CDA looked more robotic than Quinton's avatar, as if it was a much earlier model. The chassis was humanoid in appearance and roughly the average size of a human. Corvax's CDA had a masculine physical appearance, but the exterior was chrome-colored with green accents. Quinton wasn't sure if the accent colors were a user preference or not.

Corvax looked at him, and his optics glowed a brilliant green. The CDA was a similar model to that which Quinton had expected to be reactivated in.

"Your ship is quite impressive. I knew the ACN loved their ship designs, but this star class jumper has capabilities beyond anything we had in the Alari Navy," Corvax said appreciatively.

Corvax's entire demeanor had changed after they'd authenticated with each other and he'd learned that Quinton was a Galactic class PMC.

Quinton was about to reply to Corvax when shouting erupted from the other side of the cargo area.

"What do you mean it's not here!" Harper shouted.

"It didn't make it to the ship; otherwise, it would have been in the hold," Guttman replied.

Quinton hastened past a row of cargo containers.

"You did this on purpose," Harper said with a scowl. The spider-drone's legs tapped the ground in irritation.

"I didn't sabotage the delivery. The cargo never even made it to the hold. You better back off," Guttman growled.

Quinton saw Guttman glaring at Harper. Several of the spider-drone's legs shook, as if they were getting conflicting signals from Harper.

"Harper," Quinton said, "what happened?"

The spider-drone was poised like a coiled spring, ready to explode.

Guttman looked at Quinton. "He's barely keeping it together."

"There was a CDA for Harper that made it to the hangar," Quinton said.

Guttman nodded but kept an eye on Harper. "I know. That's what I'm trying to tell him. It never made it to the ship."

Quinton winced inwardly. Damage from the Sentinel bombardment must have prevented the cargo drones from bringing it to the ship. There had been so much happening at the time that Quinton hadn't checked before they left.

"Harper, it's not his fault," Quinton said.

Harper didn't respond. He didn't move at all, which Quinton found more disturbing than if he'd begun shouting.

Becker and Simon came into the cargo area.

"What's going on?" Becker asked.

Quinton stepped toward Harper. "It's not his fault," he said.

Guttman exhaled explosively. "This is bullshit! I don't have to stand here and take this from him. I'm getting out of here," he said and stomped his way past Harper.

Quinton heard a faint muttering coming from Harper. It was so soft that he doubted anyone else could hear it.

"Yes, it is. Yes, it is. Yes. It. Is," Harper said in a harsh whisper.

Quinton opened a comlink to Harper, but it was refused. Harper had closed himself off.

"Harper," Quinton said softly. "Are you still with me? We'll find you another body."

"I had a body," Harper replied, finally. He turned around slowly, and the spider-drone's optics seemed to regard the others.

Quinton turned toward the others. "Give us a minute."

Maelyn corralled the others into the workshop. He heard Corvax say that the integrity check of Chloe Bradshaw's PMC was nearly complete.

Harper looked at Quinton and said, "I should have gone out and retrieved the CDA myself."

"You were doing what I asked you to do—monitoring the Sentinels and making sure the ship was ready to leave," Quinton replied.

"I could have done it. I should have."

"No, you couldn't have."

"Why! Is it because you don't trust me either?"

Quinton drew himself up. "You're not giving me much of a reason to. Now knock it off."

Harper didn't reply.

"First thing," Quinton said, "no one is trying to prevent you from getting a body. Guttman may be… well, he's Guttman. He may not like you, but he's not out to get you. Is that understood?"

Harper remained silent.

"Is that understood, Lieutenant?"

"The ACN doesn't exist. Remember? I'm not a lieutenant anymore," Harper replied.

Quinton watched the spider-drone very carefully. Dissociative disorder was a prevailing cause for PMC failure. It led to insanity.

"All right," Quinton said.

The spider-drone's optic bobbed up and down as it regarded Quinton. "It's just Nash. No, I'm just Nash Harper. Quinton, I don't think I can stay in this drone much longer."

Quinton knew what it was like to hold on to your sanity by your fingertips. If Harper lost it, then it wouldn't matter if Quinton forced him into standby because Harper would be gone.

"I promise I'll get you a replacement. The next place we're going to will be a station that will have something for you, even if I have to steal it. I just need you to keep it together. Can you do that?"

Harper was silent for a few long moments. "I believe you. I think it might be better if I go into a long-duration rest cycle. The ship's VR helps, but it's not perfect."

"I understand," Quinton said. "Just stay away from Guttman for a while, okay?"

He watched as the spider-drone left the cargo area. He felt helpless. He should have made sure that the unoccupied CDA had made it to the damn ship. After he'd gotten confirmation that it had reached the hangar bay… The attack.

He heard the others speaking in the workshop and joined them.

Another CDA stood in the room. The exterior chassis had adjusted to being more feminine. Artificial azure eyes shifted toward him. A PMC authentication comlink registered with

Quinton, and he acknowledged it. There was a brief exchange of data to confirm their identities.

"Commander Aldren," she said.

"It's just Quinton."

"Negative, Commander. I can't do that," Bradshaw replied.

"This isn't… Never mind. We'll bring you up to speed."

Bradshaw looked at Corvax, and her metallic lips lifted in wry amusement. "You really thought he was an Agent of Harding?" she said and shook her head a little. She turned back to Quinton. "I've been brought up to speed, sir. Walsh filled me in."

Quinton glanced at Corvax for a second. "She just woke up."

"Yes," Corvax said, understanding. "As part of the PMC integrity check, I uploaded what I'd learned so Bradshaw could hit the ground running."

Quinton glanced at Maelyn, Becker, and Simon.

"It's knowledge-sharing. In short increments, it's safe."

"What about larger increments?" Becker asked.

"Not safe," Corvax explained. "There is a high risk of corruption with mergence protocols."

Quinton frowned. "That's news to me."

Corvax looked at Bradshaw. "He predates the Federation Wars."

Bradshaw nodded. "Oh, I see," she said and looked at Quinton. "Mergence protocol was expected of you, right?"

"In my training, it was encouraged, but Radek just informed me that those protocols had been disabled by the time I was reactivated."

"That must have been Admiral Browning's work then," Corvax said.

"What makes you say that?" Quinton asked.

"Because if you were an Agent of Harding, we'd all be dead."

Becker cleared his throat. "Now, wait a second. You said this before about Harding being the enemy. Are you talking about *the* Miles Harding?"

"Are there any others?" Corvax replied.

Simon glanced at Maelyn, and she gave him a nod. "Miles Harding created PMC technology. He was the first PMC ever."

Becker nodded. "Yeah, if my galactic history is right, Harding was pivotal to the ACN defeating the Jordani Federation."

"That is true," Corvax said.

Becker looked at Quinton with raised eyebrows.

"Why do I get the feeling that our whole world is about to get turned upside down," Quinton said and looked at Corvax and Bradshaw. "As far as I'm concerned, everyone in this room has clearance to whatever information you're going to share."

Corvax looked at Bradshaw. "You might be better at this than I am."

Bradshaw nodded. "Works for me. It's really quite simple. Everything you think you know about the Federation Wars is wrong."

Quinton watched as the others exchanged pointed looks. Maelyn looked the least surprised. He'd long suspected that there was significant misinformation about the Federation Wars. Maybe Maelyn believed the same.

"This is crazy," Becker said. "You've only just gotten here. We're the ones who've lived here. We know more about what happened in the Federation Wars than you."

Bradshaw grinned. "That's where you're wrong. Walsh and I were there at the beginning of the Federation Wars, although they didn't call it that at the time." She gave them an appraising look. "First of all, thank you, Simon, for providing Corvax and me with your historical records. They'll really help us make this easier for you."

Becker looked at Simon. "When did you do that?"

"Just a few minutes ago," Simon replied.

Becker looked at Quinton.

"They can do the same things I can," Quinton said. "They

adjusted their frame rates to give themselves time to review the data."

"That's only partially correct, sir," Bradshaw said. "But we'll get to that. Your history tells you that Admiral Browning went rogue and took all his followers—about a dozen fleets under his command—and began attacking the other federations, coalitions, empires, what have you. He was credited with the most egregious war crimes ever committed. I'm here to tell you that this is all a lie. Browning didn't do those things. He tried to stop them from happening." Becker opened his mouth to say something, and Bradshaw gestured for him to be quiet. "The massacres and attacks on civilian targets, colony worlds, and military installations *did* happen. But they were because of Harding. Miles Harding Prime, to be exact."

Becker shook his head. "You're wrong. There were PMC lockdown protocols that would have kept Harding from doing those things."

"There were. He figured out a way to break free of them," Bradshaw replied. "And this is where it gets a little unclear. We think—or Browning's intelligence apparatus thinks—that the mergence protocol that allowed PMCs to build up the intelligence and experiences of other PMCs is what led Harding Prime to betray the ACN and every other galactic civilization."

"Harding went insane?" Quinton asked.

Bradshaw shook her head. "That's the thing. We don't know. All those attacks that Admiral Browning was accused of were orchestrated by Miles Harding. We tried to stop them. We succeeded in the beginning, but that's when Harding got creative. He was too methodical to be insane." Bradshaw paused for a moment, considering her words. "He's different."

"You've encountered Miles Harding?" Simon asked.

"Yes, and no," Bradshaw replied. "I'm an operations officer and logistics are my specialty. PMCs who came into contact with

Harding's forces had to be isolated, but I never came into direct contact with Harding."

"They were compromised," Quinton said and frowned. "Harding could infiltrate other PMCs! That means that he could've... Did he create the Sentinels?"

Becker's mouth hung halfway between denial and indignation.

"That's where we're unclear. Harding may have had a hand in their creation, but he didn't need to be actively involved. He might have provided remaining federation navies with the tools to create them."

"You don't know for sure," Maelyn said.

Bradshaw shook her head.

Maelyn pursed her lips. "If the galaxy was already uniting against Admiral Browning, there was no way he could defeat Harding."

"Harding had somehow spread himself among the other federations," Bradshaw said. "They were eager to get their hands on PMC technology. It was a huge tactical advantage. We can compartmentalize ourselves to function in any computer system. Warship weapons systems became much more efficient with PMCs than they had been with virtual intelligences alone."

"He gave it away to everyone and they lined up to get it," Quinton said bitterly. "But he also included a way for him to take control later on." He looked at the others. "Browning must have seen it first. The Federation Wars were some kind of elaborate plan of Harding's."

"He tried to warn them," Corvax said. "In the beginning, he tried to warn the ACN and then anyone who would listen."

"But he was discredited and chased away because he couldn't stop it," Simon said. His eyes were wide.

Becker grunted. "You all sound like conspiracy theorist nut jobs. This is crazy. Why would Harding do any of this?"

"He's got a point," Quinton said. "Did Browning figure out Harding's motivation?"

"I don't know," Bradshaw said.

"Me either," Corvax replied. "That's why Commander Isobe Misako was crucial to our mission."

"Who?" Becker asked.

"The CDA that attacked us," Corvax said. "Communications had become impossible to secure, so we'd started using PMCs to carry mission briefings for combat operations, but Misako was different."

"How?" Quinton asked.

"Because…" Corvax began but paused, thinking. "Browning had come up with a way to stop Harding. I think it has to do with you."

Quinton blinked several times. "Me?"

"Him?" Becker asked almost at the same time.

Maelyn nodded. "You predate the Federation Wars, Quinton. You're a Galactic Class PMC. As I recall, you weren't sure what that was, so it must have come after you were uploaded."

"I didn't know. That wasn't part of my training."

Becker looked at him and narrowed his gaze. "It sounds like *they* don't know either," he said, gesturing toward the two CDAs.

"We'd know more if Misako had survived," Bradshaw said and looked at Quinton. "But you do have command authority, sir."

"Because of his rank?" Becker asked.

"That, too, but also because of the type of PMC he is," Bradshaw said.

All of them looked at Quinton. "There are quite a few assumptions being tossed around."

"There are also a lot of good points. It makes sense," Maelyn said.

"Just because we like an explanation doesn't make it right," Quinton replied.

Becker's shoulders slumped a little and he sighed. "I'm glad you're at least questioning this."

"I'm gonna need some time to think about it."

"No, you don't," Maelyn said. "Increase your frame rate. Have Radek run his analysis and you'll see that there are a lot of kernels of truth."

Quinton frowned. She was right... again. It was beginning to be a habit. "I'll get to that, but first, Harper needs a body."

"Quinton," Maelyn said and stepped closer to him. "You're meant to command them. Browning had a plan. You're part of it. It all makes sense."

"Yeah, a dead man had a plan to continue fighting a war that ended long ago," Quinton said. "I'm not saying there wasn't a plan, but that doesn't mean I have to drop everything and take up his cause."

Maelyn opened her mouth to reply but then pressed her lips together. "What are you going to do then?"

"I'm going to help Harper. We have a list of space stations in the Sector that will have what we need. That's first. Then Crowe has to be stopped," Quinton said.

Maelyn rolled her eyes, and Quinton could guess what she was about to say. He couldn't dock at any spaceports because they're afraid of a Sentinel attack. But he'd failed to help Harper before, and he wasn't going to ignore him because of what they'd just learned.

"We'll dock with the *Nebulon* in a few hours," Quinton said and left the workshop.

No one followed him.

This was his ship. If they didn't approve of where he was going to fly it, they could leave.

CHAPTER TWENTY-THREE

It was easy to get lost in the vastness of the galaxy, which was why Quinton wasn't too concerned that they'd been tracked. With most of the passengers gathered near the portside airlock, the bridge of the *Wayfarer* wasn't as crowded as it had been a few moments ago.

The *Nebulon* was about to dock with his ship, and Quinton resisted the urge to look over at navigation. Oscar wouldn't be sitting there. Becker, Guttman, and Oscar were all going to the *Nebulon*. He didn't know what Maelyn had offered them, but it wasn't too hard to guess.

"The *Nebulon* has docked," Bradshaw said.

Quinton stood up. "I'm going to see them off. Corvax, you have the conn."

"Aye, Commander. I have the conn," Corvax confirmed.

Quinton left the bridge and headed toward the portside airlock. He could hear the others talking from all the way down the corridor.

"You can't be serious," Guttman said. "You still have that creature aboard ship?"

"Yeah, you're going to be bunkmates," Simon replied and grinned.

"Like hell we are. What was its name again… Thing?"

"Stumpy."

"That's right. It's got gimpy little legs. If it comes near me, I'm going introduce it to the wrong end of my blaster."

"That would be unwise," Simon said.

"Yeah, right," Guttman replied.

"No, seriously. Captain Wayborn made Stumpy an official member of the crew. You're just visiting, so…"

"Official member of the crew?" Guttman said. "Is that true, Captain?"

"Quite true," Quinton heard Maelyn reply.

He'd forgotten about the furry little creature that had hitched a ride with him. He was glad Simon had kept him.

"Come on, you're joking with me."

"Nope," Simon said. "His official title is pest control. He scampers all over the ship."

"I'm still not bunking with that creature."

"I'm sure it wouldn't be able to stand the smell," Becker said.

Oscar stepped into the corridor. "Quinton," he said.

"Are you ready to go?" Quinton asked, hoping Oscar wouldn't reveal that he'd been listening to their conversation.

"Just about. Listen, I wanted to talk to you."

"Don't worry about it, Oscar. You stayed when it counted, and you don't owe me anything."

Oscar eyed him for a few moments, then nodded. Without another word, he headed back inside.

Quinton followed him in and looked at the others. They were gathered around the airlock doors. They all looked at him. Simon appeared as if he had something to tell him but couldn't seem to pick the right moment. Guttman kept checking his gear and the same pockets a few times, then gave Quinton a nod. Becker regarded him, as did Maelyn.

Quinton sighed at the awkwardness. "I guess I lost all the kids in the divorce."

The airlock doors opened and Kieva stood on the *Nebulon* side. She was short, blonde, and cute. "Hello, *spacer*," she said approvingly.

Guttman frowned. "You know this is Quinton."

Kieva's lips lifted. "Oh, I know," she said. "You're cleared to come aboard."

"Thank you, Kieva," Maelyn said.

Kieva gave her a two-fingered salute, waved to Quinton, and started to head back through the airlock.

"It's a shame we didn't have more time," Quinton said.

Kieva's laugh echoed down the corridor.

Quinton looked at the men who'd been his companions for the past few months.

Guttman's face became serious. "Be careful."

"One step ahead. Right?"

Guttman nodded. Then he went onto the *Nebulon*.

"Quinton," Simon said, "I made a navigation update available to the *Wayfarer*. You'll need to acknowledge it."

"Thanks, Simon."

Simon nodded and went back to his ship.

Becker walked over to him. "Are you sure about this?"

"Harper needs help. This is something I have to do," Quinton said. Becker nodded. "But if I hear about any ships for sale, I'll send you a message."

Becker shook his head. "If it's up for sale, it's probably not worth flying."

"That's right. You want to find the ones that are about to come on the market."

Quinton watched him for a second, then looked at Maelyn. "So, this is it."

Maelyn regarded him. "For now."

"If I learn anything that could be useful to you, I'll reach out. I promise," Quinton said. It was all he could do. She thought he was making a mistake, and he saw the resignation in her gaze.

"I would welcome it, Captain Aldren," Maelyn said.

Quinton smiled. "Safe travels, Captain Wayborn."

She walked through the airlock and Quinton watched as she secured the *Nebulon's* airlock. She looked at him through the small window. Then, the *Nebulon's* docking clamps released and the two ships separated.

Quinton walked back toward the bridge but stopped at the galley. All the food and supplies had been stored away, and the galley looked abandoned. He'd spent hours in here with the others. It was their meeting place.

As he watched the *Nebulon,* he wondered if he was making a mistake. But he wasn't second-guessing himself—at least not completely.

The door to the bridge opened.

"Ready to execute jump, Commander," Corvax said.

Quinton walked to the captain's chair and sat down. "Very well. Take us away."

MAELYN WALKED AWAY from the airlock where Becker was waiting for her.

"What do you think he'll do?" Becker asked.

"Exactly what he said he'd do," she replied.

Guttman let out a long sigh of relief and smiled. "Thank you, Captain. I don't think I could have taken being on a ship with a crew of PMCs for much longer."

Maelyn looked at him with a surprised expression.

"Quinton is fine," Guttman said quickly. "It's the others. Especially Harper. There's no saving that one."

"Indeed. We'll see."

Becker looked at her and frowned. "I can't figure out what you're doing."

Maelyn smirked. "You could just ask."

"I think I just did."

"You can follow me to the bridge," she said.

Guttman left them, heading toward the crews' quarters.

"Now, don't be like that," Becker said, speaking to Oscar.

Maelyn raised her eyebrows, and Oscar shrugged. "It still doesn't feel right. We're abandoning him."

Maelyn nodded. "Oh, I see."

"I get why you're mad at him, but he's—"

"Going to do exactly as he thinks best," Maelyn said. They reached the bridge, and she looked at Oscar. "For what it's worth, getting you guys off that ship is probably for the best."

"Why?" Oscar asked.

"Because Quinton has a black hole's worth of stubbornness. Once he's made up his mind, there's no convincing him to do anything else."

"He's just trying to do the right thing for Harper."

Maelyn nodded. "I know," she said gently. "I understand why he's doing it."

"But it's not what you want him to do," Becker said.

Maelyn shook her head. "It's not what you think. I'm going to show you what I shared with Quinton."

"This has to do with increased Sentinel activity," Becker said.

"And the PMC activation signals," Maelyn confirmed. "I don't think it's the last we'll see of Quinton. He's stubborn, determined, and sometimes irritating, but he's a good man. Sometimes even the best of us have to learn things for ourselves. The sooner he realizes he's pursuing the wrong goal, the better off he'll be."

"The wrong goal," Becker said and frowned. "You mean Lennix Crowe?"

Maelyn nodded. "Crowe might be part of all this, but he's not the real problem."

"Who is?"

"I don't know."

"Then what are you going to do?"

"We're going to look for PMC activation signals," Maelyn replied sweetly. "Don't look so alarmed. It'll all make sense soon."

Becker snorted. "Guttman is going to flip out. He's gonna lose it when he hears what I think we're going to be doing." He leaned back on the nearby workstation and gestured toward the main holoscreen.

Oscar crossed his arms and did the same.

Maelyn had hoped she could convince Quinton to go with her. She never expected to see him again. She'd thought he'd died on that starbase, and seeing him on that outpost, alive, and in some kind of prototype body... She gritted her teeth. He seemed genuinely sorry. Regardless of her own feelings, they all needed Quinton. She just hoped he learned it quickly enough that the real players of the Federation Wars didn't catch up with him first.

Becker held up his hand. "I'll get Guttman up here. He's going to want to hear this, too."

Maelyn nodded. "All right, gentlemen. Get ready to blow the airlock doors wide open."

CHAPTER TWENTY-FOUR

TERACOM INDUSTRIAL SPACEPORT was just under five astronomical units from the *Wayfarer*.

"They're firing on us," Harper said.

"Warning shots only," Corvax replied.

Quinton activated the comlink. "Captain Alina, I thought we were going to be friends."

A squadron of Conda scout ships on patrol had swooped to their location almost as soon as they'd jumped into the system.

"Transfer your ship registration and your credentials immediately, or I'll order my squad to fire on your ship," Captain Alina replied in a no-nonsense, trigger-happy voice.

"I have a firing solution," Harper offered.

"Negative," Quinton replied.

"Have it your way then, Captain," Captain Alina said.

Quinton hadn't muted the comlink when he'd replied to Harper. "Wait a second. I wasn't talking to you. I'm sending our registration and credentials to you now."

"Hold your position," Alina said.

Quinton muted the comlink.

"Sir," Corvax said, "we're within range of the Conda's frag-cannons."

Frag-cannons were capable of firing three-round bursts, which could penetrate the armored hull.

Quinton looked at the tactical plot on the main holoscreen. The squadron of Conda Fighters had staggered their approach. They were agile and could get up to speed quickly.

The comlink went active again.

"Star class jumper *Wayfarer*," Captain Alina said. "Your ship is unregistered with any of the common ship registries in the sector. Teracom Industrial Spaceport is closed to you. You will leave this area immediately, or we will destroy your ship."

"Captain," Quinton said, "as I already included in the data I sent you, this is a prototype ship that we salvaged from wreckage on an outpost. That's why it's not on any of your registries."

"Oh, is that all?" Captain Alina said mockingly. "Well, why didn't you say so?"

"Captain, I can tell that you're a formidable woman. We'll leave immediately as ordered, but is there anyone who could deliver what we need?"

The comlink went dark.

"Weapons systems are powering up on all of them. I have point defense systems on standby," Corvax said.

Quinton cursed. This was the fourth spaceport they'd been to and the receptions had all been similar. Spaceport security was operating at the highest severity.

"I have a firing solution," Harper said.

"I already said no," Quinton snapped.

He engaged maneuvering thrusters and throttled up the mains, and the ship quickly increased its distance from the Conda Space Fighters.

"We could have made a run for the spaceport," Harper said. "We could have slipped past their defenses. There's no way they can secure every docking platform."

They'd already tried to gain access to four other spaceports. They'd even come close to reaching a docking platform with two of them. Maelyn was right. The spaceports in this sector were in tight lockdown.

"We can't take out civilian security forces," Corvax replied.

"I was just going to disable their ships. They can survive on life support until a repair ship arrives," Harper replied.

"The moment we fired on them, they would have alerted the spaceport and the rest of their security forces," Quinton said.

He watched the tactical plot. The Condas hadn't left. They were making sure the *Wayfarer* departed the area, so he engaged the jump drive and did just that.

"We could try raiding a warehouse facility," Harper said. "I could reprogram a few drones to break in and retrieve what we need."

Quinton looked at him. "We don't have drones that can do that. Warehouse facilities are huge. We wouldn't know where to look even if we were able to get inside one. We tried scouting before and were detected."

"So, we're giving up?"

"No," Quinton replied. "Never, but I don't want to keep doing the same thing and failing. That's just a waste of time."

A message indicator appeared on Quinton's personal holo-screen. He frowned. They hadn't received any comlink requests, but the message had made it through his own security measures, so he knew it was safe. He opened it, and a recorded message from Simon came to prominence.

"Simon," Quinton said quietly. He put the recorded video up on the main holoscreen. "I just got this. I don't know what it is, but I think all of you should see it too."

"Quinton," Simon said, "I put this message on a conditional subroutine to be presented after the ship made a certain number of jumps," he paused and lifted the edges of his lips a little. "I know you're determined to help Harper get a more suitable host for his PMC. Sounds familiar, doesn't it? Anyway, I wanted to give you another option. I've cleared this with Maelyn, and chances are you might have already thought of this. But, just in case you haven't, I'm hoping you'll carefully consider what I'm about to say." He paused again as if wanting to give them a moment to take in what he'd said. "Okay, here it is. We—or Maelyn, that is—have copies of your DNA data and also the entire DNA archive from Endurance Starbase. It was one of the first things we transferred when... Well, you know when. Harper's or even the others' DNA might all be in there. It's an option if you want to pursue it. That's all I wanted you to know."

The video recording ended and the screen became dark.

"I see what he did. How he stored the message," Bradshaw said. "Quite clever, actually."

"Simon is one of the good ones," Quinton said.

"They have copies of our DNA?" Harper asked.

"Mine for sure," Quinton said and smiled a little. He leaned back in his chair and shook his head a little.

"What are you smiling about?" Harper asked.

"Because sometimes people know you better than you give them credit for," Quinton replied. "Never mind. We have a choice to make."

"Why didn't they just tell us about it then? Why wait?" Harper asked.

"Also," Corvax added, "what good is having the DNA data if they don't have the means to grow the body?"

"They can't do it on the *Nebulon,* but the DUC has the resources for it. Simon wouldn't have sent this if they didn't have the transference protocols to offload our PMCs," Quinton replied.

"I still don't see how this helps," Harper said.

"Really? You don't?" Quinton asked and paused for a moment, giving Harper time to consider it. Harper didn't reply, so Quinton continued. "Because, if they have your DNA on record, we can safely get you out of the spider-drone. If they don't, they have mine. I can offload this avatar and you can use it."

The spider-drone's optics regarded him. "You'd do that?"

"Of course. That's what I was going to do anyway, but I was hoping to do it without help from the DUC."

"You can't do that, sir," Corvax said, and Bradshaw echoed the same. "You're a Galactic class PMC. Admiral Browning must have had plans for you. If you give that up, we might not be able to find another."

"Maybe he did, but there might not be any other option."

"He's right," Harper said. "I can't let you do that."

Quinton regarded his new crew for a few moments. "It might not even be an issue."

"It's not, because I'm not going to let you do that," Harper said.

Quinton glanced at the others. Sometimes a CDA's facial expressions could be so deadpanned that they might as well not exist. He thought he saw some kind of understanding pass between them that Quinton could only suspect, and he certainly didn't like where this was going.

"Fine, let's move on, but before we do, there's something I need to show you guys," Quinton said.

He showed them the Sentinel tracker data Maelyn had given him.

"Where did the data come from?" Corvax asked.

"Dholeren United Coalition. The DUC. They have an extensive network of ships and contacts."

"That makes sense since they're a nomadic civilian space fleet," Bradshaw said.

"Multiple fleets, outposts, and hopefully a few colonies by now," Quinton said.

"This data is old," Corvax said. "Without more current updates, all we're seeing is that these Sentinels exist. Albeit, there are more of them now than before."

Quinton nodded. "And these new data points are from PMC activation signals."

"This is what we should be focused on," Corvax said.

"Could this be Polaris?" Quinton asked.

"Maybe," Bradshaw replied. "We can't be sure, but if Misako told it to you, then it must be important."

"I was thinking the same thing, but it could also just be the Sentinels trying to trap us," Quinton said.

Corvax cleared his throat. "Commander, if you're looking for our input on what we should do next, then mine is that we pursue these activation signals. One of them could lead us to the source."

"I agree with Walsh," Bradshaw said. "Browning had a plan. We should trust it."

"They're right, Quinton," Harper said. "This is more important than finding me a better host."

Each time Harper used the ship's VR during a rest cycle it performed a PMC integrity check. Quinton had added this command without Harper being any the wiser. Since he'd first rescued Harper, there had been a steady decrease in the stability of his PMC. The VR helped slow it down, but the trend was going in the wrong direction. Harper didn't have a whole lot of time before the damage was irreversible.

"There could be more Galactic class PMCs. I can't be the only one," Quinton said.

The others remained quiet.

"Don't you think so?"

Bradshaw nodded. "Of course. Browning wouldn't have hinged a way to defeat Harding on so slim a chance."

"True," Corvax said. "But we can't know that until we find

out what's triggering the PMCs. Wherever the activation signals occur, these Sentinels aren't far behind."

"That can't be a coincidence," Quinton agreed. "We can't do this on our own. We're going to need help."

The others agreed, and Quinton sent a subspace comlink to the *Nebulon*.

CHAPTER TWENTY-FIVE

THE MAIN HOLOSCREEN showed a video comlink of the bridge on the *Nebulon*. The *Wayfarer* had just emerged at the waypoint. Quinton looked at Maelyn.

"Captain Wayborn," he greeted.

"Commander Aldren," she replied, choosing to use his ACN rank in acknowledgment that he was more than just an independent ship captain.

Becker stood nearby Maelyn and tossed a nod his way. Oscar waved, and Guttman was sitting next to Kieva.

Quinton looked at Simon. "I got your message. Top marks. We all agreed."

Simon tilted his head to the side a little by way of acknowledgment. "I had help."

Quinton's gaze flicked back to Maelyn. "You were right."

Maelyn raised a dark eyebrow, and the hint of a dimple appeared next to one of her delicate cheekbones. "About what?"

Quinton chuckled and leaned forward. "You already know. We had a hell of a time trying to reach any spaceports in the sector. I'll save the details for another time."

"I'll look forward to it," Maelyn replied.

He just bet she would. "Do you have the DNA data?"

"I do."

"Is Harper listed in it?"

"I don't know, and I can't search for it. The data isn't aboard the ship."

One of the spider-drone's legs began tapping the floor, but Harper remained quiet.

"Time is an issue here, Maelyn. If we have to negotiate with the DUC for access to the data…"

Maelyn shook her head. "No, it won't come to that. I promise you. They have their own copy, and I have *my* own."

That was as much of a confirmation as he was likely to get from her, but it was enough. Maelyn wouldn't lie to him. "I trust you," he said.

Her lips lifted and her eyes gleamed. "Thank you, Quinton."

The spider-drone's leg stopped tapping the floor.

"I've shown the others the Sentinel tracking data and the PMC activation signals that've been reported or detected by the DUC," Quinton said. "Can you send us updates for it? If we're going to track the PMC activation signals, I'd like to target a system farthest away from Sentinel activity."

"Of course," Maelyn said. "We've been working on this. Simon can give you an update."

A data burst was added to the comlink channel and Quinton authorized it.

Simon stood up. "We've been trying to track the activation signal since the starbase attack. The signals occur more frequently than ever before, but the pattern seems to be random. We think this is by design," he paused and glanced at the others. "I'm just going to say that this is Admiral Browning's design instead of referring to it as something else. If this is incorrect, then I'll adjust accordingly." Simon turned back to the holoscreen. "So, the activation signal is random, at least by our analysis, but I think yours might be different."

"We tried this before," Quinton said, "the first time around."

"We didn't really pursue it before," Maelyn said. "The coordinates for the starbase came from you."

"Let's not get sidetracked," Simon said. "Time is of the essence, right? Okay, here's my theory, but I'll need you—all of you—to confirm it. I think the pattern of the activation signals also contains coordinates for finding the source."

"How would that work?" Guttman asked.

"The pattern itself contains an encoded message that they can decipher," Simon replied, gesturing toward Quinton and the others.

"I think the Sentinels would be able to figure this out," Becker said.

Quinton considered it and agreed with Becker.

"I know what you think," Simon said to Becker. "I want to know what *they* think."

Becker didn't reply.

"What do you think of Simon's theory?" Maelyn asked.

"I hate to say it because it's Becker, but I have to agree with him," Quinton replied.

"Knowing a pattern exists is a lot different than understanding what it means," Corvax said.

"I agree with Walsh," Bradshaw said.

"If the Sentinels had already figured it out, none of us would be here," Harper said.

Quinton chuckled softly. "This is what I get for making snap judgments. You all make good points. All right, let's have a look at what you've got, Simon."

"Great," Simon replied. "The data is time-lapsed, so you can try and see the pattern."

"No need. Just send all of it. Radek and the other VIs will take that into consideration," Quinton said.

A new data link became available. Quinton routed it into the *Wayfarer*'s computer systems and gave access to Corvax, Bradshaw, and Harper. Then Quinton increased his frame rate and began an analysis of the PMC activation signals. First, he focused on where they appeared on a galactic star map. The pattern was random and completely unpredictable. He then shifted his attention to the frequency of the signals as they were detected.

"Some of the signals are reactionary," Bradshaw said.

"I see it, too. Filter those out," Corvax added.

Quinton created a filter that ignored PMC activation signals that occurred after an initial signal was detected. Radek presented multiple iterations of data subsets because some of them filtered out so much information that there was nothing left.

The reaction from the other PMCs was almost immediate. The advantage of PMCs was their ability to create predictive algorithms that had any number of applications. There was a pattern to the PMC activation signals. Each of the PMCs aboard the *Wayfarer* contributed to the refinement of the filter until they couldn't break it down any further. Quinton saw the beginnings of it first, but then the others added their own interpretations.

Quinton and the others returned their frame rates back to normal time. Less than a minute had passed.

"Simon, you're a genius," Quinton said. "There *is* a pattern that contains information for us to find the source."

"That was fast. Are you sure you've got it?" Becker asked.

Quinton nodded. "It was a team effort. We all contributed to it. I think that might have been a requirement."

"There were also a great many false activation signals," Corvax said.

"Yeah, someone is triggering them," Quinton replied. "There's a strong correlation between those and Sentinel activity."

"Are the Sentinels capable of doing this or not?" Maelyn asked.

"I don't think so," Quinton replied. "They only respond after the signal is triggered. If they could do this on their own, there would be no length of time between the activation signal and when the Sentinels showed up to investigate."

"That makes sense," Maelyn replied.

"So how do we find the source of the activation signals?" Becker asked.

"It's complicated," Quinton said and looked at Maelyn. "Captain Wayborn, is your jump drive charged?" he asked and sent a set of coordinates to the *Nebulon*.

"Of course," she replied.

"Wait a second," Becker said. "We're just going? No discussion?"

Maelyn looked at Quinton.

"Trust should work both ways," Quinton said.

Maelyn gave him a slight nod. "It does."

"Good. I have a request."

"What do you need?"

"I need a pilot. Do you happen to have an extra?" Quinton asked and looked at Oscar. "I need your help."

"That won't be necessary, Oscar," Maelyn said before Oscar could answer.

"It's fine. I'll go back over there," Oscar said.

"I'll take care it," Maelyn replied. Quinton looked at her and frowned. "I'll be coming to your ship, along with Simon. Becker can help Kieva look after the *Nebulon*."

Quinton wasn't sure what to say. "If you're sure, then welcome aboard."

Becker stared at Maelyn for a few moments. "*I'll* go with Oscar back aboard the *Wayfarer*. We already know the ship. You should stay here."

Quinton hadn't anticipated any of this. He just needed a backup pilot in case he was preoccupied with something else. "He's got a point."

Maelyn smiled. "That he does. We'll do it your way, Becker."

Quinton had to hand it to Maelyn. She certainly knew how

to motivate people to do exactly what she needed them to do. They shared a knowing look as he watched Becker and Oscar leave the bridge.

Quinton looked at Simon. "Next time."

The young spacer nodded. "I'm picking my moment."

Once Becker and Oscar were back aboard the *Wayfarer*, Quinton executed a jump to a nearby star system. The binary star system was uninhabited and showed no signs of anyone having ever been there.

The pattern Quinton and the others had deciphered showed them how to find where the PMC activation signal was going to occur next.

"Nothing detected on the scanners," Corvax said.

"Understood," Quinton replied. "Starting broadcast."

Quinton accessed the ship's comms systems and initiated a data comlink broadcast. A challenge protocol presented itself, and authentication codes contained within Quinton's ESS responded with the proper authentication codes. This back and forth went on for almost a full minute before he was granted access.

Confirm PMC identity.

Commander Quinton Aldren, G-Class.

Acheron Confederacy Navy, SP.

Quinton increased his frame rate, and multiple data windows appeared on his HUD.

"I'm accessing the comms drone," Quinton said.

PMC conditions have been met.

Access granted.

Data update available.

Provide Activation Code.

Quinton sent over the data he had for his own activation, then received the following reply.

Multimode authentication required. Provide additional activation codes to proceed.

Quinton requested the data from Corvax, Bradshaw, and

Harper. All three replied with the data and Quinton sent it to the comms drone. The comlink interface showed him that the comms drone had been recently constructed, so this wasn't some remnant tech left over from the Federation Wars that was simply being reactivated.

Multimode authentication granted.

Stand by for updated configuration.

Quinton had put the data session on the main holoscreen, which was also mirrored on the *Nebulon* so the others could see what was happening.

Polaris Operation authorized.

Salvation initialized.

A set of coordinates appeared in the data session, along with a thirty-six-hour countdown timer.

The comms drone then began broadcasting a series of subspace comlinks, and a few moments later these were acknowledged by the other comms drones. Then the comms drone went offline.

Quinton returned his frame rate to normal. "I think it initiated a self-destruct protocol. I'm not able to reach it."

"What happens in thirty-six hours?" Becker asked.

Quinton reviewed the data upload he'd received from the comms drone. "It's the Polaris Operation," he said and looked at Corvax and Bradshaw. "We have to get to those coordinates."

"What's there?" Maelyn asked.

"I think I just triggered the broadcast of PMC activation signals everywhere. In thirty-six hours, it'll spread to enough drones that they'll begin broadcasting at the same time."

The drone hadn't self-destructed. It simply wouldn't accept another comlink from him.

Becker leaned forward. "Are you sure? Why would Browning do that?"

"It's a recall for PMCs," Quinton said and updated the star map on the main holoscreen. "This is a tracker for the subspace signal that came from that comms drone. See the spread? It's contacted all comms drones in range. Then the process repeats. We have to stop this."

"Why?" Corvax asked.

"Because if all those PMCs come online at once, this will cause another Sentinel incursion. They'll be slaughtered before they can be recalled."

"What's at those coordinates?" Becker asked.

"Hopefully, a way to stop the broadcast," Quinton said. "I've uploaded the coordinates to the nav computer. You should be receiving them now."

"Confirmed," Maelyn replied. "Synchronized on your mark."

"Execute," Quinton said.

The two ships initiated a space jump at precisely the same time.

CHAPTER TWENTY-SIX

ADMEN DESHER SAT in the command chair on the bridge of the stealth star-class jumper. The CDA he occupied was perfectly still. His specialized protocols had negated the micro habits that maintained the illusion that he was human. The comlink session to the comms drone linked to Browning's Polaris Operation had just been authorized. He was rarely in the same star system that the hyper-jump-capable comms drones traveled to. They never stayed anywhere for long, and in the mere months since he'd been reactivated, neither had he.

Admen had been triggering PMC activation signals from these drones since he'd been brought back online. He glanced over the storage container full of spent leuridium ESS cores of the PMCs he'd questioned. They hadn't known anything. Browning had kept all his PMCs ignorant of his plans. If there was a PMC in his vicinity, he'd retrieve it, but things were seldom that convenient. If any of the Sentinels found a PMC worth pursuing, he'd be informed.

Admen knew his own activation hadn't been the product of some random occurrence. Browning's Polaris Operation had begun to be initialized with the destruction of an ACN starbase brought back online by a Galactic class PMC. All of Admen's own predictive algorithms put him on a direct intercept course with the G-class PMC known as Quinton Aldren. None of the records that he had access to contained any information about that PMC. He was outside of Admiral Browning's last known command structure. Admen wondered how many of the PMCs Browning had scattered across the galaxy had been detached from his original fighting force. Admen was as likely to find a PMC created from Browning's original command as he was to find a completely new one, and he'd spent quite a bit of time considering how it had been done. Browning must have found a way to modify PMCs under his command, and they'd been altered so they couldn't be traced by the Prime.

The comms drone received a massive subspace broadcast. If Admen hadn't infiltrated the drone's systems, he'd never have detected the occurrence. Dozens of realizations stemmed from that one data session. He stopped his own scheduled broadcast to allow the comms drone to carry out its own protocols initiated by the broadcast it had received.

Polaris Operation authorized.

Salvation initialized.

The comms drone prepared a new data broadcast and Admen copied it. Within the broadcast were a set of coordinates. His predictive algorithms indicated the highest probability that these actions were by Browning's design. Admen carried a subset of the Prime's VIs that authorized him to investigate these coordinates. His alpha priorities were updated.

The ship's scanner detected several gamma bursts as warships entered the system. Admen had their ship signatures on file. Tactical alerts came to prominence as his own scans reported the active weapons statuses of the Union warships.

Admen had anticipated the chance that he'd encounter Union

warships. They were hunting for him. He'd used Crowe's Union to help trigger Sentinel activity throughout the galaxy. He could have engaged his jump drive and escaped, but there was an opportunity being presented to him, and he wasn't going to let it slip through his fingers.

CHAPTER TWENTY-SEVEN

QUINTON HAD EXPECTED the jump coordinates they'd received from the comms drone to lead them to some far-off star system on the fringe of the galaxy. Instead, it was the opposite. They traveled along one of the spiral arms of the galaxy that led them to a much more volatile and dangerous region of space. These star systems weren't inhabited by anyone because galactic expansion hadn't exhausted the most habitable star systems. The great diaspora led to the creation of multiple federations, star unions, imperiums, and just about any other words where a group of people settled into the galactic sectors of known space. There was still room to grow, and there were plenty of mysteries left to discover in the galaxy.

Quinton had limited the range of his ship's jump drive so that the *Nebulon* could stay with them. They were under a time constraint, but they would arrive well before the countdown timer for Polaris expired. The *Nebulon's* jump drive had an impressive range, but because the damage to the *Wayfarer* from their encounters with the Sentinels limited their effective jump range, it brought the disparity of capabilities between the two ships to something they could work with. They had tens of thousands of light-years to cross and very little time to do it.

Another reason for traveling across the deep dark with another ship was to displace the risk of solitary traveling. They were pushing both ships hard to cross the vast distance to the source of PMC activation signals. Data communications via subspace could cover much greater distances quicker than any starship could travel, and Quinton thought the initial thirty-six-hour countdown hadn't been an arbitrary amount of time. It must have been based on their location relative to the coordinates they'd been given. He could appreciate the subtle nuances of a plan that tried to account for an awe-inspiring number of variables. Browning couldn't have done this on his own, but regardless of how many people had been involved, it was an impressive feat.

Each jump disrupted the comlink channel between the two ships, so they'd re-establish communications, perform a quick diagnostic of critical systems, and then execute another jump that brought them ever closer to their final destination. More than thirty hours had passed, and they were finally about to execute their final jump. To reduce the likelihood of an encounter with hostile forces, Quinton had chosen to avoid populated star systems. Maelyn had received updates from the DUC's Sentinel and PMC activation signal trackers. There were increasing reports of Sentinel ships in populated star systems even as the PMC activation signals had decreased. Quinton surmised that the decrease in detection wasn't because all of the specialized comms drones had gone dormant; it was because they'd stopped broadcasting activation signals as part of the Polaris Operation. He had no idea what Salvation meant, but since it had been part of the data he'd received from the comms drone, he knew it was significant.

"The nav computer is giving us the green light, but that star system is a mess," Oscar said.

Quinton glanced at him.

"I'm just saying we need to be careful."

Quinton nodded. "Be careful. Got it," he said and looked at Maelyn. "Ready, Captain Wayborn?"

"At your discretion, Commander Aldren."

Quinton checked the jump coordinates for the umpteenth time. "Execute Jump."

The two ships' jump drives engaged, folding the distance and they emerged on the other side. A few seconds went by while scanners raced to map out the star system. They had been two thousand light-years from the star system, so the data they had was out of date, but it did indicate volatility. Navigation systems on both ships had the benefit of a huge data repository to compare the visible galaxy against. Those systems took the scan data, as well as the high-resolution images of their destination, and attempted to match them up for known star-system types. They weren't blind going into an unexplored star system, even though they could never be fully prepared for what they would find. A couple of thousand years in galactic terms was less than the blink of the eye. It had taken humanity thousands of years to expand out into the galaxy, and they weren't finished. However, what the scanners reported was the mashup of multiple star systems. Each of the galaxy's spiral arms became denser as they drew nearer to the galactic core. Stars, both common and rare, planets, and vast nebula-forming clouds made the area within twenty thousand light-years of the galactic core rich in materials but not stable enough to allow for life to evolve for very long.

The data from the scanners were funneled into a map of the star system and displayed on the main holoscreen. Three separate star systems were merging to form a new singular star system. The process would take a long time. Two of the star systems were binary, but they were being devoured by a blue giant star. The five stars were in a celestial tug of war as they orbited each other. The system of planets orbiting each of those star systems had become the near chaotic mess that was only just beginning to form a new system. Remnants of over a hundred rocky planets were in the process of colliding while trying to re-form, only to begin the cycle all over again. They stretched out over eighty light-minutes from stars battling to the death. Beyond them were dozens of gas giants, some of which had an elliptical orbit that pulled them closer to the dueling stars, only to be flung far away. Some of them would never return, but they wreaked havoc on the star system's already chaotic interior.

"Not the safest place to fly," Quinton said.

"It's no place to take a ship," Becker replied.

Quinton peered at the main holoscreen. "And shockingly, that's exactly where we need to go."

Becker didn't offer any more comments.

The waypoint had them going to a mass of former planets that had clumped together amid the scattered remnants of even more planets.

"The nav is going to struggle with this," Oscar said.

"We're going to help it," Quinton said. "Be ready to take over, but don't hesitate to input course corrections after we micro-jump."

"Won't that interfere with what you'll be doing?" Becker asked.

"We can account for it," Quinton replied, and looked at the video comlink to the *Nebulon*. "Keep that data link open. I'll make sure a course is uploaded to the *Nebulon*, but if the link goes offline, you'll have to take over."

"Understood," Maelyn replied.

Quinton increased his frame rate, and so did Corvax, Bradshaw, and Harper. They only increased to a point where they could multitask but still communicate in real time with the human crew. Quinton's avatar was the most capable of the four of them, but the CDAs were doing extremely well. Harper did the best he could within the capabilities of the spider-drone.

All of them were fully integrated with the ship and the scan data that came in from both ships. Integrating with the ship in this way meant there was no latency in accessing the data. With the assistance of Radek, who was the primary VI for Quinton, as well as the others' own virtual assistants, information overload was offset. Multitasking in this way was what PMCs were designed to do. It was what they excelled at.

Quinton accessed the flight controls for both the *Wayfarer* and the *Nebulon* and executed a micro-jump. When he emerged farther into the system, they immediately flew on an intercept course that would take them to the waypoint.

A data comlink broadcast was detected, and the ships' scanners quickly identified another ship in the system.

No sooner had Quinton brought up the signal analysis of the broadcast than an alert appeared. It was a PMC broadcast, but it had the same infiltration code that the Sentinels had used.

"It's an Agent of Harding. It must want control of Salvation," Corvax said. Whoever that other PMC was, Quinton had to agree with Corvax's assessment. It wasn't one of them. For the first time, Quinton had to categorize another PMC as the enemy. It was one thing to know about a potential enemy, but it was another thing to come face-to-face with one.

"Targeting enemy ship," Harper said.

The unknown ship executed a micro-jump. They must have detected them.

"We need to get there first," Quinton said and kept them on course.

"The ionized gas cloud is interfering with our scans, but I'm able to detect a power core signature. Multiple power cores. There's something huge in there," Corvax said.

The Agent of Harding was trying to get access. The only thing Quinton could do was try to beat him to it.

"There isn't a way to fly through that mess," Bradshaw said.

"I'm going to try to communicate with it," Quinton replied.

They couldn't see what it was. The scan data and the high-res images all showed only a mass of remnant chunks of former planets that had clumped together, but something in there was generating power. This is what they had come for. It was certainly enough power to generate a massive broadcast that could spread to all the Galactic sectors.

Quinton broadcasted his own comlink and received the same challenge protocols he'd gotten earlier from the comms drone. He sent his PMC identification and rank, and then invited the others to do the same along his comlink. The authentication to Salvation pulled codes from each of their energy storage systems.

A data update became available, and Quinton acknowledged it. It was a flight plan that took them right into the heart of a crushing debris field. Quinton hesitated. If he was wrong about this, both ships would be destroyed. But if he didn't go inside, the enemy would control whatever was on the other side. He couldn't be sure how many fail-safes Admiral Browning had put in place. Not going at all meant that the timer for Salvation would expire, which would activate every PMC scattered throughout the galaxy. This would trigger a Sentinel incursion, and the galaxy would be thrown into chaos. Quinton put the new course into the nav computer and pushed both ships' throttles up to maximum.

CHAPTER TWENTY-EIGHT

QUINTON HAD ENABLED the *Wayfarer's* point defenses to help protect the ship from the debris field they were flying into.

"I suggest you enable your point defense systems," Quinton said to Maelyn.

"Already engaged."

She knew her stuff. Quinton had access to the *Nebulon's* navigation system, but not any weapons systems.

"We still don't know what's inside," Becker said. "What do you think is in there?"

"We're going to find out," Quinton replied.

Simon cleared his throat. "Power core readings are incredibly high, but there are multiple sources, some of which are large shipyards. If there's a tech base, there could be a fleet."

"A massive factory for creating warships?" Becker asked.

"Could be," Quinton said. "There's certainly enough material here to use. Don't forget, whatever's in there has been around for a while, considering the secret location, an abundance of materials, and time enough to do something constructive with it all."

"It's a miracle it's still there," Becker said.

"That's a good point," Maelyn said. "Look at the destruction. How could anything survive here for long?"

"Polaris Operation," Corvax said. "This is a place to coordinate Polaris Operation."

"This is where we stop whatever Salvation is," Quinton said.

"Multiple ships detected entering the star system," Corvax said.

"Jordani class heavy cruiser design," Harper said. "I have a firing solution."

The others glanced at the spider-drone in bewilderment. Harper was becoming too eager to shoot first and ask questions later.

"How many ships are there?" Quinton asked.

"Twenty-two—make that thirty-two ships, sir," Harper replied.

"We're not going to engage those ships," Quinton said.

On the main holoscreen, he could see Guttman's 'I told you so' look. Becker frowned, and Quinton gestured for him to take it easy.

"I'm sorry," Harper said. "That was foolish. I'll work on a firing solution in case we need to make a hasty retreat."

"Understood," Quinton replied.

"They're Union ships," Maelyn said.

"Crowe!"

"How the hell did Crowe end up here?" Becker asked.

Quinton's mind raced while he considered it. How had Lennix Crowe even learned about this place, much less made it here at virtually the same time they had? "It can't be a coincidence, so it must have to do with that other ship we detected."

Corvax looked at him. "If this Lennix Crowe is involved with an Agent of Harding, then he's a pawn, willing or otherwise."

Quinton nodded. "Someone desperate enough to figure out a way to use the Sentinels as his own personal attack force."

"You think Crowe had help luring Sentinels to attack Collective targets?" Maelyn asked.

"It makes the most sense. Crowe had Sentinel code to help capture me on Endurance Starbase, and he must have gotten help with adapting it so he could use it for something else."

"Why is he here then?"

"He's in over his head," Quinton replied.

"What do you mean?"

"Would an Agent of Harding hesitate to create the conditions for a Sentinel incursion if it meant flushing us out?" Quinton said, gesturing toward the other PMCs, as well as himself.

"That would mean they were the ones attacking other targets besides the Collective," Maelyn said and nodded.

"Like I said," Quinton replied, "he's in way over his head. I have no idea why he came here, but it must have something to do with the Agent of Harding."

Quinton heard Maelyn reply, but it sounded distant, as if he were listening to her speak from another room. He also heard the others shouting, and he thought he heard Becker call his name, but he couldn't reply. The data comlink to whatever Salvation was had suddenly become active, and it pulled him inside an abyss that had taken him away from the bridge of the *Wayfarer*.

Something was doing an analysis of Quinton's ESS, and he thought it must be an integrity check. Even though he recognized the access and flow of information, it didn't seem to be taking anything away from him, but Quinton felt as if it was reviewing his actions. Within moments, the utilization of the data comlink lessened and he regained more control.

"It's all right," Quinton said. "I'm fine."

"What happened?" Maelyn asked.

"It was a data connection to them."

"Them?" Becker said. "Who?"

"Not a 'them'—it. Whatever's on the other side," Quinton said.

The two ships flew through the dense asteroid field. Some of the asteroids were the size of dwarf planets, and even though they flew quickly, they gave themselves enough time to alter course if needed.

"Simon," Oscar said, "are you getting an automated guidance request?"

"I just got it," Simon replied.

The same request had appeared on Quinton's internal HUD. "Give it access. We're being guided inside. We must be close enough for an automated docking procedure."

Oscar hesitated for a few moments, then acknowledged the request.

"Do it," Maelyn said to Simon.

Simon also acknowledged the request, and both ships' flight control systems were handed off to the Acheron Confederacy Navy installation they were heading to. Quinton recognized the ACN protocols used for guiding visiting ships to space stations, starbases, and even large warships.

Their velocity increased, which confirmed what Quinton was thinking. "They must already have a course planned for us."

Becker groaned. "I just wish I knew who *they* were. Has there been any other contact?"

Quinton shook his head. "No."

Becker looked at the others. "Anyone else?"

No one else had been contacted.

"Our scanners just went dark," Oscar said. "They're operating normally, but we can't see anything."

"We must be inside a dampening field," Quinton replied.

Both ships were on their own now, and there was no going back. They had to see this through. The ships' engines throttled down, but their velocity increased, and the motion wasn't even registering on the ship's inertia dampeners. The ships raced at such speeds that Quinton could only track their progress by increasing his frame rate. They flew between dwarf-planet-size asteroids, some of which had molten cores from deep fissures along the surface. They flew toward an area that was completely devoid of light, as if all the light had been swallowed, but the scanners still reported data of their immediate vicinity. They were flying into a mighty tunnel that was a good two hundred meters across and lit by a brilliant strip of lights. As it enveloped them, they noted stone walls that glittered with an odd sheen, as if they'd been fused glass-slick, but before long the tunnel walls became suddenly metallic. It was a gray metal, gleaming with a bit of yellow in the light, stretching so far ahead that its mighty bore dwindled to a gleaming dot with distance.

Their speed dropped, and Quinton was able to make out the shapes of hatches sliding past—dozens of hatches, with most as large as the one they'd flown into. The occupants of both ships' bridges were silent as their minds reeled at the structure's sheer size. This was beyond anything they'd ever experienced.

One huge hatch suddenly flicked open, and both ships were guided toward it. They slipped neatly through the open hatch, and the *Wayfarer* settled onto a floor comprised of the grayish-yellow alloy. Quinton watched as the *Nebulon* followed.

The image on the main holoscreen showed that they were in a dimly lit metal cavern more than a kilometer across. Nearby were rows of neatly parked combat spacecraft with the ACN's black and gold emblem on their sides. Quinton peered at the floor and saw the two golden triangular halves that angled away from a sphere on a black background. The letter of the first word was underneath.

"Perseverance," Quinton said quietly. He stood up and walked toward the holoscreen.

Corvax joined him. "Endurance," he whispered.

The lighting in the massive hangar increased.

"Fortitude," Bradshaw said.

Rows of combat fighters gleamed under the lights.

"Readiness," Harper said.

Quinton glanced at Becker and then Oscar. Both men watched the video feed with stunned reverence. Becker looked at him and nodded once.

"What do we do now?" Guttman asked.

Quinton caught a glimpse of movement as a double-ended, bullet-shaped aircar came to a stop between the two ships. Counter-grav emitters kept it hovering one foot or so above the floor. A large hatch opened on the side and light spilled from the opening, bright and welcoming.

"Quinton," Maelyn said, "has there been any other contact?"

"No, but the data connection is still there. I think we're being invited to go somewhere."

The spider-drone's armored body spun toward Quinton. "I'm not staying behind," Harper said.

"No one is staying behind this time," Quinton said. He looked at the holoscreen, and Maelyn nodded in agreement.

Becker stood up and cleared his throat. "Is anyone worried about the Union ships in the star system?"

"I think we're pretty well protected for now," Quinton replied.

"He's right," Oscar said. "Did you see what we had to fly through to make it here?"

"Let's go," Quinton said.

They left the bridge and exited the rear loading ramp of the *Wayfarer*. Maelyn and the others met them outside the aircar. The air was crisp, with a slight chill.

"I'm getting atmospheric readings," Maelyn said. She pulled off her helmet and the others did the same.

Guttman checked his weapon and kept looking around as if he expected to be attacked at any moment. "This is just like that starbase, except there are more ships here. If these star fighters are here, there must be other ships."

"They're not yours," Corvax said.

Guttman frowned. "I don't see anyone here claiming them."

"Let's not divvy anything up just yet," Quinton said and entered the aircar.

The others followed.

"What's the matter with you?" Simon said to Guttman.

"What?"

"You're a real piece of work. You think everything is just there for you to take."

Guttman shrugged. "What do you think *they're* doing here?" He jutted his chin toward Quinton. "And if it's not us, then it'll be someone else. There's no room for being high and mighty."

The spider-drone began tapping one of its legs on the ground, and the drone's red optics swung toward Guttman. "How about showing one iota of respect."

Corvax and Bradshaw looked at him with the artificial eyes of the CDA.

Guttman bit his lower lip for a moment and looked at Quinton. "I apologize," he said and looked away from them.

The aircar's hatch closed, and several chairs rose from the floor near everyone except Harper, Corvax, and Bradshaw. The others sat down.

"They're so comfortable. We need these on the *Nebulon*," Kieva said.

Maelyn agreed.

The aircar accelerated away from their ships and sped across the cavern, heading straight at a featureless metal wall that popped open an instant before they hit. The aircar then darted into another brightly lit bore.

Quinton glanced at the others. "Reminds me of traveling in some of the moon stations in the core star systems," he said and paused. "What's wrong?"

"There's so much metal," Becker said. "I've never seen this much in one place before."

Guttman blew out a breath. "I'm glad someone finally said it. I'm barely keeping it together here."

"We're heading toward another wall," Simon said.

Once again, a hatch opened at the last minute. There was a brief darkened area and then they emerged into another brightly lit bore, this one no wider than two or three of the aircar in which they rode.

The walls weren't featureless, but speed reduced those features to a blur. They traveled for so long that even Quinton was wondering just how big this place was. It easily dwarfed any space station he'd ever seen. He glanced at Maelyn, and her eyes gleamed with excitement. There was a fresh spurt of acceleration and a sideways surge of inertia as the aircar swept through a curved junction and darted into yet another tunnel.

A status window appeared on Quinton's HUD.

Pre-Check of Personality Matrix Construct Integrity Complete.

Confirm identity is Quinton Aldren.

Acheron Confederacy Navy.

Rank: Commander.

Galactic Personality Matrix Construct.

Authentication Procedure Step Two: Virtual Intelligence Integrity Check.

Are you ready to proceed?

Quinton stared at the question for a few moments. "Radek," he said sub-vocally. "What do you make of this?"

"It's an additional integrity check for a virtual intelligence. I would have expected this to happen as part of the other check, but since that was designated a pre-check, they might have changed the procedures."

Quinton tried to think of a reason to take one all-inclusive integrity check and divide it into multiple steps, but he came up short.

"These checks are prerequisites for assuming command of an Acheron Confederacy Naval vessel or installation, such as a star-base or space station," Radek said.

This place was much too big to be a ship.

"This tunnel is going on forever," Guttman said.

"I saw a chamber earlier that contained more ships," Simon said. "We're traveling so fast that I hardly got a good look at them. They might have been Condor class."

The aircar scooted down the very center of the tunnel.

"I keep waiting to arrive," Maelyn said.

The others agreed. The PMCs were quiet.

Quinton looked over at Corvax, Bradshaw, and Harper. "Have you gotten anything through the data comlink about integrity checks for your VIs?"

Corvax and Bradshaw exchanged a glance and shook their heads.

"I haven't received a data comlink," Harper said.

"Same here. There's been nothing since I provided my identification on the ship," Corvax said.

Bradshaw nodded. "You're the Galactic, Commander."

"It might be because you're the ranking officer here," Maelyn said.

Quinton considered it. He just needed to find a way to stop the massive broadcast that would reactivate the PMCs scattered across the galaxy. Without those signals, the Sentinels would go back to the deep dark.

"Why would they run a separate integrity check for your VI?" Simon asked.

"That's the thing," Quinton replied. "They're like the psychological evaluations commanding officers go through before assuming command of anything—a ship, a fleet, a starbase. The PMC integrity checks are similar. I've just never had a specific request for Radek before."

"What's wrong with that? Wasn't this part of your training?" Maelyn asked.

"It's usually part of..." Quinton began and stopped. "Never mind. To answer your question, no it wasn't. Radek, or any VI, is integrated into a PMC. They bridge the gap between the human-to-machine interface. If I grant the request, I might be unresponsive for the duration of the check."

Becker frowned, leaned forward, and rubbed the palms of his hands together. "Let me see if I understand this. We're being taken somewhere, and you haven't even finished authenticating to whatever this place is yet?"

Quinton pursed his lips while he considered it for a moment, then nodded. "When you put it like that, it sounds... There's no turning back now."

Becker sighed and shook his head, then turned toward the window to stare at the dark tunnel. The aircar began to slow and the entire cockpit swiveled smoothly until they were facing back the way they'd come. Quinton felt the drag of deceleration, which continued for almost ten minutes, and then the blurred walls beyond the transparent canopy slowed. He could make out the details once more, including the maws of other tunnels. The aircar slowed virtually to a walk, and they swerved gently down an intersecting tunnel that was only a little wider than the vehicle itself. It slid alongside an entrance and stopped. The hatch flicked soundlessly open.

The others looked at Quinton expectantly. "I'll go first," he said with mock enthusiasm, stepping out of the vehicle and looking around. Then he gestured for the others to follow. Once they were all out, the vehicle's hatch closed and it slid silently backwards, vanishing the way it had come.

Guttman cursed as he looked longingly in the direction the vehicle had gone.

The flashing light of a small sphere appeared, hanging in midair. It bobbed a few times to attract their attention and then headed down a side corridor at a comfortable pace.

Quinton tried to open another comlink session, but they were all denied. The only connection available was the one waiting for his response.

"Let's go," Quinton said and followed the sphere.

It guided them down a corridor past numerous closed doors until they came to an expanse of black walls where thin, pale, glowing lines traveled the length of the long corridor. Quinton peered at the lines and saw that they were actually tiny words written in a flowing white script.

Quinton slowed down and looked at the words. "They're names of people," he said and looked at the others. He turned back toward the names, quickly reading. Many had ACN ranks associated with them.

Maelyn went to the other side of the corridor. "Oh my," she said and leaned closer to the wall. "There are other federations listed here—Tilion Empire Marines, Ixander Star Collective, Alari. And Dholeren United Coalition!"

Becker walk over to her. "The DUC was part of this?" he asked and peered at the wall.

Simon joined them, gesturing toward the wall a few moments later. "The list of spacers here were part of the DUC's lost fleets. I recognize the ships' names. They were lost during the Federation Wars."

"Why would they be listed here?" Becker asked.

"There are Jordani ships and spacers listed over here," Guttman said. "The ships have JFS in the names. That has to be them, right?"

"They helped Browning," Quinton said. Silence nearly swallowed the hallowed halls. "These names are honoring soldiers who died in battle. This corridor is a monument to the fallen. Whoever built this place wanted anyone who came down here to understand the sacrifice of so many. Browning had help, and by the looks of it, he had it from…" Quinton's gaze swept the walls. The flowing cursive script went on and on. He hesitated to guess how many people were listed there.

"Most of these federations or unions are gone," Maelyn said.

Quinton's eyebrows pulled together and his gaze became hard. The white, flowing script was tiny, and yet it filled up the walls from floor to ceiling. Each of these names, ranks, ship references, alliances, and places were tied to the people who'd tried to help Elias Browning—Grand Admiral Browning who had allegedly betrayed the Acheron Confederacy and raided countless worlds on some kind of destructive tirade. The survivors of the Federation Wars believed Browning was a monster, but if he was, why would this monument even exist? If Browning had been so evil, why would so many spacers fight alongside him?

Corvax and Bradshaw watched him. Their metallic faces conveyed a grimness forged in battle and sacrifice in a war Quinton had never been part of. He felt like an imposter, intruding upon the halls of the dead. Corvax and Bradshaw had fought in the Federation Wars. He looked at Harper. The spider-drone stood in the center of the corridor with its optics forward, but Quinton knew he could see all around him. Did they recognize any of the names written on the walls? He wanted to know but wouldn't ask. Some information should only be volunteered, and it was a struggle at times when his past caught up with him.

Even now he felt all those memories of a life long gone bubbling to the surface of his thoughts. He knew the others felt it, too. He remembered the agricultural bot he'd been forced to use. His access to his memories had been severely limited because it hadn't been designed to house a PMC. But for all the agricultural bot's flaws, the limited access to his memories had been both a blessing and a curse. In the avatar he used now, he had no such limitations. Quinton had full access to his life from before, and this monument was just another reminder of what he'd lost. He looked at the others, and his gaze lingered on Maelyn for only a moment before moving on. He just needed to stop the signal and figure out how to get all the resources here to the people who could use them. There had to be a CDA here for Harper to use. Once he did all that, he could move on.

Quinton continued, his footsteps echoing through the long corridor, and the others quietly followed him. The corridor eventually curved and then ended abruptly at a hatch that was large enough for a shuttle to fly through. The middle of the hatch bore the ACN black and gold emblem in stunning clarity. The ACN motto was written in elegant cursive script that surrounded the planet, and beneath it was the word *Salvation*.

Their disembodied guide twitched impatiently and drifted closer to the hatch. Quinton followed, and the massive door slid open as he approached. The door had been constructed of a thick metallic alloy that formed an immensely strong barrier. He followed the guide down the silently opening passage. Once they were all through, the door shut behind them, equally silently, and he tried to suppress a feeling of imprisonment.

The interior lighting began to glow brighter, revealing a spherical chamber that felt as open as the cavern they'd been in before. Smooth walls surrounded them in a colossal display of strength. They stood on a platform that had been thrust out from one curving wall. The platform was transparent, dotted with dozens of comfortable couch-like chairs before what could only be control consoles. The consoles were blank, as if they were in standby.

A holoscreen winked into existence at the edge of the platform.

Authentication Procedure Step Two: Virtual Intelligence Integrity Check.

Are you ready to proceed?

Quinton walked toward the holoscreen on a platform so transparent that he seemed to be striding on air as he crossed. His guide flew toward the display.

He turned to see Corvax, Bradshaw, and Harper fanned out behind him, but the others remained near the chairs. Quinton heard the spider-drone's legs begin to tap the floor in a nervous tick. Turning back toward the holoscreen, he sent an affirmative, and then everything went dark.

CHAPTER TWENTY-NINE

A FLASH of code scrolled so quickly down the holoscreen that Maelyn couldn't read it before it disappeared.

"Dammit all!" Guttman groused, glaring at his wrist computer. "This thing hasn't worked right since we were on that damn outpost."

Maelyn blinked several times. Then her eyes widened, and she stormed toward Guttman. "What did you say?"

Guttman leaned back, frowned a little, and glanced at the others for a moment. "It's nothing. I just need to get this thing fixed, is all."

Maelyn's gaze swooped toward Guttman's wrist computer and then to Quinton. She closed the distance to him, startling both Corvax and Bradshaw.

"Something's not right," Maelyn said.

The two CDAs regarded her and then looked at Quinton. Maelyn moved to stand in front of him. He was completely still. Frozen. Lifeless.

"Quinton!" she shouted.

It was a feeble attempt to get him to respond, and it didn't work.

Her gazed darted to the others, frantically searching for a way to help him. Becker and Simon came towards her with questions emerging from their lips that she couldn't hear. She lifted her wrist computer and tried to open a comlink to Quinton, snarling when it failed. Stalking back and forth in front of him, she shook her head as a tangle of ideas came to her mind and were dismissed, one after the other.

"I can't get a connection," Corvax said.

"Me either," Bradshaw said.

Maelyn flung her arm toward the blank holoscreen. "Well, what about there? Can you connect to that?" Her voice echoed throughout the vast chamber.

Corvax and Bradshaw focused on the holoscreen, but nothing happened.

Maelyn inhaled explosively and stormed in front of them. "You find a way to help him," she said through gritted teeth. "I don't care what you have to do. Do you hear me! Help him now!"

She scowled toward Quinton. The cybernetic avatar that made him look so human now held him prisoner.

"Quinton isn't the only one who's not responding," Simon said.

Maelyn looked in his direction, and he gestured toward Harper. The spider-drone was frozen, just like Quinton, with one of its legs stopped in mid-motion.

A data window flickered on the holoscreen—snippets of something she couldn't quite see.

"Uh, guys," Guttman said in a shaky voice. "This doesn't look right." He held out his arm, showing them his personal holoscreen. It flickered with code just like the holoscreen in front of Quinton.

"What did you do?" Becker asked.

"Nothing," Guttman replied. "I didn't do anything. You think I could do something like this? I don't even know what this thing is doing."

Simon darted over to him. Maelyn looked at Corvax and Bradshaw. "Check that out," she ordered.

The two PMCs did as she told them. Maelyn gritted her teeth and glared at Quinton for a few moments, then joined the others.

SOMETIMES IT WAS the little things that could sneak up and really have a huge impact on your day. One moment Quinton was consenting to having Radek's integrity checked, and the next he was fighting for his life. In the briefest of moments, Radek's security measures went on full alert, but Salvation's computing core must have sensed the danger and quarantined both of them into some kind of virtual holding area. He stood in a virtual reproduction of the chamber his avatar was in with all the others. Harper was with him, but there was something wrong with him.

Radek's security alert referred to the same Sentinel control signal they'd encountered on the Alari Outpost. Quinton tried to connect to Harper's PMC. He'd given all of them the same protections he had in place, so he couldn't figure out how or why Harper was compromised now.

Quinton tried to move, but nothing happened. He was cut off from the cybernetic avatar that housed his PMC, trapped in this virtual environment.

"Harper, can you hear me?"

"Quinton!?" Harper said, sounding confused and disoriented. "Something's wrong. Someone's trying to control me, Quinton. I don't know how to stop it."

Quinton detected another PMC's presence trapped with them. It lurked in the virtual environment but was part of Harper at the same time.

"I'm going to help you, Harper. Listen to me. I'm going to get us out of this."

"Just tell me what to do." Harper was quiet for a few

moments. "Commander? No, you already told me the firing solution was wrong. We're not going to attack the Union ships."

"There aren't any ships. What are you talking about?"

Quinton was stuck in the middle of authenticating with Salvation, and it wouldn't allow him to proceed. Something was stopping him.

"The others are plotting to kill me," Harper said. He wasn't even looking at Quinton. "They want to trap the drone by the airlock. Once I'm gone, they think there's nothing you can do about it. Guttman is the worst. I hate his beady eyes. He always thinks I'm trying to get him. He'd never know it if I was. I've sneaked up on him before. I like how afraid he is when I do that."

Quinton tried to open a comlink to Harper, but it was denied. He tried to force his way in.

"It's so hard," Harper said. "I've been trying to keep pushing forward. All those damn diagnostics had the same result. PMC degeneration is inevitable."

Quinton almost found a way to reach Harper, but then it was closed off. He cursed.

"Radek, can you reach Greta?" Quinton asked, hoping that Harper's VI was at least able to communicate with them.

"Yet another in a long line of mistakes, Commander Quinton Aldren."

Quinton scanned out, trying to find the source of the other PMC. Harper whimpered incoherently.

"You can't help him."

"Shut up!" Quinton snarled.

He was able to find the source of the third PMC. It was coming through Harper. The two were linked. It was the only thing that made sense.

"So, you're the Agent of Harding."

"Is that what they call me? Then I guess I am. I suppose *you* might be called an Agent of Browning." He paused, considering.

"I don't think you're quite there yet, so there is still hope for you, but this exchange will get tedious if we keep on this way. I'm Admen Desher."

His tone dripped with the pure arrogance of someone with an unshakable certainty of the superiority of their position. Quinton hated it, even if it was partially true.

"You say that like it's supposed to mean something to me. I didn't know Sentinels used PMCs."

"Wrong again," Desher said with wry amusement. "I've reviewed Harper's ESS, particularly his experiences with you. Quite revealing."

"Leave him alone. Get out of his ESS," he snarled.

"That temper is going to get the better of you, but let's not get sidetracked here. I can do what I want with Harper. You've encountered the infiltration protocol before. Yes, I see it now. A Sentinel encounter. Another PMC named Misako. I know that one. Commander Isobe Misako, Intelligence Officer. She was a high-priority target. Sentinels occasionally get the job done, it seems," Desher said scathingly.

Harper's whimper turned into a growl. "Get out of my head!"

"Give it up, Lieutenant Harper. Your PMC was corrupt long before I got here," Desher scorned.

"Don't listen to that asshole, Harper. Let me in, and I can help you fight him."

"Oh yes, do that, Harper. Commander Aldren is going to make everything better."

Quinton tried to force a connection to Harper's PMC but was blocked by Harper.

"That's not going to work," Desher said. "Let's try something else. I think we can be reasonable."

"Go to hell!"

"You're a Galactic PMC—one of Browning's prized Galactics. I thought PMCs like you might have been just a ruse to throw off the Sentinels," Desher said.

Quinton needed to calm down. Flying into a rage wasn't going to help anyone. Desher seemed keen on talking, so maybe he could learn something. "What do you want?"

"The way I see it is that we're stuck here with no end in sight. No one is going to get what they want like this," Desher said.

Quinton would have liked to see what Desher actually looked like, but his voice was coming through Harper. "Get to the damn point then."

Harper looked at Quinton, and Desher's voice came through his lips. "You never wanted this. You're one of the earliest iterations of PMCs meant to fight the Jordanis. I can clear things up for you. The Acheron Confederacy humbled the Jordanis in the most humiliating way possible. The ACN crushed their vast military. Browning was a hero. You would have been, too, if your ESS had gotten to where it was supposed to go. There, that's all done now. Regardless, you can walk away from all of this."

"And leave Salvation to you?"

"I don't want this place. It has no value to me or my mission at all," Desher replied.

"I don't believe you. Haven't you—"

"I had no idea this place was even here. Some kind of automated construction VI with access to too many resources must have built another ACN starbase."

"Then why did you come here? You arrived before we did. How did you find this place?"

"I would have thought that was obvious," Desher said in that same scathing tone that made Quinton want to kick something. "I came here because you triggered the Polaris Operation—part of Browning's pathetic attempts to change the outcome of a war that was decided long ago," Desher said and paused for a moment. "He lost. I'm not going to argue the point with you, but he did. You came here to stop the Polaris Operation. You want to prevent the broadcast of PMC activation signals across the galaxy."

Quinton hated that Desher had access to Harper's ESS. All the chips were stacked in his favor.

"You've got me all figured out," Quinton replied evenly.

"How are you going to stop the broadcast from here? This is just another ACN starbase, albeit a much larger one than the fleet records indicate, but a starbase all the same."

Quinton thought Desher was being a little too insistent on what he professed to know, which made Quinton doubt what he was being told.

"Let's take it a step further. Why would Browning make you a Galactic PMC? Why reactivate you in a galaxy you don't even know and not give you any help at all? The Federation Wars have already been fought and lost. We're in the final cleanup phase of that conflict. You'll never be able to defeat the Prime."

Quinton laughed. "The Prime. That's what you call Miles Harding?"

"The Prime has never been defeated. Everything that has happened is according to his plan."

"His plan, you say," Quinton sneered. "Really? You think he controls everything. Is this place part of his plan, too?"

"Yes," Desher replied without hesitation. "This variable was one of many that could occur. Let's not get hung up on the details. But think about it. The situation is hopeless. You've encountered the Sentinels before. They have hundreds of thousands of warships at their disposal, with more coming online, especially now with all the PMC activity going on. After this broadcast, they'll all be deployed. Also, why would Browning entrust Polaris and Salvation to an ACN Commander who's probably only commanded a small battle group against the Jordani Federation before volunteering for the PMC program. Does any of that sound like a brilliant strategy?"

Quinton let Desher's words penetrate deep into his mind. How many times had he said he just wanted to find a way to become human again? Find another DNA vault and download his PMC into a body that was as close as he was ever going to get to the one he'd been born with. Desher was right. The Federation Wars had been fought and lost. All Quinton wanted to do was put all this behind him and move on with his life, finding a way to coexist until they could combat the Sentinels in a way that wouldn't get them all killed.

"Do you have any idea how many Sentinel fleets must have arrived at this star system by now?" Desher asked. "After the broadcast is sent and all the PMCs scattered across the galaxy start coming here, we'll mop them up in droves. We won't even have to hunt them down, but we'll do that, too, Commander Aldren."

A maelstrom of memories spun up from the depths of his mind—recollections of his life before becoming a PMC, coming back online in a dying world, his time aboard the *Nebulon*, and then more recent memories of commanding the *Wayfarer* with his friends. Becker, Oscar, and Guttman could be wearing on anyone who spent time with them, but so could he. It was messy and it was real. They'd fought together and had even gone their separate ways, but they'd come back together.

Then he remembered obsidian walls along a long corridor and the countless names of the people who had died, people who had sacrificed, people who had made a stand in the face of over-whelming odds. He felt them all as if he were slamming his fists against battle steel, and each recollection brought a piece of knowledge that seemed to snap into place. He knew what Salvation was. He'd figured it out, and judging by Desher's comments, the Agent of Harding hadn't. Desher didn't have the slightest clue, but Quinton did, and the knowledge settled on him like the most hardened battle-steel-armored hull of the most colossal warship ever created.

Quinton focused on accessing the Salvation's systems, but he was still locked out. They wouldn't allow him to assume command with Admen Desher infiltrating Harper's PMC. He tried to think of a way to help Harper and couldn't. He kept remembering Misako leaping out of the Alari Outpost's hangar bay, choosing to sacrifice herself rather than remain controlled by the Sentinels. Now Harper was faced with a similar choice, except his PMC might have deteriorated so much that it was impossible to predict what he was going to do.

"You must know that it is hopeless," Desher said.

Quinton gritted his teeth.

"All that remains now is whether you'll admit it to yourself or not," Desher continued.

"I know exactly what I'm going to do," Quinton replied, hating it.

"I'm waiting."

"You're not even inside this place, and you don't know what it is. You probably followed us through the asteroid field and are using your docking clamps on the outer walls. You're within the dampening field, so somehow you've got a subspace comlink to penetrate all the way here."

"Bravo, Commander. You've got me all figured out," Desher replied.

"Probably not all, but I've got a few things to say to you. First, you almost had me convinced that you knew what Salvation is and what it was meant for. Also, you're so certain that your precious Harding Prime has already won the war. You're wrong."

"Take a look at the galaxy. You're on the losing side."

Quinton laughed. "I wouldn't be so sure about that. I figured out what Browning's plan was, and now I'm going to take this fight to your precious Prime. Wherever he's hiding, I'm going to find him. I bet *you* don't even know where Harding Prime is, do you?"

Desher didn't reply.

"Well, do you? Do you know where he is? Where's he been? If he's already won the war, why hasn't anyone seen him? You don't know."

"Neither do you."

"Maybe Lieutenant Nash Harper can help settle this."

Desher snorted. "You can't save him."

Quinton scowled. "Listen to me. If you somehow survive what's about to happen, make sure you send my regards to your superiors."

"You seem quite sure of yourself. We're in a stalemate. That hasn't changed. None of us wins."

"That's the problem with supreme arrogance. Not only does it make you an asshole, but it blinds to what you should have already realized," Quinton said, and hated what he was about to do. Then he spoke with the command authority of a Galactic PMC. "Lieutenant Nash Harper, Acheron Confederacy Navy, you're hereby relieved of duty. Your service to the Acheron Confederacy is complete. It's time for your PMC to go into standby. Thank you for your service."

Harper let out a soft sigh and disappeared from VR. Quinton heard the beginnings of Desher's venomous scream before it was cut off. At the same time, Salvation's authentication protocols completed Radek's integrity check and began transferring command authority to Quinton.

CHAPTER THIRTY

THE SPIDER-DRONE COLLAPSED to the transparent floor. Maelyn spun toward it and the others stepped back.

Corvax stepped toward it and squatted down. "His ESS has gone dormant."

"Dormant? But that means he's…" Maelyn said and hastened to Quinton.

"Harper is dead? Are you sure? How?" Becker asked.

Maelyn stared at Quinton's chest and scanned for the avatar's power core, but the shielding prevented her from seeing it.

Bradshaw came to stand next to her. "His ESS is still working," she said.

Maelyn frowned and bobbed her head a little. Quinton still looked as lifeless as he'd been for the past fifteen minutes. On the far side of the chamber, a tremendous holoscreen flickered to life, and a vast array of data feeds began popping up.

"I don't know what happened to him," Corvax said.

Maelyn looked over at them, and Becker lifted his eyebrows questioningly.

"He's still alive," she said.

Becker let out a huge breath and looked at Corvax. "Can you

remote-access Harper's ESS and figure out what happened to him?"

"That won't work," Simon said. "If the core is dead, the ESS is gone, along with all the data on it."

"Maybe Quinton found a way to transfer him to a CDA somewhere," Guttman said.

Maelyn saw Quinton move. He took a few steps forward and rocked on his feet, disoriented, then squeezed his eyes shut and slowly shook his head.

"Just give me a second," Quinton said. His voice sounded slightly modulated, reminding her of when he multitasked within a computer system and stretched his capacity to the limit.

They gathered around him.

"We're here," Maelyn said. "You've been out of it for over fifteen minutes."

Quinton's eyes flashed and tracked back and forth as if he was reading at a fast pace.

"Harper?" Quinton asked. He started to turn but halted.

"His core is depleted. We thought maybe he was transferred out of it into a CDA," Maelyn said.

Quinton pressed his lips together and narrowed his gaze. "No, he was…" He jerked toward Guttman, and the spacer's eyes went wide. "Give it. Your wrist computer is compromised."

Guttman hastily took it off, but Becker intercepted it as Guttman tried to hand it off.

"I'll take that," Becker said. He dropped it to the floor and shot it with his hand-cannon. "No need to take any chances."

Quinton nodded and thanked him.

"What happened to Harper?" Maelyn asked.

"I couldn't help him. His matrix was too corrupt, and when he was infiltrated…" Quinton said and paused. "I'm sorry, the ship is transferring command authority and it's complicated."

"What ship?" Becker asked.

Maelyn lifted her eyebrows.

Quinton smiled, his eyes gleaming, and she felt her own lips lift in response.

"This place is a ship. It's one massive ship. Welcome to the *Salvation*."

Maelyn thought about how long it had taken them to get this far, trying to estimate the size, but she couldn't.

"Did he say 'ship'?" Guttman asked.

Becker nodded.

"Corvax and Bradshaw, I'm sending you a comlink with authentication protocols. I need you integrated ASAP," Quinton said.

"Yes, Commander," Corvax said.

The two CDAs walked away from them and then stood still.

"What's happening?" Maelyn asked.

"The Sentinels are here. There are thousands of them. I'll explain everything."

"Sentinels!" Guttman nearly shrieked. "We've gotta get out of here. This thing must have a heck of a jump drive. Let's skedaddle."

Quinton shook his head. "Not this time," he said with a hungry gleam in his gaze. "This time, we send a very clear message to the Sentinels, with Admiral Browning's compliments."

"What can we do to help?" Maelyn asked.

"Go over to those consoles and we'll get started."

QUINTON WATCHED the others for a moment and then turned toward the massive holoscreen on the far side of the bridge. Even with Radek managing the data feed from the *Salvation*, he still felt as if he was filling up to the breaking point. Knowledge of the *Salvation's* operation and weapons' systems and capabilities, along with live data feeds from their sensors, needed to be throttled or it would overwhelm him. His knowledge expanded with the vast data repositories aboard, and he chased after it because the answers were there—answers about the *Salvation*, Admiral Browning, and the Federation Wars.

"You must pace yourself," Radek warned.

"I know, but there's so much here," Quinton replied.

He couldn't afford to get distracted. Sensor data was still coming in, showing that thousands of Sentinel ships had entered the star system. He searched for the Union Ships that were attempting to flee, but they were within the dampening field. He had to set aside the paralyzing knowledge that he was about to fly a planetoid-class starship that was six thousand kilometers in diameter. He checked the specs multiple times, even though he knew they were accurate. Questions kept mounting, but he had to ignore them. He was going to fly a ship meant to be crewed by half a million people.

The dampening field protecting the *Salvation* was maintained by millions of field generators located throughout the remnant planet clusters, shielding the ship from the rest of the star system. The clusters maintained their formation due to the artificial gravity field powered by an array of the *Salvation's* power cores.

Quinton maintained a comlink with the others but could group them as needed; otherwise, they'd never get anything done. He activated Corvax and Bradshaw. Integrated PMCs could communicate much faster than the spoken word. Once they understood what Quinton wanted, they began to build targeting, and the tactical plot began to update.

Corvax queried Quinton regarding the Union Ships, and he told him to make sure they weren't harmed. Sentinel targeting only.

Bradshaw began to integrate with the *Salvation's* complex engineering components, focusing on the power core infrastructure.

Quinton uploaded multiple versions of his VI assistants into the *Salvation's* systems to scratch the surface of the command shortfall because they didn't have a full crew. He then immediately turned his attention to the tactical plot. Corvax was feeding targeting data in, almost at the same time that the sensor data reported it.

"Time to show ourselves to the galaxy," Quinton said.

He executed an update to the artificial gravity controls and his VI assistants took over. A multitude of the *Salvation's* power cores reported a huge spike in energy draw as the massive artificial gravity field reversed with startlingly accurate precision. The sheer gravitational forces tore apart the remnant planet clusters, expelling them out into the star system. Rocky chunks that had been clustered together suddenly broke apart as the gravitational field reversal pushed them outward at thirty percent of the speed of light. Everything in their path was destroyed. Thousands of Sentinel ships were blindsided by a colossal bombardment that their powerful control VIs had never anticipated. Even with the benefit of increased frame rate to facilitate supercomputing processing power, whole fleets of Sentinel warships were destroyed.

Located in the heart of what had been a cluster of dead remnant planets was the *Salvation*. All the infrastructure that had been used to build the ship had been part of the massive asteroids now pummeling fleets of Sentinel ships. The rearmost ships attempted to evade, but there was nowhere for them to run.

A holographic image of the ship appeared on the main holoscreen. The *Salvation* had triangular halves that swept away from the sphere in the middle.

"Would you look at that?" Guttman said.

"They replicated the emblem of the ACN," Becker said.

Quinton regarded the image with grim determination.

"They're running," Simon said. "The sentinel ships are trying to flee."

Multiple volleys of hyper-missiles burst from missile tubes across the *Salvation's* hull. The hyper-missiles transitioned into hyperspace, delivering antimatter warheads to Sentinel heavy cruisers. Quinton created a firing solution for the Sentinel Dreadnaught class ships, which had the equivalent mass of seven heavy cruisers each. Hundreds more hyper-missiles left their salvos armed with gravitonic warheads. Within moments, Sentinel Dreadnoughts began to drop from the tactical plot as the warheads detonated, creating short-lived black holes that tore the warships apart.

Quinton observed the Sentinels trying to escape, but the *Salvation* discharged its weapons with deadly precision. As he watched the tactical plot, a piece of knowledge sprang to existence. No doubt, Radek thought he needed it. The Sentinels had been the solution to a galaxy overwrought with corrupt PMC-controlled warships. They'd been constructed by pooling the resources of the surviving federations and star unions. They couldn't have known that the wars had been instigated by Miles Harding. Browning had exhausted his resources trying to stop it and couldn't. Admen Desher hadn't lied about that—Browning had been losing the war. He quit the field so they could rebuild, and the *Salvation* had been his solution. Quinton thought about the monument of the fallen that lined the corridor leading to the *Salvation's* main bridge. He and his companions hadn't been alone. They were standing on the shoulders of trillions of people who had died for this. They'd died for a chance to free the galaxy of not only the Sentinels but Miles Harding.

Quinton accessed the communication systems and found the protocols used for Polaris. They were hours away from recalling the PMCs scattered across the galaxy.

Maelyn walked over to him. "Is that all of them?"

Quinton nodded. "Their last known locations."

"What are you going to do?"

"If I let Polaris initiate, many of them are going to die. There are too many Sentinels. We can't get to all of them in time."

"Then don't," Maelyn said. "Stop the signal."

"We need them."

"Yes, but do we need them right now? Like this?"

Quinton considered it for a few moments. She was right. There was a better way than signaling a massive recall. He stopped Polaris and authorized a broadcast to stop the communication drones deployed throughout the galaxy as well. Radek gave him a report. "The signal won't be stopped everywhere in time."

"Then we should go there first."

"Yes, but we can't do everything ourselves. We need to coordinate with others."

Maelyn smiled and turned back to the tactical plot. "Look at them run. I've never heard of Sentinels retreating before."

"It's a tactical retreat, but it's no less satisfying. We should get underway ourselves."

CHAPTER THIRTY-ONE

ADMEN DESHER FLEW his ship through the asteroid field. Union ships were also flying through the area, trying to escape the Sentinel fleets he'd gathered there. He regarded the tactical plot, feeling spikes of rage as thousands of Sentinels were destroyed. This wasn't a battle; it was a slaughter. The dampening field had ceased just before the attack, and his ship had happened to be among the Union ships. He guided his ship to stay with them, easily blending in.

The scan data showed him an impossibly deadly creation. He'd been so close to discovering this secret, and to have it snatched away made him want to spit fire. Commander Aldren had beaten him. Galactic PMCs had command authority over their ranks, and it had been able to give Nash Harper a chance to deny the corruption. Admen had lost all control when Harper went offline. Aldren had proven to be a shrewd opponent.

A subspace comlink registered from a Sentinel warship and uploaded a data package with new commands for him to follow, but the warship went offline before Admen could reply. It must have been unable to escape the star system in time. Admen executed a micro-jump that took him away from the chaos. By the time the Union ships noticed, he would be somewhere else. Commander Aldren may have won the battle, but the war was far from over.

"THE DAMPENING FIELD IS GONE, COMMANDER," Pierce said.

Lennix looked at the data on the main holoscreen. The Sentinel fleets were being destroyed. Huge swaths of their numbers had simply disappeared.

Nate Carradine turned toward him. "Analysis of the attack indicates that we're not being targeted."

Lennix had watched in complete and utter shock as clusters of asteroids, scattered by some unseen force, began decimating Sentinel warships. They'd been pursuing his small fleet, and they must have been just as surprised by the attack as he was.

"Commander, we're being hailed," Pierce said.

"By whom?" Lennix asked.

"He wants to speak to you, sir. He knows you're on this ship, specifically."

Lennix sat down and inclined his chin toward the main holoscreen. A video comlink appeared, showing the head and shoulders of someone he hadn't expected to see again. "Aldren," he whispered.

The PMC smiled. If not for the slight glow of the eyes, Lennix would have thought he was human.

"You and I need to talk," Quinton said.

Lennix leaned forward, but his mouth went dry.

"I'm not going to fire on any Union ships."

Lennix looked confused. "Why not?"

"Because you're not the enemy," Quinton said. "At least, you don't have to be. I know what you did with my ID. It's not going to work anymore."

Lennix knew better than to deny it. All their lives were

dangling by a very thin thread. "It was the only way to fight the Collective, but when similar attacks began happening elsewhere…" He paused and shook his head. "We tried to stop it. The information broker we used—Admen Desher—he double-crossed us."

Quinton frowned. "Admen Desher was your information broker?"

Lennix nodded. If he kept Quinton talking, maybe there would be enough time to get away.

"I want to know everything about that, but I don't have time right now," Quinton said and leaned closer to the camera. "You owe me, Crowe. The only reason the Sentinels didn't destroy your fleet was because of me. Do we have an understanding?"

Lennix swallowed hard and nodded. "What do you want?"

"I want you to get your fleet out of here. The Sentinels might come back, and it's best you're not here. But I don't want you to throw your ships away trying to take on the Collective."

"I might not have a choice."

"The Collective is the least of our worries. But I need to be clear with you here. If you start raiding Collective targets again, Trenton Draven will be the least of your worries."

"Why do you care about the Collective?"

Quinton shook his head. "I don't. I care about fighting the Sentinels, and you're going to help me do it. So is Draven. There's a lot you don't know, and a briefing is being prepared to explain it all."

Lennix glanced at Nate, who kept his gaze locked on the main holoscreen. He didn't have a choice. He had to do whatever Quinton said, at least for the moment. "All right, we'll cease all hostilities against Collective targets as of right now."

"Good," Quinton replied. "I've cataloged all of your ships here, as well as the reserves that aren't here."

"You don't know where my reserves are," Lennix said.

Quinton regarded him. "Don't make me regret this," he said

and shook his head. "You know what? Never mind. I think you're more trouble than you're worth. Goodbye Crowe."

"Wait!" Lennix cried. "Wait. Just tell me what you want."

"First, I want you to leave this star system. Second, you're to continue building up your fleet strength. I'll be in contact with you."

"Why are you doing this?"

"Like I already said, you're not the enemy. You've got a lot to answer for, Crowe, but that can come later. You'll get your chance to balance what you owe me."

Lennix regarded him for a few moments. "All right."

Quinton nodded once. "Good. Now get your people out of here. They have important work to do."

The comlink severed and Lennix looked at Nate.

"We better do as he says," Nate said.

"Give me a broadcast channel to the fleet," Lennix said.

After he was through giving orders to clear the area, he leaned back in his chair.

Nate looked at him. "He could have killed us."

"But he didn't, which means he was telling the truth. He needs us."

"To take on the Sentinels," Nate replied. "He's simply delaying our deaths to a more convenient time."

"That gives us time to prepare. I have no intention of dying."

CHAPTER THIRTY-TWO

QUINTON STOOD several meters outside the *Salvation's* primary bridge. He'd just added a name to the monument of the fallen, and he looked at the others for a moment before turning back to the obsidian-colored wall that was almost covered with white script. He saluted in the tradition of the Acheron Confederacy Navy. Corvax and Bradshaw followed suit while the others watched in silence.

Among the long list of people who'd died during the Federation Wars was a new name.

"Lieutenant Nash Harper," Quinton said. "Gone but never forgotten."

"Never forgotten," the others echoed.

Quinton looked at the name and wondered how many more would be added to it. After a few moments' contemplation, he returned to the bridge and couldn't help but be impressed by the sight of it all.

"I've heard back from Admiral Brandt. He confirmed that Sentinel activity has decreased everywhere," Maelyn said.

Quinton had expected it.

"Where did they all go?" Becker asked.

"They were probably recalled. Admen Desher must have gotten away and reported to Harding Prime," Quinton said.

"You're really going to do it? You're going to take on the Sentinels?" Becker asked.

Quinton bobbed his head once. "Hopefully not alone. I was expecting the rest of you might help, but I don't have a choice."

"What do you mean you don't have a choice?"

Quinton looked at them. "It's part of taking command of this ship. Do you think Browning was just going to leave it with whoever ended up here first? No, he had a bunch of constraints associated with it."

Becker regarded him for a moment. "So, you couldn't walk away even if you wanted to?"

"I'm not walking away from this. There isn't anyone else."

Becker rubbed the side of his face. "But all those other PMCs. I guess I just thought that maybe there *would* be someone else."

Quinton arched an eyebrow and half his mouth lifted. "Thanks for the vote of confidence. I really appreciate it."

"No, that isn't what I meant."

"Yes, it was."

Becker rolled his eyes. "I just thought maybe there was someone with more experience or someone who knows more about this ship."

"Then I guess it's do-or-die time," Quinton said. "Besides, there are entire training libraries on all the ships' systems, so we can all catch up."

"I guess we'd better get to work then," Maelyn said, smiling at both of them.

Quinton returned her smile. "You should see the orientation program videos. They're something else," he said and gestured toward the main holoscreen.

Two video windows appeared. One of them showed Oscar

singing while pretending to fly an aircar that was locked on a maintenance hold.

"Then, there's this one," Quinton said.

A video feed of a small bridge appeared, and Guttman ran into view. He stopped suddenly and stripped off his EVA suit, wobbling on his feet a little.

"Oh, come on!" Guttman said. "You promised you wouldn't do that anymore."

On the holoscreen, Guttman began galloping around while shouting at the top of his lungs. Then he looked as if he were replying to someone. "Servitors are coming? Woohoo!"

Laughter bubbled up out of all of them. Oscar went to stand beside Guttman and the two bowed.

"When did this happen?" Maelyn asked.

"It wasn't all that long ago," Quinton said.

He updated the video feed so they played on a three-second loop. More rounds of laughter bubbled out of all of them.

"As God as my witness, I'm going to find a way to get back at you," Guttman said.

"That's what I keep hearing," Quinton replied.

"He'll have help," Oscar replied.

The two shared a knowing look and Quinton grinned. It felt good. He killed the video.

A few minutes later, Simon called them over to his workstation. Quinton lingered behind and Maelyn strolled over to him.

"They needed that," she said.

"So did I."

Maelyn eyed him. "Is it true? You really don't have a choice?"

Quinton shrugged. "There's always a choice. I just might not like the choices I've got," he said, and Maelyn nodded. "You saw what the *Salvation* is capable of. Would you just hand that off without a way of keeping them in line?"

"When you put it like that, I guess not."

"We've got a lot of work to do," he said, thinking about the endless list of tasks that were still filling up his "To Do" list, and learning more about the ship only added to it. The *Salvation* also carried hundreds of smaller warships in its hangar bays.

"It's a good thing you've got a strong second-in-command."

Quinton frowned. "I do?"

Maelyn smiled sweetly and gave him a teasing look. "Would you rather it was Becker?"

Quinton chuckled and glanced at the others. They were watching Simon's holoscreen with interest, still wrapping their minds around everything that had happened.

"No, he's not ready for this, although neither are you nor I," Quinton said.

Maelyn raised her chin. "I know, but we'll all have to be quick learners."

Quinton considered it for a few moments, then nodded. "I already am, but I'm not sure about you."

Maelyn narrowed her gaze. "I can do whatever you can, except for..." she said and gestured toward him.

"All I'm saying is that there's an extensive interview process so I can be sure your strengths match up with the rest of the team's."

Maelyn's mouth opened a little and then she laughed. "You're... Fine. Let's start right now."

"We can't."

"Why not?"

"Oh, because I need to put together an advisory committee."

"Now I know you're lying. You hate decisions by committee."

Quinton sighed. "Damn, you saw through it. Well, that means you've passed your first test."

"How many tests are there?"

Quinton smiled. "Admiral's Privilege."

AUTHOR NOTE

Thank you for reading Acheron Salvation, Federation Chronicles Book 2. I hope you enjoyed the story. Quinton and the team will be back in Federation Chronicles book 3. Please consider leaving a review for the book. Reviews help my books get discovered by other readers. Also, consider telling a friend about the book or share it on social media. Word of mouth is crucial in helping authors write books that readers want to read.

Again, thank you for reading one of my books. I'm so grateful that I get to write these stories.

If you're new to my work, here is a little bit about myself. This is the 24th book I've written since 2013. It took me years to write that first book, mostly because I couldn't get out of my own way. Over the years, I've worked to improve my craft, so I can deliver quality stories on a regular schedule. I aim to write 3 to 4 books a year.

I worked in IT Security for 20 years, and in 2013 I decided I wanted to change careers. I'd had enough, so I picked up the bones on an old book I'd started writing a long time ago and finished it. For about four years, I wrote in the early morning hours before my workday began for my day job. By the summer of 2017, I'd released 10 books, and then life threw me a curve-ball. I'd found out that I was going to be let go from my job in the next round of layoffs. My employer gave me six months notice, which, while not ideal, wasn't as bad as it could have been. I had to decide whether I was ready for my hobby of writing books to be my new career. I wasn't an overnight success story when it came to writing books. Between 2013 - 2017 I wrote, improved my craft, and more people read my stories, but it wasn't enough to replace my salary. I have a family and respon-sibilities that needed to be fulfilled. After quite a bit of soul-searching, I decided that I wanted to take the leap to see if I could take my hobby of writing books and make it my career. I had six months. I wrote the first two books in the First Colony series, and on my last day at my old job, I started writing the third book in the series. I said a few prayers and released the first book in the First Colony series. That book and the other books in the series skyrocketed to the top of the charts and stayed there. I was awestruck, and although it's been a few years since that happened, I still am. I plan to be around for a long time writing books, and I hope that you find some fun escapism in the stories that I write.

Thanks again for reading one of my books. If you wouldn't mind, please consider leaving a review for this book. Reviews really do help, even it's just a few words to say that you really liked this book.

https://kenlozito.com/my-books/

The series continues with the 3rd book.

Acheron Redemption - Federation Chronicles Book 3

I do have a Facebook group called **Ken Lozito's SF readers**.

Answer two easy questions and you're in. If you're on Facebook and you'd like to stop by, please search for it on Facebook.

Not everyone is on Facebook. I get it, but I also have a blog if you'd like to stop by there. My blog is more of a monthly check-in as to the status of what I'm working on. Please stop by and say hello, I'd love to hear from you.

Visit www.kenlozito.com

THANK YOU FOR READING ACHERON SALVATION - FEDERATION CHRONICLES BOOK 2.

If you loved this book, please consider leaving a review. Comments and reviews allow readers to discover authors, so if you want others to enjoy *Acheron Salvation* as you have, please leave a short note.

The Federation Chronicles will continue with - Federation Chronicles Book 3

Visit KenLozito.com to learn more.

If you're looking for something else to read consider the following series I've written.

First Colony - A story about humanity's first interstellar colony.

Ascension - A story about humanity's first alien contact.

ABOUT THE AUTHOR

I've written multiple science fiction and fantasy series. Books have been my way to escape everyday life since I was a teenager to my current ripe old(?) age. What started out as a love of stories has turned into a full-blown passion for writing them.

Overall, I'm just a fan of really good stories regardless of genre. I love the heroic tales, redemption stories, the last stand, or just a good old fashion adventure. Those are the types of stories I like to write. Stories with rich and interesting characters and then I put them into dangerous and sometimes morally gray situations.

My ultimate intent for writing stories is to provide fun escapism for readers. I write stories that I would like to read, and I hope you enjoy them as well.

If you have questions or comments about any of my works I would love to hear from you, even if it's only to drop by to say hello at KenLozito.com

Thanks again for reading *Acheron Salvation - Federation Chronicles Book 2*

Don't be shy about emails, I love getting them, and try to respond to everyone.

ALSO BY KEN LOZITO

Rising Force

Ascension

Safanarion Order Series

Road to Shandara

Echoes of a Gloried Past

Amidst the Rising Shadows

Heir of Shandara

Broken Crown Series

Haven of Shadows

If you would like to be notified when my next book is released visit kenlozito.com

Made in United States
Orlando, FL
28 August 2022

21675819R10183